THE ESCAPE

ᴛʜᴇ ESCAPE

A NOVEL IN FIVE PARTS

ADAM THIRLWELL

JONATHAN CAPE
LONDON

Published by Jonathan Cape

2 4 6 8 10 9 7 5 3 1

Copyright © Adam Thirlwell 2009

First published in Great Britain in 2009 by
Jonathan Cape
Random House, 20 Vauxhall Bridge Road,
London SW1V 2SA

www.rbooks.co.uk

Addresses for companies within The Random House Group Limited can be
found at: www.randomhouse.co.uk/offices.htm

The Random House Group Limited Reg. No. 954009

A CIP catalogue record for this book
is available from the British Library

ISBN 9780224089111 (HARDBACK)
ISBN 9780224089128 (TRADE PAPERBACK)

The Random House Group Limited supports The Forest Stewardship Council
(FSC), the leading international forest certification organisation. All our titles that
are printed on Greenpeace approved FSC certified paper carry the FSC logo. Our
at www.rbooks.co.uk/environment

impsest Book Production Limited,
Grangemouth, Stirlingshire

ted and bound in Great Britain by
Clays Ltd, St Ives plc

TO ALISON,
FOR MY FAMILY

Contents

PART ONE   1

Haffner Unbound
Haffner Amorous
Haffner Amphibious

PART TWO   63

Haffner Enraged
Haffner Soothed
Haffner Timeless
Haffner Roman
Haffner Buoyant

PART THREE   151

Haffner Interrupted
Haffner Banished
Haffner Delinquent
Haffner Guilty
Haffner Jewish

PART FOUR   217

Haffner Gastronomic
Haffner Drunk
Haffner Defeated
Haffner Translated

PART FIVE   279

Haffner Harmonic
Haffner Fugitive
Haffner Mortal

PART ONE

Haffner Unbound

And so the century ended: with Haffner watching a man caress a woman's breasts.

It was an imbroglio. He would admit that much. But at least it was an imbroglio of Haffner's making.

He might have been seventy-eight, but in Haffner's opinion he counted as young. He counted, in the words of the young, as hip. Or as close to hip as anyone else. Only Haffner, after all, would have been found in this position.

What position?

Concealed in a wardrobe, the doors darkly ajar, watching a woman be nakedly playful to her boyfriend.

This was why I admired him. Haffner Unbound! But there were other Haffners too – Haffner Pensive, Haffner Abandoned. He tended to see himself like this; as in a dream, in poses. Like the panels of a classical frieze.

A tzigani pop album – disco drumbeats, accordions, sporadic trumpets – was being broadcast by a compact-disc player above the minibar. This weakened his squinting concentration. He disliked the modern combination of sex and music. It was better, thought Haffner, for bodies to undress themselves in the quiet of the everyday background

3

hum. In Naples once, in what, he had to say, could only be described as a dive, in the liberated city, the lights went suddenly out, and so the piano stopped, and in the ensuing silent twilight Haffner watched a woman undress so slowly, so awkwardly, so peacefully – accompanied only by the accidental chime of wine glasses, the brief struck fizz of matches – that she had, until this moment, more than fifty years later, remained his ideal of beauty.

Now, however, Haffner was unsure of his ideals.

He continued looking at Zinka. It wasn't a difficult task. Her hair was dark; her nipples were long, and almost black, with stained pools of areolae; her stomach curved gently towards her hips, where the bone then steeply rose; her legs were slender. Her breasts and nose were cute. If Haffner had a type, then this was it: the feminine unfeminine. The word for her, in his heyday, would have been *gamine*. She was a *garçonne*. If those words were, he mused, at the end of his century, still used for girls at all.

They were not.

A suckling noise emerged from Niko, who was now tugging at Zinka's nipples with the pursed O of his mouth.

Haffner was lustful, selfish, vain – an entirely commonplace man. It was the unavoidable conclusion. He had to admit it. In London and New York he had practised as a banker. His life had been unremarkable. It was the twentieth century's idea of the bourgeois: the grey Atlantic Ocean. The horizontal fretting waves of the grey Atlantic Ocean. With Liberty at one extreme, and the Bank of England at the other. But Haffner wasn't straddling the Atlantic any more. A hotel in a spa town was now Haffner's temporary home. He was landlocked – adrift in the centre of Europe, aloft in the Alps.

And now he was hidden in a wardrobe.

He was not, however, the usual voyeur. It was true that Niko was unaware of his presence. But Zinka – Zinka knew all about this spectral form in the wardrobe. Somehow, in a way which had seemed natural at the time, Zinka and Haffner had developed this idea of Haffner's unnatural pleasure. The causes were obscure, occasioned by some random confluence of Haffner's charm and the odd mixture Zinka felt of tenderness for Haffner and mischief towards her boyfriend. But however obscure its causes, the conclusion was obvious.

So, ladies and gentlemen, maybe Haffner was grand, in a way. Maybe Haffner was an epic hero. And if Haffner was a hero, then his wallet, with its creased photographs, was his mute mausoleum. Take a look! Haffner in Rome, wonkily crowned by the curve of the Colosseum, a medusan pile of spaghetti in front of him; Haffner and Livia at a garden party in Buckingham Palace, trying to smile while hoping that Livia's hat – a plate on which lay a pile of flowers – would not erupt and blow away; Haffner's grandson, Benjamin, aged four, in a Yankees baseball cap, pissing with cherubic abandon – a live Renaissance fountain – in the gardens of a country house.

All photo albums are unhappy, in the words of the old master, in their own particular way.

2

And me? I was born sixty years after Haffner. I was just a friend.

I went to see him, in a hospital on the outskirts of London. His finale in the centre of Europe had been a decade ago. Now, Haffner was dying. But then Haffner had been dying for so long.

—The thing is, he said, I just need to plan for the next forty-eight hours. We just need to organise the next few days of the new era.

And when I asked him what new era he meant, he replied that this was exactly what we had to find out.

Everything was ending. On the television, a panel was discussing the crisis. The money was disappearing. The banks were disappearing. The end, as usual, was continuing. I wasn't sorry for the money, however. I was sorry for Haffner. There was a miniature rose in bud on the table. Haffner was trying to explain. Something, he said, had gone very very wrong. Perhaps, he said, we just needed to get this closed – pointing to a bedside cabinet, whose lock was gone.

He was lower than the dust, he told me. Lower than the dust. After an hour, he wanted to go to the bathroom. He started trying to undress himself, there in his armchair. And so I called a nurse and then I left him, as he was ushered into the women's bathroom, because that bathroom was closer to the room in which Haffner was busily dying.

Standing in the hospital's elliptical concrete drive, as the electric doors opened and closed behind me, I waited for the taxi to take me to the trains – back to the city. Across the silver fields the mauve fir trees kept themselves to themselves. It was neither the country nor the city. It was nowhere.

And as I listened to the boring sirens, I rehearsed my memories of Haffner.

With my vision of Haffner – his trousers round his ankles, his hands nervous at his cream underwear – I began my project for his resurrection. Like that historian looking down at the ruins of Rome, in the twilight – with the tourists sketching their souvenirs, and the bells beginning, and the pestering guides, and the watersellers, and the sun above them shrinking: the endless and mortal sun.

3

His career had been the usual success story. After the war Haffner had joined Warburg's. He had distinguished himself with the money he made in the exchange crisis. But his true moment had arrived some years later, when it was Haffner who had realised, as the fifties wore on, the American crisis with dollars. Only Haffner had quite understood the obviousness of it all. The obtuseness of Regulation Q! Naturally, more and more dollars would leave, stranded as they were in the vaults of the United States, and come to Europe – to enrich themselves. This was what he had explained to an executive in Bankers Trust, who was over in London to encourage men like Haffner to move to New York. In 1963, therefore, Haffner left Warburg's for America, where he stayed as a general manager for eleven years. He was the expert in currency exchange: doyen of the international. Then, in 1974, he returned as Chief General Manager in the London office of Chase Manhattan. Just in time for the birth of his grandson – who had promised so much, thought Haffner, as another version of Haffner, and yet delivered so little. Then, finally, there came Haffner's final promotion to the board of directors. His banishment, joked Haffner.

Haffner, I have to admit, didn't practise the usual art of being a grandfather. Cowardice, obscenity, charm, moral turpitude: these were the qualities Haffner preferred. He had bravado. And so it was that, a decade ago, in the spa town, when everything seemed happier, he had avoided the letters from his daughter, the telephone calls from his grandson, the metaphysical lamentation from his exasperated family. Instead, he continued staring at Zinka's breasts, as Niko clumsily caressed them.

Since Zinka was the other hero of Haffner's finale, it may be useful to understand her history.

To some people, Zinka said she was from Bukovina. This was where she had been born, at the eastern edge of Europe – on a night, her mother said, when everything had frozen, even the sweat on her forehead. Her mother, as Zinka knew, was given to hyperbole. To other people, Zinka said she was from Bucharest; and this was true too. It was where she had grown up, in an apartment block out to the north of the city: near the park. But to Haffner, she had simply said she was from Zagreb. In Zagreb, she had trained in the corps de ballet. Until History, that arrogant personification, decided to interrupt. So now she worked here, in this hotel in a spa town, in the unfashionable unfrequented Alps, north of the Italian border – as a health assistant to the European rich.

This was where Haffner had discovered her – in the second week of his escape. Sipping a coffee, he had seen her – the cute yoga teacher – squatting and shimmying her shoulders behind her knees, while the hotel guests comically mimicked her. She was in a grey T-shirt and grey tracksuit trousers: a T-shirt and trousers which could not conceal the twin small swelling of her breasts, borrowed from an even younger girl, and their reflection, the twin swelling of her buttocks, borrowed from an even younger boy. Then she clasped her hands inside out above her back, in a pose which Haffner could only imagine implied such infinite dexterity that his body began to throb, and he felt the old illness return. The familiar, peristaltic illness of the women.

Concealed in a bedroom wardrobe, he looked up at what he could see of the ceiling: where the electric bulb's white light was converted by a dusty trapezoid lampshade into a peachy, emollient glow.

He really didn't want anything else. The women were the only means of Haffner's triumph – his ageing body still a pincushion for the multicoloured plastic arrows of the victorious kid-god: Cupid.

4

Reproductions of these arrows could now be found disporting on Niko's forearms, directing the observer's gaze up to his biceps, where two colourful dragons were eating their own tails – dragons which, if he could have seen them in detail, would have reminded Haffner of the lurid mythical beasts tattooed on the arms of his CO in the war. But Haffner could not see these dragons in detail. Gold bracelets tightly gilded Niko's wrist. Another more abstract tattoo spread over the indented muscles of his stomach – a background, now, to his erect penis, to which Zinka – dressed only in the smallest turquoise panties – was attending.

Situations like these were Haffner's habitat – he lived for the women, ever since he had taken out his first ever girl, to the Ionic Picture Theatre on the Finchley Road. Her name was Hazel. She let him touch her hand all through the feature. The erotic determined him. The film they had seen had been chosen by Hazel: a romance involving fairies, and the spirits of the wood. None of the effects – the billowing cloths, the wind machines, the fuzzy light at the edges of each frame, the doleful music – convinced sarcastic Haffner of their reality. Afterwards, he had bought her two slices of chocolate cake in a Lyons Tea House, and they looked at each other, tenderly – while, in a pattern which would menace Haffner all his life, he began to wonder when he might acceptably, politely, try to kiss her.

He was mediocre; he was unoriginal. He admitted this freely. With only one thing had Haffner been blessed – with the looks. There was no denying, Haffner used to say, mock-ruefully, that Haffner was old – especially if you took a look at him. In the words of his favourite comedian. But Haffner knew this wasn't true. He was unoriginal – but the looks were something else. It was not just his friends who said this; his colleagues acknowledged it too. Now, at seventy-eight, Haffner possessed more hair than was his natural right. This hair was blond. His eyes were blue; his cheeks were sculpted. Beneath the silk weave of his polo necks, his stomach described the gentlest of inclinations.

Now, however, Haffner's colleagues would have been surprised.

Haffner was dressed in waterproof sky-blue tracksuit trousers, a sky-blue T-shirt, and a pistachio sweatshirt. These clothes did not express his inner man. This much, he hoped, was obvious. His inner man was *soigné*, elegant. His mother had praised him for this. In the time when his mother praised him at all.

9

—Darling, she used to say to him, you are your mother's man. You make her proud. Let nobody forget this.

She dressed him in white sailor suits, with navy stripes curtailing each cuff. At the children's parties, Haffner acted unconcerned. As soon as he could, however, he preferred the look of the gangster: the Bowery cool, the Whitechapel raciness. Elegance gone to seed. His first trilby was bought at James Lock, off Pall Mall; his umbrellas came from James Smith & Sons, at the edge of Covent Garden. The royal patent could seduce him. He had a thing for glamour, for the mysteries of lineage. He could talk to you for a long time about his lineage.

The problem was that now, at the end of the twentieth century, his suitcase had gone missing. It had vanished, two weeks ago, on his arrival at the airport in Trieste. It had still not been returned. It was imminent, the airline promised him. Absolutely. His eyesight, therefore, had been forced to rely on itself – without his spectacles. And he had been corralled into odd collages of clothes, bought from the outdoor-clothes shops in this town. He walked round the square, around the lake, up small lanes, and wondered where anyone bought their indoor clothes. Was the indoors so beyond them? Was everyone always outdoors?

He was a long way from the bright lights of the West End.

Zinka leaned back, grinned up at Niko, who pushed strands of her hair away from her forehead: an idyll. He began to kiss her, softly. He talked to her in a language which Haffner did not know. But Haffner knew what they were saying. They were saying they loved each other.

It was midsummer. He was in the centre of Europe, as high as Haffner could go. As far away as Haffner could get. Through the slats on the window he could see the blurred and Alpine mountains, the vague sky and its clouds, backlit by the setting sun. The view was pricked by conifers.

And Haffner, as he watched, was sad.

He lived for the women. He would learn nothing. He would learn nothing and leave everyone. That was what his daughter had said of him, when she patiently shouted at him and explained his lack of moral courage, his pitiful inadequacy as a husband, as a father, as a man. He would remain inexperienced. It seemed an accurate description.

But as Zinka performed for her invisible audience, Haffner still felt sad. He thought he would feel exultant, but he did not. And the only explanation he could think of was that, once again, Haffner was in love. But this time there was a difference. This, thought Haffner, was the real thing. As he had always thought before, and then had always convinced himself that he was wrong.

5

The pain of it perturbed him. To this pain, he had to acknowledge, there was added the more obvious pain in his legs. He had now been standing for nearly an hour. The difficulty of this had been increased by the tension of avoiding the stray coat hangers Haffner had not removed. It was ridiculous, he thought. He was starting to panic. So calm yourself, thought Haffner. He tried to concentrate on the naked facts – like the smallness of Zinka's breasts, but their smallness simply increased his panic, since they only added to the erotic charge with which Haffner was now pulsing. They were so little to do with function, so much to do with form – as they hung there, unsupported. The nipple completed them; the nipple exhausted them. They were dark with areolae. Their proportions all tended to the sexual, away from the neatly maternal.

Haffner wasn't into sex, after all, for the family. The children were the mistake. He was in it for all the exorbitant extras.

No, not for Haffner – the normal curves, the pedestrian features. His desire was seduced by an imperfectly shaved armpit, or a tanning forearm with its swatch of sweat. That was the principle of Haffner's mythology. Haffner, an admirer of the classics. So what if this now made him laughable, or ridiculous, or – in the newly moralistic vocabulary of Benji, his orthodox and religious grandson – sleazy? As if there should be closure on dirtiness. As if there should ever be, thought Haffner, any shame in one's lust. Or any more shame than anyone else's. If he could have extended the epic of Haffner's lust for another lifetime, then he would have done it.

In this, he would confess, he differed from Goldfaden. Goldfaden would have preferred a happy ending. He was into the One, not the Many. In New York once, in a place below Houston, Goldfaden had told him that some woman – Haffner couldn't remember her name, some secretary he'd been dealing with in Princeton, or Cambridge – was the kind of woman you'd take by force when the world fell apart. Not like his wife, said Goldfaden: nothing like Cynthia. Then he had downed his single malt and ordered another. At the time, helpful Haffner's contribution to the list of such ultimate women was Evelyn Laye, the star of stage and screen. The most beautiful woman he had ever laid eyes on, when she accompanied her husband to his training camp in Hampshire, in 1939. They arrived in a silver Wolseley 14/16. Goldfaden, however, had contradicted Haffner's choice of Evelyn Laye. As he contradicted so many of Haffner's opinions. She was passable, Goldfaden argued, but it wasn't what he had in mind. And Haffner wondered – as now, so many years later, he watched while Niko stretched Zinka's slim legs apart, displaying the indented hollows inside her thighs, the tatooed mermaid's head protruding from her panties – whether Goldfaden would have agreed that in Zinka he had finally found this kind of woman: the unattainable, the one who would be worth any kind of immorality. If Goldfaden was still alive. He didn't know. He didn't, to be honest, really care. Why, after all, would you want anyone when the world fell apart? It was typical of Goldfaden: this macho exaggeration.

But Haffner no longer had Goldfaden. Which was a story in itself. He no longer had anyone to use as his silent audience.

This solitude made Haffner melancholy.

The ethos of Raphael Haffner – as businessman, raconteur, wit, jazzman, reader – was simple: no experience could be more pleasurable than its telling. The description was always to be preferred to the reality. Yet here it was: his finale – and there was no one there to listen. In the absence of this audience, in Haffner's history, anything had been known to take its place; anything could be spoken to in Haffner's intimate yell: himself, his ghosts, his absent mentors, even – why not? – the more neutral and natural spectators, like the roses in his garden, or the bright impassive sun.

He looked at Zinka, who suddenly crouched in front of Niko, with her back to Haffner, and allowed her hand to be elaborate on Niko's penis.

As defeats went, thought Haffner, it was pretty comprehensive. Even Papa never got himself as messed up as this.

Was it too late for him to change? To undergo one final metamorphosis? I am not what I am! That was Haffner's constant wish, his mantra. He was a man replete with mantras. He would not act his age, or his Age. He would not be what others made of him.

And yet; and yet.

The thing was, said a friend of Livia's once, thirty years ago, in the green room of a theatre on St Martin's Lane, making smoke rings dissolve in the smoky air – a habit which always reminded Livia of her father. The thing was, he was always saying that he wanted to disappear.

She was an actress. He wanted this actress, very much. Once, in their bedroom with Livia before a party, he had seen her undress; and although asked to turn away had still fleetingly seen the lavish shapeless bush between her legs. With such memories was Haffner continually oppressed. It wasn't new. With such memories did

Haffner distress himself. But he couldn't prevent the thought that if she'd undressed in front of him like that, then it was unlikely that she looked on him with any erotic interest – only a calm and uninterested friendliness.

Yes, she continued, he was always saying how he'd prefer to live his life unnoticed, free from the demands of other people.

—But let me tell you something, Raphael, said Livia's friend. You don't need to disappear.

Then she paused; blew out a final smoke ring; scribbled her cigarette out in an ashtray celebrating the natural beauty of Normandy; looked at Livia.

—Because no one, she said, is ever looking for you.

How Haffner had tried to smile, as if he didn't care about her jibe! How Haffner continued to try to smile, whenever this conversation returned to him.

Maybe, he thought, she was right: maybe that was the story of his life, of his century.

And now it was ending – Haffner's twentieth century. What had Haffner done with the twentieth century? He enjoyed measuring himself like this, against the grand categories. But that depended, perhaps, on another question. What had the twentieth century done with him?

6

The era in which Haffner's last story took place was an interregnum: a pause. The British empire was over. The Hapsburg empire was over. Over, too, was the Communist empire. All the ideologies were over. But it was not yet the time of full aromatherapy, the era of celebrity: of chakras, and pressure points. It was after the era of the spa as a path to health, and before the era of the spa as a path to beauty. It was not an era at all.

Everything was almost over. And maybe that was how it should be. The more over things were, the better. You no longer needed to be troubled by the constant conjuring with tenses.

In this hiatus, in the final year of the twentieth century, entered Raphael Haffner.

The hotel where Haffner was staying defined itself as a mountain escape. It had the normal look. It was all white – with a roof that rose in waves of red tile and green louvred shutters on all three floors, each storey narrower than the one below. The top storey resembled a little summerhouse with a tiny structure made of iron shutters on the roof, like an observation post or a weather station with instruments inside and barometers outside. On top of it all, at the very peak, a red weathercock turned in the wind. Every window on every floor had a balcony entered through a set of French doors. Behind the hotel rose the traces of conifered paths, ascending to a distant summit; in front of it, pooled the lake, with its reflections. Beside this lake, on the edge of the town, there was a park, with gravel diagonals, and a view of a distant factory.

Once, the town had been the main location for the holidays of the Central European rich. This was where Livia's family had spent their summers, out of Trieste. They had gone so far, in 1936, as to purchase a villa, with hot and cold water, on the outskirts of the town. In this town, said Livia's father, he felt happy. It had style. The restaurants were replete with waiters – replete, in their turn, with eyebrow. Then, in the summer of 1939, when she was seventeen, Livia and her younger brother, Cesare, had not come to the mountains, but instead had made their way to London. And they had never come back. Seven years later, in a hotel dining room in Honfleur, where Haffner had taken her for the honeymoon which the war had prevented, she described to Haffner, entranced by the glamour, the dining rooms of her past. Crisp mitres of napkins sat in state on the tables. The guests were served not spa food but the classics of their heritage: schnitzel Holstein, and minestrone. The

Béarnaise sauce was served in a silver boat, its lip warped into a moue. There was the clearest chicken soup with the lightest dumplings.

And now, when this place belonged to another country, here was Haffner, her husband: alone – to claim the villa, to claim an inheritance which was not his.

The hotel still served the food of Livia's memory. This place was timeless: it was the end of history. The customer could still order steak Diane, beef Wellington – arranged on vast circles of china, with a thin gold ring inscribing its circumference. Even Haffner knew this wasn't chic, but he wasn't after the chic. He just wanted an escape. An escape from what, however, Haffner could not say.

No, Haffner could never disappear.

In 1974, in the last year of his New York life, when Barbra – who was twenty-nine, worked in the Wall Street office as his secretary and smoked Dunhills which she kept in a cigarette holder, triple facts which made her desirable to Haffner as he passed middle age – asked him why it was he still went faithfully back every night to his wife, he could not answer. It didn't have to be like that, she said. With irritation, as he looked at Barbra, the steep curve between her breasts, he remembered his snooker table in the annexe at home, its blue baize built over by Livia's castles of unread books. He knew that the next morning he would be there, at home: with his breakfast of Corn Chex, morosely reading the *Peanuts* cartoons. He knew this, and did not want to know it. So often, he wanted to give up, and elope from his history. The problem was in finding the right elopee. He only had Haffner. And Haffner wasn't enough.

Zinka turned in the direction of the wardrobe. Usually, she wore her hair sternly in a pony tail. But now she let it drift out, on to her shoulders. And Haffner looked away. Because, he thought, he loved her. He looked back again. Because, he thought, he loved her.

No, there was no escape. And because this is true, then maybe in my turn I should not always allow Haffner the luxury of language.

He was burdened by what he thought was love. But therefore he did not express it in this way. No, trapped by his temptations, Haffner simply sighed.

—Ouf, he exhaled, in his wardrobe. Ouf: ouf.

7

In this vacant hotel room to which Zinka had lured Niko, Zinka had arranged things so that she was facing the mirror which hung above the bed. Behind her, stood Haffner – in the wardrobe. Before her, sat Niko, his legs and his testicles dangling over the edge of the bed. His foot protruded close to Haffner's lair. One of his toenails, Haffner noted, was blackened – the badge of Niko's fitness, of the dogged distances he jogged every day.

But Haffner felt no grievance at the disparity between their bodies. He had perspective. This was one reason to love him. He had the sense of humour I admired. It wasn't just that it was possible to imagine that what was higher could derive always and only from what was lower – in the words of another old master. No, one could go further. And so it was also possible to imagine that – given the polarity and, more importantly, the ludicrousness of the world – everything derived from its opposite: day from night, frailty from strength, deformity from beauty, fortune from misfortune. Victory was made up exclusively of beatings.

This defeat, therefore, could be a victory too. It seemed unlikely, perhaps, but Haffner rarely wanted to be burdened with the problems of probability. Haffner found perks everywhere.

Niko's face was now smothered by the dark nipples of his girl-friend. He was blinded by her body. He therefore couldn't see that, in the mirror, she was looking at the wardrobe, where Haffner was looking at her. Her lips were parted. She was smiling at him: at the invisible Haffner she knew was lurking there, having first splashed a tangle of coat hangers hurriedly into a drawer. Haffner happily smiled back. Then he stopped himself. It felt obscurely comical for a man to be smiling when concealed in a wardrobe. So, shyly, Haffner looked away. He gazed at her thin back instead, gently imprinted with vertebrae.

A thought arrived to Haffner. Was this it? he considered. Was this love?

When he was seventeen – so Haffner once told me, when we were both drunk on vodka cokes, at a golden-wedding party themed for no obvious reason to gangster films of the American 1970s – Haffner had gone to sleep each night imagining the girl he would meet, who would be his perfect girl. This was very important, he said. She would be a woman of the world, attractive, with a hint of something more, if I knew what he meant. I knew what he meant: he wanted the urban, he wanted a vision of cool. And, he told me, he continued to do this – even after the advent of his wife (and his girlfriends, his collection of lovers). Even there, in this spa town, at seventy-eight, he still calmed himself to sleep imagining this girl who would be so infinitely charmed by him. But now, something had changed.

As of now, this girl was simply Zinka.

This was not, of course, what Haffner was meant to be thinking. But then Haffner had a talent for not thinking the orthodox thoughts.

It wasn't enough that Haffner was failing to accomplish the bureaucratic task, which was why he was here, in this spa town: to oversee the legal restoration to his family of the villa – appropriated first by the Nazis, then by the Communists, and finally by nationalist capitalists – which now, in the absence of any other surviving relative, belonged theoretically to Haffner and his descendants. No, even here, in the centre of Europe, he had managed to complicate matters even more mythologically. In addition he had already managed to concoct this unusual story with Zinka. Not content with this, he had also managed to concoct another more ordinary story: an affair with a married woman, staying at the hotel. Her name was Frau Tummel. She said that she adored him; and one aspect of Frau Tummel's soul was its sincerity.

Haffner, however, at this moment, didn't care about Frau Tummel's soul. He knew that he was meant to have been with her – regarding a sad sunset. But Zinka's sudden plan had possessed an overwhelming power of persuasion.

He was not a good man. He didn't need to be told. The jury wasn't out on Haffner's ethics. The case was closed. As a businessman, he had tended to the risky; as a husband, to the unfaithful. He hadn't really cared about his duties as a father or a grandfather. He cared about himself.

How fluently Haffner could self-lacerate! Then again: how easily Haffner could be distracted from his tribunal.

Niko began to whimper, gently. Why, thought Haffner, in his cupboard, did Haffner have to be old? It was devastating; it was Sophoclean. How could this love for Zinka have arrived so late in his life? Yes, Haffner was lyrical. He understood the language of inspiration. Here it was. Yes, here it was. He was inflated: a Silenus raised from his stupor, made buoyant by a force which was beyond him, as he stood there, neatly framed by a hotel wardrobe.

8

I should pause on that adjective Sophoclean, that noun Silenus.

Haffner was an admirer of the classics.

He had always watched the television dons; he had listened to the radio intellectuals. And now, at this late stage, in his retirement, Haffner had embarked on a programme of enlightenment – a succession of evening classes. Even if he would learn nothing about himself, he still wanted to know everything about anything else. So there they were: the old and unemployed, the desperate to learn. Into this group came Haffner. In these classes, Haffner read history. That was his idea of the classic. Occasionally, after he had returned to London, until Haffner's dying took over, I came with him. We grappled, in the introductions to the classics, with the concept of philosophic history. History which was ironic, clever, unimpressed.

The course on the *Lives of the Caesars* was Haffner's late education. He listened to a man berate the Caesars for their immorality. What a lesson it was, said Errol – sitting behind a desk which was too small for him, being made for a lissom teenager, not a distended middle-aged man – what a lesson in vanity, in the way power corrupted. To which the group, all seated at miniature desks, solemnly assented. A poster on the wall displayed a range of fluorescent vegetables and their appropriate names in German. Then Haffner asked if he could say something. He understood that they had all been very moved by the book which was the subject of this course. And he would like to say that he had been the most moved of them all. He had been converted, he said: and now he fully understood the grandeur of the Romans. He hadn't cared for them before, but now, said Haffner, reading about the glorious crimes of the emperors, he saw how truly great they really were.

At this point, Haffner paused for the expected laugh. It did not come.

Blissfully, Haffner had roamed along the shelves of the hotel library, parsing its eccentric selection of the classics. Beside his bed, there was now an abridged edition of Edward Gibbon, underneath his copy of the *Lives of the Caesars*. By his lounger at the side of the pool, with its view of the snow-shrouded mountains, was a novel by Thomas Mann. He liked to stretch himself. Only after a week here had Haffner realised he was the only one who read. Everyone else favoured sleep; they favoured chatter. But Haffner respected those things over which he had no authority. Those things made him want to accrue their authority too. His will was all vicarious.

Haffner hadn't been to university. His daughter had been, and his grandson, but not Haffner. He had been to war instead. But

Haffner felt no insecurity. He had his own triumphs. It was Haffner, for instance, who had persuaded the Chancellor of the Exchequer, the Governor of the Bank of England and the Emeritus Professor of Economic Theory at the LSE – Goldfaden, hero of the Brains Trust, doyen of the radio lecture – to be gathered in one unheard-of trio at the annual dinner of the City branch of the Institute of Bankers, in 1982. He wasn't nobody.

And now he was a student of philosophic history. With this know-ledge, he weighed up his biography: he studied the story of Livia, his wife; and Goldfaden, Haffner's friend and counsellor. Goldfaden: the celebrity economist, famed on both sides of the Atlantic.

Goldfaden was a capitalist; but a capitalist who liked to tease. Where, Goldfaden would ask his baffled listeners, was the greatest monument to international *esprit*? Who had inherited the mantle of Isaac Leib Peretz, the Jewish cosmopolitan? The man who had once argued, at the beginning of the century, that it was a unique culture rather than its patrolled borders that guaranteed a nation its independent existence. True, maybe. But you couldn't beat patrolled borders to help you sleep at night, thought Haffner. Couldn't beat them. While Goldfaden carried on his party trick. They couldn't guess? They couldn't say which was the most cosmo-politan country on earth? The Soviet Union, of course! The greatest federation of nations this world had seen since the Roman empire. Communism! The highest stage of imperialism. What Jew wouldn't love an empire? An empire, continued Goldfaden, was the greatest political system on earth – a confederation of states, blithe to the problems of ethnicity. The zenith of liberalism. But its era was now over; and Goldfaden mourned it. Or so he said, thought Haffner.

But Haffner was still not ready to consider the problem of Goldfaden.

One time, having finished the classic novel I had told him to read, Haffner told me that it had prompted certain thoughts. Think about it: the novel of education was lost on the young. It was the old who were the true protagonists. It was the old, thought Haffner, who deserved the love stories. Return, Monsieur Stendhal! Let yourself go, Mr Dickens! Feast on Haffner! Write a sentimental education for the very old, the absolute advanced.

But no one would.

It was a pity, because Haffner was a folk hero. These were the stories I grew up with – about Haffner. He was a man of legend: his anecdotes were endless. Like this, his final story.

Because there it was, once more, the lust – extravagant: like a sprinkler in the rose garden of Haffner's suburban home, automatically turning itself on to soak the lawn already soaked with rain.

9

Niko was now spread on the bed, his legs twitching. His eyes were shut. Zinka was poised, leaning over his face. His mouth was blindly searching – a kitten – for her breasts.

Then Haffner swayed and chimed against the hangers.

Niko was stilled. Haffner was stilled, his heart an amplification. Only Zinka continued as if nothing had happened. She tended to Niko; she asked him to carry on. And Haffner stood and listened to his heart as if he were only an outsider – as if he were the minicab driver waiting outside a nightclub, in the dawn, in the East End of London, or the Meatpacking District of New York, listening to the deep bass rhythm through the guarded doors while swapping two Marlboros for two much stronger and harsher cigarettes illegally imported from Iran.

To Haffner's slow relief, he noticed that slowly Niko was slowly distracted, slowly.

He really should have been somewhere else, thought Haffner. He should have been with Frau Tummel. Or, even more morally, he should have been in his own room, in his own bed, asleep, with his head slipping off the bolster's irritating cylinder – before returning once again, the next morning, to the Town Hall and its endless offices, where the subcommittees sat, the subcommittees which included the committee on Spatial Planning. The committee over which Haffner was here to exercise his charm. Yes, he should have been performing his role as a family man. But Haffner, somehow, still preferred this wardrobe with a view.

Livia's own erotic style, he remembered, watching Zinka, had been subtler. She would meet him in the foyer of the municipal pool in Golders Green, having just performed a synchronised swimming routine, and Haffner would say to her, laughing, that she was his emissary in the world of women. He would beg her to tell him what she saw, in the changing rooms. Livia sat him down. She touched him with the tips of her fingers absently resting on his penis through the button fly of his trousers, for this was how gentlemen dressed, and she told him about the girls in their changing room, the ones who shaved the hair between their legs into neater triangles, the ones who stood there, naked, pretending nobody could see, a festival of women. And Haffner would ask her not to stop, not to stop, and Livia would say that she wasn't stopping, dear heart: she wasn't stopping.

Then Zinka and Niko came to their own conclusion.

Haffner relaxed, relieved. He was beginning, he realised, to be too preoccupied by the practical difficulties of this display. Now that it was over, he began to long for his own bed. But Niko, to Haffner's irritation, seemed to be in a languid state of abandon. He wanted to lie there; he wanted Zinka to rest in his arms.

This was not, thought Haffner, at all what he had been led to expect.

And Haffner waited, in a wardrobe, while a couple held each other: amorous.

Oh Haffner had stamina! So often, in the bedroom, Haffner surpassed everyone's expectation. So many people thought they knew him! As if anyone could really know him. But Haffner would often argue that in this matter of Haffner's monstrosity one could draw some distinctions. He wasn't, for example, a monster like Caligula. The incest didn't move Haffner. Whereas Caligula used to commit incest with each of his three sisters in turn. And very possibly his mother. And his brothers. His mother and his brothers and his aunts.

Haffner was the generalissimo of hyperbole. Unlike a real generalissimo, however, he had to perform the hyperbole himself.

My poor Haffner: his own shill.

No one else, for instance, was so sure that the obvious comparison to Haffner was Caligula. It wasn't so much Haffner's monstrosity which troubled his family, but his absolute mundanity. Whenever his daughter, Esther, brought up the issue of his adultery, his bed tricks, she said he was banal. She would stand there, in her business suits, with their badly cut trousers; her silk blouse; the sleek blonde bob which Haffner regretted, taming as it did the cuteness of her curls. This belittling idea of hers had always unnerved Haffner. He felt a distant sense of pique. Surely, he would reason, unconvincingly, afterwards – to an unconvinced Haffner, or an unconvinced anonymous drinker, or the indignant husband of his daughter – the infidelity had contained infinite riches, if only you knew how to look? From one perspective, pure vanity: yes maybe. But from another – what gorgeous vistas! What passes, what valleys, what pastoral hillocks!

Was there really anything so wrong, thought Haffner, in a crescendo of impatience, as he waited for Niko and Zinka to leave, as Zinka paused in the doorway, looking back to the innocent wardrobe – was there really anything so wrong, thought Haffner, as he finally emerged, with being a man of feeling?

The classics were full of it. The loves of the gods were various. The loves of Jupiter, for instance, were a festival of costume change, of metamorphosis. He mated with Aegina as a flame, Asteria as an eagle, Persephone as a snake; with Leda he took the form of a swan, with Olympias a snake. To Semele he appeared as a blazing fire, to Io as a fog, to Danae as a shower of gold. When he first slept with Juno, his wife, he became a cuckoo. Alcmena and Callisto were won by his impersonations of humans. Yes, the loves of Jupiter were famous. They had heft.

With these stories Haffner sought consolation.

But, I have to add, in the many stories of Haffner, he was always only himself.

Haffner Amorous

1

Returning to his room, Haffner rounded a corner and passed a coiled roulade of fire hose pinned to the wall, as he happily imagined his bed and its crisp sheets, a single circle of chocolate laid out on one diagonal fold. And then he discovered the weeping monumental form of Frau Tummel.

For what was up was also down, and what seemed a victory, after all, was really a defeat: so Haffner's happiness must always be subject to swift reversals.

Frau Tummel was in a cotton nightgown, with ruched lace at the breasts, and a cotton bathrobe stitched with pink tight roses. There, in front of his door, Haffner confronted her – outlandish in his sky-blue and pistachio ensemble. He looked around, to see if anyone else might be there. He felt burdened with concern: for Frau Tummel, and for himself. He didn't want to explain why it was that he had returned to his room this late, in such exhaustion.

Frau Tummel raised her face, displaying the ravages of her mascara: a harlequin.

—What are you doing here? said Haffner, brightly.

—We had a rendezvous, she said.

—Come now, said Haffner, less brightly.

Maybe it was over, she said, sadly.

—Over? said a Haffner transformed into the sign for a smile: a single reclining parenthesis.

Yes, continued Frau Tummel. It would end with him leaving her. She knew this. And it was right. For sure. It was understandable.

He tried to reassure her. Of course he wasn't going to leave! The idea of it! And Frau Tummel said that yes, she knew this. She knew he thought this was true. But how could he know this? There were so many complications. She really thought they needed to discuss this.

The sign for Haffner was no longer a supine parenthesis.

He knew what he was meant to say. He didn't want to say it. He wanted to be alone; to go to sleep. But Haffner had his code of honour. This was one aspect of his undoing. He was an admirer of the classics, and no man with a classical education could deny the wills of women. The classics taught one, he had decided, to trust in the pagan gods. Trust Cupid. Trust him in all his other guises, as cherubs, or as Eros. The men must always allow themselves to be led by the women. So he said what he was meant to say. He wondered if she would like to come into his room.

Frau Tummel raised her ravaged face: a joyful harlequin.

So ended, in one swift exchange, the swift moment of Haffner's happiness.

2

The imbroglios seemed so fluently to come to Haffner.

He was here to claim his wife's inheritance – therefore, naturally, he became involved with other women. This seemed to be the logic of his life.

They had met two weeks ago, on the second day of his stay, at the swimming-pool complex in the hotel's basement. There were three pools – three adjacent water lilies, each attached to the other by a miniature set of steps. The smallest was a jacuzzi – for the indolent, or the fat. In it could therefore be found Haffner, who was indolent, and Frau Tummel, who was fat.

The voice of Frau Tummel, he soon discovered, was husky, it was rasping. She had class. She wrapped herself in a towel to go and lie on a lounger outside, to smoke three rapid cigarettes, pinched in the contraption of her extravagant cigarette holder – which unfolded and then unfolded one more time, just when you thought it could not be extended further. Then she relapsed into the boiling jacuzzi, to Haffner's charmed curiosity.

He wasn't normally so devoted to swimming pools. He preferred the gyms – the exercise machines which prolonged to such a surprisingly toned extent the overlong life of Haffner. The gym was another place where we had fleetingly made conversation. Occasionally, I would happen on Haffner in the changing room: and, delighted, he maintained a naked conversation – our penises dolefully looking away – while I stood there on the bobbled tiles wishing I were not faced by the superior nature of Haffner's so much older muscles. Although the gym was really a place of yearning for Haffner. It was, quite frankly, most often a place of rest. In the gym, a slothful primate, he could let his arms droop over the bars on the chest press. Below the slope of his T-shirt, his arms were white and darkly speckled, like a photocopy. From here, he could observe the varieties of breast movement – some solid in sports bras, others fragile, unsupported, tenderly visible. He developed a stare for this purpose, an alibi – heavy-lidded with exhaustion, hypnotically unfocused, unable to look away.

Frau Tummel worked in the perfume industry. She was here in this spa hotel with her husband – whose nerves, she told Haffner, were gone, whose blood pressure was abnormal. He spent his days on the veranda, looking at the silent mountains: sipping peppermint tea. It was, thought Haffner, the old old story: the loyal wife who was bored of her loyalty – the century's normal story of a spa.

When Frau Tummel had gone, Haffner leaned back in the jacuzzi, letting the movement of the bubbles absorb his concentration with their frantic foam – and then he padded off, leaving dark echoes of his feet on the floor's lukewarm tiling. In one room, he discovered a table with flowers: gentian, violets. In another room there was a sauna, where a woman was lying, motionless, on the pine slats of the highest step. Haffner paused, considered not. And then he pushed open another door, and discovered Frau Tummel again, in the process of being massaged. She was lying on her front, on a towel monogrammed in stitched gold thread with the hotel's invented crest. And in her shock she leaned up, so exposing to Haffner's gaze the moles on her breasts, the beginnings of her pink areolae, cobbled with cold.

He apologised, and went outside. Twenty minutes later he apologised to her again, in the rest room, illuminated by low lighting, and inventively perfumed candles – tuberose, lily, pomegranate. They decided to go for a walk. They made for the peak of the mountain. Light shimmered on her hair. She was uninterested in Haffner's ability to name the varieties of Alpine star, the daisies and the grasses – names he had culled from a colour-coded children's botany book, the white flowers in one section, the pink in another, bought in a fit of nostalgia for Haffner's earnest youth when buying chocolate in a tabac. She wanted to talk about love. She wanted to talk about her marriage, which entailed discussion of Haffner's marriage. It involved so many sacrifices, did he not think? The conversation so absorbed them that soon she was back in the hotel with Haffner, sitting on his bed. This did not surprise Haffner. Nor was it surprising that, as she lit a final cigarette, then stubbed it out, Haffner discovered that, without realising, as he kissed her, he had gone too far. He had overstepped, or overreached.

Yes, because nothing in this world occurs without a backstory: and what is higher always derives from what is lower and every victory contains its own defeat.

That day, Frau Tummel's feelings had been a little depleted. She had been demoralised by a fractious meeting with her husband's doctor in the morning; and then by an unhappy phone call from her mother at lunchtime. The massage had been suggested by her husband – it would, he said, cheer her up. The casual flirting with Haffner was an improvised addition of her own. But nothing, thought Frau Tummel now, as she stubbed out her final cigarette, was improvised. Nothing was casual. Everything was fate.

Like Haffner, she saw signs everywhere.

She turned round, and Haffner kissed her. And Frau Tummel kissed him back – for he was the magical combination of clever and kind. He understood her. But at this point, her body overtook her.

Frau Tummel was fifty-five. Her periods, as she used to tell her girlfriends, in a spirit of European openness, were becoming more and more erratic. Her cycle was unpredictable. The night before, after an absence of three months, a period had begun. And so she did not want to have sex with Haffner. She did not even want to undress. He must not touch her. Gently, Frau Tummel tried to explain her feelings to Haffner.

She didn't want to say, she said. He should not make her say.

And Haffner did not mind, he told her, gently. For he knew why – the constant coyness of unfaithful wives. So Haffner continued to kiss her. Through his trousers, hesitantly she touched the nub of his penis, blunted by his briefs.

Born with a different kind of soul to Haffner, Frau Tummel's husband was repelled by her periods. Quickly they had developed an unspoken rule that they would never have sex at these times; nor would he even touch her. Frau Tummel was therefore amazed when Haffner was so undisgusted. Such elegance!

Such delicacy! It even tempted her, for a moment, to relinquish her scruples. But no, she thought, gathering herself, she really shouldn't.

Perhaps if she had slept with Haffner, she might not have been so moved. But she did not. So Frau Tummel could nurture her feelings, invulnerable to complication. On returning to her husband, she could wonder why it was she was so impatient with desire.

Haffner didn't know how seriously Frau Tummel took her moment with Haffner. He thought this was what she did. He thought she had done this before. She would go so far, and then back off.

Frau Tummel, however, had never been unfaithful. She was not trained at it. The guilt of it confused and overtook her, the next morning, as she woke up beside her husband, cutely rumpled in a mess of pillow and pyjama.

The guilt of it confused and overtook her – Frau Tummel! who was fifty-five! but at fifty-five you can still, after all, be inexperienced – that this feeling she felt for Haffner must be love.

3

She didn't know that love was always the beginning of Haffner's downfall. She didn't know that this was what Haffner was gloomily concluding, as he observed Frau Tummel's weeping form, sipping a gin and tonic he had invented from the minibar.

Mainly, the love belonged to other people. Once, it had been Haffner's.

When he was courting her, in the summer of 1939, Haffner used to take Livia dancing in metroland, the green and pleasant suburbs of north London. Since Haffner was a little perturbed by this girl who had the glamour of a foreign accent, Italianate, a flutter, he tried to impress her with the gorgeousness of his dancing, for at that time Haffner – so Haffner said – had the finest pair of feet in north London. And in Highgate once they sat down after a dance, and looked at each other, while Haffner worried about the visibility of his erection, mummified in his underwear. They had been dancing a foxtrot. He crossed his legs, making sure that Livia could not see or know about it. But she knew. And it intrigued her. She sat there, and she wondered if Haffner would do anything so bold as try to kiss her. They had been courting for some time now. She had just turned eighteen. And she wondered if she would be interested if Haffner did indeed do something. Yes, she thought, she would. But it needed Haffner first. While Haffner, who was shy despite his fleet feet, his slick blond hair, decided that he could do nothing without her visible approval. And so Haffner and Livia sat together and neither touched nor talked.

Two weeks later, at a dance hall in Hendon, they argued about this.

She was sorry, concluded Livia, but it didn't happen and if it didn't happen then it couldn't happen. Haffner asked if this had to be true. Yes, said Livia, it did. And she left Haffner outside, and went back in on the arm of another man. There was a small wart on the right-hand side of his neck, like a piece of gravel. So Haffner had nowhere to go. He walked away from home, towards the river, for an hour, into the dismal city. He reached the Gray's Inn Road, then High Holborn, where the family law firm was, the family law firm which he was destined never to enter, and then wandered back, finding himself in Clerkenwell. This, he discovered, was a mistake. All the Italian shops made him even more nostalgic for his Livia. He passed Chiappa & Sons, the organ makers on Eyre Street Hill; the working men's club – the Mazzini Garibaldi – where her brother, Cesare, would later sit and play morra: teased for his elegant accent, his neat small hands. In the cab shelter opposite Hatton Garden, by the Italian church, Haffner sat at a table beside an initial pool of gravy which he mopped up with the folded triangle of a napkin. He looked out of the window. Up on Leather Lane, a jumper was caught in a tree. It settled, sodden, between a collection of branches. And as he gazed at this wrecked jumper, improbably in the branches of this silver birch, Haffner realised that it wasn't a kiss he wanted: it wasn't even the body of Livia. He wanted her for ever. He wanted to marry her. And so he concocted an imaginary conversation between an imaginary Haffner and an imaginary Livia, as he looked at the way the foggy rain made the occasional lamp outside a sieved and shimmering haze, a delicate gold.

These thoughts returned to Haffner, sentimental, in the Alpine rain, observing the different gold of a Central European desk light.

4

He knew this was all very wrong, said Frau Tummel.

—Oh I don't know, said Haffner, airily.

She had decided that she really must cheer up. She must not be so down. She must not show him this face of hers.

What he did to her, what he made her feel: was wrong, said Frau Tummel. He was a bad man, she said – tapping him on the nose: a disgruntled, startled puppy. He was a bad man.

She may have been delicious, thought Haffner, sadly – with her joyful breasts, her trembling thighs – but her concerns were not his concerns. It was undeniable. The flirting surely could have possessed slightly more *élan*. But Frau Tummel didn't want sophistication. Frau Tummel's thing was love. She went for the serious. And Haffner was not in the mood for love; or the serious. Or maybe I should say: he didn't go for love now, with her. With Frau Tummel he would have liked, instead, to be delirious with appetite.

The love was all for Zinka.

—Yes, yes, said Haffner. You told me that.

And maybe this was not fair. Maybe this wasn't accurate to the difficulty Frau Tummel was feeling.

Did he know, she asked him, how lucky they were?

—How lucky? queried Haffner.

Yes, how lucky they were, repeated Frau Tummel.

He looked at her. She stepped forward, let the belt of her bathrobe undo itself, pushed it off her shoulders, on to the floor. Then she unbuttoned her nightgown to her breasts, and pulled it down over her shoulders. Now, therefore, she was naked – except, to Haffner's surprise, for her bra. The bra saddened him; it added to her pathos. Like the bathrobe, it was dotted with stitched pink roses.

In this bra, Haffner confronted the problem of love.

Haffner was not all barbarian, not all the time. He was helpful. He tried to please. Weakly, not wanting to sadden her, he wondered if they should order some champagne.

Stricken, he watched Frau Tummel smile.

—Oh, said Frau Tummel, it is a good life, is it not?

Haffner's deepest wish was to possess the total independence of a mad imperator; a classical god. But the stern line of Haffner's cruelty was always complicated by the kink of his kindness.

Frau Tummel leaned across the bed, on to her stomach, and picked up the phone. She talked to reception as she lay there, her legs kicking in the air. It was such a girlish gesture, this kicking in the air.

While somewhere else – but where? Dubrovnik? La Rochelle? – a younger Livia opened the wardrobe in their hotel room so that the mirror reflected the bed on which she flung herself, face down, thus able to be ravaged from behind by her marauder, the angel Raphael, while simultaneously watching her angel rear devastatingly above her.

But where? Dover, in 1949!

Haffner leaned forward, and spread Frau Tummel's legs apart:

revealing their symmetrical Rorschach stain – like a picture of a butterfly once solemnly presented to him by his grandson, Benjamin, constructed by pressing one half of the paper over the other – already stained with Benji's idea of a butterfly's smudged if multicoloured pattern. Haffner began to lick her, gently, as she tried to finish the call. And as he licked her, as he parted her, she started to invent more and more food. They would have champagne, she said, yes – and also caviar. And blini. And a Russian salad. And pickled cucumbers. And oh, she said. No, oh, she said. She was fine. She was very well. If they could bring everything in, if they could just come up and put everything in her room. If they could bring it up. If they could bring it up. And put it in. Then she put the phone down, and revelled in the pleasure of Haffner's flesh.

If he was touching her like this, then of course it was love. No one except her husband had ever touched her in this way. Not even her husband had touched her in this way.

Too soon, the room service arrived. She gathered herself back into the bathrobe. Haffner, in his dishevelled tracksuit, tipped the waiter, wondering if he could induce him to stay, deciding that he couldn't.

—You aren't angry with me? she asked.

But why, asked Haffner, would he be angry?

But it was so complicated. She was sorry. She was sorry for being so complicated. But he had to understand. She had a husband.

Haffner understood.

He must think it was like Romeo and Juliet, she said.

Haffner did not reply: he had no idea how he could reply.

—You know, she said, I am not. This is not me. But it is difficult to hide the secrets of the heart.

—Hide what? said Haffner, appalled.

—Raphael! said Frau Tummel. You are too much.

And Haffner considered the extraordinary way in which a life repeated itself. For Livia had used this phrase for him. Just once. Or a phrase resembling this phrase. Maybe he was too much for her, she said. Maybe in the end he was too much even for her. And when he had tried to tell Livia, this was in 1982, the night of his triumphant dinner for the Institute of Bankers, that all he wanted was her, she turned away. They were sitting in the kitchen. She was in a nightgown which Haffner had never liked – being made of a blue towelling, which tended to make her look, he argued, unattractive: he never wanted the cosy, the comfortable, only the erotic. That was one form, he now considered, of his immaturity. So maybe everyone had him right. He could understand it. He was too much for himself.

He put his fingers to Frau Tummel's lips. She began to kiss them. Each finger she curled into her mouth.

What could really go wrong, thought Haffner, in a hotel, in a spa town? It seemed safe enough.

But then he had to correct himself. He allowed his will to follow the wills of women. That was his classical principle. But he knew that this had its problems too. He freely admitted this. When the women were in love with him, then Haffner was no longer safe. This was one aspect of his education. It had happened with Barbra. It had happened before Barbra. And now, he worried, it was happening again.

This was one aspect of his education. But Haffner would never learn.

5

Haffner acceptingly approached the women who approached him as if they were portents. They were Haffner's irresistible fate.

He didn't, he once said – in a conversation which was now legendary in Haffner's family, when confronted by Esther after

36

Livia's death with accusations of his truly infantile excesses – he didn't want to regret anything. No, he didn't see why he should be left with any regret. He said this without really thinking, as he said so many things. Or so argued Haffner afterwards – after it had become his definition. As if a man's marriage, said Esther, triumphantly, with the absolute agreement of her family, should ever make him regret anything. Esther's husband, Esmond, did not continue the conversation. And although it had passed into the annals of his family as the epitome of Haffner's selfishness, as recounted to me once by Benjamin, I was not so convinced. Awkward he may have been, but Haffner was not malicious. And Benjamin, with his new-found devotion to his religion, his new-found devotion to the family, was not, I thought, a reliable moral guide: he had lost his imagination.

Nor, I tried to say to Benjamin, had Livia ever been public with her disapproval. If she really disapproved. So maybe this should make us pause as well.

One can be so rarely sure, Haffner once said to me, that what one has done is right. So maybe it was possible that in his self-defence Haffner was being truthful, rather than self-deceiving. He was simply being faithful to his refusal of self-denial; his absolute distrust of the philosophy on which it was based, the puritanical certainty.

Which was one reason, surely, why Livia might love him. For Haffner's absolute sense of humour.

6

Oh, the comic pathos of dictators! Haffner's sense of humour!

Maybe they were never really given their moral due. More and more, as Haffner lay beside the swimming pool, or sat on a bench in front of an Alpine view, he approved of the scandalous emperors. He couldn't understand the world's astonishment.

Like Augustus, who had absolute faith, so wrote his historian, in certain premonitory signs. Once, when a palm tree pushed its way between the paving stones in front of his home he had it transplanted to the inner court beside his household gods, and lavished care on it. Just as Haffner found it difficult to reject the women who entered his sphere of orbit. Who could have the hubris to reject the artistry of chance? If Augustus didn't, then why should Haffner? Even if it was unclear how much his meetings with women were to do with chance, rather than the machinations of Haffner's will. But then again, Augustus could be a mentor here as well, since it was Augustus who justified his adulterous affairs as the necessary burden of an emperor – charged with knowing the secrets of his subjects, his closest advisers. Of course an emperor had to sleep with his counsellors' wives! How else would he know what they were thinking? There was nothing in it for Augustus: his sexual life was all in service to the state.

And in fact this was not a new discovery of Haffner's. Perhaps he had forgotten, but the emperors had entered his moral universe before. Years ago, Livia had been reading about these Roman dictators. They were all in Dubrovnik, in the wilds of Europe, during one of Esther's summer holidays. They lay underneath a parasol, moving their position in relation to it as the day wore on, a live performance of a sundial – and, to the shuffle of the sea, Livia read aloud to Haffner from the book which her brother had given her. A new translation. Haffner was slowly sunburning. And she had mischievously read out to Haffner the story of Tiberius – the man who had built a private sporting-house, where sexual extravagances were performed for his secret pleasure. Hundreds of girls and young men, whom he had collected from all over the empire as adepts in unnatural practices, and known as *spintriae* – but what did *spintriae* mean? wondered Haffner: it must have been dirty; it must have been good, or the man would have translated it: no, said Livia, there was no footnote, nothing – would perform before Tiberius in groups of three, to excite his waning passion. Some aspects of his criminal obscenity were almost too vile to discuss, much less believe, read Livia. Imagine training little boys, whom he called his minnows, to chase him while he went swimming and get between his legs to lick and nibble him! Or letting babies not yet weaned from their mother's breast suck at him – such a filthy old man he had become! So wrote his historian. But neither Livia nor Haffner was so prone to judgement.

Filthy old man or not, they seemed to get Tiberius. The experimenter with pleasure: a pioneer of power – always minuscule before the infinite.

A few years later, at the time of the Brazilian coup, they had been in São Paolo – some deal with a bank which didn't work out. The deal, and the bank. With their host, who impressed Haffner with the beauty of his wife, and the cultural beauty of his life, they were sitting in a theatre, watching a classic of contemporary theatre. And even Haffner was amused when the police burst in, and called up everyone involved on stage. They took a programme and began to intone the names: the actors, the stage manager, the lighting designer. Dutifully, the arrested provocateurs lined up on stage. And finally, stated the policemen, confident in their authority, they demanded that the arch instigator, the impresario of this whole production should present himself to the police as well: a man with the unlikely Brazilian name of Bertolt Brecht. Everyone looked concernedly around. Mr Brecht appeared, they thought, to have disappeared.

And what Haffner now remembered was how that night, in their hotel room, Livia had confessed that however much she found it funny, however much she had laughed with their hosts, with the audience, with the entire tropical night – deep in her worried thoughts was a regret. She still felt sorry for the deluded dictatorial policemen.

The poor dictators! Even the dictators, after all, were the dupes of accident and defeat.

7

At this moment, for instance, Frau Tummel was trying, in the words of the comics, to offer Haffner pleasure. Perhaps this might not obviously seem like a defeat. But look closer, dear reader – look closer. Enter Haffner's soul. Haffner was beginning to feel melancholy. Soft in Frau Tummel's mouth, his penis had no point to it.

If the ghost of Livia were looking down, at this moment, perhaps she would have found this funny, thought Haffner. And so could he. It was just another instance of the accidental.

He touched Frau Tummel, gently, on her grey and golden hair – on the combed grey roots. Could he ask her, politely, he said, to stop doing what she was doing?

Frau Tummel looked up, the head of his slumped penis slumped on the slump of her lower lip. A thin trail of saliva, unnoticed, connected the two. Haffner tried to be romantic: he tried to maintain the tone. She still loved her husband, he told her. She was being silly. But no, said Frau Tummel. It was over a long time ago. And she bent down, continuing to show her affection to Haffner. While Haffner despaired. His soft penis was not moving. It hung there: obeisant to the law of gravity.

It wasn't, obviously, the first time this kind of event had occurred. The despair was local. It had placed Haffner in a difficult social situation. On the one hand, it meant that he could not experience the pleasures he had previously experienced with Frau Tummel. But, on the other hand, he could not ask her to leave. His pride would not allow it. So he was trapped into a conversation – where Frau Tummel had the power. She pitied him; she pored over him; she looked after him. She stated the permanence of their love.

His impotence had trapped Haffner in a conversation he wanted to be over. This sadness was creating so much more intimacy than he ever wanted. He tried to concentrate on images of the erotic: he tried to think about Zinka's breasts. But Zinka eluded him. He remembered the way Livia had touched him, the first time, at the ponds on Hampstead Heath – her hand dipping under his briefs, under the curve of his tense strained penis, a hand which he delightedly and immediately made wet with his semen. Neither of them had spoken. She simply withdrew her hand, took out a handkerchief, wiped it gently – a gesture which for Haffner still seemed fraught with tenderness.

And maybe that had been the moment when he decided to marry Livia: when he knew that he was in love. Just because it had happened so fast. All his triumphs, he began to think now, were just defeats reconfigured. Like the time he batted for five hours in Jerusalem, in 1946, thus securing an improbable draw on a pitch destroyed by three days of tropical rain.

He looked at Frau Tummel. Frau Tummel was looking with tenderness at him: an absolute maternal tenderness. A tenderness which made Haffner afraid with its intimacy. And she bent down, kissed his penis, at its tip.

—Whatever you want, she said. Whatever you want, I will do.

He looked down at his drooping penis – once faithful in all his infidelities. Its defeat now should not, he reflected, have surprised him.

—You can have me, said Frau Tummel, anywhere. If that will help. You can have me where my husband has not had me.

Frau Tummel believed in the reality of their love. She believed that this love was truth. Frau Tummel was not a libertine: for her, the erotic was an aspect of love. She was a Christian woman. She had been brought up to trust and worship the instincts of her soul.

Or was now not the right time for her little lamb? she wondered. Perhaps not, replied her little lamb. Perhaps not.

—We must, said Frau Tummel, talk to my husband. It is the only right thing.

She said this with no enjoyment, no glory. She had come here with her ill husband. She was a model wife. And she would leave with her life destroyed, she thought. She could not live without her husband, and now she could not leave without Haffner. To Haffner, however, it seemed so unnecessary. He talked about the need to take their time. He talked about the need not to injure the blossom of their love.

The dawn was just beginning, in the window. There was a light sparse rain.

But maybe it was possible, she added, for Haffner to forget. If he would only let another woman into his life – to care for him, to be his companion.

8

Frau Tummel's will was just another way in which the twentieth century was conspiring to entrap Haffner. Once more, he had entered *Mitteleuropa*. It was a place which had always amazed him. Its endless capacity for seriousness! The intellectual fervour! Whenever he thought about the Europeans, he became hysterical with exclamations. Ever since he discovered, through Cesare, that the Russians wrote to each other with exclamation marks, Haffner had liked this theatrical way of talking. The European vocative – addressing absent abstractions. Love! Death! Fame! Bohemia! Wherever Bohemia was. It was how he always thought about Cesare. Whom Haffner had loved. Of whom Haffner despaired.

Cesare used to come up with Livia from Charlton, in south London, where they were boarding, at the home of a paint salesman from Trieste. Haffner used to sit with him on Wimbledon Common.

He was about twenty; Cesare was about eighteen. Cesare delighted in deckchairs. And patiently Haffner explained the rules of cricket. Cesare was slightly deaf in one ear – after an accident when he was a child. He didn't mind, however, because in Cesare's opinion it added lustre to him. His deafness was distinguished. He listened to Haffner with one hand cocked, like the flower of an ear trumpet. A hollyhock, thought Haffner. Patiently, he convinced Cesare that just because the two batsmen were at opposite ends of the wicket, this didn't mean that they were on different sides. Cesare could not understand this. He tried, but he could not.

Haffner loved him, but had never quite got him. Never, in his entire life, did Cesare lose his comical Italian accent. His hair was white by the time he was twenty; but his eyebrows forever were black. And Haffner never asked him if this was due to nature or nurture. Yes, Cesare would sit there, reading *War and Peace*, while Haffner watched the cricket. This must have been 1940, thought Haffner. When the BBC was supporting the Russian cause with its radio version of Tolstoy's novel. Haffner must have been on leave, or about to ship out. He would test Cesare on the characters' names from the bookmark – on which was printed each family, and a guide to pronunciation.

And then, as always, they discussed the politics of Europe. To Cesare, this was natural. So natural that from that point on it had marked his life, thought Haffner, these discussions of European politics: the endless problems Cesare found with any kind of state. Problems to which Haffner was oblivious. He had the arguments with anarchists, with socialists, with social democrats and liberal democrats. He had talked them through with fascists and with communists. Cesare himself had preferred a modified form of communism. Haffner, the Englishman, had demurred. He wouldn't be swayed by Cesare's assertion that Haffner, like Cesare, was a Jew, not an Englishman; that as a Jew he really should be more mindful of the rights of minority peoples.

Cesare was European; and Haffner was not.

Haffner did care about the rights of minorities. His way of displaying this was simply less exhibitionist than others – or so Haffner told himself. In 1938, for instance, at the Scarborough Cricket Festival, a week or so before Chamberlain set off for Munich, he had remonstrated with his father, who had offered the opinion that a Nazi Britain might have its advantages – less obsessed with money, less nouveau riche – unconvinced as he was that Hitler really meant to do away with every Jew. First, Raphael had reminded him, Hitler really did want to do away with every Jew; and secondly – he continued – what was so wrong with the plutocrats? Who had a problem with the City of London? He wasn't bothered by the vulgar, Haffner. He didn't see why Papa should so look down on people.

But then, sanity had never been Papa's hallmark. In the Great War, he had joined up in the Rangers. He served in the Dorsetshire Regiment, a machine-gunner. He served throughout the battle of Passchendaele, until he was wounded.

—Anything is better than war, said Papa. Anything.

And although Haffner thought he was the opposite of Papa, I am not so sure. No, like Papa, Haffner never took the Europeans seriously. Like Papa, he never quite understood its rages.

—My theory of course is that Cohen is not a real Jew, Haffner once said to me, talking about Goldfaden's friend, a Canadian Marxist Jewish academic: the son of immigrant pioneers. He's too Jewish to be true. My theory is, continued Haffner, that at a certain point in, say, the 1950s, he realised that his career could flourish if he were Jewish – not true now, of course, not true now – and that he therefore took on the persona of a Marxist Jewish intellectual.

—In reality, he concluded, his ancestry is Polish. Working-class anti-Semitic Polish. He denies this, of course. But then, finished Haffner, pouring himself another drink, smiling at me, ignoring my empty proffered glass, he would.

Haffner was silent. He kissed Frau Tummel, gently, on the cheek.

—I have an idea, said Frau Tummel. We will swim. Yes? We will have eine kleine dip. You have a wife. I have a husband. We must forget them both. For an hour.

But Haffner, he was realising, could forget nothing. Haffner was still ancient. He was wondering if Trajan had come here. Was this the land of Dacia, or Dalmatia? Pannonia? The Romans had conquered everywhere; their triumph was total. So presumably the legionaries had ended up in these mountains too – blistered, their groins chafed, their cracked nipples greased with duck fat to protect them against the coarse fabric of their shirts – and then afterwards, on their return to Rome, they had set up that column with its curving wrap-around frieze, like a stick of candy – or like the lighthouse on Cape Hatteras in the Outer Banks, where Haffner had spent a weekend with Livia, where they had seen the dolphins shimmying after each other, their sheen dappled and mottled in the water. Yes, that column which Haffner had seen when he was twenty-four and remembered nothing about the Romans except the fact that an orator called Cicero made many speeches – speeches, Livia told him, which had been delivered in that sad and empty brick building on the edge of the Forum. It hadn't moved Haffner then. It seemed to move Haffner now.

He had understood Livia, and Livia had understood him. She had borne with fractious grace the obvious signs of infidelity; the crazy signs of infidelity – like the moment when she saw a woman driving down the high street in Hendon, in Haffner's car. A car, he told her that evening, he had donated to the garage because it was out of order. How could he control what the garage had done with it next (folding his napkin, finding his pipe, leaving the room, aggrieved)? Yes, she understood the dictators. Livia – the most naturally elegant woman he ever knew: who once played tennis naked, he suddenly remembered, in the rain, after two gimlets and three martinis, at some friend's house in the Cotswolds. Oh he was stricken!

—Raphael! said Frau Tummel. Are you listening?

And yes yes, said Haffner, in another world entirely – where a rejuvenated version of Haffner issued giggling directions from the passenger seat, as Livia drove them back to London, tipsy and still naked except for a towel across her waist, the seat belt tight between her freezing breasts.

Haffner Amphibious

1

The lake in this town was not the kind which Haffner admired: it had no follies – no ruined grottos, no temples to Venus. Its spirit was civic, not aristocratic. Politics possessed it, not pleasure. It lay in front of the hotel; on the edge of the park. In the distance, made fuzzy to Haffner – bereft, as ever, of his glasses – were the twin peaks of the mountains, and their thinner silhouettes, the twin peaks of the factory chimneys. And all the cement apartment blocks: the random codes of their illuminated windows like the punched cardboard sheets for street organs.

Beside this lake, as the dawn freshened, Frau Tummel began to undress. Haffner looked around, nervously. They were sheltered, here, by two clustering beech trees. They did not reassure him very much. He looked at Frau Tummel, who was bending over, folding her nightgown. The tuft of hair between her legs was visible then invisible as she leaned further forward, arranging her bathrobe on top of the nightgown: a neat arrangement of squares.

An echo in Haffner's mind, Zinka bent over to extract her stocking from the bed's scalloped valance.

Reluctantly, Haffner undressed. He displayed his slighter breasts to the gathered winds: the voyeuristic zephyrs. They made for his pink nipples, the droop of his ghostly pectorals. He let his shirt drop where it wanted: it tumbled to the ground, a dying swan.

Just as after yet another late night of working he would undress in his dressing room, or on the landing, leaving puddles of clothes behind his tiptoeing footsteps – and then enter the bedroom, feeling the carpet on his bare feet, the densely corrugated metal strip at the door where the carpet ended, and then be suddenly surprised by Livia turning on an enquiring lamp, so that he paused there, a satyr, stalled in the pursuit of an invisible prey.

2

At the jetty, Haffner paused. The wood was greasy. Frau Tummel was already in – treading water, only her head visible. Her face had transformed itself into a smile.

—It is delicious, she said. You must come in.

Haffner was not amphibious, not normally. But nothing, at the moment, seemed normal. Their affair had been marked by water. Water was its motif. First the swimming pool, the jacuzzi: and now this. It was unusual in the life of Haffner. In general, he avoided water. Although it was true that there had been that night in the baths at Rome – the day after they had liberated the city. The opened city.

Silk reflections from the water had unfolded on the ceiling. The building was Haffner's most exalted idea of the grand. It was monumental. It was imperial. The largest bronze eagle he had ever seen was spread, like a mounted butterfly, against a wall.

There had been other moments in jacuzzis, whirlpool baths. There had been, also, Livia's love of swimming competitions, with her hair invisible in its sleek white cap. But, in these scenes, the water was an accessory. It was almost furniture.

He put a foot in, holding on to the jetty's post: paused. He retracted his foot.

—It is very cold, he said, gravely.

He looked around. The wind was breathing through the trees. But Haffner didn't want the nymphs, the naiads and dryads: the sylvan pastoral.

It wasn't that Haffner was immune to nature. Haffner was a member of the Royal Horticultural Society. Its journal would arrive, a precise oblong, in its plastic wrapper. It was the only society to which he felt allegiance: a community which shared his love of the cultivated, the meekly tended – the romance of the rose.

Haffner was an expert in breeding roses. He loved the extra-ordinary lottery of each new specimen. All the textbooks talked of the evolution of a species in temporal terms; for them, everything proceeded in a logical order. The first was always the most import-ant. But breeding, Haffner decided, proved this could not be true. It was a pure fluke, if a new variety of rose was formed, and there-fore propagated, before another one. Its place in the species had nothing to do with time. It was much more like a jigsaw puzzle. In nature, Haffner found the self-sufficiency of art. But he didn't describe it like this; which is how I might have described it. For Haffner, this insight had other vocabulary. That things could happen according to a logic which one could not understand was no argu-ment against that logic's existence. But perhaps this was not right, either; perhaps Haffner didn't use words to describe the pain it caused him, the lush pain as he looked at the photographs of gardens in exotic places, full of grace, these places in another hemisphere – Persia, Pakistan, Afghanistan.

You have no idea how therapeutic it can be – he would tell bored Benji, bovine – to take the secateurs and go out into the garden, after a hard day's work. Everyone, he would add, must have a hobby; and Benjamin, who at this point, when he was fifteen, wanted no hobbies, no bourgeois attributes, absently nodded.

Now, however, Haffner was oblivious to the pastoral: he wanted to be anywhere but here. He wanted sirens, emergencies, the asphalt and the smoke. The asphalt jungle and the big smoke. He wanted the transparent lethal purity of carbon monoxide.

So Haffner looked away, into the landscape, and there discovered to his dismay a shape which was walking with a staccato lilt, and which therefore would soon resolve itself into the more solid flesh of Zinka. Presumably, thought hampered Haffner, she was on her way back to work at the hotel. He looked down: at his slight breasts, his bright nipples, the hair around his belly button: his penis dwindling in the cold. An acorn, it blended in with the arboreal theme. There seemed no obvious hiding place, thought Haffner, rapidly assessing the bleak and empty parkland – and in any case it was too late. Zinka had seen him. Shame possessed Haffner – a shame that she was seeing him like this, so unclothed; and a greater shame of seeing her so soon after the escapade of the night before. He was not quite sure how one was to behave, when one has just concealed oneself inside a wardrobe in a vacated hotel room, to watch a woman nakedly converse with her boyfriend. But most of all, he felt embarrassed of her seeing him with Frau Tummel: in this illusion of intimacy. Because love was his downfall. And with Zinka, he was concerned that the love this time belonged to Haffner.

If only he could have explained how little Frau Tummel meant to him! Then, perhaps, he would have been glad to see Zinka. But he could not. So, in an ecstasy of embarrassment and shame – the only forms of ecstasy which seemed still available to Haffner – he jumped in.

3

As he sank, the everlasting problems of Haffner's life concentrated themselves into more particular problems of the body. He felt sheathed in cold; enveloped. It seemed unlikely that he would ever feel warm again. The water was dark, slubbed with weeds.

At first, Haffner thought that he was only sinking. But this was premature. Gradually, he felt his body ascend: gifted with buoyancy.

Finally, he reached the surface, where Frau Tummel joyfully greeted him. He tried to tread water. It seemed harder than he remembered. His heart was gripped by cold. He felt it slow, then slow some more. This scared him. His breathing became more difficult. He looked around for safety. No safety seemed visible.

—It is wonderful, no? said Frau Tummel.

Carefully, trying to swim suavely, Haffner made as if to disport himself, a porpoise, in the water. He tried to move towards the jetty, where he could cling to a step, or a pole.

—And how are you? asked Zinka: above him.

—Oh we are very well! said Frau Tummel. Is it not wonderful?

Zinka smiled at Haffner: a bubble of intimacy. Haffner, his hair slick over his forehead, a bedraggled pony, tried to smile winningly back.

Then he felt the weather begin. It started to rain on Haffner, and his mistress, gently, in the lake.

He clung to the jetty, and found no solace. He was out of his depth, thought Haffner. In all the possible senses.

They seemed to be having fun together, said Zinka. They weren't together, said Haffner. They thought it would be charming, said Frau Tummel. That wasn't right, Haffner tried to say.

The rain became stronger. In response, Haffner maintained a casual grin. Glancing with mock-helplessness at the heavens, Zinka said that she really had to be getting to work. Was it really necessary? asked Haffner. Frau Tummel glared at him. Yes, said Zinka, she felt so – after all, they didn't want her there, did they, interrupting them? Oh, said Haffner. He was sure that wasn't true. Was it? he asked Frau Tummel.

She didn't want to make Zinka late, said Frau Tummel.

It wasn't special to Haffner, the desperation he felt as reality crowded in. Haffner was special only in his hyperbole: his unusually stubborn refusal to accept the order of the facts. And because he was determined in his refusal of reality, hyperbolic with effort, Haffner said to Frau Tummel that of course Zinka wouldn't be late. It really wouldn't happen. In any case, if there were any trouble, he would take care of the matter. Indignantly Frau Tummel splashed away. Haffner looked at her. Zinka looked at her. Then, before Haffner could turn back to Zinka, Zinka had looked away.

—I should be going, said Zinka.

Surely, thought Haffner, he could think of something to say? Surely at this point he could come up with the sentence which would charm Zinka, and make her stay?

No, said Zinka. She really had to go. Frau Tummel splashed noisily in the calm water. Momentarily, Zinka was distracted. But she would see them later, no – perhaps for the aerobics? She smiled at Frau Tummel; then at Haffner. It would be at twelve. And she turned around, while Haffner gazed after her: her retreat in the grey towelling of her tracksuit.

Well, that went well, he thought, brightly. One should build on that. They weren't far off, he decided, mordantly, from reaching an understanding.

And this was how I could have depicted Haffner as an allegory, if I had wanted to make Haffner an allegory – with a woman walking away from him and a woman swimming away from him, while he clung to a jetty, frantically thinking, failing, possibly dying.

4

Now, announced Frau Tummel, they must swim. She offered Haffner the prospect of catching her, and then set off, with swift strong choppy strokes – the fat shaking beneath the curves of her biceps – towards what might, to Haffner's straining eyes, have been an island: or might have been just debris, floating in the lake.

Around him, the horizons gathered, and their attendant mountains.

He set off. Mistakenly, he swallowed some cold and soiled water. Very soon he wallowed back. If he could only move his arms, thought Haffner, then he might survive. The prospect seemed unlikely. It seemed improbable that Haffner's body would ever work again.

He was not, it was true, famous for the accuracy of his self-diagnosis. The day he thought he had cancer, he asked Livia if he could show her his testicles. She had just come out of the shower – in a perfume of synthetic citrus fruits. Her hair was flattened against her face, which emphasised the way her face with its perfect cheek-bones looked old, looked mournfully mature. He proffered her a testicle, asked her to feel it. She declined. Over breakfast, he pointed out that he should probably go to see Ordynski. Livia tightened the lid on the marmalade and agreed that he probably should. If it was absolutely necessary, then of course he should. And so it was that Haffner went to his doctor, who told him that no, there was nothing to worry about: there was no evidence of any tumour.

Haffner corrected Ordynski.

—Not yet, he sadly said.

He was the recorder on the grandest scale of all the ways in which life was unjust to him. These ways were mainly physical. And maybe Haffner was right: maybe this was one way of living healthily – minutely to record a list of all the unfair weaknesses he endured: a heart murmur, an attack of asthma, exploratory tests on his kidneys and aorta in an effort to discover the causes of Haffner's exorbitant blood pressure. Then the possible cancers, the lingering viruses. If this made him a hypochondriac, so be it. So what if he was still alive? It didn't prove the irrelevance of his symptoms. It didn't prove that one day they wouldn't unfurl themselves into truths.

What no one seemed to understand, he used to tell his daughter, as they watched Benjamin play cricket, on some sports ground in the bucolic environs of London – before Benjamin developed his intellectual difficulties with the idea of sport – was how the imagination of disaster was such a burden. He wouldn't wish it on anyone. It was no joke, living with illness in the way that Haffner lived with it. It was debilitating. Churchill, in Marrakech, got through his pneumonia on pills. He knew that. But that was Churchill. And Esther had simply got up, silently, straightened the creases in her slacks, and gone to buy herself a tea.

And as he mournfully watched the distant image of his grandson perform the neat parallelogram of a forward defensive stroke, Haffner considered the sad truth that his fears were never believed. Haffner was always alert to the way a life became a system of signs. It didn't seem unreasonable to Haffner. Greater men than Haffner, he reminded the now imaginary Esther, had been caught in the trap of a justified paranoia. Wasn't it well known, thought Haffner, that an emperor, of all people, was the most miserable of men – since only his actual assassination could convince the people that the manifold conspiracies against his life were real? This was one resemblance of Haffner to the emperors. Only Haffner's death would convince his family that he had been right all along.

In the mercurial water, this death seemed finally imminent. Frau Tummel had swum back. Such a kitten he was, to dislike the joys of water! And angrily Haffner had gestured at Frau Tummel – a gesture which was meant to signify absolute irritation, but because this gesture meant that he let go of the jetty, he suddenly found himself underwater, then hoisted by Frau Tummel in an ungainly manner back towards a pole which he grabbed at, gratefully, spouting water like a respiring whale.

Frau Tummel asked after him, but Haffner could not speak. Breathing heavily, he looked across the lawns. On the edge of the park, there was what to Haffner seemed another park. This one was an area of tarmac, for children's games. Yearningly – because Haffner adored all games – he imagined the roundabout, the swings, the rocking horses with their bellies pierced by springs. The springs beneath one swaying horse were creaking in the wind: as if, thought Haffner, the horse were neighing.

This playground seemed a refuge to Haffner.

Frau Tummel had plunged underwater, to tug at his legs, pulling him away from the safety of the jetty, into the abysmal open water. There was sun as well, true, but the sun was no help to him now. The rain was coming down, thought Haffner, really quite hard.

Behind the hills arc'd a fuzzy rainbow.

—You are so Englishman! said Frau Tummel. Enjoy yourself, my love. Express your feelings!

He couldn't help thinking that Frau Tummel was angry with him. No other explanation seemed plausible for her oppressive joyfulness. Swimming wasn't how Haffner expressed himself. When he wanted to express himself, he turned to his clarinet.

He wouldn't do it, he told Frau Tummel. He wouldn't swim. He was finished. And he raised himself gradually out of the water, the sheen streaming off him in the pale beginning sunlight.

5

And as he stands there, rubbing at his body with a towel which seemed of an unnaturally limited size, gathering his clothes about him, I feel a little sad that Haffner's moments of self-expression should be so absolutely historical. Let Haffner be allowed his chapter of jazz!

For he played his clarinet with abandon, in the suburbs of north London. Dutifully, he studied Benny Goodman's exercises for the modern player: the complex intervals of his jazz arpeggios. The greatest melody of all time, thought Haffner, was 'Begin the Beguine', as rendered by the genius Artie Shaw. For its outlandish, unhummable length. Its reckless shape which defied all normal ideas of the proper lifespan of a melody. That was self-expression. But self-expression, so often, was banned for Haffner. Gently, Livia would beg him to think of the neighbours. And Haffner would reply that he was thinking about the neighbours: it was a generous gift, this perform-ance by Haffner of 'Begin the Beguine'.

Some saw in his love of jazz songs an irrevocable flippancy. He had no respect, Goldfaden used to say, for authority. It was quite extraordinary. But Haffner wasn't so sure that this was true. His authorities were simply different to those of other people. Pfeffer tried to find authority in his wife; his grandson found it in his rabbi. Other people depended on their manager, their marriage-guidance counsellors. Haffner found it in jazz. He took what he could. How strange was it anyway to listen to Cole Porter? Had anyone else come up with better descriptions of the heart's affections? Not Shakespeare, as his daughter argued; not the writer of the Psalms, as Benjamin now argued.

Every time we say goodbye, I die a little. That was all it took for Haffner to shiver with emotion.

There was a stringent division in the record collection which Haffner shared with Livia. Haffner owned the jazz. Livia admired her opera singers, her great conductors. She was the one who owned the cumbersome box sets – the collected symphonies, the complete quartets. As an encouraging birthday present, she had given Haffner Mozart's *Haffner Symphony*. He had tried to listen, but he had to confess that he saw no interest in it. Not even with such a title. No, if Haffner tried to improve himself, he preferred to read. That was his chosen domain of education. Whereas when it came to music, he preferred the songwriters: Arlen, Gershwin, Mercer. The songs from the era when Haffner was young: the songs from before the era when Haffner was young.

According to the liner notes on the record Haffner loved most – of Ella Fitzgerald singing Cole Porter – the qualities which made Porter great were Knowledge, Spunk, Individuality, Originality, Realism, Restraint, Rascality. Haffner had no problem with this list. Its last term, however, was a problem for Haffner's idea of the aesthetic. The last quality on the liner notes was Maturity. And Haffner could do without maturity. As if that was an ideal. The greatest education possible, thought Haffner, would not lead its citizens into an age of responsibility, but instead would escalate them to the rarefied heights of dazzling, starlit, spangled immaturity.

6

He was saying goodbye, said Haffner to Frau Tummel: and then he turned away.

—Raphael, said Frau Tummel.

Haffner turned back.

But Frau Tummel did not say anything. She smiled at him, in a way which she hoped was happy. And Haffner, once more, turned away.

He had finally become his father. The man who drifted away. It had never been his aim. He had done his best to avoid becoming Papa. At least, for instance, it had only been the one wife for Haffner. He had that over him. But still, all the motifs were there.

His father had been the quietest man he ever knew. One finger was missing, due to an accident in the Great War, for which Papa never offered an explanation. A photograph survived somewhere – in a box in some attic, acrid with asbestos – of Solomon Haffner, smiling as he held a grenade in his muddy hand: like the proud cultivator of a prize marrow at a provincial gardening show. But Solomon never talked. So Haffner had been forced to imagine the reasons for his missing finger: chewed off in hunger, blown away by a bullet, poisoned to the root by acid. The word for his father, said his mother, was *destroyed*. Some of Papa had been destroyed. Raphael had to understand this. She said this to Haffner when yet another cook was sitting in the hall, waiting to be interviewed, since her predecessor, along with several others, had condescended to treat Solomon Haffner in ways which went beyond the normal domestic duties of domestics. She only hoped (oh Mama!) that Raphael would not behave in this way when he was a man.

And as if the powers governing Haffner wished to demonstrate how comprehensively he could be entrapped, Haffner's phone went – stowed in his tracksuit pocket. The voice of his grandson asked him if things were fixed yet. Had he managed to get any further?

Really, thought Haffner, Mama had been correct all along. It wasn't right, for Haffner to be adult. The duties were beyond him.

At the moment, the twenty-three-year-old Benjamin was in Israel, somewhere near Tel Aviv. He was at a summer school in a rabbinical seminary, where he was educating himself about the history of his people. His people and their invented traditions. As Haffner argued. In Tel Aviv, in his self-imposed isolation, Benjamin had taken on – for reasons which were obscure to his grandfather – the burden of his family's disappointment in Haffner. Every day, he had called Haffner: wondering when the matter would be fixed. Because no one understood, said Benjamin, why it was taking so long. He couldn't understand it himself. He really thought, he said, that Haffner should at least be explaining what was going on.

—Your mother put you up to this? said Haffner.

Benjamin assured him that this wasn't true. He was only, he was only trying to understand what was going on.

Everyone was tired of the grandfathers. Everyone was bored with the everlasting males. This seemed fair.

Was it possible that Haffner wasn't the father of his child? He envied his brother-in-law, Cesare, who had lived his life only for himself, unencumbered. Cesare's lone state had always worried Livia. It had never worried Haffner. Or there were those other men, the cuckolds, with their blissful state of non-paternity. He could see the point of that as well. Oh, Haffner so wanted to desert! It was just, he never had a clear idea of what he would desert for: no, he was not a natural elopee. Haffner had never joined the truant train of Bacchus – Bacchus, with his gang of heartbreakers, his absconding crew. Always, the final disappearance had been beyond him.

7

The first time he had heard the music of Artie Shaw was in his training camp in Hampshire, listening to the wireless with Evelyn Laye. She had expressed admiration. So, quickly, Haffner became a connoisseur; he developed a taste for the lyrics of Johnny Mercer, the music of Hoagy Carmichael. Haffner loved the USA – that land of opportunity, of the Ritz, and razzmatazz. One night, waiting to find out what to do next at Anzio, when the options seemed decidedly limited, Haffner chatted to a black man in a US cavalry unit. His name was Morton. He was Haffner's double; his twin. They spent the night amusing themselves by coming up with the names of the great women songwriters: Kay Swift, of course; and Alice Wrubel. The geniuses for the standards.

But Morton was now dead too. Like everyone else whom Haffner loved, including Haffner's wife.

Haffner walked home, to the hotel. In the distant landscape, there were concrete buildings. These were the buildings of the socialist renaissance. Their facades were stained concrete and patched glass. There was no ornament. A small sports complex, with its dank swimming pool and dark sauna. A home for the mentally ill. And out on the absolute edge of the town, where the motorway began, were the beginnings of the capitalist renaissance: the warehouses and their associates: the strip club, the pool hall, the strangely Chinese restaurant.

It was hard to see the attraction of this spa town. It was melancholy: chlorinated, salty, sulphuric. It wasn't the spa town which Haffner had imagined. It wasn't for Haffner. He wished he were anywhere else but here. He'd rather, quite frankly, be in a provincial town in Britain, standing at a bar where coked-up girls drank Malibu through fluorescent plastic straws. Haffner's image of the sanatorium had been a lustful, tubercular hothouse. That was surely what it had been like, in the era of the Great War – before Haffner had even been born. The stories Livia had reported! Of docile and female patients, their legs akimbo in stirrups. The women would invent symptoms, just so they could be treated by the stern philandering doctors, there, on the examination table. They would lay themselves out, tense specimens to be relaxed and galvanised by massage. Or even, wondered Haffner, they would begin to enjoy the tenderness of the speculum. Because it was very possible, Haffner had once been told, by a girl whom he believed was flirting with him, that one could climax through these examinations: it had once been very embarrassing for her, but the nurse assured her it was entirely normal. A fact which, when relayed idly to Livia, received only an abrupt refutation.

On Livia, Haffner paused.

She used to refute him, often. She was Haffner's educator. This seemed like Haffner's ideal of marriage. Without her, he was adrift. But adrift as he was, now that she was absent, he could still admit that not even in Haffner's moral philosophy was it possible to argue that his attempt to secure her inheritance should have transformed itself into this Haffnerian farce: the bored affair with a married woman; the excited affair with a girl who was half a century younger than him. In neither of which, thought Haffner, did Haffner seem to be in control. No, it rather seemed to be Haffner on the massage table, supine: Haffner himself in stirrups.

A cold remorse flowed through him. Today, he thought, would be the day he finished this business of Livia's villa. Let his grandson be proud of Haffner! He would go back to that committee room, he would try once more. No one would vanquish Raphael Haffner.

And so he strode in his damp sportswear through the hotel's uniform gardens. The electric doors of the entrance hissed open, and Haffner hurried in, only to be called back by the receptionist. He hadn't, presumably, forgotten about his early massage?

Mr Haffner, thought Haffner – who? Him? That schmuck could forget anything.

But Haffner was in a new era of maturity. He asked if the massage could wait. The receptionist thought that it could. So Haffner strode on, and returned to his room.

He stood there, looking in the mirror – contemplative at the sketchy portrait of Haffner. The diminutive slope of his belly seemed suddenly sad to him now: the fat, the mark of the human. His penis hung there, in its brief tuft of hair, so oblivious, thought Haffner sadly, to the history of its glories and disasters. The veins on his chest were turquoise behind his skin. Bruises, like passport stamps, lay on his shins and arms.

It seemed unlikely, he admitted, that Zinka could love him.

But Haffner was not downcast. He was unmockable when it came to his body. And in this, truly, he was greater than Julius Caesar, who was so disturbed by his lack of hair that he combed the thin strands forward over his head. Which was one reason, and perhaps the most important, why Caesar, it was said, so coveted the laurel wreath.

Haffner was not vain. He dismissed the love Frau Tummel felt for him; he dismissed the love he might feel for Zinka. He was an emperor, a dictator.

Now, he had to deal with his inheritance.

PART TWO

Haffner Enraged

1

Haffner walked into town. At first, he proceeded through a suburban and universal neatness – past the front gardens embroidered with roses; the garbage cans topped with sedge hats; the open garages displaying workbenches and shelves of car accessories: the serried oblongs of oil cans – like the retrospective Manhattan skyline as one stands on the ferry, and the sun is everywhere, and everyone is in love. Haffner's Saab 900 returned to him, isolated in the car show of his memory: the avant-garde slope of its trunk, the sky blue of its paintwork, the luminous orange quiver of its speedometer. A car which Livia had driven into their garden wall. Which Haffner had driven into the new glass frontage of an evangelical church. Thus continuing a grand family tradition, begun in 1922 when Papa crashed the new Mercedes, blaming first the wind conditions, then the road conditions, and finally an assortment of malevolent historical enemies, the most powerful of whom were the Bolsheviks.

Two men walked past him, carrying a wardrobe, one of whose doors had fallen open, so exposing to the outside world a mirror which was now reflecting the unimpressed landscape, behind which disported the tremulous picturesque mountains.

A variety of apartment blocks arranged themselves around an absent centre. Then a road adorned with nothing: no building, no monument, not even slick patches of well-kept grass. Just dust and the sky and a view of a factory. This landscape then softened into more apartment blocks. By the side of the road was a cement mixer and its accompanying builder – in T-shirt, socks and jeans – who was slapping the soles of his trainers together to dislodge the dry mud, his arms flapping up and then down.

He really did have no idea why the family so insisted on reclaiming a villa in this benighted country. He hardly envisaged the family holidays, the relaxing weekend breaks. But then Haffner, having reached this obvious conclusion, could see the force of an obvious question. If this was the case, then why was Haffner here?

Haffner was disinclined, at this point, to undertake the self-examination. Already, too many people seemed to want to understand his motives. It didn't need Haffner to enquire into them as well.

Instead, Haffner entered into the old town. Just off the main square, in the courtyard of a church, there was a kiosk topped with a cross, with lit candles for the dead. The air was weeping above the flames. A woman lit a small stub then changed her mind. She plucked then dabbed its wick, then selected the tallest, most powerful candle. Beside the church, set back in its railed-off enclosure, stood the Writers' Club. It advertised coffee. Haffner wandered in. The Writers' Club was also marked by candles, which lit the dining room, pointlessly illuminating the coffered dark ceiling, the mahogany sideboards. In the foyer were gilt candelabra, gripped in their mouths by silenced lions. At each corner of the room, there was a mirror; caryatids in the eaves of the roof, which displayed a peeling fresco of a fleshy muse, airborne in a toga. On the terrace, an emblematic writer was scribbling at a table, throwing away crumpled carnations of paper. On the table beside him, two slices of melon rind had been laid crossways over each other by an artistic vanished diner: an impromptu four-pointed crown.

Yes, here Haffner was: in what he only knew as Bohemia. It wasn't Bohemia, of course. But Haffner's idea of geography, like his idea of history, was eclectic. It had been taught to him by his Uncle Ernie. Uncle Ernie! – who ran a brewery business and whose hatred of women developed intricate disguises, so that once, from Nice, he sent a postcard to the young Haffner describing how Mrs Jay had once more collared him for a dance, but thank goodness this time she didn't have her monkey with her. Haffner always wondered if this monkey were real, or allegorical. Uncle Ernie's theory of Europe was simple: there was England, there was France, and then began Bohemia – a land which stretched from Gdansk to Vienna, from Strasbourg to Odessa. A minute version of Haffner tried to query this, but was rebuffed. So although Bohemia had disappeared in 1918, before the era of Haffner, it was now Haffner's central country: wherever Haffner was in Europe, that place became Bohemia.

He couldn't really say that the architecture of this town was truly modern. It was, he thought, as he left the club, a place which seemed unobtrusively to have opted for excess. What might have been a palace or at least the grandest of condos rose proudly in the sunlight. Over the porch curved a glass shell, with strutted ribs, a petal of glass: on either side of it were twin balconies, made of iron: these balconies were furious with detail. Curlicues of foliage melted into each other, in black mazes, twisted into dripping florets and stems – like the rose bushes Haffner had so coveted, in Pfeffer's garden. Pfeffer, Haffner's schoolfriend, was a lawyer in the City. His rose bushes were all tended by a gardener – and yet it was Pfeffer whose picture was found in the horticultural journals, Pfeffer who wrote in with exquisite botanical notes describing impossible species; Pfeffer who sentimentally named each of his new breeds with the name of one of his grandchildren. Above these railings, the brickwork was scrolled and crenellated. The facades had terracotta highlights, small statues which carried flaming torches in an upstretched hand, dead goddesses, proud heroes. The entire classical corpus. And the walls of the Town Hall's foyer bore bas-reliefs, mosaics. *Industry Leading the Spirit of the People. The Triumph of the Working Man. The Fecundity of the New Woman.*

No, nothing here was modern. But then, Haffner's twin domains – the islands of Manhattan and the City of London – weren't modern either. Everywhere was decorated in the junk of the Hapsburg nineteenth century. The junk was inescapable.

2

On his arrival, Haffner had come to the Town Hall, and been given a variety of forms to be filled out. These confused him, but Haffner persevered. Yes, Haffner had tried to do the dutiful, the proper thing. He had never planned on his private imbroglio. He had just thought that the legal process would be a formality: his last duty to the dead, which he could be done with in one day. For it had been Haffner who had placated his rivals at J.P. Morgan with artfully capped and collared contracts; Haffner who had perfected the art of the butterfly spread. These residential forms, he thought, could therefore not be beyond him. They simply involved him proving that he was who he was; and that Livia had been who she had been; and the house was what it was. With these forms neatly completed, he came back, to be told that the only person in the building who could translate for him was away. She was having a hernia operation. Two days later, by this time embroiled with Frau Tummel, and touched by Zinka, he had returned once more, greeted his oddly healthy translator, handed in the forms, and been told that the process was still in its initial stages.

Now, then, for the fourth time, he ascended the stairs, slowly, and entered the building. A security guard, sitting inside a plastic box, with a dog asleep at his feet, acknowledged him with a movement of one eyebrow. Haffner waved at this man, cheerily. For one should always be good to the staff. You never knew when they might become useful. He had been taught this by his first ever superior at Warburg's, in the Long Bar at Slaters in the welcome spring of 1947: and Haffner had never forgotten. The bellboy, the receptionist, the driver: Haffner knew them all by name. Even if, so often, he reflected, Haffner got it wrong: the temping busboy, the relief lift attendant . . .

Haffner's goal was the Committee on Spatial Planning. The room which contained the secretaries to the Committee on Spatial Planning was adorned by no painting, no mirror, no poster. Its walls were bare, except for a cork noticeboard, pinned with reminders of rota systems, memos about departmental protocol. A handwritten invitation to a party from two months ago was beginning to curl at the bottom: a stalled wave.

The single window seemed to offer a view of nothing: a back garden, a washing line. Just as on the tenement roofs below Grand Street the washing used to hang there like the urban signal for surrender. Haffner would look out over the shining city: at the World Trade Center, and its ancestor, the Chrysler, all his beloved monuments. The feats of prowess! The tricks of engineering! He looked out and basked in that new capital of speed.

But was the villa worth it? This was the question which Haffner still pursued. After all, the villa didn't belong to them: not any more. Long before the death of Livia's father and mother, in Buchenwald, in 1944, it had been transferred to the Nazi authorities. A German family had lived there for two years, until the Soviets arrived, and instituted their Communist utopia. The villa was then occupied by a functionary in the department of education. His soul was bucolic. He had relandscaped the gardens. Then, following the events of perestroika, and all its unintended consequences, the new democratic regime had auctioned it, and it was bought by a Czech microchip company – who used it as a vacation cottage for their favoured, bonus-earning employees. And now, following the policy of reappropriation, the villa was legally to be returned to Livia's family.

None of this, thought Haffner, explained why the villa was worth his protracted effort. The history of this century, in Haffner's opinion, was rarely an adequate explanation. Instead, the private history of his century seemed more relevant. Haffner knew the concealed grievances of his family. He didn't believe that Esther really wanted this villa: not for herself. No, it wasn't about the villa. Haffner was here as a symbol. His daughter's constant theme was that Haffner should pay for his mistakes: the carelessness of his parenting; the flippancy in his friendships; the breakdown of his marriage. Just once, as Esther put it, he would act unselfishly.

Yes, thought Haffner sadly: it was always about Haffner. And the judgement on Haffner was simple: Haffner had failed.

2

Livia had not shared this mournful disappointment in Haffner. Her moments of reproach occurred more unexpectedly, there where Haffner felt most safe. Like the time when she rebuked both Haffner and her brother – in the seclusion of a booth in Sheekey's, watched over by a black-and-white scene from a drawing-room farce – after a night out in theatreland. She was unconvinced by Haffner's lack of commitment to an omnipotent God. No, she said, as Cesare tried to talk, let her finish. This was not because she was an orthodox believer. She was simply unconvinced by Raphael's refusal to believe that this world could not be the only world. But then, Cesare defended him, he thought that Raphael was very right to be unconvinced by their inherited God – that bearded legal system. Here, he accidentally dropped a piece of bread under the table. Together, both Haffner and Cesare motioned to pick it up. They bent; they paused: they left it to its fate. No, continued Cesare, he had always preferred a certain Jewish renegade, Spinoza (—Who?

said Haffner; Spinoza, repeated Cesare, refusing all explication), who had observed that humans were mistaken if they thought that God was a superman, an elongated version of your average Joe. Absolutely! agreed Haffner. He couldn't agree more – rebending down to recover the bread, avoiding Livia's unimpressed gaze – thus hearing from between the stockinged calves of Livia, the trousered calves of Cesare, how there was no more reason to believe in such a myth, in Cesare's opinion, than there was to believe that God's form was that of a benign and bearded anteater, or a trident-wielding koala.

3

With this koala still perched on a branch of his mind, chewing on a eucalyptus leaf and resembling uncannily the koala which the young Benjamin had adored until its polyester fur lost all its shine and volume, Haffner went to a guichet. He loped over in a now stilted imitation of the walk which had marked the heyday of Haffner: suave, indolent, assured. Or all the other adjectives to which Haffner had aspired. He was told that he needed a ticket, with a number. Haffner questioned this. He pointed out that he was the only customer in the room. He asserted that no one had minded before. But no, said the woman: he still needed a ticket. He went to the red plastic box on the wall, which was sticking its tongue out, and extracted a ticket; sat down, and waited. He waited for ten minutes. No one else came in. Finally, his number was called. He returned to the guichet. At this point, he was told that if he had to speak in English, then they must wait for the interpreter. And so Haffner sat down again.

Such vacancy of waiting rooms! When Haffner wanted something done, it had been done. The fluency of the West – this was Haffner's expectation. He came from a world of anxious secretaries, divine stenographers. Not for him the sullen service, the dejected functionaries. The office as a place of pleasure – this was Haffner's norm. He sighed. He tried to read the notices. The notices gave nothing away.

With a heartbeat of flickering anticipation, Haffner saw a man come in: he was tall, and he looked tired. His air was Slavic. Perhaps, thought Haffner, this was his interpreter. The man began to talk in an incomprehensible language, then switched to Italian, then switched, to Haffner's relief, into English. His name was Pawel, he said. He was not an interpreter. Like Haffner, he was here as an applicant. He was here because his wife had – he was here to manage his wife's estate. Haffner nodded. In a way which he hoped indicated a funereal solidarity.

Together, they sat in silence.

Finally, Haffner's interpreter entered the room. Her name was Isabella. She was blonde. Her legs were long. Perhaps not the longest that Haffner had ever seen – in the matter of women only, he was not given to hyperbole – but they were extensive. She looked at Haffner, looked at the woman framed in the guichet like the image of the most venerated saint, and then nodded. Haffner moved over to the window. A relay involving sentences by Haffner and Isabella tried to reach the infinitely receding finish line of the woman in the guichet. Haffner was told that if he wished to discover information on the stages of the Committee's deliberation, he was at the wrong guichet. The room he needed was two doors down, across the corridor.

Haffner smiled encouragingly to Isabella.

They entered the new office. An anglepoise lamp, without a bulb, was folded in on itself. A woman was filing her nails with slow long strokes. Another woman was staring at what looked like absent space, but which was really the image of her daughter, playing trombone, who did not practise enough, and who therefore was unlikely to succeed in the brass competition in four days' time.

The lassitude of the ages spread its stain through Haffner's soul. He went up to the woman who was staring into space. As he spoke, she began to categorise papers into nine piles on her desk.

He began with what he considered to be a minuscule request.

Haffner wondered if at least it might be possible for a visit to be arranged inside the villa, even if the process were not yet fully complete. He had only, as it happened, seen photographs.

The woman then spoke in what seemed to Haffner to be a paragraph. A long, eventful, dense paragraph. He looked inquisitively, hopefully, at his translator.

—No, said the interpreter.

Haffner sighed.

There followed a much shorter sentence from the woman inside the guichet.

—Perhaps we could do this without a bribe, but maybe you don't need the stress, said the interpreter, interpreting.

There was a pause. They looked at Haffner. In this pause, the trio considered how corrupt this Haffner might be.

4

Haffner's moral code belonged to the previous century – to the tsarist world of his great-grandfathers. His ideal was his great-great-grandfather: the emigrant – off the boat in the north of England, at a seaport no destitute Lithuanian cared or knew about. A miracle of survival, of charming strategy. Which was to be found also, he had to admit, in the history of Goldfaden and his family – unintentionally escaped from Warsaw in May 1940, their only possessions being two trunks of holiday clothes. For Goldfaden had only avoided the terror of the Ghetto because he had been in London with his family, to celebrate his sister's marriage. Strategic corruption, then, was Haffner's ideal: not the guarded lavishness of Haffner's parents, or the slick luxury of his contemporaries.

No, Haffner had no problem with the bribes. It was all a matter of survival. But in this case, he doubted if a bribe was worth the effort. He doubted if this woman really did possess the power she tried to flaunt.

And so, as often happened in Haffner's life, he accepted the facts and tried to recreate them according to Haffner's version of reality: he tried to discover an ally. He had never been hampered by the British ethos of the queue – its hopeful stance, its doleful allegiance to the scarcity, the want. He very much doubted, he used to say, if there was anyone who couldn't be corrupted. He went for friends: the deep connection. In Isabella he saw this possible ally in his route to justice. He offered to buy her a coffee. She looked at him. Resolutely, he did not look at her legs. And she said yes. Why not?

—Just five minutes, said Haffner, to the woman inside the guichet.

There had been many stories of Haffner. According to Haffner, this was because events conspired to ruin him. His innocence was always unimpeachable. But perhaps this was not so true. Was Haffner not to blame for the series of amatory notes sent to the rabbi's wife, which culminated in her flight to his house and the much talked about scene with Livia, who talked her through the crisis, and sent her home? Was it not Haffner who had spontaneously suggested an orgy in the London office after a retirement party – before swiftly and unobtrusively absenting himself? He couldn't deny it. All the facts of his legend were true.

5

She was so sorry, said Isabella. This was her country! So what could they do? He was Jewish, yes? And his wife as well. Such terrible suffering the Jews had faced. She felt very close to the Jews. She understood. She felt, she said, very close to every people that had suffered. For so many others had suffered too. This Haffner had to understand. Her people had also suffered so very terribly.

Once more, the horrified angel of history had come to roost on Haffner's shoulder: its wings gently flapping.

No, she said, it was true. Her grandmother was put into a cattle truck and taken to Siberia. Did Haffner know of this? Her grandmother saw a woman give birth to a child and then throw it over the side of the truck. These were horrors. Was he going to deny this?

Haffner was not going to deny it.

Her grandmother, she continued, had started smoking to make herself less hungry. She was hungry every day, in this Russian state. As if her country ever had anything to do with Russia! How she hated the idea of Eastern Europe – an invention of the West. This was the kind of tragedy her people had suffered. And no one cared.

—Well let's be precise here, said Haffner.

Like everyone else, she wanted to burden him with a past which was not his.

So, wearily, Haffner sat down to talk. But Haffner had not understood. He thought she wanted to deny the Jews their suffering. He thought she wanted to subject it to some diminuendo. All his life, he had tried to give this up – the talk of Jews and those who hated them. It belonged to a place which Haffner did not want to visit. It belonged to the conversations of his relatives. But now here he was, trapped: in the former Hapsburg empire, the former Soviet empire: high in the Alps, deep in the problem of grievances: and Haffner, if he had to, would fight.

—I don't know why, said Haffner, we need to be talking about the Jews.

—But I am not, said Isabella.

—Yes, said Haffner. You are. I know this is what you are saying.

—But I am not, said Isabella.

And she was right.

6

I should say this now, in this chapter on Haffner's inheritance: Haffner was not Jewish in the way that other people were Jewish. He was a minor sect of one. He always said that he never really cared about his religion at all. If Haffner had been an intellectual, if Haffner had been Goldfaden, the ever so fucking verbal Goldfaden, then perhaps he would have tried to explain his sympathy for the half-Jews, the non-Jewish Jews. Haffner could even see the worth of the self-hating Jew. It didn't seem reprehensible to Haffner. It had a rationale: the refusal to be burdened by the past of other people. But he wasn't an intellectual. This wasn't his way. He just knew that he only found amusing the attempts by the Orthodox communities of London to recreate a shtetl. When it was decided, late in Haffner's life, to recreate an eruv in the suburbs of north London, Haffner found this deeply comical – with Esther, as they walked to the car, having lunched at some new and disappointing Chinese eaterie, Haffner sarcastically pointed out the string hung from lamp posts, a dejected line which sagged like the bunting at the saddest village fête, in the rain, in the centre of England, in the absent summer. He was bored by his friends who kept kosher, by the women who married and then developed a religious side, by the friends who wanted to visit historic synagogues, or remnants of ghettos, on their otherwise bourgeois summer holidays. Schmaltz! All of it! They weren't for him, the Jewish museums – with their nineteenth-century oil paintings of Torah scribes; the postcards thrown from moving trains, with the saddest phrases (*We must always think of the good things in life*) underlined. He wouldn't let it sadden him. It was not, he thought, his heritage: this European disaster.

Haffner had no sympathy for the manias of the twentieth century. The grand era of decolonisation; the century of splinter groups. All the crazed ethnicity. Was this such a triumph for the human spirit? It seemed to Haffner that it was a distinct defeat. All Haffner wanted was the conservative; the inherited; the right.

But the twentieth century was all he had.

And at this point I must describe a final loop in this aspect of Haffner's character. He disliked the burden of a tragic heritage.

He wished to live in a world free of this kind of inherited loyalty. But if anyone else, who was not Jewish, tried to agree with Haffner, he rebelled. No one else, he thought, had the right to criticise.

This was one of the marks of Haffner. Disloyal among his friends; and loyal among his enemies.

And so once more, in his exile, against his instincts, Haffner was becoming more Jewish than he wanted to be. Hyper-English among the Jews, this was Haffner – the blond and blue-eyed boy. But Jewish with everyone else.

7

As he prepared to defend his people, to argue the case of his embattled race, in a trance of passionate and unnecessary boredom, Haffner's phone rang. Hopefully, he looked at it, wishing for a respite from the history of Europe. For a brief moment, before remembering that this was impossible, he imagined it might be Zinka. But it was Europe all over again.

Once more, he heard the voice of Benjamin: the disappointment of Haffner's old age: as Haffner was the disappointment of Benjamin's youth.

—Poppa, said a voice which emanated from a payphone in some Tel Aviv hall of residence.

The recent mystery of Benjamin still confused Haffner. Each time Benji called, he said he wouldn't call again. And then he called again. And maybe if Haffner had only paused to consider this, then he might have seen the mute obviousness of Benjamin's behaviour: the slapstick of his reticence. He might have seen that Benjamin was in a crisis of his own. But Haffner was rarely good at that kind of thinking. He tended to believe that everyone said what they wanted. Just as, he maintained, he always said what he wanted. So it did not occur to him to wonder whether Benjamin might have more personal reasons for calling Haffner, the family's legendary immoralist. No, he did not imagine, for instance, ensconced as he was in his own romantic crisis, that Benjamin could be in a romantic crisis as well. Since Haffner never chose to believe in his own mysteries, why should he be forced to believe in the mysteries of others?

—Call me back, said Haffner, swiftly. I'm busy.

The voice of Benjamin swooned into silence.

And Haffner, in the unexpected glory of his triumph in so peremptorily dismissing Benjamin, returned to Isabella. He couldn't understand it. Yes, let him change the conversation for just one moment. He had now been to this office four, perhaps five times. And no one seemed interested. Did they realise they had a legal duty? Had they no respect for the law?

Isabella replied that there was no reason to raise his voice.

He demanded that they stop this conversation, he said to Isabella, and that they go back in. She would smoke one final cigarette, said Isabella. And Haffner loped away: to fume.

This pause lasted for as long as Haffner could contain himself, while staring at Isabella, angrily, with Isabella staring back. The pause, therefore, was short. He walked over to her again.

Why, he enquired, did she have to care so much about the past? It wasn't difficult, after all – remembering the past. It hardly needed to be an obligation.

You didn't need to remind Haffner about remembrance. He couldn't help it. So many of the atrocities were his. But why then should Haffner remember them? What use was the guilt? Since when, he asked Isabella, was suffering the criterion of a life? Why not the charm? Why not the fun?

—This country! sighed Isabella.

The smoke on her cigarette, noted Haffner, listlessly, was being redundantly echoed by its imperfect twin, the smoke from a distant chimney.

What kind of civilisation was it, she asked Haffner – who had no answer, just as he so rarely had answers to the absolute questions – where a girl was scared to go to church? Where a girl was told never to tell her friends that her family went to church? Because if they heard about it, they would send her family away. What kind of civilisation? This was reality, she said. This was real.

Could he have a cigarette? he asked. Moodily, Isabella extracted one. She lit it behind Haffner's hand. He inhaled: and felt sick.

It was the first cigarette he had smoked for twenty years. That seemed right. Smiling, therefore, in this moment of complicity, Haffner tried to create a truce.

Isabella pressed her cigarette out against the wall with her thumb: the butt bent. They went back into the cool of the building, and its humidified air.

8

This time, Haffner received a new answer.

There was, they had ascertained, a problem which no one had quite anticipated. He had not given them all the information required. Haffner paused them here. He could assure them, he said, that all the necessary information had been supplied, on more than one occasion. Perhaps, they said. But they needed to be sure. And Haffner was then asked where his wife had been born. He replied that he had given them this information already. Nevertheless, they said. Nevertheless what? said Haffner to Isabella, who declined to reply or to translate. If he gave this information again, thought Haffner, he gave it only to show how generous he could be. He wasn't one to bear grudges.

It turned out that, as they had feared, they could not help him at all.

His wife, you see, said Isabella, his late wife was a citizen not of this country but of Italy. He understood? So it was very difficult. They understood. But it was very difficult.

He had come, he pointed out, a very long way. They appreciated this, said Isabella, but their hands were tied. It was a problem of citizenship.

Were they serious? said Haffner. Isabella replied that absolutely. She was very sorry, she added. These were the ways of the world.

But did they understand, Haffner wondered, that the question of ownership was completely separate from whatever problem of citizenship they wanted to invent?

Isabella asked him to slow down. Could he please repeat himself?

Haffner, in his fury, rose from his chair: an avenging, unsteady god.

He had no intention, he announced, of repeating himself to these people. He had had enough.

—Everyone is very sorry, said Isabella.

—It's not happening today? Haffner asked her.

—Today, no. I do not think so, she said.

—I just wanted to know, said Haffner, coldly.

As the gambler who plays cards, knowing they are rigged – the deal-box, coffee mill, loaded dice, top-tell – yet still believing in the efficacy of his luck, so Haffner confronted the miniature conflicts which the century placed in his path. That one had lost before the game had started was no reason not to play. And after all: surely he was still owed one great win: one absolute and effervescent triumph? He believed in it as other people believed in the more likely cascade of the slot machines: a parallel line of green apples, with jaunty stems.

—I am so sorry, said Isabella: melancholy for all the exiled and dispossessed.

Haffner only wanted a triumph. This was true. In the full panoply of his Jewishness, he had now experienced a moment of conversion. He wasn't doing this for Esther. Now, he was going to recover this villa in a gesture of piety. Yes, Haffner's triumph now consisted in his vision of the villa. And he knew his record when it came to obtaining triumphs. They proved, so often, beyond Haffner's talent. But Haffner, thought Haffner, was ready for the fight.

No wonder, thought Haffner, the emperors all went manic. He sympathised; he understood their frustration at reality's recalcitrance. No wonder they amused themselves with killing sprees.

9

In the lives of the Caesars, the only ones who interested him were the monsters: Caligula, Tiberius, Nero. He liked the overreachers. How could you choose between them? If pressed, however, maybe Haffner would have gone for the god Caligula – who was happy to do it with anyone, male or female, active or passive. Caligula, continued Haffner, talking to himself, was famous for the comprehensiveness of his taste. He would give dinners to which he invited all the noble couples: the couples of the blood. This story in particular commanded Haffner's respect. It displayed a grand disregard for the niceties of public opinion. The wives would have to process up and down, passing a couch on which lay – untroubled by its stains, its cheap upholstery – the emperor Caligula. If one of them tried to avoid his gaze, he lifted up her chin. Like an animal. When the moment seemed right, he would send for one of them, and then the happy couple would retire. On their return, he would talk about her performance; mentioning a flaw here, a perfection there. He listed the movements for which she had no talent.

That, concluded Haffner, was the moment when Caligula rightly deserved his deification.

Perhaps he thought he only meant to shock. But Haffner was never coarse. If he shocked the general public, it was always because of a sincere misalignment in relation to the orthodox. So that even though I am not sure, as he said it, how much Haffner believed in this, it contained – perhaps unknown to Haffner – its own inverted logic, which was Haffner's deepest unexplored motif. He didn't really admire Caligula for the purity of his cruelty: he might have wanted his audience to think this, but Haffner was rarely sincere to his audience. No, Caligula was to be admired for his publicity. Haffner loved him, if he loved him, for the lack of shame.

No one understood the emperors. No one saw how humble they were – free from the deeper vanity of concealing one's own vanity – like Haffner before his family, refusing the illusion of maturity.

Haffner Soothed

1

As Haffner arrived back at the hotel, intent on his newly discovered decisiveness, like an infant intent on the helium balloon
clutched in a tight hand, a man emerged from an inner sanctum
behind the reception desk. He was in a bright white T-shirt and
blue tracksuit with silken sheen – his upper lip stained by a black
and inadequate moustache. This was his masseur! the receptionist
told Haffner, excitedly.

Haffner eyed his masseur, utterly indifferent. The helium balloon
of his decisiveness floated up into the empty air.

Haffner allowed himself to be led downstairs, to the candlelit,
scented day spa: and there, prone on the massage table, his face
ensconced in its padded lasso – wrapped in tissue paper, to absorb
the unguents of Haffner – he lay down.

As he did so, a montage of previous Haffners lay down with him.

2

There were the Kodaks of Haffner reclining on towelled beds in
his sports clubs, then the black-and-white photos of his white
body on a black bench in his army barracks. But the film stopped

on the image of him in New York, at the Russian Bath House on Avenue B. He used to go there with Morton. The steam secluded them. They would sit there: heating up – on the steps of the sauna, as if awaiting some spectral performance, some senatorial oratory. Cleansed, they would go to a bar in the Village – the name escaped Haffner's stuttering memory. Not often, but sometimes. And, in this bar, they would continue their discussion of the Jews and the Blacks. This was why Haffner settled on this image, as he relaxed from his struggle in the committee rooms. He was het up with the century's usual argument. But there it was. Haffner loved the Blacks, and Morton loved the Jews. Enough of this! Haffner would say. Enough of this sectarian rubbish. The race was unimportant. He could go further: there were people with charm, and people without. That was the only division one ever needed to contemplate.

Maybe to him, Morton replied. Maybe to him.

Morton put down his bottle of beer. It rested there, in front of Haffner's tired eyes. A bubble stretched, a condom, over its rim.

He didn't understand, said Haffner. He didn't get what Morton was implying.

—You've made it, said Morton. So you're cool.

—I'm cool, said Haffner.

—Not literally, said Morton. I'd never say you were cool in the real sense of this word. No. But yeah, you're cool. You've won your fight. So you don't care.

Haffner wondered if this was fair. Certainly, he could see the accusation's force. Catholic only in his hatred of all Protestants, all splinter groups – to which Haffner preferred the international art of business: an art to which he felt a strong allegiance, an art of which his central principle had been his insistence, in the wreckage of 1950s Europe, that one could not capitalise, as it were, if an economy wanted to remain national. The future was international. That was all he believed. He warmed to cosmopolitans, like Cesare.

—Is he Jewish? Haffner had asked Livia once, about an acquaintance at their tennis club.

—Oh, interrupted Cesare. Did you not know that the whole concept of the non-Jew is strictly inapplicable?

He had always admired Cesare. Always been fond of him. Cesare, in Haffner's opinion, lived up to his name.

—I mean it, continued Cesare. Every time I meet someone new, I discover they are Jewish. It's true what they say: the Jews are everywhere. It's a problem for the anti-Semites. Everyone hates the Jews; but then everyone *is* a Jew. It's a dilemma.

And Haffner called that fine.

3

In his padded lasso, Haffner began to talk to his masseur. His name, it turned out, was Viko. It was really Viktor, he said: but everyone called him Viko.

—Niko? said Haffner.

—Viko, said Viko.

As if he were Niko's twin.

—Your name, it is like you are Hugh Hefner! said the masseur, delighted.

—You think you're the first person to make that joke? said Haffner, grimly.

—You know him? asked the masseur, undeterred. Relation?

It had been an exhausting morning, a very stressful morning, said Haffner. He could feel it, said Viko. There was much tension in him. But Haffner, as he always did, chose to turn the conversation away from his internal tensions.

He supposed, Haffner therefore observed, that it was a very difficult thing, to live in this country after the Communists had wrecked everything. And before Viko could reply, Haffner began to tell him a story about the Communists, which was a story about his brother-in-law: Cesare.

But maybe this was still a way of Haffner talking about Haffner.

Cesare, after the war, and his degree at Cambridge, had eventually decided to return to Italy, where he worked for the next two decades as a professor in sociology. The anecdote might interest Viko, said Haffner – raising himself up, patted back down. He was a Communist, Cesare: a Party man. But to understand this story, one also had to understand, said Haffner – talking into his lasso, to Viko's bright new trainers – that this man had a cold streak. He was hard. But there it was. In Italy, he began an affair with a girl whose name, Haffner tended to think, was Simonetta. Perhaps Simonetta. When it began, she was twenty-five. So Cesare must have been in his forties, in his fifties.

And Haffner suddenly noticed how this disparity in age, which had always struck him as tinged with a Hollywood seediness, was nothing when compared to the disparity between his age and Zinka's.

For Cesare, he said to Viko, it was everything he wanted. This girl of his wore leather; she rode a Honda bike. She was an assistant lecturer at the university. Could anything be more alluring? At the time, Cesare was editing a journal of revolutionary sociology. He made Simonetta his deputy editor. Cesare was a man of the world, said Haffner. A Communist, yes: but a Communist who loved the shops in the Quadrilatero d'Oro. A Communist who bought himself handstitched shirts, or shoes made from a single piece of leather. He loved his life. He was happy.

Then this girl wanted a baby. It made Cesare pause.

—I would love one, he said, absolutely love one. But first I must divorce my wife.

Dutifully, Viko chuckled.

In revenge, continued Haffner, unbeknown to Cesare, she stopped taking the Pill, and got pregnant. But Cesare didn't care about this difficulty. He simply got her sacked from her deputy editorship of the journal; and also from her job at the university. But then, a year later, when Cesare was in the process of manoeuvring for the university rectorship, the Italian Communist Party issued a list of approved yet not affiliated intellectuals. These were the kosher ones, though not confirmed. Cesare was duly admitted as being ideologically pure. But Simonetta campaigned. Using her contacts in the women's section of the Communist Party, she held meetings, she published denouncements.

Of all the intellectuals duly nominated by the Communists, said Haffner, only Cesare failed in his bid for election.

But the greatest moment of all, he concluded, was when Cesare told this story to his mentor at the university in Rome – who, on being told by a mournful Cesare the full dossier of the facts over a lavish dinner at a restaurant in a side street off the Spanish Steps, asked him if this was really how it would be from now on. Were they, said his mentor, to be ruled now by their mistresses?

Haffner! So sure that he was charming! So intent on making conversation – even though, of course, Viko was not interested in his anecdotes about communism. He didn't care about Haffner's urbane distaste for all the politics.

The anecdote, therefore, did not receive the applause which Haffner thought it was due. A little shocked, perhaps, he tried another conclusion.

That, said Haffner, was the best he could say for communism. But before Haffner could gratify himself with a murmured smile – as he remembered Cesare ruefully saying that the whole adventure had at least produced one benefit, because his wife, having found out, had finally made him a free man – Haffner felt a moment of alarm. It felt to Haffner's worried senses that Viko might be going too far.

The range of Haffner's body available to massage seemed to be becoming more expansive.

4

Haffner was lying on his stomach: a warm towel over his legs and feet. He was naked. At first, he had toyed with the idea of wearing the briefs he usually swam in. But then had thought that really he should not care. They were hardly the most comfortable of items. The important thing, he always thought, was a comprehensive massage. As if he needed to be worried about his modesty! No, not here, not with a man.

But now, he felt Viko let his hands splay and drift with the oil further up his thighs. At first, as Haffner chatted, he had interpreted this as invigorating. Then he began to wonder. But he was too confused to make a sign, to tense his thigh muscles in the ordinary mute gesture of irritation. He could not be sure how European this was – how much to do with the health spa, and how much to do with something else entirely.

His penis was trapped there, under his thigh, its squashed head protruding under his testicles.

And then he felt the man's hand flicker on to the head of his penis. He really could not be sure if this were still an accident. These accidents, felt Haffner, were becoming so much less accidental than he had first imagined.

5

He was rarely successful in his active search for what he considered to be bohemian. Whenever Haffer metamorphosed into the bohemian, it tended to be the result of someone else's choice. He strayed into it. He had understood the streets in Soho – but he had never felt quite at home on Wardour Street, or Frith Street. He went to the French House sometimes. But not the Colony Room, not the Gargoyle Club. Never had the wisecracking hostess Muriel Belcher eyed him from behind the bar, admiringly, as he went promiscuous with a male prostitute who came from the satellite towns around Glasgow. Nor had he drunk with Francis Bacon, vomiting into the gutter, each supporting the other's bent body, wildly applauding.

No, thought Haffner: bohemia, when it came to Haffner, always came in such strangely bourgeois costumes: a moustached man in a tracksuit, say, surrounded by candles.

This confusion was one instinct which he had inherited from Papa. Early on in Haffner's career, in Haffner's marriage, they had sat in the rose garden, in the pale sunshine, a police siren tumescing and detumescing in the background, and Papa had expounded on life. The thing was, a man could either waste his life or live his life. And in the end it was better to live it than to waste it. Did he understand this? Haffner answered that he thought he did. But what was wasting, and what was living? Was it Livia, or not Livia? A marriage, or not a marriage? It was hardly as if Papa had been an expert in distinguishing the living from the wasting – in knowing what was a place of safety, and what was a place of harm. In Haffner's opinion, these terms had a habit of turning themselves upside down. He seemed isolated in this uncertainty. The only other person who shared his bewilderment, in the end, was Livia herself. More often, it led to arguments like the one which had occurred the day of Livia's funeral: sitting in his kitchen with his daughter and her husband, Esmond.

He was, Esther told him, simply impossible. Haffner tried to disagree. She interrupted him. He was impossible. Like an infant. Haffner did not try to disagree.

He cared for nothing, said Esther. And angrily Haffner had replied that in fact it was he, her father, who was the only person in this family to think about other people. Yes, let him speak.

No one was more conceited than Haffner, said his daughter. No one cared more about himself. Did he know what Mama used to say? She had married a Greek god, and had left a Roman emperor. A monster of ego.

—Humble! roared Haffner. I am the humblest person I know.

No one could think what to say next. The chutzpah of it dazzled them. So no one spoke. Haffner simply glared at Esmond. Esmond silently glared back.

It amazed him, thought Haffner, how vanquished this man was: the absolute son-in-law.

Esmond wore the steel rectangular spectacles sported by fundamentalist spokesmen and the vice presidents of Midwestern software companies; but Esmond was neither a vice president nor a fundamentalist.

He admired Esmond for only one thing, did Haffner: his hair. This, he conceded, was splendid – the way it flowed and oozed, a miracle of liquidity. But nothing else. Not the liberal moral certainties; nor the obsession with football borrowed from the newspapers. Yet this was the man who had made Haffner's daughter into a meek provider: who had seduced her into the temptations of orthodoxy. This was the man who had made his grandson rabbinical.

He still saw no reason, said Esmond, why that other woman should have presumed to come. Barbra, Haffner interrupted, was a very dear friend. Esmond ignored this statement. If that was what Haffner wanted, then he was welcome to continue this friendship, he said. He looked at Esther. She was arranging the cutlery in front of her – which had been laid for a breakfast no one, now, except Haffner, would eat: the rustic basket of *pains au chocolat* before him, the snorting coffee machine on the counter behind him. But there was no reason, Esmond said, for them to have to witness this. He saw no reason why they should have to deal with Haffner's, with his – but Esmond had no word for Haffner's delinquency.

And for a moment, Haffner, on his massage bed, felt a rare tenderness for Esmond. He understood the difficulty – since this was how Haffner had felt too, when trying to contemplate the moral life of Papa.

History, thought Haffner, was simply a playground of repetition. It really did amaze him how limited were its motifs.

Hurt as Haffner was by Papa's reckless behaviour, with the women, and the money, he tried to understand his impulses. Papa was terrified of waste. It was the only lesson he had ever learned; the only one he could ever impart. Haffner thought he understood, therefore, why his father had acted with such theatrical self-pity when selling off the only other inheritance with which Haffner had been involved. Papa had been the greatest collector of cricketana the world had ever seen: he bought engravings, handkerchiefs printed with the laws of the game, mugs, memoirs, the technical manuals. In cricket, Papa found his reason for being. It made him safe. He compiled bibliographies, small monographs on centenary tankards. Haffner had inherited this love – a love he had passed on to Benjamin, his grandson and heir. Then, before Papa died, in what Haffner regarded with tacit admiration as an act of grand malevolence, but which was interpreted by everyone else as an act of petty and vindictive spite, he auctioned the entire collection. So that in the course of Haffner's life, in random provincial museums, he would observe a small typewritten card marked neatly in a bottom corner with his ancestral name.

When Haffner's mother died, no one expected his father to be sad. Only Haffner. It didn't amaze Haffner to receive a noble letter from his father in which Solomon told him that had he never known his wife, that grief would have been even greater than the grief he now felt at this temporary separation imposed on them. And maybe this was not so wrong. Maybe this was the only way in which Solomon Haffner could have loved his wife, in this exorbitant way – writing to posterity. Whereas Haffner's love for his mother had been different. It was all nostalgic. Whenever he remembered her, it was only as an idyll.

But then maybe every idyll is remembered: maybe memory is a condition of the idyllic.

So Haffner had sat there, his father's letter beside him, and remembered how his mother used to lay the lemon meringue pie on the stone floor of the larder, so that it could set.

6

The previous section, dear reader, as Haffner is lost in his memories, is a way of describing Raphael Haffner asleep.

For although to Haffner's dismay his penis had begun to burgeon towards Viko's hand, thus creating, in Haffner's opinion, a situation of the utmost delicacy, he couldn't think what to do. The solutions seemed absent. Previously, when faced by situations which disturbed him, Haffner had consulted his mental library of exempla. So now, desperate, with his face down, Haffner tried to consider his mentors. But, once more, the external forces which tended to disrupt the straight line of Haffner's life overtook him.

Worried, Haffner fell asleep. He relaxed. He drifted into a place of absence, emptiness. Drifting further, his legs spread slightly more apart, in a gesture which was unmistakably flirtatious, thought Viko.

Viko was used to these situations. They occurred often, in his candlelit basement. They followed an ordinary pattern.

Viko, poised above Haffner's back, couldn't see that Haffner's eyes were closed. He assumed that the greater deepness of Haffner's breathing meant only one thing: the masseur's skill at finding individual ways to please the gratified client. He continued to move his hands around Haffner's thighs, the tops of his thighs, brushing his penis and testicles with slow abandon. All the signs were there.

The fact that Haffner had made no protest; the fact that he had positioned his penis deliberately so that its tip was softly available to Viko's touch; the fact that now he was even moving his legs apart to allow the masseur easier access: these were the ordinary, done thing.

His fingers ran up and down the shaft of Haffner's penis. As Haffner slept, Viko touched him, slid his hand in such a way that Haffner half woke, aroused, descending into thoughts of Livia: the only woman who had ever touched his penis so deftly. Who, even before their wedding in the Abbey Road Synagogue, as Haffner never tired of remembering, slipped her hand beneath the tightness of his waistband, just as she had done before: a gesture which remained the erotic zenith of Haffner's marriage.

7

Haffner's wedding! At this zenith, while Haffner remains there, happily asleep, with his penis in a stranger's hand, I am suddenly reminded of another Haffnerian story.

Haffner used to tell his stories in the car, while he was driving. Haffner drove like they drive in the ancient movies: inexplicably watching his passenger, and not the road. Between rows of parked cars, Haffner drove – as if before a pre-recorded backdrop – courageously oblivious to the malice of wing mirrors.

And, one night, Haffner told me the story of his wedding.

The service had been taken by his rabbi: the Reverend Ephraim Levine. The kindest man in the world, said Haffner. A very fine man. Who in fact, strange as it may seem, became the legal guardian of every Jewish refugee to London from Germany before the war. But that was another story. Yes, that was another story, which involved the story Haffner preferred to forget: of a girl upstairs in a locked bathroom, young Raphael adding up his batting average in the dining room with a pencil stub, its end wrinkled where he sucked it. Whereas a story Haffner always remembered was his father leaving the wedding service and asking for theological guidance.

—Ephie, why do we have two days Rosh Hashanah?

And the Reverend Ephraim Levine looked at him and said:

—Solly, why do we have five days Ascot?

It was very fine, said Haffner. Very fine. He was the wittiest of men. You never knew what to expect. And after the wedding, after his mother had by mistake drunk the wine which was meant for the bride, thus causing a dumbshow, a hiatus in the service, there was a tea dance at the Rembrandt Hotel, in Knightsbridge. Haffner's padre from his unit shared a taxi to the reception with the Reverend Levine. And did I know, Haffner asked, what the padre had said to him, astonished, when they returned to the unit? The padre took him aside. The things he had been told, the padre confided in Haffner, afterwards, refusing to enlarge this statement with detail. The things the Reverend Levine had told him. He had been shocked, said the padre: absolutely shocked.

And now, I think, I know what Haffner liked in this anecdote. He liked the revelation that all men were men of this world. Because every story, for Haffner, was the same.

Haffner was an admirer of the classics. He went to the classics for the higher gossip. Haffner, humble Haffner, wanted to understand how everything declined and fell. The history of the classical era was the history of decadence. Curious, Haffner read of Nero and his monstrous appetite – which overruled his reason so comprehensively that Nero devised a pretty game. He was released from a den, dressed in the skins of wild animals, and would then gnaw at the penises and exposed pubic bushes of servile men and women who had been bound naked to stakes. Haffner appreciated the underlying philosophy. For, in the vocabulary of Solomon Haffner, the patriarch of Haffner, to live one's life was the same thing, in the end, as wasting it. This was what the stories taught the gentle reader. Just as the classical, in the end, wasn't really classical: it led forever to the Goths, to the Picts and the Saxons; the Visigoths and Ostrogoths: all the savage barbarians. The classical only existed in retrospect, when everything was over. You couldn't separate the classic from the decadent. No, the defeat might seem to come from nowhere, but really there was no escape from it: because it was visible, really, all along, from the beginning. So every story was a story of defeat. Even the stories about the victories.

Yes, I think now, as I contemplate the stories of Haffner, this seems true. Victory is only a series of slow defeats. Defeats so slow that for a moment they could seem like a victory.

Or maybe it was only true of Haffner. Maybe this was only the principle of Haffner's exorbitant life.

8

For this was how the farce of Haffner's finale continued. As Viko tended to Haffner's penis, Haffner's phone began to ring, pulsing where it lay – the shrill twin to his penis which was pulsing, contentedly, in Viko's hand. Blearily, his heart pounding with an ill heaviness in his chest, he raised his head and – a gecko – stared at Viko.

Haffner never did anything wrong – not willingly. It was just he was so often trapped by forces which were beyond him. But no one believed him.

The degree to which this scene seemed his fault was debatable. Perhaps Haffner, in some way, was guilty. Usually, the guilt came from women. The list of the women who felt disappointed by Haffner was one which Haffner usually preferred to ignore. At its head, there was Barbra, who had given up, she said, so much for him: but then there were all the others – Cynthia, with freckled hands; Joan, who only drank champagne; Hyacinth, who cried whenever Haffner called her; and Pilar, who was happily married, she said, happily married.

But Haffner would never join this resigned lament. When it came to guilt, Haffner was immune.

This wasn't to say he regretted nothing. Not at all. Naturally, there were things he regretted. Regret was the territory. But regret, he wanted to assure the absent gods, the cartoon gods, was not responsibility.

Once more, he tried to convince the world that the world was a menace for Haffner. Hazily, he explained to Viko that he had just dropped off there. He had no idea, really. To which Viko, a professional of politesse, simply replied that but of course.

There was a pause of awkwardness.

—I should take this, said Haffner – pointing to the telephone: relieved in relation to the masseur; depressed in relation to the fact that, once more, it was Benjamin.

—This is the third time I'm calling you, said Benjamin.

—Really? said Haffner.

—I'm just saying, said Benjamin. You could at least be polite.

—I don't think, Benjamin, said Haffner, that you should be lecturing others on how to live their lives.

Haffner's opinion of Benjamin had once been more forgiving. When Benji had been into sports, Haffner had adored him.

Like Haffner before him, Benji was a goalkeeper. Haffner would watch him from the touchline, in the Jewish soccer leagues. Benji possessed poise. He had the weight. He was noted for his bravery. As colossal boys jinked and trampled towards him, Benjamin didn't hang back. He didn't remain stymied on the goal line. No, he closed down the angle. He tumbled down at their dangerous feet. Haffner applauded. Benjamin pretended not to be pleased. Mimicking the great goalkeepers of the past, he pretended to care only about his team. Having gathered the ball, he would ferociously bowl it to a free player on the wing, or kick it back into the opposing half. With the back of his gloved hand, Benjamin would smear the mud across his sweating forehead. Then, silhouetted at the far end of the pitch, in splendid isolation, Benjamin leaned against a goalpost. He observed the flow of play. He lined up the fingers of his padded gloves on each hand, as if in prayer.

At the weekends, when Benji was meant to be learning the piano, studying some piece by Mendelssohn, with a bordered cream cover, Haffner read the paper. In the adjoining study – called so boyishly and pathetically his den – Esmond looked at X-rays in his lightbox. As soon as Esmond wandered away, then Haffner began with the weighty discussion of sports.

Then, a few years later, a change occurred. Or not so much a change in Benji's character: just a change in the objects of its affection. The reasons for this affection had always been the same. There he was, on the outskirts of London, in the northern suburbs, and Benjamin discovered drugs. Not the terrifying, working-class drugs: not the crack and the glue and the marker pens. Instead, he discovered the recreational drugs, the ones with intellectual pedigree. Benjamin discovered the lure of cool. It upset Haffner, but he coped. It was, at least, a pastime he could understand. Now, even that had changed too. Now, for reasons which Haffner could not understand – in fact, he did not believe there was any actual reason – Benjamin had adopted his race's religion. He had adopted it, said Haffner, with a vengeance. And this vengeance, thought Haffner, was continuing.

—It's not me, said Benjamin. I'm not lecturing anyone.

—You tell me this, said Haffner. Is it really a way to live your life, to do what you're doing out there? With your missiles and your lunatics.

He hadn't phoned, said Benjamin, to have this conversation. He wasn't having this conversation. They'd had this conversation.

—Are you ever going to tell me how things are going? said Benji. Are things fixed yet?

—No, said Haffner. They're not.

—I really think, said Benjamin, if you're having so many problems, then I should come and see if I can help.

Haffner considered Frau Tummel, and Zinka, and felt alarmed.

He couldn't bear it. Youth, he thought, was the spirit of the petit bourgeois. Of course, thought Haffner, the young needed their myth of adolescence, their myth of sixty-eight – of course they needed the romantic movements. Without the romantic movements, the young would have to see themselves for what they were: always the most punitive, the most envious, the quickest to judge. So Haffner, as he lay prone, on the massage table, opted to ignore Benjamin's proposal of a friendly visit. Instead, Haffner asked Benji if he'd ever heard of the celebrated Peter Ustinov. Benjamin said that he hadn't.

—He's never heard of Peter Ustinov! said Haffner: possibly to Viko, but almost definitely to himself.

—Now, let me tell you something, continued Haffner. Peter Ustinov possessed a quality which is in very short supply nowadays. In very short supply.

—And what's that? asked Benjamin.

—Charm, said Haffner. Now listen, old chap, I have to go.

—This is ridiculous, said Benjamin, and continued the conversation: in which he told Haffner that he could get a flight that day. He really thought he should. He could be with him by tomorrow. But Haffner never heard this conversation, nor Benjamin's frustrated squawk when he realised that Haffner was no longer listening, because he had hung up.

Haffner turned to the masseur. Suddenly, he felt naked. But he felt calm.

—Thank you, said Haffner.

—Mais merci, smiled the masseur.

—Absolutely, said Haffner.

A change seemed to happen within Viko: a ripple, a sigh. He turned away. He seemed to be smiling to himself. Haffner questioned him on this. He denied that he was smiling.

Sitting on the table, Haffner gave Viko all the money in his wallet. It was not much. It seemed ungrateful.

Not for the first time, Haffner felt overtaken by an exhaustion. He looked at the chair beside the massage table, at the arms of his tracksuit top, helplessly hanging down. Clutching his towel to his waist, Haffner gathered up his clothes – a hunchback. And then Haffner – who so wanted sleep, and rest – shyly shuffled out of Viko's salon.

9

There could be courage in retreat. Think, pacific reader, about Napoleon. The wars of Napoleon led to a million bushels of bones being taken from the plains of Waterloo, Austerlitz and Leipzig, then shipped to Hull, there to be sent to Yorkshire bone-grinders and converted into fertiliser for farmers. Haffner knew this. But he also knew the greatest bon mot ever, when Napoleon, recounting to the Polish ambassador the story of his retreat from Moscow on a sledge, observed that from the sublime to the ridiculous was only a step. No experience, after all, could not be transfigured by the telling. No retreat, therefore, was always shameful.

Yes, to Haffner, who admired the war books, the manuals on strategy, Napoleon was not so much the emperor of Europe, but more an expert on an empire's inevitable decline and fall.

Many years ago, on the French Riviera, when he was there for the jazz festival at Juan-les-Pins, Haffner had seen a waistcoat of Napoleon's, worn in exile on St Helena: it had charmed Haffner with its miniature size. Everything he loved in Napoleon was embodied in this waistcoat: he understood the littleness of things. Napoleon: the man who, at the Battle of Borodino, stayed in and issued orders from his tent. Yes, that man knew about the tactics of withdrawal: just as Bradman, another of Haffner's imaginary mentors, when faced with batting on a disintegrating wet pitch at Melbourne, in 1937, sent in his batting order entirely reversed, so that by the time Bradman went in at number seven the pitch had dried out, and he made a double century and won the match. That was the action of a true genius of victory: a man who was an expert in the mechanics of timing, a connoisseur of retreat.

With these reflections, Haffner returned to the hoped-for safety of his room, where he discovered a chambermaid, in an abattoir of her own devising: surrounded by the intestines of the Hoover cabling; the wet towels on the floor, like tripe.

And so Haffner, homeless, retreated further: he turned round and walked away, searching for somewhere to sleep.

Haffner Timeless

1

Haffner went out on to the veranda. Finally alone, Haffner lay in a lounger and looked at the mountains. He saw nothing which might interest him. Should he go so far as to say that he was exhausted? Yes, Haffner was exhausted. The sun was softening. And Haffner only wanted rest. For what a night it had been! What a morning! In the distance, the dogs in the village were yelping. He willed them to be quiet. Just as he had often willed Livia's pets to be silent: the moody schnauzer, the bulimic borzoi.

A tree was leafing through itself, anxiously.

Into a doze went Haffner. He drifted and looped as if through a dream of an endless sky. In his sleep he could rest and then fall, fall further, rest and then fall. His doze was a dream of diving.

Peace for Haffner! Let him rest!

While Haffner falls asleep in the midst of the afternoon, maybe I should let him be – reclining in my invisible deckchair, my imaginary lounger.

Haffner's sense of time was often subject to odd absences. Now that he was older, his time spans had lengthened. Benji, for instance, felt grand when he thought in terms of months. Haffner was used to thinking in decades: the decades seemed more accurate to the nature of the facts. They were the more useful unit of measurement. But here, in the mountains, these problems with time involved new proportions entirely. At moments, and this was one of them, he could not tell how long he had been in this spa town, in this hotel. Everything up here had become timeless. The usual co-ordinates were lost.

At what point had Haffner been innocent? Haffner, who could still remember with more vividness than he experienced many other things how on his eighteenth birthday, during the Scarborough Cricket Festival in 1938, Papa had invited the greatest opening batsman in England, Herbert Sutcliffe – a Yorkshireman, and a professional – to dine with his wife in the Grand Hotel. He was the first professional ever to be invited to dine, during the Cricket Festival, at the Grand Hotel. Before Papa's invitation, it had been strictly reserved for the amateurs. But Papa could not be denied. For Papa believed in cricket more than he believed in class. So into the dining room of the Grand Hotel walked Papa, followed by his wife and son, behind whom came Herbert Sutcliffe, with his wife, Emmy. Haffner danced the Lambeth Walk with Emmy. And around nine months later Sutcliffe phoned up to ask Solomon Haffner if he remembered that evening in the Grand Hotel, and Emmy and the champagne? —Well today, said Herbert Sutcliffe, Emmy presented me with a son. And Sutcliffe started to laugh.

This was how Haffner's soul functioned – through these anecdotes which everyone else had forgotten, which no one else had noticed: like the ballet of electrified shrugs and ripples given off by the fringe of a beach umbrella, on a terrace, at midday, while everyone lies there sunbathing, with their eyes closed against the light.

There were two methods for the historian to record the history of Haffner. The obvious way was to follow the chronology: the annals of Haffner. But then there was the more philosophic way, which happened to coincide with the way Haffner really thought about it: with events overlapping, grouping themselves into themes. In his privacy, suspended in the fluid of his memories, Haffner approached the philosophical himself: a medium of total objectivity.

So it was only right, perhaps, that he should perform his finale up here, in the mountains, where everything seemed turned upside down: in the endless light of midsummer. Up here, as Haffner would have read if he had begun the novel beside his bed – but he had not, because he cared too much about the lives of the Caesars – life is only serious down below. Up here, all the being ill, all the dying and recuperating, all the endless and serious work at the spa was just weightless: life was just another way of wasting time.

He was not who he was! Not an aged patriarch. No, Haffner was so much younger than he looked – and he looked younger than he was. With Morton, as they sat and steamed, he used to turn the conversation to the women: at what point, he asked Morton, did he think they would lose their right to try it on with the women? At what point did Morton think the lust would leave the body of Raphael Haffner? Morton only looked at him, with an infinite amused pity in his eyes. He pointed out that one thing he loved Haffner for, indeed he would go so far as to say it was definitely what he loved him for, was that Haffner always thought there was so much more to Haffner than anyone else ever thought. He had the arrogance of potential. He was a romantic, said Morton.

It didn't seem so unreasonable. What was down was up, and what was up was down: so that Haffner, who boyishly soared above the hills in his usual dream of flight – the sky turned underwater, with dolphins in the trees – was really this aged Haffner, in a lounger, as the sun declined and the clouds bunched and pooled together, while Zinka – the dream of Haffner's youth – approached his prone form, accompanied by Niko.

Haffner was never left alone by the world for long.

Zinka nudged him, then nudged him again, until he spluttered himself awake. With depression, he realised that he was still so very tired. With elation, he realised he was looking at Zinka.

And then, to Haffner's startled gaze, Zinka said to him, with a grin, that this man of hers was refusing to chaperone her that night. It was always like this with him – impossible. Haffner nodded, slowly. He tried to understand his role in the conversation; but he could not.

So, said Zinka: he knew what he could do. Haffner smiled, benignly. Think about it, bonza. Haffner tried. He still could not.

He could ask her to dinner himself, said Zinka. Haffner looked at Niko. His face betrayed no expression. He shrugged. Haffner looked at Zinka. Was it dinner time? he asked her, wonderingly. She tenderly smiled.

Was this a dream? thought Haffner. He could not tell. Carefully, Haffner considered his options. His adagio was over. This seemed obvious. There would never be a period, he worried, when adagio would exist again. His options seemed limited to one.

Prestissimo, Haffner said yes.

3

The maître d' ushered Haffner to his table, where Haffner's bottle of wine from the night before was settled in a shallow silver salver, the cork stuffed in at a jaunty angle. Swiftly, declining to express his inner smile, his inner shock at seeing Haffner so publicly tend to Zinka, he then gathered an extra chair.

Haffner began to talk to the waiter, offering Zinka an aquavit. No, she interrupted. It would be better if she took care of this.

He must, for instance, try the cuisines of the region. And Haffner, as she conversed with the serious waiter, the marvelling waiter, took the opportunity to wonder about this continuation of his syncopated adventure with Zinka.

There had been the incident of the wardrobe, then the incident of the lake. Neither of these episodes, he thought, had enabled Haffner's true charm to shine. But now, here she was – opposite him in the elegance of a dining room. This was Haffner's more usual backdrop. He considered Zinka: in the residual glow of his amazement. The persistent, grand desire for her disturbed him. And yet, he sadly considered, he could not think for a moment that Zinka desired him. He possessed no liberating craziness about his erotic attraction. He knew that Zinka represented the unattainable. Even if, he wanted to add, there had been the improvised escapade with the wardrobe. This, surely, was not without some kind of wordless flirtation? Although, he corrected himself, it could so easily have not involved any wordless flirtation. She had been talking to him about his wife, all the melancholy reasons why he was here, in this spa town where everyone, she said, was so unhappy. Haffner was drinking some kind of grappa. And, as normal with the women, Haffner asked the intimate questions: because he was always intent, with women, on understanding their hidden sadnesses, the depth of their secrets. Which he perhaps inherited from all the imprecise conversations with Mama. And Zinka told him about her love life, and together in this conversation they knitted and clothed a rag doll of Zinka – unfulfilled, sarcastic, mischievous. So it had seemed somehow natural for her to lean in and propose – in English so accented and asyntactical that Haffner worried he had utterly misunderstood – that Haffner should conceal himself in a wardrobe and see how brutishly Niko treated her. If he wanted. And Raphael Haffner very much wanted indeed.

No, thought Haffner, the episode was not about him. And there he paused, because he had no wish to spoil this image of the two of them there – dining together: this image of the old and the young entranced. He didn't want to do anything which might disturb this dream of Haffner.

He discovered that Zinka was already involved in conversation. In Zagreb, she told him, she had trained as a ballet dancer. This he knew. Evenings, she used to practise trapeze. The trapeze was what she really loved.

Haffner mentioned that all the same he thought he would order an aquavit for himself.

Patiently, she explained to Haffner the various terms – the French vocabulary: the *croix*, or crucifix; the *grenouilles*, or candlesticks; the *soleil avant*, which in English was the skinner; the *chutes*, the drops. The *tour du monde*. And then the important *sorties* – as you extricated yourself from the tangle of movement.

Haffner, concealing his excitement at this vision, these outlined movements, asked her if it weren't dangerous. Zinka said no. Not at all, on the flying trapeze? Haffner had always imagined . . .

—Not the flying trapeze, said Zinka. Just trapeze.

There was a pause.

—I was on the stage once, said Haffner.

4

It was towards the beginning of the war, in 1939 or '40. In Haffner's battalion there were many actors. Since he was in a London regiment. Many famous actors. And one day the actors said that they ought to get the whole battalion together and put on a variety show. Did she understand? She thought so. And they put it up to the second lieutenant – who went on, added Haffner, to become a very eminent newspaper editor, as it happened – who agreed, and so they put on this show which couldn't have been put on at the Palladium. No. There was Max Miller, and. And. No, Haffner had forgotten.

—How can you be a name-dropper, wondered Haffner, if you can't remember anyone's names?

He looked out of the windows at the sky: out of the grand windows at the grand sky.

There was Enid Stamp Taylor, Renée Houston, Oliver Wakefield, Guy Middleton, Stanley Holloway, Hugh 'Tam' Williams. These names probably meant nothing to anyone now. These chaps were putting on their own little sketch. And one of them, who was a well-known producer, Wallace Douglas, fell ill and Guy Middleton came up to Haffner and said that Wallace Douglas was unwell and he wanted Haffner to take his part.

Should Haffner tell this story?

In this sketch Middleton was a colonel and Haffner was a subaltern. And all that happened was that Middleton would ask Haffner where he had got his breeches. And all Haffner had to reply was that he had got them in a shop in the Strand, sir.

No, thought Haffner. He should not.

He was so old, so woebegone, thought Zinka. She felt a tenderness for him. Tenderly, she tried to retrieve the conversation.

—You were in the war? asked Zinka.

—I was in the war, said Haffner. Of course. Everyone was.

He paused. He looked at her.

Zinka was wearing a grey boiler short-suit, with black tights and rouge noir fingernails. Her hair was brown and her eyes were blue. The style was beyond Haffner: he had no idea, any longer, whether this was a style at all. He no longer cared. She was so utterly and completely beautiful, thought Haffner. So absolute in her body.

Then Zinka took hold of his hands, and looked at his palms.

Haffner, amazed, asked her if she was reading his palm. Meditatively, ignoring Haffner's scepticism, Zinka said that he was intelligent.

—Unintelligent? misheard Haffner, depressed.

He shouldn't have been shocked. The women he wanted were so often unhurt by a feminine self-hatred. Instead, they were happily confident in describing how Haffner could fail.

—Intelligent, repeated Zinka.

A paper flower of relief unfolded itself in the solution of Haffner's soul. He smiled at her, as she continued to read from his hand. But, she added, sombrely, he was unlucky.

—Unlucky? repeated Haffner.

—Well, said Zinka, trying to reconsider. Yes. Unlucky. I am sorry. I tell things as they are.

Haffner looked round, in an effort to find comfort in the view. But the view had disappeared. All that was visible was human. There, as usual, were the usual diners. At the table by the opposite window sat Frau Tummel, and her husband. They sat silently, in their marriage of silence. So Haffner turned back to Zinka.

—You do not wish you were eating with her? said Zinka.

—Her? said Haffner. No no.

—I am glad, said Zinka.

He knew his place in the art of love: the comic figure, forever grasping after the women who fled him. Just like Silenus, whose comically old flesh concealed the youth of the lust within.

He tended to see himself in poses. This was true. But I saw him as something else. Like the hero of every legend – you had to gnaw on him, like on a bone, to discover the richness, the inner meaning. So I preferred my private image. Haffner was his own *matrioshka*: concealing within himself the other, diminutive dolls of Haffner's infinite possibility.

5

Zinka used to live in a village with her grandmother. Haffner considered if he could think of any questions about this arrangement. He paused. So, asked Haffner, were her parents dead? Not at all, replied

Zinka. She described their characters for him. Her mother was hysterical. Her father was calm. That was all he needed to know. Haffner paused again. In this pause, Zinka asked if he believed in God. Did she? asked Haffner, avoiding the question. She replied that she believed in an energy. And Haffner? He did not believe, said Haffner.

—I will tell you what you are, said Zinka. You are realistic, but also a dreamer. I think you are easy to melancholy. Is this true?

—Oh it's true, said Haffner.

—Yes, said Zinka. Now you tell me about myself.

—Oh, said Haffner. I think you are: I think you are tough, but you are not as tough as you want to be. Something softer there.

—Oh, said Zinka, you are fifty per cent true. No. No, you are much closer. Too close perhaps.

Haffner wondered what he was really doing here.

—I have no regrets, said Zinka. People have to live the moment.

Haffner murmured something indistinct.

And because Zinka seemed suddenly sad, Haffner asked her, delicately, if she were sad. Yes, she replied, she was sad. But she did not want to talk about it.

—My country, it is destroyed, said Zinka. The baddest country in Europe.

But Haffner had seen worse.

The light outside, as usual, still persisted. It was as if the light went on forever. In this light, Haffner looked down at his plate. He had to confess, the food here distressed him. He had never been one for the Jewish food, the food of Eastern Europe. He preferred nouvelle cuisine to the heaviness of starch. In a sauce of sour cream and oil lay a dumpling, stuffed with pork. Haffner considered if at this late stage he should return to keeping kosher. It seemed desirable. The dumpling outdid him. First, it had been fried. This fried dumpling had then, surmised Haffner, been boiled. Nothing else could have created this texture, of the softest rubber. He did not understand it. In the sauce of sour cream and oil, small moments of bacon were visible.

In what way, thought Haffner, could this hotel be said to care about health? What was the point of the massages, the waters, the sauna?

He looked across at Frau Tummel. She was staring at him, angrily; and Herr Tummel was staring at his wife. He also seemed to be angry.

There had been a woman in love with her in Zagreb, Zinka was telling him. Did he understand this? He did, he assured her, he did. But why should she seem so proud of this fact, thought Haffner. It wasn't so strange, to fall in love. It just needed, in the end, someone else to be there. Oh Zinka was so tired of love, she said. And Haffner raised an eyebrow: a self-interested, altruistic eyebrow. He mentioned, for instance, Niko. Yes, she said: but Haffner knew Niko too. That boy. She was not sure he understood her. But no. She did not want to talk about this.

—No? said Haffner.

He began to worry that she wanted to mention the wardrobe, and all the pleasures which Haffner had seen. On this subject, he worried, he had no conversation.

No, she said. There were things it was good not to talk about. The matters of the heart. It was complicated. He did not want to hear this. Haffner tried to assure her that he did.

—No, she said. Not now.

The sex scene which was not a sex scene: this was the recent story of Niko and Zinka. The idyllic scene in the hotel room had been only theatre, after all. They were absent from each other. They coupled only in disguise, in the dark.

How could Haffner know this? Was it Haffner's fault, dear reader, if he did not know the inner history of Zinka?

6

No, Haffner wasn't free. Unlike the transparent and liberated reader, he couldn't be everywhere, like the bright encompassing air.

For these were the nights of Zinka. The concrete balcony to her apartment was covered by an advert, a scrim hung down ten floors from the roof. The scrim was printed with a woman on a cell phone, in some countryside, surrounded by birds. On Zinka's balcony, therefore, the reverse of a savage, eight-foot swallow looked in on her – observing the television in its mahogany hutch; a garden chair, forever folded, in a corner; the reproductions of Impressionist paintings, from the era when leisure was invented. In the apartment block opposite hers, the forgetful cleaner – who returned home on the buses, disliking the organic smell of her shoes, the chemical smell of her hands – would leave random lights on, illuminating the darkness for the potential spectator. But there were no other spectators. Except for Zinka's books – an illustrated translation of Pushkin, a novel in Russian by Dovlatov, a history of ballet – which looked down on her and Niko in their bed.

And Niko would touch Zinka's thigh, gently – which began their new game. In response to Niko's roughness, Zinka now never gave him permission. He could do what he wanted, she said: just so long as he expected her to do nothing.

And so, sadly, Niko did.

7

Perhaps this, then, was one reason for her silence. Perhaps this was one reason why she said to Haffner that she didn't want to talk about herself. Instead, she wanted him to tell her about Haffner's war.

And she looked up at Haffner.

So Haffner began where he always began, with the long night of

Haffner's spring in Italy: in the foothills around Anzio. Haffner got there on Valentine's Day. They were in the woods, on the flat ground, and the Germans, with the Ukrainians, were on the Alban Hills outside Rome. So they could see everything. There was nowhere you could escape. Everything was bound to hit something. The Germans had one wonderful gun – an 80 mm. Much better than anything the British had. They were sending over these great big heavies called Anzio Annies. Going for the docks. But it was much worse when they came over at night with the cluster bombs. On the whole, said Haffner, the British were very well dug in. But just about the time that Haffner got there, on Valentine's Day, was when the Germans made their one last big effort. They couldn't use their armour in that sort of mud. He didn't know it at the time. He didn't realise that those four or five days were the Germans' last chance to push the British and the Americans into the sea. They put everything into it. The noise, said Haffner. The noise. Their artillery was very good. The British had some destroyers outside the docks who were firing as well. And years later, on holiday in Madeira with his wife, he met a naval chap, who said: it was him. He was helping them. So there it was. Things got better when they began to see their own planes.

It was amazing, thought Haffner, how you settled down to a life: truly amazing. The chaps in the front were machine-gunned, killed in hand-to-hand fighting. And yet soon this seemed like a *façon de vivre*. His job as the second in command was to take up all the rations and things. And there was really only one way, which the Germans knew about: an alley.

Haffner paused. He considered himself. What could he tell her about Haffner's war? It seemed indescribable.

He remembered the yard in a town outside Alexandria, where he had enjoyed the greatest shrimp of his life, its flesh a white fluff inside the charred shell: there was a concrete reservoir, and a wind pump pumping water into it, clacking as it turned, casting a flickering shadow on the house.

This was all he could really tell her.

The problem about catastrophe, he had learned from the silences in his conversations with Papa, and then had learned for himself, from the silences in his own conversations with other people, was the incomprehension. There was the incomprehension of those who had seen nothing; and then there was the incomprehension of those who had seen everything.

Everyone persisted in the safety of flippancy. But maybe the flippancy was right.

At home, when the war was over, Livia would ask him why he was so private. She used to ask him this as if it were a fault, remembered Haffner – only idly noticing the fact that Frau Tummel was suddenly talking with animation to her husband. Livia expected Haffner to behave like a hero – to revel in his war stories. But Haffner never felt like a hero; not when he was being heroic. It had only bred in him a certain humour: a wit which could enjoy the gags of the emperors, like the one who, when a man asked for extension of his sick leave, ordered that this man should have his throat cut – for if the medicine had taken so long to work, then the man needed to be bled. With this humour, Haffner preserved his version of privacy. Livia used to upbraid him for his gaucheness at parties. He was always ready for his tête-à-têtes, she said. So why could he not be charming when there was more than one person present? And Haffner tried to explain that he had never been one for parties: for all the social whirl.

But maybe it was more of a problem that after the war Haffner's sense of humour had been replaced with something no one, really, wanted to know.

In Rome, Haffner had admired the triumphal column on which was carved a panel displaying a German baby being screamingly torn away from the arms of its mother by a stern Roman soldier. But most of all, he admired the Roman talent for the comic. Because – wrote a scholar in a booklet which Cesare bought and then translated out loud for Haffner, over a coffee in Piazza Navona – although a modern viewer might see this panel as deeply affecting, for the Romans it would have been amusing. It would have been sitcom.

And maybe Haffner and his Romans had it right. A war as a farce: this doesn't seem to me to be so implausible – with its mismatched exits and entrances, and its grandly outflanked speeches.

8

No, he hadn't told Livia about certain things. So he was hardly going to be able to do it here, thought Haffner, with a girl he hardly knew.

His anecdotes faded away.

But then Zinka said that her friend, she too had been in a war: the recent war. Haffner nodded. She once told Zinka that she had seen such a horrible thing: she had seen one of her neighbours with his mouth propped open with a piece of wood. Then they made him swallow sewage water. This was the woman who loved her.

—She committed suicide, said Zinka, thoughtfully.

—Who? said Haffner.

—That woman, said Zinka.

—The lesbian? asked Haffner.

—Yes, said Zinka.

—In what way, said Haffner?

—Drinking pills, said Zinka.

—It's easier, said Haffner.

The conversation paused.

This wasn't something that she told people, said Zinka. But she would tell Haffner.

This struck Haffner as strange, but he was feeling so unsure of what was happening that he decided to let this thought go. So intent was he on constructing his own escape, his desertion from his duty, he didn't consider that, for Zinka, Haffner could represent an escape too.

There was one time, said Zinka, when she was walking down the street in Zagreb. And some soldiers were outside an embassy. And she was with her friend. As they approached, the soldiers began to raise their rifles. This was true.

He didn't doubt it, said Haffner.

And this was what she had never forgotten, said Zinka. They were shouting that they were nothing: they were only walking home. And eventually, of course, as he could see, nothing happened. But at the moment when it seemed possible the soldiers would shoot, said Zinka, she stepped behind her friend. And although immediately she stepped back out, level with her, she could never forget this moment of self-betrayal.

There was a pause.

And at this moment, Haffner – timeless – felt everything returning to him.

The beach at Anzio strewn with bodies, as if everyone were sunbathing.

But most of all, in the series of women who had graced the life of Haffner, here, at its zenith, there was Zinka – for whom he felt such absolute adoration. Yes, at this moment, thought Haffner, extravagant through nostalgia, ignorant of Zinka, he could have endured anything, if only she would love him. Even if there was, I feel, little left for Haffner to endure. Yes, this was Haffner's ideology now. Maybe it could even borrow a slogan. *Love me as little as you like* – this was Haffner: *but just love me as long as you can.*

For Haffner believed in coincidence – he saw his life as a system of signs. He scanned each new acquaintance for the meaning they were trying to figure in the everlasting life of Haffner. So here, in his finale, he could only see in Zinka a kindred spirit, the twin for whom he had been searching all his life. The twin whom Haffner tried to align as closely as possible to himself.

—Oh, but that was nothing, said Haffner.

There were so many ways, he said, that you could feel ashamed. Not just the obvious betrayal. In Anzio, he said, at night, they had to leave the bodies on the beach: it was too dangerous to go back for anyone. So Haffner had to lie there. And a boy was calling, quietly: Mama Mama Mama.

—Mama Mama Mama, said Haffner.

All he wanted, said Haffner, was for this boy to bloody shut up.

It was only some years later that he realised how much he was like his father – when Esther reminded him of the story her grand-father had once told her. He described to her the wailing you could hear from no-man's-land, at night. At this point, he recalled, Papa would begin to shout. Because Papa was still angry at the disparity between this wailing and the official British telegrams, informing the anguished families that their heroes had died instantly, from a bullet in the heart.

—Sometimes, Haffner said to Zinka, one has conversations which are impossible with one's wife.

—But you're not married, said Zinka. Your wife, she is dead.

—It's the principle, he said.

And Haffner smiled.

—She's still alive in spirit, said Haffner.

And Zinka smiled too.

And in the sudden pause of their understanding, Haffner could still not prevent himself remembering the first time he had used this line about impossible conversations. It was one of his ordinary lines: in the Travelodge, at the business convention. Each time he used it, even now, even though he could remember all the times he had used it insincerely, he believed in it as true.

9

As if to celebrate this moment of Haffner's glory, the small jazz band serenading the hotel's residents began a melody from the oeuvre of Haffner's hero, Artie Shaw; and, cushioned by this melody, Frau Tummel descended on him, as if from the highest clouds.

Haffner looked to Zinka. Zinka looked away, staring at the indifferent mountains, as if finding in their indifference some kind of solace.

Frau Tummel was simply here, she said, to have the smallest word with Haffner. She beamed at Zinka. She did not want to interrupt.

He was all ears, said Haffner. She was sorry? said Frau Tummel. He was listening, said Haffner.

But this was not entirely true. The melody began to bother Haffner. He couldn't remember the title. Even as Frau Tummel stood in front of him. It suddenly seemed important. And maybe this wasn't just a ruse of Haffner. For his only dates left were the songs. The songs in which dead people sang about their immortal love. As soon as he heard a song, then everything came back to him. With the songs, he could happily wallow in the wreckage of Haffner.

She just wanted to check that they still had their arrangement for the next day, said Frau Tummel. And Haffner nodded: a toy dog.

That was wonderful, exclaimed Frau Tummel. Because if he didn't want to, then he only needed to say.

It was a conversation Haffner was practised in. Of course he wanted to see her, he said, fluent and abstract with flattery.

In that case, said Frau Tummel, she would leave them be. Or perhaps, she added, she could take a glass of aquavit with them – glancing over at her husband making pencilled notes in his guidebook.

Zinka sighed. Haffner was silent. Encouraged, Frau Tummel motioned to the distant waiter. She pointed to Haffner's glass of aquavit. She mimed her desire for another. Then no, she reconsidered: she called the waiter over and ordered a glass of dry white wine.

—The aquavit, she explained to Haffner and Zinka, it is not for me.

She smiled, at Zinka, who did not smile back.

Frau Tummel, thought Haffner, was the absolute bourgeois. She embodied strength: the statuesque matronly repression. There was nothing, thought Haffner, which Frau Tummel could not sublimate. And perhaps this, if he were honest with himself, was also why Frau Tummel so appealed to him. He liked the effort of her strength. Her strength enchanted him. Yes, he realised, for Frau Tummel he felt a spreading tenderness, welling under Haffner's soul, like a bruise.

Frau Tummel was talking about her husband. She was playing the part of the wife. One never knew, she said, how much one was doing the right thing.

—Perhaps, said Frau Tummel, I am not the right woman for him.

—Come now, said Haffner. Of course you are!

And perhaps if he had thought more precisely or extensively he might have decided that this was not exactly the right tone; that seduced as he may have been by Frau Tummel's calm he should still have understood its fragility. He should still have expected that his pity was not what Frau Tummel wanted.

He really didn't need to talk to her like this, she said. It was hardly elegant. To this accusation, Haffner made some kind of noise. In this noise, he hoped to register a charming protestation. Frau Tummel regarded him. He was useless, she observed.

—No denying it! said Haffner, cheekily. He opened out his arms in a happy gesture of surrender.

And in her irritation at Haffner's refusal to offer her even the most minimal affection, Frau Tummel informed Haffner that she really should be returning to her husband, and so rose swiftly from her chair, thus colliding with the waiter who – as if he and Frau Tummel were a carefully rehearsed double act, a famous pair of clowns – tipped the wine gently over Zinka, as if in benediction.

Frau Tummel, in a flurry of mortification, tried to apologise to Zinka, who waved her irritably away, pressing her napkin to her top. Haffner looked out of the window, at the sunset, at the inexpertly murdered sky.

He scanned the horizon – like isolated Crusoe, with the craziest beard, wishing for a rescue which he never, now, expected.

10

Haffner was timeless. Perhaps this moment where Haffner scanned the horizon was one small proof. As he watched, he wondered to himself how far this scene was his fault. He searched the scene for hidden motives. And as he did so, all the previous allegations against Haffner fluently returned to him – trapped on his stage, in his follow spot, the ripples of a sequinned backdrop behind him, facing the disdain of his miniature audience: one couple waiting for another act, the manager himself, the confused splinter group of a stag party, one baffled drunk soldier on leave. In Haffner's lone state, Frau Tummel multiplied into the other women – like Barbra, or Esther – who had found Haffner so disappointing.

His efforts were rarely enough, thought Haffner – as he stood up with a superfluous napkin which he held out to Zinka, who did not see it, occupied as she was in preventing Frau Tummel from offering advice, while wiping off the sticky sheen of alcohol from her skin. It was so often the same, he thought – picking up his own wine glass, correcting himself, putting it gently down: like the confrontation with Livia, after the Allied liberation of Rome, who was wild with jealousy, having been sent a photo of the Colosseum.

It was not the usual tourist cliché.

In the centre of the photo was a jeep, on which an Allied soldier was sitting, at the wheel: a white carnation was a badge in his beret. A suntanned woman in a navy dress, with large sunglasses up on her blonde hair, was showing something to this Allied officer, which was making him contentedly smile. While beside them an assortment of elegant coiffed sunglassed Italians were clapping.

Haffner had always denied that this was Haffner.

The photo had been sent to Livia – whom Haffner had at that time not seen for two years, not since he had been mobilised straight after their marriage in 1942 – by a so-called friend of hers who had seen it in the newspapers. She was jealous, said Haffner. She was mad with jealousy. It was a spiteful thing to do.

It was true that there was some ambiguity. The man in the photograph was looking down, in profile: so there was room for doubt. And this doubt also left room for Haffner to escape the accusations. When, fifty years later, Benjamin discovered this photograph too, going through a pile of Haffner's things, Haffner repeated his excuses again. Why then, thought Benji, had Haffner kept this photograph for fifty years, if it wasn't of him? Why would you preserve the triumph of another man?

But I thought I knew. I tried to tell Benji; but Benji was unconvinced. For I was the only one who believed in Haffner's innocence.

This photograph marked Haffner's jazz. His ultimate in pure freedom. It represented every moment in which Haffner had escaped, momentarily, from the observing world.

Like the riffs he had heard played on Artie Shaw's masterpiece 'Nightmare', in the rundown clubs of the Via Margutta. At some point, after all, you lost your moral compass. This was true. But it was difficult to know where. The borders of the bourgeoisie and bohemia were so hard to identify – like the manic jazz tune of Artie Shaw which was now returning to Haffner, as he sat there in the dining room, flanked by two gilt mirrors so that an infinite regress of Haffners looked with joyful affection at Zinka: her wet hair slicked to one side, like all the androgynous fashions of Haffner's century: the flappers and the *nouvelle vague*, the *movida* after Franco, the perverse and civilised *dolce vita* of the Fascists and the Communists in Rome.

11

Zinka stood up, and said that he could follow her. And Haffner, who wanted no fuss in his public life, who wanted no attention to be drawn to him, followed mutely after Zinka, nodding adieu to Frau Tummel.

The air above Zinka smelled of florals and herbs: the intoxicating warm forest contained in the wine she had been doused in. Safely alone, in the hotel foyer, she contemplated her ruined hair, the map of stains forming on her dress. And Zinka said to Haffner that perhaps he could escort her to his room, so that she could wash.

Oh Zinka! Haffner would have bathed her himself. He would have prepared baths of asses' milk, vials of perfumes. He was an old man still piqued by lust, by love. Of this, Haffner had no illusions.

He had so often believed in the counterlife, the myth of Haffner's excess. A Haffner untrammelled by his marriage, his Atlantic existence. Haffner unencumbered! Like the most distant tropical sunset, reached by regal Concorde, supersonic – its front wheel propped under its chin, like the solid goatee of a monumental pharaoh. But his escapes were always so fleeting. A night with a girl, a night at the opera: these were Haffner's *Cinco de Mayo*; his Risorgimento: the Parisian *événements* of Haffner's savage uprising.

These were the new life which Haffner dreamed of – but it always needed, he felt, someone to take him there. And no one, in the end, had really wanted to go.

So maybe, Haffner thought, he understood. The problem had been that he always wanted an elopee. Which meant that the problem, really, was Haffner. He could conjure with time as much as he liked, but the anecdotes only proved one thing. They were a strip cartoon which always involved the same dogged character: a Haffneriad. For the metamorphoses which lust invented in Haffner were never permanent. The glimpses of other Haffners – Haffner the New Yorker, Haffner the Roman, Haffner the free – did not transform him: just like Silberman, in Palestine, in 1944. Haffner had been told to do something with a couple of the other Jewish soldiers in his platoon. Surely something could be done to tone them down? Which Haffner contested. For nothing could be done with Silberman – disguised as a non-Jew with his clever costume of yarmulke, tefillin, and the extraordinary rapidity with which he entered arguments in Hebrew at roadside cafés frequented only by Russian Zionists and the occasional Zionist mule. Now, fifty years too late, Haffner had some sympathy for Silberman: disguised only in the guise of himself.

Haffner Roman

1

After Haffner had located the key – with its tasselled mane – Zinka immediately made for Haffner's bathroom. She went in, slammed the door. From within the bathroom, then came the sound of running water.

Haffner sat on the edge of the bed; took off his shoes; discovered *The Lives of the Caesars*, in paperback, underneath the scalloped valance; placed the book on the bedside table, beside his edition of Gibbon; and he sighed.

Three eras, he decided, marked any possible grandeur he might have ever had, the eras when he was most true to himself: there was the war; then the glorious 1970s; and maybe, he considered, now. At this coda to his life – as if his life had been extended, in a moment of grace, just slightly too long.

Zinka had a mole on her left cheek, tusked with twin hairs. It was the same mole, with the same tusks of hair, as the one which had belonged to a girl whom Haffner had met when the war in North Africa was over. This was 1942, or thereabouts. The regiment had gone to Bone, a lovely little place. And there it was, somehow, that he had met a lovely Jewish family who gave two or three of them a dinner. Haffner often wondered what happened to those nice people in North Africa, after the war was over. He always remembered the girl, with the darkest skin Haffner had ever seen, playing 'Invitation to the Waltz' on the piano. The next day the family arranged for them to be called up to read a portion of the Torah at the synagogue.

An echo in the bathroom, Zinka asked him if he wanted to come in.

He didn't think that this was his right – this openness which women so often displayed towards him. He never felt so confident as that. It was why the women loved him: his inherent modesty. He knew that this was happening by a grace which was beyond him.

Joyful, as he stepped into the bathroom, on stockinged feet, he paused at his window – where the sky was now one single shade of red, like a colour sample.

2

And Haffner was transported.

For just as the sky was now a painting of paint, to Haffner's distracted eyes, so he remembered how, in 1973, he had seen an exhibition of pure colour: at MoMa in New York. The exhibition was of paintings which were simply called *Colors*. The trip, on this Sunday afternoon, was Livia's idea. Haffner, always eager to discover new maps of his cultural ignorance, happily agreed.

Thin slabs of colour were laid next to each other: like in a paint catalogue. There seemed no genius, thought Haffner, no sublime. It was the absence of hyperbole – but precisely at this point Haffner found himself warming to this painting. Yes, this – so Haffner once told me – was the only art which he had ever liked. Livia had expected him to act with his normal grumpy chutzpah in the face of the masterpieces of modernism. But Haffner was transfixed. He was transfigured.

Long after Livia had left him for the cafeteria, where she sat with a filter coffee and three shrugs of sugar, Haffner still stood there, gazing into colour.

Such freedom! Although Haffner also enjoyed trying to trace the patterns in the grid – trying to work out if the repetitions of the yellow or the red could be predicted. He wasn't sure they could. So he let his eyes go endless.

Livia had disliked this abstract art: this most abstract of abstract art. It seemed emotionless, she thought. It was cold. This was what she told Haffner in the leather nook of a banquette at the Plaza, in the Oak Room. It had nothing to do with the real world. And Haffner had discovered a tirade within himself: that what the fuck did she care about the real world; that as far as Haffner was concerned there was no such thing as the real world; that this painting – to which, he reminded her, she herself had taken him, it wasn't Haffner's idea – this painting was as real as anything else; that in fact it seemed to Haffner an accurate portrayal of the real world in its clarity, its order; that quite frankly he saw little difference between the world which Livia called real and the world of colour in the grid on a wall at MoMA.

In the colours, Haffner found something he loved. He didn't understand it. But he knew that he admired it. This world beyond the world: where everything was pure.

3

There in her bath, Zinka was a vision of bubbles. Haffner knew the word for this. It was a fantasia. The vision of Walt Disney, the master of cartoons.

From the costume of her bubbles, Zinka said that first he must blindfold himself. Haffner queried this. Yes, she said. If he wanted to stay. He could take that stocking from over there. Haffner looked: a sliver of black pantyhose was slumped under her dress. He looked back at her. She nodded. That was the condition, she said.

These were the trials, thought Haffner. He was happy with the trials. Yes, for pleasure, Haffner could undergo anything.

With clumsy hands, Haffner tied the stocking limply over his eyes: a robber baron. But Haffner didn't care. He could still see: cloudy, in black and white. The peep shows of his maturity.

Haffner transformed by lust! Haffner crowned with the head of an ass!

If Haffner wanted, she said, he could now come and help to wash her. Would he like that? If he wanted, he could take that sponge and wash her back. Just so long as he was careful.

The fragrances from the water overtook Haffner. He stood over her. He wished he could have seen more. There her outline was, like the coyest vision of Hollywood, submerged by infinite foam. Her hair was done up in a hazy bun. One hand was leaning over the rim of the bath. She was looking up at him.

She told him to tighten the stocking. Haffner obeyed.

Then he took off his jacket, pushed the cuffs of his sweatshirt up – a bad imitation of his father, whose billowing sleeves were always secured with two silver bands, like the neat cuffs for napkins. He took a sponge, and dunked it: then expressed the water in warm rivulets over the curve of her back, with its peeling patches of foam.

An incubus, Haffner hunkered over Zinka. Perhaps this was another image which Haffner thought he should have minded. Haffner, however, never minded the embarrassments in his pursuit of pleasure. The embarrassments were just the acknowledged debt one owed.

Just below the disintegrating level of foam, he could see – through the thin blindfold – the momentary beginning of Zinka's breasts. He could see the side of her left breast, but the slope was some- thing else. Pretending not to look, he tried to notice as much as he could: to preserve it for the playground of his memory, while Zinka told him that he was being very kind. He was quite the gentleman.

Haffner wondered how long he could maintain a courtly conversation with a woman while blindfolded with her stocking. Its scent was odd: a mixture of must and shoe leather and the faintest last echo of her perfume.

Yes really, she said. He was a civilised man, and she liked that.

She flattered him. As Haffner had been flattered all his life, by the women. The women loved to flatter him: they loved to exercise his ego. He was cosseted. Not every woman, obviously. Not, most importantly, Livia. But the women Haffner went for in his secret life, his private life, were images of his mother. They told him how wonderful he was. They wrapped presents for him, surprises. On his sixtieth birthday, a woman for whom Haffner had only the most vestigial of passions privately presented him with a giant trunk of presents: sixty, each wrapped inside the other. A present of presents for the birthday boy. But maybe Livia had praised him like this, at the beginning. Maybe she simply got tired of his demands for flattery: or simply realised the untruth of all her praise – the practised way in which he enticed her with his vulnerability.

But there was another explanation. Her love was quieter because it was more true. Unlike everyone else, she trusted in Haffner's love. She would never, she once whispered to him, be loved by anyone else in the way that Haffner loved her. So how could she refuse him?

Zinka looked at Haffner's hand on her shoulder, drowning it in droplets. It was a girlish hand, she said. And Haffner wondered if at this late stage in his life he should waste himself in exercising his vanity on this kind of phrase. He decided that he had no choice. How could he invert the habits of a lifetime? He was not up to it.

So Haffner felt silently annoyed, silently exercised on behalf of his masculine hands.

Zinka asked if he were satisfied. He repeated the word to her: a question. Was he happy? she asked. But of course, replied Haffner, with a delirious grin. Then he paused. But maybe. Maybe what?

she asked him. No, it was nothing, said Haffner. But he had to tell her, said Zinka. Well then, maybe, Haffner wondered, he might be allowed to kiss her.

<h1 style="text-align:center">4</h1>

Now that, said Zinka, would be a very improper request. And Haffner, downcast, agreed. But, he added, contemplating how far down the path of humiliation Haffner might be prepared to walk, it would make him very happy.

He discovered that the path of humiliation had unexpectedly scenic views.

For although Zinka eventually said, from the depths of her silence, that yes, he could kiss her, it was not the kiss which Haffner was expecting.

She raised her left knee so that it rose from the water, crested with scintillating foam.

—You may kiss me on the knee, said Zinka.

Haffner considered Zinka's knee. At its tip, there was a small scar, translucent. A blurred and miniature map of France.

His own knees hurt him, cramped there on the bathroom tiles. He tried to ignore this. He bent his head to Zinka, hoping to see beyond the clouding bubbles: to the dark crevices of Zinka. He could not.

And Haffner kissed her.

His mouth filled with a froth of foam. It gilded his upper lip with a stray moustache. It embittered his mouth with chemicals.

How pleasurable was this? Haffner asked himself. Was it enough? For her part, Zinka thought it was. But Haffner wanted to lick her until her true smell returned: the delicious bare smell of her skin. Not the sterility of artificial foam. He asked if he could kiss her again. She said no. She was going to wash now. It was time for him to go back into the bedroom.

Haffner tried to stand up. He could not. Like some immovable sphinx, with buried paws. He could only turn his head away. He tried to explain this to Zinka, with the utmost maintenance of his dignity. In that case, said Zinka, she would just get out and dry herself. He must not look, she said. He promised this? Haffner promised. He turned his head.

There was a surge of water beside him. He tried to wrench the stocking away. Too late, he gazed at Zinka, with her back to him, wrapping herself in the softness of Haffner's towels: a Roman matron, in her flowing toga.

5

Sourly, he tasted the foam in his mouth. There was no doubt, thought Haffner, that his dignity was in danger. And yet, he was discovering, he seemed curiously avid for this degradation. It seemed, this ruin of Haffner, to be a kind of triumph too.

This wasn't a new motif in the life of Raphael Haffner.

In Rome, after the liberation, while Haffner waited for an infinitely postponed decision on his regiment's movements, he used to go up to the Pincio Gardens, and smoke his traded cigarettes, dropping the butts in the sand. Even up there, the smell from the sewage was heavy. The cigarettes, among other things, were Haffner's improvised pomander.

The light up there was pulverised; it was dust. The Tiber below Haffner was sluggish mud. A breeze made the leaves on the poplars silver themselves. Their pollen floated whitely on to the ground.

And Haffner looked down on the ruined, eternal city. It was the ruins, considered Haffner, which were precisely what was eternal.

Yes, this seemed to be Haffner's pattern.

Up from Anzio, before they reached Rome, they had ended up sleeping in the grounds of Ninfa. At that time, Haffner had not been horticultural. He had not admired the romantic unkempt wilderness. Kept awake by mosquitoes, Haffner instead found himself oppressed by the death of kings.

The gardens of Ninfa were built on the ruins of Ninfa – a town which had been sacked by its neighbours in the thirteenth century. The basilica had once held the coronation of a pope: now it was a dismantled heap of stones. Then, in the twentieth century, the town had been made into a true romantic garden: a meditation on the ruins of time. But Haffner had been troubled. There was no romance for him in ruins. They made him sad. Although this sympathy could so easily have been a more inward form of sympathy: Haffner's empathy for himself. In these cities' destruction, he only saw the futility of Haffner. The hollowness of Haffner.

—I will be remembered, he once told me, for my after-dinner speeches.

And then he paused.

—But that's worth nothing, he said.

And then Haffner smiled, glorious in the knowledge of his defeat.

6

Awkwardly, Haffner unfolded himself upright, via the rim of the bath, then the rim of the basin. He looked around – at the emptying swirl of the water, the deliquescent towels on the soaked mat. His masculine cologne was sitting on the shelf, its bottle embossed with a white tear of toothpaste foam. The toothpaste itself lay there, its tail twisted like a comma – like a fortune-telling miracle fish: its red plastic curled into the sign for passion, for jealousy, for sadness. The scenes of pleasure usually ended up this wasted, like the hotel in Venice where Haffner and the girl who had chosen him from his perch at the bar proceeded to order a feast of room service, one bottle and dish at a time, delighted by the maid's growing confusion between curiosity and distaste.

You should be happy for the things you get, Mama had said. No man should think he could have more than the Lord intended. So Haffner was humble. For at least the worship of women was a brave and noble aim.

Methodically, he laid out the full range of his medicines, in preparation for the night ahead. They included pills to combat the intensity of his blood pressure, pills to lower the ratio of bad cholesterol to good, antidepressants. Then the more soothing medicines: the ones to relieve Haffner's body of pain; the ones to make him sleep.

He picked up the wet towels, scented with Zinka's body. Then she appeared in the doorway.

Did he want to walk her home? asked a clothed and beautiful version of Zinka. To which a reduced version of Haffner wailed in response that the idea that he should ever be parted from her oppressed him with an absolute melancholy. If this miniature Haffner were to be allowed to rule reality, they would never be parted.

So Haffner said yes; and went out with his chaperone into the midsummer night.

Haffner Buoyant

1

To kiss a girl's knee, while on one's own knees, might have seemed, to the outside observer, a little pitiable, thought Haffner. To the outside observer, it might well have seemed to indicate some incipient breakdown. But Haffner tended to disagree. He admired the effects. The sound and light. The softly spattered fireworks above the ruined chateau: the fading and luminous palm fronds, thistles, water lilies in the sky.

For Haffner was in love.

They had left the lake behind; and the park, with its watchful factories. In what looked, to Haffner's bourgeois eye, like a shanty town, a tzigane was carrying a blue gas canister and a gold can of beer, following the dug-out route of a possible but phantom pipeline. Then they found themselves in another, less private park. It was a shortcut, said Zinka. At the centre of this park was a boating lake, embossed with a fountain, a fraying plume of foam. The rowing boats by the side of the lake crossed their arms neatly; the pedalos were chained together, clopping. Yes, there they were, at midnight: with the monuments to the source of the river; the monument to the unknown soldier. All the angels in stone, their wings in imitation of the earthly wings of pigeons.

Haffner's knees, aching from their bathtime antics, made walking difficult for Haffner. As they passed a sinuous bench, he asked if they could sit down, just for a moment.

—Not yet, she said. Not yet.

He was so old. And Zinka was so young. These facts were undeniable. But Haffner did not care. He looked at her, she smiled and Haffner did not care if this girl were using him; if she looked on him as an old fool. He was an old fool. There was no shame in that.

—How old am I? asked Zinka.

—Thirty? hazarded Haffner, baffled utterly.

—So old? said Zinka, disappointed.

—I was wrong? asked Haffner.

—A little, said Zinka.

And she, beckoning to tired Haffner, began to climb some small and artificial hill. Wincing, Haffner followed her. They sat for a while, to ease Haffner's legs, in the bandstand. But no band could stand this bandstand – thought Haffner. Dejectedly he regarded the signs of a struggle, a flight in haste: two condoms; a cigarette packet and its scattered assortment of butts, some blushing with lipstick, some not; a bottle of beer, without any beer. He looked out over the landscape.

From this point, perched on an artificial mound, Haffner saw the fields outside the city; the yellow rape fields, now blue in the dark, against which were dabbed the cypresses' black Japanese brushmarks.

From here, Zinka told him, she was fine. She was just in that apartment block – the one he could see, on the other side of the park. Haffner slowly nodded. She kissed him goodbye on his cheek.

Around him clouded his life: its particles – as usual – suspended, motionless. He hardly knew where he was: or to whom he belonged.

2

But no, just right now, I'm not quite in the mood for Haffner, and his confusions. Instead, I am into the different confusions of Zinka.

For Haffner suspected that to Zinka it was simply a matter of the usual story: an old man being used by a young girl. But this, I think, was not fair to the complicated romance of Zinka.

He was, thought Zinka, the first man she had ever met who enjoyed it when she teased him. He did not mind when one praised him for the smallness of his hands. He did not mind when you asked him to follow you, when you refused him the kisses you knew he wanted from you.

To Zinka, Haffner represented freedom. He had a politesse which she admired. This would have seemed unlikely to the women who had known the previous incarnations of Haffner: the forgetter of birthdays and anniversaries, the man incapable of returning a phone call. But maybe Zinka was not so wrong.

In front of her apartment block there was a water feature which she had never seen working: in its trough lay a ready-made of garbage. So she looked up instead, at the giant advert covering her balcony: the manic woman, the manic birds.

He didn't need his pride. This, she thought, was why she liked him. At last, she had discovered a relationship which could be improvised by Zinka.

And as Zinka went into the kitchen, to find some food – emerging with a packet of crisps – above her hovered the moon, the clouds in a cirrus formation which watched over the buildings with their scaffolding, their satellite dishes and air-conditioning units, the adverts (*Heineken: Meet You There*), the raised blinds and the shut blinds: all the domestic paraphernalia.

She turned back the two folding doors to the television. She switched on some form of American TV. A baseball star was showing the camera crew round his house. They were approaching the bedroom.

He was going to say, thought Zinka, that this was where the magic happened.

She reached in the empty packet for some crisps; her fingers emerged empty, but dandruff'd with salt.

—This is where the magic happens, said the baseball star.

And Zinka marvelled, silently, looking out at the suburbs by night, through the advert's gauze: wishing she could have told someone. First, she thought of Niko. But she wasn't sure Niko would understand any humour, let alone hers. And then she thought of Haffner.

And there she paused.

On the packet of her paprika crisps, a slice of potato with arms and legs beckoned to her with delirious eyes.

3

Alone in the midsummer night, Haffner had wandered off towards the hotel – on a road marked only by stray houses, then a Service Auto, beside a shop which seemed to sell the million varieties of cigarette, displayed behind glass cases, like extinct species of insect. Then a pizza place. And then a strip joint.

The twenty-four-hour bar (*Service Non-stop!*) into which Haffner descended, down a steep flight of stairs, was apparently in its busiest period. A group of possibly Polish truckers and a couple of policemen off duty made up the front row. Behind them, amphitheatrically, were ranged an assortment of men.

Haffner, however, wasn't here for the men.

He watched the women extend their legs around a stainless steel pole. He observed the way their breasts fell forward, elongated pyramids, as they leaned over – touching their toes in some strange imitation of an eighties aerobics routine, without the pink legwarmers, the turquoise sweatbands.

Then, in the crowd, Haffner recognised Niko: Zinka's boyfriend. He felt a descending qualm, a chime inside his chest. Niko gestured to him, warmly. He wanted him, it seemed, to join Niko's group. Haffner wondered about this.

He decided he had no choice.

—You all speak English? said Haffner to Niko.

—Of course we speak English. Fuck you, said Niko.

—That's a good accent you've got, said Haffner.

—Merci, said Niko.

It was the world of men.

—This man, said Niko, he look after my mad girl tonight. She bored you?

—No no, said Haffner, brightly.

—Yes, she bored you, said Niko. It's OK. We all understand.

And everyone, including wistful Haffner, laughed.

—You want to play a trust game? said Niko. It is what we are doing. You can zip the person next to you – zip zip. Only zap the person across from you.

—No, said Haffner.

—Zap, said Niko.

—You mean zip, said Haffner.

—Yes, said Niko.

—Can we stop this? asked Haffner.

On stage, a girl was now entirely naked, apart from a pair of translucent platform heels, on which she was balancing with a grace and ease which charmed old Haffner's heart. But not Niko's. She lacked flair, he argued. If, however, Haffner wanted her . . . He indicated that he had not finished his sentence. Haffner, however, was beyond the innuendos now. The masculine, and its zest for the tight-lipped, no longer charmed him.

He sadly nodded no.

—This is what you are here for? asked Niko.

Wearily, Haffner explained that, in fact, it was not why he was here. Or not officially. Nor primarily. Haffner was in this town to secure his heritage, his inheritance. He was here to do honour to his wife.

Angrily, he began a tirade against the state. He could not understand it. The bureaucracy bewildered him. It demeaned the

136

human spirit. Why did no one seem to care? What, he asked Niko, did you have to do in this country to get anything done? He only wanted what was his due. He was hardly demanding the moon.

—You know, said Niko, I like you.

—I like you too, said Haffner.

—Yes, I like you, said Niko, then wandered off, leaving Haffner with Niko's friends, who did not seem to share his pure love of Haffner.

4

Ignored, listening to Niko's friends talk freely about him in a language he could not understand, Haffner sat and watched the women. If these men wanted to mock him, then so be it. He could do abasement. The silent pattern of his life had been delicately training him, thought Haffner, for these moments of humiliation. Like the time when he came home to discover that his father had sold all his bar mitzvah presents, arguing that they only took up space in the house, declining to discuss the possibility that he was going to use the money for some selfish gain. Yes, Raphael Haffner was used to the destruction of his hopes.

Then Niko came back.

—You want this place? said Niko. Maybe we can do this for you. But it costs.

—I'm sorry? said Haffner.

—You want this place? said Niko.

—I don't understand, said Haffner.

He understood, of course, that Niko had a proposal. It wasn't the deal which was beyond him. It was the fact that Niko seemed to think he could effect such a deal: this was beyond the limits of Haffner's scepticism.

—Simple, said Niko.

He began to explain. It all depended on knowing the right people; and Niko knew the right man. It was not so difficult. It all depended on the right things getting into the right hands.

—You are not from here, said Niko.

This was just the way things were. Everyone knew how this worked. Either you could go through the ordinary ways of doing things, or you could enter the speed road. It was just a question of speed. Then the papers could get handed over, and the villa would belong to Haffner. The wheels would be oiled.

—No questions ask, said Niko.

There was a pause. In this pause, Haffner considered the perfect bodies of imperfect women.

—I am your patron, said Niko.

—Cash? asked Haffner, suspicious.

—Cash, said Niko. —You crazy or what?

Niko didn't really understand, he said, why Haffner needed any more detail at all. He only needed to know this. If he was so impatient.

—I'm not impatient, said Haffner.

If he were so impatient, said Niko, then things could be worked out. He had seen this problem before. He knew how to fix it.

Haffner had to understand, said Niko, that it was still the same people in charge. Yes, Niko knew what had happened. Haffner's papers would be sitting there, ignored, in someone's office. Just waiting for a reason to be dealt with.

—Let me think about it, said Haffner.

And as he tried to balance his doubts as to Niko's efficacy – his general untrustworthiness, the danger of relying too much on a man whom he had spied on only the night before, and whose girl-friend had only an hour ago been soaping herself in Haffner's bath – against the obvious benefit of having, as he used to say, a man on the ground, Haffner excused himself: desperate to find a toilet, a cubicle where Haffner could think.

But reality continued to pursue him. He took a few steps, into a corridor which bore graffiti, torn posters, an exhibition of faulty plumbing. Then all the lights went out.

And Haffner was in the dark.

5

Practical, Haffner told himself that he mustn't get this wrong: he didn't want to lose his way. To his surprise, in a basement, in a bar, in a wasteland, he found himself wishing he had the practical wisdom of Frau Tummel. He stopped. He considered this thought.

To whom was Haffner loyal? It seemed unsolvable. There seemed so many ways for Haffner to demonstrate his disloyalty. Livia, the obvious candidate, was so fluently replaced by all her avatars, her rivals.

In the dark, Haffner edged his way along the wall – his hand extended, palm flat: directing invisible traffic. Distant whoops of masculine joy reached him from the main area, whoops which were tinged, now, for Haffner, with a poignancy. It seemed unlikely he would ever see humans again. Then suddenly the wall gave way, as it transformed itself into a door. Haffner peered into the black. Soothing plashings from what he thought could be urinals echoed throughout the room. Was this a bathroom? wondered Haffner. He could not be sure. It might have been, for instance, the hideout of the janitor.

Then he discovered one tiled wall. It decided Haffner on the question of a bathroom. Where else did one find ceramic? He ignored, for instance, the possibilities of storerooms, the opportunities of kitchens. Facing this wall, Haffner stood, unbuttoned his fly, and began the lengthy process of unburdening himself – telling himself that, after all, it wasn't as if Haffner disliked the dark. Bourgeois he may have been, but Haffner wasn't spoiled. He started working at Warburg's in the winter of 1946: the nightmarish winter, when the electrics failed and everyone in the City worked by candlelight. The clerks sat with their feet encased in typewriter covers stuffed with newspaper – gigantic and ineffectual slippers, improvised snowshoes. That spring, the streets were still a mess of rubble sprouting woodland plants – ragwort, groundsel. The dark had nothing on Haffner.

When he emerged, the lights were still not on. Now, however, a selection of torches had been discovered, and lighters, and solitary candles. A man was savagely strumming an acoustic guitar.

—Like a refugee camp? Niko breathed into Haffner's startled ear.

Haffner stared at him.

—So wonderful, no? said Niko.

Haffner looked around. In chiaroscuro, a girl was holding a flashlight above her head, like a handheld shower. In the sway of its light, she was dancing. As the light swayed, her breasts swayed with it. Another girl was on all fours, while a man mimicked the act of whipping her: his whip ascending in flourishes, an undulant lasso. The shadows made momentary blindfolds on the man's face; or the girls acquired sudden grimaces, as if from the painted masks of Venice, which Haffner had looked at, in wonder, in 1952, at the carnival with Livia – while she began to cry beside him, describing the carnivals she had seen before the war. Which seemed so long ago, she said. And already, at this point, Haffner had considered if he could ever leave Livia – because this was how he tested all his affections, by imagining him leaving them behind – and had realised that, for him, it was unimaginable. She was the only person he would never leave.

—Vodka? asked Niko.

—Perhaps not, said Haffner.

—Maybe you prefer tea? asked Niko. It is more British?

—A double vodka, said Haffner.

Returning with a plastic cup awash with vodka, Niko asked Haffner if he knew that they had all survived radiation. Or survived as much as they could. Oh yes, many years ago, when they were children, a factory had blown up a hundred kilometres south of here, but the distance was nothing, said Niko. The radiation was everywhere, all over the countryside.

—The motherfuckers, they killed us. Fucked us, said Niko.

His sister, he told Haffner, was born with only four fingers on her left hand. He moved closer to Haffner. He understood this? Only four fingers. On her left hand.

Unwillingly, Haffner inhaled the alcohol of Niko's breath. He drank a gulp of vodka, for equilibrium.

Haffner, said Haffner, understood.

It wasn't as if Haffner hadn't seen the horrors: he had seen the rulebook torture – the forced standing for twenty-four hours, so that the prisoner's ankles swelled up, blisters developed on the soles of the feet, the kidneys shut down. In one village in Italy, the soldiers had just gone mad. They dressed up in women's clothes. They hung clothes in the trees. They went through the houses. Soon, there was nothing left to eat. Once, on the edge of the desert, they came across a food truck, carrying fruit. The people inside were crushed. Haffner and his unit stopped. They wiped the fuel and blood off, and started to eat the peaches, the heavy grapes. They hadn't eaten for a day. There was a girl there who had a dress but no legs. This was one of the women to whom Haffner felt closest. At a checkpoint in Syria, a kid was in an abandoned truck, cowering. He went to help her. He picked her up. Her head slumped off the neck on to his arm, heavy, like a pumpkin.

It wasn't then that Haffner threw up. It was ten minutes later, after he had buried her. After he had buried her just there, by the side of the road – because what fool would wander off to find a place to bury the dead? Just as what fool went off to seek his necessary privacy if he wanted to shit? The sniper fire on the way out; the friendly fire on the way back. Instead, you squatted there, in front of everyone, discussing the imaginary world of sports.

And Haffner discovered in this moment with Niko its secret twin, which already existed in the story of Haffner.

In another blackout, the universal blackout of 1977 – the summer Haffner came back to New York after being away for three years – he had argued with Goldfaden about sport. They were in Chinatown. Goldfaden had just outlined his theory that genetically the Jewish race was programmed to adore Chinese food. And Haffner felt no urge to disagree. He was happy. Before him, sat a plate of crispy shredded beef: a pile of orange twigs – which was Haffner's most reliable delight.

Then the lights went out. And Haffner found the conversation turning to sports.

It was escapism, said Goldfaden. There was nothing wrong with this, he wanted to add. He believed that everyone, at some time, needed a way of escaping. For Goldfaden, it was love. For Haffner, it was sports. Where, then, was the argument?

The argument, thought Haffner, was precisely in this idea that anything could be imaginary. Nothing was imaginary. This was Haffner's idea. So often accused of being divorced from real life, Haffner always maintained that – on the contrary – he would love to be divorced from real life, but the divorce was impossible. There was no counterlife.

As waiters began to scurry round for candles, Haffner talked.

The accusation of escapism was not a new one. Normally, however, this was seen as a bad thing. Esther used to accuse him of a lack of seriousness. Sport wasn't, said Esther, real life. She asked her new husband to agree with her. And Esmond did. But Haffner now maintained, in front of Goldfaden, in the dark, that there was no difference between a sport and real life: how, he wondered, could there be? In what way was real life suspended by the act of kicking a football, that would not mean that the act of sipping a coffee also represented a suspension of real life? The theory was ridiculous. What escapism was it to be battered by emotion, scarred by defeat, elated in victory? In Haffner's opinion, this proved a further and deeper truth: there was no such thing as escapism. No, never. How could you escape? Where did Goldfaden think he could go?

Well, said Goldfaden: he supposed he was much more of a romantic than Haffner.

Did he really want to talk about football? said Haffner, ignoring this comparison. Because he could. The Norwegians, for instance, who refused to play Nazi football. So the quislings watched each other in desolate stadiums. How was that not real life? So OK, said Goldfaden. But Haffner wasn't finished. Let us not, said Haffner, forget the Viennese genius Matthias Sindelar, known as The Wafer, who was said to have brains in his legs, and many unexpected ideas occurred to them while they were running. For instance, said Haffner, there was the last ever match between Austria and Germany, a month after the Nazis had annexed Austria in 1938. Everyone knew that Sindelar had been told not to score. For the whole first half, therefore, he pushed the ball a little wide of each post, sarcastically. And then, in the second half, he couldn't stop himself: so Sindelar scored. And then another man scored a free kick, thus sealing the game, and Sindelar, because he had ideas in his legs, went to celebrate by dancing in front of the Nazi directors' box.

That, said Haffner, was sport. It could never be an escape from life. Life was everywhere.

No, there was no such thing as a counterlife, Haffner wanted to argue. Just as there was no such thing as a real metamorphosis. In the end, you only had yourself to work with. Wherever you went, it was still you.

While around them, the city of New York was looted. Though whether this proved or disproved Haffner, in his imaginary nostalgic lecture hall, he didn't know.

7

He carried on looking at the girls. In Italy they had called them *segnorini* – the girls who went with the Allied soldiers: they mispronounced them, *a l'inglese*.

When she bent down, you could see the neat fur between her legs.

Behind him, the light of a candle flickered. A girl was standing beside him. She was tall, she had straight black hair, she was what the world would consider the pornographic ideal. Whatever her breasts were made of, Haffner liked it. She told Haffner her name. He could not hear it. She told him again. She thanked him for buying her a drink. He raised an eyebrow. Behind her, Niko raised a glass, gaily.

—You have a drink? she asked Haffner.

Haffner had a drink.

—So, she said, you are good to go.

He couldn't deny it. Like one of Benji's wind-up toys, which could unleash its skittering movements wherever it was placed: on the neat chevrons of blond parquet in a country-house museum or the linoleum of a kitchen floor – with damp stains, starry splashes of coffee, and one irrevocably non-matching square of concrete, where the lino had given out.

The girl who now thought of herself as Haffner's – or who thought of Haffner as her own – led him into what seemed a cave, or tunnel. It ventured into the underground. She told Haffner to sit – on a crate, or possibly an upturned bucket. It was difficult to tell. Haffner only knew that it had some kind of rim. It hurt him.

Haffner had never been into the pornography, nor the pubs to which his City friends used to go: where angry women undressed and despised their spectators. All his pleasure was more traditional. He disliked the obscenity of modern film, the sexual glee of modern literature. There were things which shouldn't be written down, said Haffner. There were certain forms to be observed. Pleasure was all about privacy, he thought: the burden of the boudoir.

And even if I disagreed, I still agreed with Haffner's motive – it wasn't from primness that he thought this, but from a wish to preserve the erotic as a secret which one kept from other people. This didn't seem unreasonable.

But now, in this unstaged intimacy, Haffner could still not discover in himself any obvious erotic surge. He should have done, he knew this. And perhaps, even recently, he would have done – but no longer. Now, Haffner was more in love with love.

This love was partly visible in the way his thoughts were tending to Zinka, in her bubble bath. But it was also visible in the way Haffner kept thinking of Livia. He sat on an upturned crate or bucket and told himself that he should simply do this so that Niko would still admire him. Because Niko was his ally. Niko was the friend who would restore Haffner to his heritage.

8

In his blackout basement, Haffner conversed urbanely with his girl. Her name, she told him, was Katya. A nice name, Haffner assured her. It was not her real name, she replied. Who needed real names? Not in here. Tonight, she said, she wanted sex, and she wanted vodka. And she had the vodka already, she said – raising the smudged plastic glass to Haffner's worried gaze. So only one thing was missing.

As usual, the god Priapus harried Haffner: with his cloven hooves, his staff entangled in ivy. His entire being a pulsing penis.

An arm was twined around Haffner's neck. He felt his lips being kissed. Then he realised that the small bikini top which Katya had been wearing was now slipping, weightless, on to his arm, then on to the floor – where it rested, invisible, unknown to Haffner, on his foot. She lifted a candle to her torso: her breasts were there, in the magical light. Katya told him that he could touch. If he were gentle.

He belonged to an older world. The older he got, the more he believed in it. Here, in the centre of Europe, in a town which was so nearly modern, and yet had been already so melancholically super-seded by other fashions, Haffner believed in romance: the candlelit dinner, the car ride home, the kiss on the cheek. This routine to be repeated, with variations.

He tried to explain to Katya that he really did not want to touch her. If she didn't mind. He wondered if perhaps they should rejoin the others.

But he was in such a rush, said Katya, sadly. Did she not please him?

He tried to look for Niko, and could see nobody. He was alone with her, in this back room. Of course, he replied, she pleased him.

Visually, it was inarguable.

Then he felt her press her breasts against him. Softly they gave against the protrusion of Haffner's nose. The rough nipples rubbed against the harsher roughness of Haffner's cheeks.

But no, it wasn't Haffner's thing. He tried to explain this to her. Really, she had been very kind, but he ought to be going. And to his unsurprised dismay, Katya seemed to feel wronged by his explanations. Angrily, she upbraided him. Never, she said, had she met such a man.

Helpless Haffner bent his head.

Did he think she really wanted him? she asked Haffner. Dumbly, Haffner shook his head. Did he think that this was her idea of love?

—You're nodding when you're not supposed to be nodding, she said.

—Ah yes, said Haffner.

—You're still doing it, she said.

They were everywhere, thought Haffner: the experts in what was real; the people who wanted to begin, or complete, his education.

Look at him! said Katya. The man was dressed in a cagoule. She could not understand how stupid he was.

And Haffner wanted to assure her that he was capable of stupidity so gigantic that she would hardly comprehend it.

Maybe, thought Haffner, he was going off sex. Once, a Texan friend of his had told him a Dallas proverb. Every time you find yourself not thinking about sex, so ran the proverb, then your mind is wandering. And this had been Haffner's philosophy, in so far as the man could have a philosophy.

My squalid Don Quixote: avid for the higher things. The higher things which Haffner looked for in the lower things: in the lust, and the vanity, and the shame.

The point was, said Katya, that she at least needed to be paid.

It was the second time that day, considered Haffner, amazed – emptying the pockets of his cagoule, presenting her with all the notes he found – when he had paid for sexual services he had never wanted. But Haffner was flexible.

He should never forget his favourite item of vocabulary. When he was in Brazil, when they were leaving the theatre, laughing to themselves at the disconcerted policemen, his counterpart in the Rio bank had tried to explain how one survived in these great times. You could do it, sure, by going underground and becoming a hero. But then you died. Or you could do it by offering up your politics to whatever came along. You preserved yourself through sacrificing your ideals. They had a word for this, he said. It was trampolin-ability. And this immediately became Haffner's favourite word. He could trampoline. Yes, this seemed possible.

To trampoline: the only form of maturity which Haffner ever recognised.

9

Rising back into the air, buoyant against gravity, Haffner made for the exit – where Niko was waiting for him. Was Niko not good to him? asked Niko. Haffner replied that Niko was very very good to him. So what, asked Niko, did Haffner think?

Haffner promised him that yes: why not? If Niko thought he could help. He didn't see why not. And Niko said that this was very good. He had perhaps said this before, but he liked Haffner very much. Now then: the practicals. He knew the snooker club? Of course, said Haffner, he didn't know the snooker club. Well then, said Niko. Well then. They would sort something out. Niko himself would take him there.

Whatever suited him, said Haffner, simply wanting to end the evening: and he walked out into the benighted dawn.

And carelessly, without thinking, the hand of fate or the world-soul nearly placed a man in a bowler hat, Haffner's twin, his arms by his side, like a sentry, at the end of Haffner's day, as Haffner turned the corner into the town's main square. But luckily this world-soul managed to arrange it so that Haffner changed his mind, did not proceed briskly back home, but lingered, looking in the window of a shop which sold domestic cleaning products, ironing boards, Hoovers, dog baskets, plastic and multicoloured clothes pegs; then the window of an adjoining lingerie shop in which was fixed a row of disembodied and cocked legs, like the Platonic idea of a cancan.

Finally, Haffner reached the hotel. He ignored the greeting of the woken receptionist – clutching a paperback and a serrated freshly burning plastic cup of coffee – walked into the lift, and pressed the wrong button, so that when he turned as normal to the left and tried to move his key in the lock, it would not work. Finally, after three minutes, he realised his mistake – oblivious to the scene he had left behind the door: a man in pyjamas, wielding an umbrella; a woman whimpering in the bed; a marriage teetering.

Haffner went to sleep, dressed in the tracksuit which now doubled as his pyjamas. Commas of white chest hair nestled in the gap above the jacket's open zip. He wanted to talk to Livia. He wanted to tell her about that conversation he had had in Chinatown, twenty years earlier, with Goldfaden. The conversation about sports. And she would turn to him, sleepy in her velvet nightgown, and tell him that of course Goldfaden was wrong. He knew that. For Livia, like Haffner, understood the majesty of sport.

Yes, it was Livia who had watched the 1980 Wimbledon tennis final with Haffner one weekend, in the early morning, in Florida – where they had gone for a summer break: featuring the American kid with the curls, and the Swedish man with the blue-eyed stare. And it was Livia who had pointed out to Haffner the obvious symbolism of the fight: the two versions of machismo. And which one, did Haffner think, was him? He thought, he said, that he was possibly the kid with the curls. And which one, asked Livia, did he think that she would go for?

The likeable kid with the curls? asked Haffner, hopefully.

No, unfortunately for Haffner, Livia's preference was instead for the resourceful and quiet man: whose machismo needed no theatricality. Even though as she said it Livia kissed him on the cheek, and grinned at him. And Haffner was glad that as he looked at her blouse – one button wrongly fastened so that the fabric bunched out and Haffner could see the beginning of a breast, the lace florets of her bra – his lust was unabated.

But Haffner's audience was gone. So Haffner lay there, on his left side, then shifted, to give solace to his heart, so placating the superstitious aspect of his soul. The aspect of his soul which believed in a soul at all.

PART THREE

Haffner Interrupted

1

The next morning, Haffner woke up late, to hear Benji in conversation outside his door.

Perhaps it was a bad dream. He tried to wake up further.

He couldn't. The dream was real.

2

—Me, Benji used to say, to his friends, his admirers, I have the greatest breasts of anyone I know. If I were a woman, said Benji, I'd want me. I mean yeah. I mean absolutely.

Yes, Benji was huge.

The hugeness had caused so many miniature aspects of Benji. It was, for example, one reason why he hadn't really had girlfriends. His emotions were distractedly doodled with shyness. Self-consciousness possessed him. This was also a reason why Benjamin was beauty-obsessed. He was always a sucker for the grand beauty. When it came to female beauty, his standards were strict. And finally, the size was why he had been forced to teach himself survival through wit.

—You want to know something? Benji said to our mutual friend Ezekiel: Ezekiel, known as Zeek.

—They look at my penis in the urinals, continued Benjamin, and they can't see it. It's like I'm pissing from my belly, you know?

—You shouldn't be too hard on yourself, said Zeek. It's not so bad. I mean, you're not circumcised, are you?

—No, said Benji.

—So you've never tried to masturbate when you're circumcised? said Zeek.

—How could I try it? said Benji.

—So then. The thing is this, said Zeek. It needs a lot of Vaseline.

—Vaseline? asked Benji.

—Or something similar, said Zeek.

—I don't need Vaseline, said Benjamin.

—But you're not circumcised, said Zeek.

—Yes, I know, said Benjamin. I told you that.

In the grey dawns after parties, we would sit out in the garden and talk: while in the living rooms, the bedrooms, the girls dozed in each other's arms, the junkies talked to themselves.

The issue of circumcision used to worry Benjamin. Once, Benjamin had talked to a girl whom he dearly wanted to kiss. As so often in the imperfectly Jewish life of Benjamin, the conversation had turned to penises, and their foreskins. She really did think, she said, that circumcised penises were preferable. They lasted longer, she smiled at him. And Benjamin, with his yarmulke, his deep knowledge of archaic law, wondered if by this she meant to flirt with him. It was possible. Come on, kid, it was possible, he said grimly, to himself. Even if, as only he knew, her hope was utterly misguided. He had to be honest. Sadly, Benjamin admitted to the intact nature of his penis, its shroud of flesh: its headscarf. It was the only way in which Esther had resisted Esmond's Orthodoxy: the practice of circumcision, she used to say, was barbaric. She couldn't countenance it for her darling son. But of course, Benji's girl then added, the circumcised penis had its own charm too. She looked at Benjamin. Confused, he looked back at her, and was quiet.

This was the boy whom Haffner could hear outside his room: while Haffner struggled to extricate himself from the placid dreams of his sleep, into the more unnatural dreams of Haffner's Alpine existence.

3

Haffner picked up the phone. He was sorry, said the receptionist to this newly bedraggled version of Haffner: his whitely blond hair awry, uncombed; his beard sprouting. Haffner asked him what he was sorry for: the receptionist explained that his grandson had said that his grandfather should be expecting him.

—No problem, said Haffner, exhausted. No problem.

And it was nearly lunchtime, added the receptionist, pedantically.

It could hardly get worse, thought Haffner. But then, as he struggled with the sheets, his shoes, the elongated dimensions of his washing routine in the bathroom, he was interrupted by the realisation that it was, in fact, worse. Benjamin, Haffner suddenly realised, was not talking to himself. Though why he had thought the boy would be talking to himself, he didn't know. No, there wasn't just Benjamin. There was also Frau Tummel. They were engaged in conversation outside his door.

And why not? thought Haffner, in dismal jubilation. Why wouldn't Frau Tummel be here as well?

It was as if the farce of his life were repeating itself, just on a diminishing scale. The interruptions of the real – the unwelcome real – which had marked his life continued even here, when Haffner was nowhere.

In the corridor, Frau Tummel was telling Benjamin that such devotion to a grandfather was rare in his generation. It was admirable, she said.

—Uhhuh, said Benjamin.

He had just arrived from the airport. And as he made himself known to reception, he had been interrupted by this woman whose appearance Benjamin felt he knew all too well, from the mothers of his schoolfriends: she was stern, and extravagant, simultaneously. When she discovered who Benjamin was, she was delighted, she said. She was ravished. She knew his grandfather, she assured him, very well. She was just on her way to see him.

He would never understand what the women still saw in his grandfather, thought Benjamin, resigned. No, he wouldn't even try. There was no point. It was part of the whole mystery of sex: a mystery which he felt was way beyond him. Though why the mystery of sex was not by now beyond his grandfather seemed an injustice too cosmic to be contemplated.

Frau Tummel asked him if he was here for a holiday as well, like his grandfather. He replied that sort of. Yes? she said. He was more here on business, said Benji. Like his grandfather.

He really did look very like his grandfather, she said. Absolutely handsome.

Benjamin simpered.

If only, thought Benjamin, she were about thirty years younger. It was always like this. If only women said this whom Benjamin thought of as girls.

Frau Tummel thought that he must admire his grandfather very much. And Benjamin replied ruefully that he could be quite different at home. Frau Tummel queried this. No, said Benjamin: it was true.

In the window, the Alpine mountains were blankly beautiful.

Well, said Frau Tummel, she had to admit that maybe there was something in what he was saying. Herr Haffner had his complications. This she would admit. But that, she said flirtatiously, smiling at Benjamin, was, after all, the signature of a man! She had no idea, said Benjamin sadly, how difficult he could be. Difficult didn't cover it.

But he did not expand on this to Frau Tummel. No, Benji was loyal. He did not tell her what he was now remembering – how once they had discovered Haffner on the island of Malta. He was with a dancer from a cruise ship. Another time, in Florence, Haffner simply wandered off; and was found two days later, in a bar on the south side of the river.

She could not believe it was true, said Frau Tummel. She had not seen this difficulty in Herr Haffner. Herr Haffner, she would at least accept, was a man with his own sense of himself, said Frau Tummel. That was one of the problems, agreed Benjamin. But there were others.

Benjamin was an expert on his grandfather. Observations of his grandfather had formed his education. Once, he had idolised him. Now, perhaps, his idolisation had become inverted: a strange form of love, which was inseparable from dislike.

5

Haffner opened his door.

—You're here? said Haffner to Benji. How?

—Surprised? asked Benji.

—Not really, said Haffner.

It was true. Nothing surprised him when it came to the decisions of his grandson, the wayward passions to which he was subject.

—Shouldn't you be in school? asked Haffner. Shouldn't you be learning something? The cultivation of forelocks? The possibility of prayer?

—You see? said Benjamin to Frau Tummel.

Anyway, said Benjamin: he had told him. Haffner questioned this.

—On the phone? said Benjamin, with his American fall and rise.

—You never told me, said Haffner.

They paused, in this silence of disagreement.

—Are you really wearing that? said Benjamin.

Yes, said Haffner, he was: refusing to explain this unusual wardrobe choice of pink hiking T-shirt and his familiar sky-blue tracksuit.

There was another pause.

—It is so wonderful, the devotion! exclaimed Frau Tummel, beaming on Haffner.

Haffner looked at her, then at Benji. He could do, thought Haffner, curtly, with losing some of that weight. But there it was. He had always been spoiled: by Esther, and then by Livia. Who always cooked the kid steak. Who made hand-cut, hand-fried fries: a treat which Haffner, in fifty years of marriage, never got for himself.

—You had breakfast? Haffner asked his grandson.

—On the plane, said Benji. Plane food.

—Hungry? asked Haffner.

—I'm hungry, said Benjamin.

Haffner's appetites were catholic. Benji's appetite had been for food. Now, unknown to Haffner, he was concerned to broaden the range of his appetites. But it was his appetite for food on which Haffner and his grandson had forged their friendship.

—You know what's happening in the cricket? asked Haffner.

—No, said Benjamin.

—Blowing a gale? said Haffner, cryptically, with an intimate smile.

Benjamin looked embarrassed. And this saddened Haffner. Mutely, he went in search of the long-lost time when Haffner had taught Benjamin his favourite routine from the movies – dialogue which they had then so often recited by heart – where a man stranded in a mountain hotel phones home to find out the cricket score.

Now Haffner had to quote to himself, in silence, the next lines in his adored dialogue – *You don't know? You can't be in England and not know the test score* – grimly thinking as he did so that it was only natural that this was how his century should end: with everyone having lost their sense of humour.

—I will leave you two boys together, said Frau Tummel.

She would meet Haffner back here, she said to Haffner: to talk. For a moment, she looked darkly at Haffner. And then, smiling more benignly at Benjamin, she left.

Haffner turned to Benjamin, and he sighed.

6

Precocious, in the heyday of his teenage years, Benjamin had listened to the hip hop from New York, the ragga from Jamaica. His favourite thing was the Los Angeles hip-hop artist, the modern saint: 2pac. Everyone loved 2pac, true. But in this love, Benji was unusual. He didn't care about the drugs, nor the women. Nor about the gold and diamanté T round 2pac's neck, a cartoon crucifix. No, for Benjamin, 2pac was an example of pure romance. His favourite song – which he played on repeat – was 2pac's elegy 'Life Goes On'. Have a party at his funeral, let every rapper rock it, sang 2pac, rapped 2pac. Let the hos that he used to know from way before kiss him from his head to his toe. Give him a paper and pen so he could write about his life of sin, a couple of bottles of gin in case he didn't get in.

The swagger had Benji entranced.

He'd be lying, continued 2pac, if he told him that he never thought of death. My nigger, they were the last ones left. But life went on.

It was so cool, thought Benjamin. Once, he tried to explain this to Haffner. Haffner tried to listen. This presented some problems: practical (the fitting of the earphones, the working of the portable

CD player); and aesthetic (the understanding of this noise as music, rather than noise).

As a teenager, Benji's ideal habitat was the urban sprawl of Los Angeles: the gang warfare, the misogyny. He spent his life in thrall to the foreign, in thrall to images to which he had no right.

This was the younger Benji – the boy whom Haffner still admired.

A hint of the devastating problem which was to ensue occurred when Benjamin, aged fifteen, decided that, while everyone else went on holiday with their youth groups to Israel – to meet girls, and sleep on beaches – instead he wanted to stay in a Buddhist monastery. This monastery was located in the countryside outside London: in Hertfordshire. It was his spiritual goal. He arrived with a smuggled packet of cigarettes, and a biography of Arthur Rimbaud. For Benji, at fifteen, was a rebel, and philosopher. But when he was confronted by the bell at five the next morning, the meditation for two hours before breakfast, the unidentified and unidentifiable breakfast itself, the work in the fields, by the afternoon he was too depressed to carry on. He couldn't even tell the men apart from the women. He went into the room of the Head Monk and asked to leave. The Head Monk looked at him. He implored him, having made the important break from the temptations of the city, to persevere in his difficult task. The worst was over, he said. But Benji was not so persuaded. There was a skull on the Head Monk's desk; and Benji did not want to be confronted by mementi mori. He could not tell, in fact, why it was he was here at all. He had simply liked the idea of it – a man above the temptations of beaches, and girls.

Two hours later, Esther had arrived to take him home.

He had at least learned something, Benjamin told everyone. He'd discovered how deeply he believed in food.

And Haffner loved him for this. The boy was independent! He understood how much more important the senses were than a sense of the serious. But the let-down came soon afterwards. Benji, after all, was in a crisis of faith. He had gone through hip hop, drugs and Buddhism. And now he returned to the most basic, the least loved. Benjamin returned to the religion of his forefathers: a lineage which began with his father, if one missed out his grandfather.

That was why, at university, he spent his vacations in the Promised Land. That was why, after university, he had entered the summer school of a rabbinical seminary.

But then, Benjamin's Jewishness, like all his other crazes, was really a form of romance. He wanted a past: he wanted a past which was more torn apart by history than the history of his happy family.

In Tel Aviv, Benjamin had met a girl who came from a family of Jewish-Algerian intellectuals. Somewhere in the Sahara, she said, there was a tribe which bore her surname. Benji wished that this girl's past were his. He didn't know what he might do with it – but he was sure that this was the missing piece of Benjamin's jigsaw, lost in another jigsaw box, abandoned underneath a sofa.

His forefathers! Who else was more like Benjamin than Haffner? Like his grandfather before him, Benji was a sucker for bohemia.

7

Haffner, however, only saw in Benjamin an exponent of the Law. He was constantly depressed by the cowl of seriousness with which Benjamin so often insulated himself: the easy *tristesse* of history which enticed him.

This judgement was true, in a way. Benjamin dearly wanted the reassuring safety of the righteous, the morally certain. But this was no reason, perhaps, to dislike him, to think that he was prim. He wanted order because he was so often overtaken by compulsions he could not understand.

His first craze was soccer. On the white gloss of his bedroom cupboards, whose moulding was painted dark blue, in imitation of the Tottenham Hotspur soccer strip, Benjamin had arranged stickers produced by Panini for the 1986 World Cup. His favourite stickers were the Brazilians – with their pineapple T-shirts, their one-word names (Socrates!), their impossible hair. Benjamin had arranged Brazil, and Paraguay, and England, gently overlapping, following the blue line of gloss along his cupboards.

Benjamin, in the youth of his youth, didn't have ripped-out pictures of film stars, or porn stars, on his ceiling. No nipples, or even bikinis, in black and white or colour, were visible in his room. True, he did possess one photocopy of a pornographic image. This picture had been given to him, as a special favour, by Ezekiel. A girl with thick, if indistinctly printed, nipples was raising a sailor-suit top towards her chin. A sailor's hat was cocked, coquettish, on her white-blonde permed hair. How innocent he was! In Benjamin's special dreams, he would touch her nipples, curiously – like tuning a radio. But this image was not public. He had simply tucked his pornographic possession, neatly folded, between pages 305 and 306 of his book which contained 1001 facts about the French Revolution, with its glossy laminated boards.

Instead of sex, Benjamin had crazes. There had been the soccer, then the drugs, and the hip hop, and the Buddhism. Then the Orthodox Jewishness. And now, finally, Benji had been disturbed by the true sexual furore – inspired by his Jewish and Algerian and French girl in Tel Aviv. With this girl, finally, Benjamin had lost his virginity. She was hairless between the legs, except for a black tuft, so that when he touched her all he felt was a slick softness. He nearly swooned. For this, thought Benji, was love.

It wasn't love, of course. Over various phone calls, Zeek tried to explain this to him. But Benji didn't care. Instead, he simply retreated into the burrow of his feelings. He told Zeek what he had not told her: that when he left her, the next morning, after they had slept together, in the taxi, he wrote in the dawn, on the back of a receipt, that this was true desire, a true passion. And passions were so rare.

This was why Benjamin was here, in the spa town. He needed an escape from the summer school, the regalia of his religion – and he needed to talk to the man who was his only authority when it came to women. The man who was his – faulty, despaired-of – authority as an adult.

But I think there was a further complication. Benji was here because he wanted permission to leave the summer school: he wanted to replace his respect for his religion with a more freestyle interest in his girl. This was true. But in his amatory crisis the family's inheritance had therefore acquired more significance than it might, perhaps, have had. For Benjamin felt guilty at his wish to abandon his religion. The villa was therefore his chance for redress: his chance to show his family and forefathers that he had not abandoned them entirely.

The villa was an excuse.

Which was, perhaps, one way in which Benji differed from his grandfather.

8

He should really stop looking at women like that, said Benjamin. Haffner said he would look where he liked. And believe him, he wasn't looking. Benjamin said that it just wasn't right.

Again, the lethargy which Haffner felt when contemplating his adventure with Frau Tummel transformed into something so much more protective. So much more like love. Such sadness which Haffner felt for the bodies of women! Such sadness which transformed into a pity of the flesh!

She was, said Haffner, a very handsome woman.

—Whatever! exclaimed Benjamin. Whatever.

Benji was here for business. So skip the breakfast, said Benji, skip the lunch: surprising even himself. They were going to sort this whole thing with the villa today. It was why he was here.

He knew, as he said this, that his motives were mixed. He knew how much he was fleeing from his summer school. He knew what a convenient excuse the story of the family villa was to him. But surely, thought Benji, the fact that he was in panicking flight should not mean he could not solve a practical problem. At least the villa was a problem whose solution was obvious.

—Not so simple, said Haffner.

—It's simple, said Benjamin.

—Believe me, said Haffner. If anything were simple, this isn't it.

Would the young not give this up? wondered Haffner. When would they learn to talk precisely? He wanted to be done with trying to bring them up. Or, maybe more precisely, he wanted to educate them out of their attempts to bring him up.

Why did no one want to believe him when he said that he had done all he could? But then, he was forced to concede, it was hardly surprising: this scepticism, this doubt in Haffner. He could understand the disappointment. As if Haffner were the omnipotent yet constantly underachieving god of the Christians and the Muslims and the Jews.

9

—I don't think you realise, said Haffner, sitting with Pfeffer, on Haffner's return to London, when the family had first discovered the existence of Barbra, the problems of living with a beautiful woman. I mean an apparition. You think it's easy?

—I don't think anything, said Pfeffer. Well maybe. I think it's easy living with the woman you love.

But no, said Haffner. Pfeffer, with his utter confidence, could never understand the problems of living with such a woman as Livia. The endless problems of self-worth. Think about it, he urged Pfeffer. You woke up every day with this noble profile. You looked across at the elegance of her face and it destroyed you. It was no way to treat a man: to emphasise the bags under his eyes, the marbled skin. It wasn't a sexual success. It was a crisis.

Pfeffer raised a philosophic eyebrow.

He wasn't blaming him, Pfeffer had said, but it didn't look good. That was all he was saying.

Only Pfeffer had tried to disabuse him of his guilt, only Pfeffer – with his retractable gold biros and pots made for him by his children – pots of beaten bronze with enamel detailing, and mahogany lids. And maybe this was a surprise. Only Pfeffer, the family man, tried to persuade Haffner that his guilt remained unproven.

They had been to school together, at prep school. Pfeffer was the man Haffner's father wanted him to be, or as close to it as possible – ever since Haffner betrayed his family by refusing to enter the family law firm. Pfeffer was a libel lawyer. He knew the secrets of showbiz. Which meant, thought Haffner, that he knew the secrets of everything, since everything was showbiz. Pfeffer lived in St John's Wood, in the largest apartment known to Haffner, with drawing rooms, and living rooms, and multiple bathrooms with multiple basins. A redundant triumph of the plural. It had always amazed Haffner, the sleek animal adaptability of these humans he grew up with: how Pfeffer, the kid he had known since prep school, who was so docile, who wore grey flannel shorts when everyone else had understood the only cool thing was trousers, could morph into this maven of luxury, silken in his deskchair. A chair in which he wallowed, his small hands neat and hairless on his blotter – whose corners were curtailed by leather bands, into an octagon.

But I don't feel like sketching Pfeffer's form. He can remain there, an outline in black, transparent against all the background colours – like some minor figure in a painting by Dufy.

Haffner was unshaven; he was in a summer suit. Beside him was a plate of biscuits brought to him by Pfeffer's secretary, a secretary whom Haffner always suspected of harbouring designs on Pfeffer. He was wearing the panama which Livia hated. It came rolled up in a metal tube. He liked to think it made him rakish.

But hey: Pfeffer added. He was the last person to be advising anyone on a marriage. What was he meant to do? His wife was in therapy. His daughter was in love with some Greek entrepreneur. Or possibly a Turk. How was Pfeffer an expert in the family? He was as much a natural family man as Artie Shaw. Or Goebbels.

And Haffner had to admit, at that moment, that he loved Pfeffer, whose idea of fun was crossword puzzles, Scrabble, memory games. The man who saw the world as a perpetual acrostic. He spent his conversations, Haffner remembered, reconfiguring each sentence backwards. Otherwise, he told Haffner, it could become boring for him. This produced no obvious vacancy in his expression, or concentration. Sometimes, just backwards was not enough. Sometimes, he had to reverse according to gaps of two or three. He was toying with implementing logarithms.

He just thought, he said, that Haffner should explain what was going on.

But what could anyone else know about the marriage of Haffner and Livia? It was a world with only two inhabitants.

When the time was coming for war, but they didn't know when, Haffner and Livia had a code – for Haffner, like every soldier, was banned from giving any prior information about his movements. He had a rich and rather unpleasant uncle, called Uncle Jonas. And the code was that if Uncle Jonas were very fit and well, everything was fine. If the prospects for Haffner to be mobilised were doubtful, then his health was not too good: and then the time came when Haffner knew he was to go abroad, and he said that he was sorry to tell her, darling, but Uncle Jonas had passed away. He was at Basingstoke at this time, in a telephone booth. It was April, in 1943. They had embarked from the docks in the west of Scotland. He didn't quite know where. He didn't really know what a dock was, if he were honest.

A marriage, thought Haffner, was the invention of a code.

No one knew the secrets of a marriage: maybe this was true. Just as Haffner didn't know the secrets of his grandson, the conundrum of his grandson, standing there in front of him: confused, like his grandfather, by the monstrous state of love.

Haffner Banished

1

The villa which belonged to Livia's family was out on the outskirts of the town, above a slope which ran down to the river. Across from its veranda was the range of snowy mountains.

In 1929, the universal crash had meant that her father took a loan from his cousin's bank in Trieste. Seven years later, his talent for money had been so adroitly employed that he had earned enough to buy this villa.

Here, Livia used to argue with her father: a nationalist when considering the Italian state, an anti-nationalist when considering the Zionist cause. He was a businessman who imported coal from Britain. Through the quiet rise of wealth, the steady progress of business, he wanted his nation to be great again.

Her father had become a Fascist after fighting in the Great War. Then, in 1922, leaving behind his daughter in her blankets and her cradle, leaving behind his pregnant wife, her father had taken part in Mussolini's March on Rome: his pedestrian coup. Her mother had cut out clippings from the newspapers. They featured grand vocative apostrophes (*O Rome!*) written in a rhetoric which even then seemed obscure (*O ship launched toward World Empire that emerges from the flux of time!*). She kept them in an album for her husband.

He believed in Italy. It was a refuge – his family's final escape from the misery of politics.

Even if this escape was a politics too.

Cesare was duly made to join the youth movements. He wore the uniform, scowling. In retaliation, he decided that when he grew up he would be a communist. If, that is, he ever grew up. As for Livia, she also wore her black pleated skirts, white piqué blouse, long white stockings, her black cape and beret. This was her Fascist youth.

Her father believed in discipline. Neither Cesare nor Livia was allowed to rest a wrist on the table when they were eating. She was told to hold two napkins under her armpits, so that she might achieve the correct deportment. His ideas of order were immutable.

She was too melancholic, her father told her, when they argued. Always on the dark side of the moon. She didn't have a positive concept of the reality of life. In reply, she would quote the Romantics to him. What else was this life but a failure? It lacked beauty. She looked forward to the one radiant light, bathed in which humanity would come together in perfect union.

In the café in the main square, Livia, when she was sixteen, had been asked to dance by a man whose eyebrows and teeth she distrusted. She had looked at Mama. And Mama had nodded her head. Her mother had never done this before. Normally, every dance was forbidden to Livia. And when she asked her mother, afterwards, why she had made her dance with that horrible man, Mama had simply said that it was because she had to: the man was a director of the secret police.

When Livia told Haffner this story, one day in 1953, he smiled at her. And did she, he wanted to know, tread on the man's toes?

—Naturalmente, said Livia. And she kissed him, her mischievous boy.

There had been a swing on the cherry tree outside the villa, stranded on an island of grass in the drive. They used to go looking for mushrooms and blackberries. In the early summer they would go to the seaside, on the Adriatic. And in August they would come up here into the mountains. That was their life.

And once, when the Buffalo Bill circus arrived in the town, Livia's mother told her that this would be the greatest night of her life. But when she told Haffner about this, forty years later, as they passed a sign for a travelling circus on the outskirts of London, following some visit to see their grandson, she did not remember the trapeze, nor the spectacle: all that had remained with her was an inarticulate concern for the living conditions of elephants.

This, then, was what Haffner was now due to inherit: the occluded history of Livia.

2

—If you had only not been so impatient, said the Head of the Committee on Spatial Planning, perhaps I help you. Not now. Now the matter is closed.

—What do you mean closed? said Haffner.

—You think this is not something I understand? said his opponent. This is something I perfectly understand.

—Really? said Haffner.

—Aggressing my staff, said the Head of the Committee.

To Haffner's surprise, within ten minutes of entering the building, they had secured an interview with the Head of the Committee on Spatial Planning. It had been to his surprise, but also to his mild irritation, giving as it did an unfortunately fluent appearance to Benjamin of the Committee's workings. This irritation, however, had been mollified when they discovered that the Head of the Committee, having dismissed Isabella as unnecessary, spoke an English which was accurate but so heavily accented that they found it difficult to follow him.

This linguistic confusion, however, was possibly irrelevant. The case, it appeared, was closed.

—First place, said the Head of the Committee, you come here earlier, much earlier. Now the window is over. Occasion gone. Doubly, I cannot do nothing for you.

—So that's it? said Haffner, banished from his estates.

—I will make to you a concession, said the Head of the Committee.

—A concession? asked Haffner, eagerly.

—Yes, said the man. I am sorry for you, I really am. But my hands are tired.

—I'm sorry? said Haffner.

—Yes, said the Head of the Committee. Tired. It is a pity for you.

—That's your concession? said Haffner. In what way does that represent a concession?

—He means confession, said Benjamin.

—What? said Haffner.

There was no goodwill. Haffner knew that. But he hoped to be surprised. And so often he was duly let down.

He indicated to the Head of the Committee that he strongly intended to pursue the matter further. In Haffner's experience of offices, this phrase was usually potent. For Haffner's threats were real. It seemed less potent now.

The Head of the Committee was blowing away the flakes of an eraser, which he had been vigorously rubbing against a mistake in his calligraphy. It was music to his ears, he said. Music to his ears. And never, thought Haffner, would he trust a man again who used this phrase. All his sense of style was outraged.

But nothing in this room was stylish.

It was situated on the first floor of a building which once housed Hapsburg bureaucrats, and had then been gutted to service the administration of Communist aristocrats. From its ground-floor windows lolled the coiled tubes of the air-conditioning units, like elephant trunks. The office looked out on to a garden, with a sparse alley of plane trees which were sickly with dust, their leaves patchy with psoriasis. A poster on the wall implored Haffner not to smoke.

Haffner had no intention of smoking. Instead, he chose escalation. His last descendant beside him, fighting for his lineage, Haffner chose defiance. Yes, Haffner began to plead and rage, while beneath the stern poster – a man palming away a proffered packet of cigarettes – the Head of the Committee smoked from his collection of Marlboro Reds: ten of them in a bleak row.

3

—How can we have a conversation, cried Haffner, reasonably, when there is no goodwill? What kind of justice is this?

In the corner of the office, there was a bucket of soapy water: a soufflé of foam disintegrating above its rim.

—Judge you? said the Head of the Committee. What else do you expect?

Once more Haffner fought against the prejudices of the ages.

After all, insinuated the Head of the Committee, it had taken him a very long time, no? To bring this suit? When it didn't seem so difficult. Haffner conceded this point. Perhaps he now thought there was money in it, said the Head of the Committee. Given his backdrop. To which Haffner replied that he didn't understand. Did he mean his British backdrop? Background?

—No, said the Head of the Committee.

But, he added, it was obvious that he was not from Britain. Haffner asked him what he meant. One only needed to look, said the Head of the Committee. Just one's eyes.

He understood. Yes, Haffner understood. Blond and blue-eyed among the Jews: and Jewish to everyone else. But just because he understood didn't mean he wasn't bewildered. Haffner wasn't used to fighting the prejudices of Central Europe. He had grown up happily in the pleasures of north London. He wasn't used to regarding himself as part of a race, rather than a nation. He was just a Haffner, not a Jewish Haffner. As he had tried to tell his driver, on their way from Haifa to Cairo – but that was another story. As he continued to try to tell various taxi drivers and financial wives, in London and New York. The cricketing taxi drivers of New York and the intellectual financial wives of London. The pattern of it, perhaps, should have made him pause. But Haffner rarely paused.

Just as he should perhaps have paused on the fact that he still possessed a *News Letter to the Forces*, dated Chanukah 5705, which he kept, he always said, not for its ethical stance but because on the back of this sheet of paper were adverts for Elco watches, from Hatton Garden; the Grodzinski chain of modern bakeries; and Lloyd Rakusen's Delicious Wheaten Crackers. He went for its nostalgia, maintained Haffner. He did not preserve it because this newsletter announced the triple burden of the continuing fight against the menace of Fascism and Nazism, the effort to rescue as many as they could of the remnants of their brethren left in Europe, and the refusal to relinquish one iota of their just claims to Eretz Israel as the Land of Israel belonging to the People of Israel. But I am not so sure. Maybe Haffner had never quite resolved the problem of his loyalties.

Was he saying, said Haffner, pounding the desk, like the grandest businessman of all time, that this committee was refusing to help him because he and his wife were Jewish? Was that the missing word? And as he did so he believed that surely now this man would retreat: surely this man would not have the temerity to disagree with Haffner. But no, even now this man preserved his calm. Of course, he said, he had not said that. He was merely observing.

But Haffner was unbowed. As Benjamin glowed with mortified pride beside him, Haffner gave a speech. He was noted for his speeches, and Haffner gave the speech that he had always dreamed of making: where the audience quails beneath the shaking fist, the pointing finger; where the righteous man can demand of the wicked man that the truth be finally told.

—These are the things you always say, said the Head of the Committee. That everyone is against you.

—Me? said Haffner. I just met you.

—Not just you, he said. All of you. That you are always prosecuted.

—Persecuted, corrected Haffner, haughty.

The secretaries, Haffner fancied, were crowding at the door. One, perhaps, was being hoisted by a sturdy palm to the rim of the door, where a crack allowed the earnest spectator to get a glimpse of Haffner in his finale: rising now, pushing back his chair, and demanding that the Head of the Committee offer him an explanation.

—Let me put a question for you, said the Head of the Committee. You think you have nothing to do with us? You think you can take what you want?

Haffner wondered what he was asking him. Was he now to take on the guilt of the entire Soviet empire? Because he and his wife were Jewish? Were the very Communists who had stolen his wife's home now to be seen as Haffner's fault?

This was Haffner's twentieth century – where the history of London was also the history of Warsaw; and the history of Tel Aviv was also the history of Paris. And so on, and so on: in the endless history of the geography. All the separate national histories were universal, if you looked from far enough away. So how could Haffner escape?

4

The Head of the Committee motioned to a man who was no doubt an assistant, an apparatchik – who had been sitting in the shadows of this vast room all along – to show these gentlemen out. He was sorry, but he really must cut short their appointment. Naturally, he said, a decision would come in due course.

Unexpectedly, as he rose passionate from his chair, Haffner discovered that he was leaving with a sense of triumph. A sense of triumph accompanied by a worry that he had rather lost the upper hand, by making such a scene – but a triumph, nevertheless, that he had been so free with his fury. He had reached a place of poetry.

He was hoping so much, thought Haffner, that Livia was watching. He had never believed in ghosts before. They had seemed gothically unnecessary. But now they seemed the only just solution to the difficult problem of death.

For Haffner was furious with loyalty. His history was Livia's too. He couldn't deny it. He had thought for so long that this villa was just a chore. And it was a chore. But it meant more to him than that. It was suddenly, he understood, all to do with Livia.

And Livia, he thought, would appreciate this fight for her cosmopolitan history. She would appreciate, above all, Haffner's unorthodox methods. For, as he confided to an astonished and worried Benjamin, he had another plan as well. To Benjamin he offered an edited version of his conversation with Niko. He perhaps exaggerated Niko's authority. He did not mention the locale where he had conducted these negotiations. But Benjamin still protested. Was he going to do something so illegal? No, Benji couldn't believe it. He mustn't do anything of the sort.

They paused outside the entrace to a jazz café in a garden – its walls graffiti'd with red and black unicorns: the arpeggios scaling the heights of the trees. They considered it; they walked on.

Maybe all of Benjamin's anxiety was his fault, thought Haffner. Maybe this was the natural consequence of Haffner: he had bequeathed accidentally to his grandson this exorbitant need for rules. In Benji's wish to be the opposite of his grandfather. Walking towards the hotel with Benjamin – as, still feeling exhausted, after two dramatic nights, Haffner dreamed of a possible nap, since exhaustion was becoming his natural state – he wondered if it was somehow in opposition to the ghost of Haffner that Benji had inherited this absolute anxiety about the feelings of others: a total timidity.

And it seemed that Haffner was right.

Only when they reached the doors to the hotel did Benjamin finally begin to talk about the fact that Benji was now in love. Yes, he said, he had met a girl whose gorgeousness transcended everything of which Benji had thought the world capable. But, wondered Benji, could he really know she liked him?

—Have you kissed this girl? said Haffner.

That wasn't the question, said Benjamin. The question was: did she want him to do this again? She seemed so cool. It was, said Haffner, an easy question to answer. He should simply see what happened next. He should kiss her again. What harm could that do? And Benjamin replied that, well, he just didn't know how much he wanted the burden of it. He didn't know if he wanted the relationship. And if he didn't want that, then he thought it was better to do nothing.

Which made him more mature than Haffner, thought Haffner. It was not a position he had so far reached himself.

—That's fine of you, said Haffner. That's very fine.

He didn't know that Benji was not quite telling him the truth. He did not know that Benji was not quite telling himself the truth. Benji's struggle against his senses was Benji's mute interior.

He needed to sleep, said Haffner. He needed to lie down, old boy. And Benji, in a gentle gesture of goodbye, kissed him on the forehead.

Innocence and experience! But which was which? The old young or the young old? Haffner wept for the things he thought he would no longer have; Benjamin for the things he thought he would never have. Both of them possessed their own comedy.

Both of them were banished.

When Livia was ill once, long before the end of their marriage, she had promised Haffner that if she died, she would come back and talk to him. He would know of the existence of an afterlife from the fact of this return; or the fact of a non-return. When she finally died and she did not, as Haffner hoped, come back to comfort him, he was not so astonished. After all, they had rarely seen each other in the two years preceding her death. Then a graver thought began to trouble him – that this was no proof of a lack of afterlife; it was only proof that she had not been able to come back. He was haunted by this idea of her trying to communicate with him, pressed to his ear, to his eyes, and Haffner unable to hear her, unable to see her. Or then an even graver and more plausible interpretation presented itself: it was only proof that she had not wanted to come back. She had decided against it.

He had mourned alone in the empty house, like the tearful queen mourning that schmuck Aeneas, as she gazed at her abandoned couch.

5

In the summer of 1938 – when Haffner was away, playing for the Old Boys cricket team of his school – Livia's father was reading, in silence, the Manifesto of the Racist Scientists. In the dining room, Cesare, who was sixteen, and believed in the greatness of his talent, was engaged on his great ceiling painting: *The Dream*, he said, *of Europa*. It featured three semi-nude women. No one was convinced of the mythological provenance: no one believed that the seriousness of the gods could compensate for Cesare's shaky technique. The pipe in his father's mouth was making him grin as he let the smoke dissolve in slow small clouds: a few smoke rings disappearing into other smoke rings. Outside, someone was beating a rug on the sill of the steps. And Livia's father was reading that Jews, according to the ninth section of the manifesto, did not belong to the Italian race.

He laid his pipe down.

At first, Livia's father, an honourable Fascist, was one of the discriminati: those discriminated from discrimination. Very soon, however, it was all over. His clients were forbidden to trade with him; his salesmen were banned from negotiating for his list. He decided to send his children to Britain, to stay with friends of his in the paint industry. They required a passport and a transit visa through France. He went to the Fascist chief of police – whose wedding anniversary he had recently celebrated at a small dinner party in town – and he said to him: either he arranged this, or he would break the law. He would buy the papers on the black market. Surely the police chief didn't want him to break the law?

The Fascist chief of police agreed that he should not break the law. So Cesare and Livia went to Britain.

Haffner still owned a photograph of Livia's mother – taken in 1915, to give to her fiancé when he went to war – dressed in a Japanese kimono. Her father owned a black Fascist fez with a silken fringe. Indignantly, he would tell her the shameful story of the Dreyfus case – from the time when Europe was imperial. And yet, on the other hand, the blue-and-white collection boxes for the nascent state of Israel: these he ignored. As if it was nothing to do with him. There was no need, he argued – unlike, perhaps, in racist France – for such drastic measures.

Yes, Livia's father believed in order. It was possible, he thought, for there to be an end of history: a utopia. But Italy, Livia wanted to say, was still Europe. Nowhere was safe from the stupidity of inheritance.

But he believed in the nineteenth century, and its bourgeoisie. The year before, in 1937, Ettore Ovazza – who was Fascist, and Jewish, and saw no contradiction in this position – wrote his reply to Paolo Orano's pamphlet which had maintained that in fact these positions were indeed contradictory. Livia's father had agreed with Ovazza. If one wanted to express one's sympathy with one's suffering fellow Jews in Germany, this didn't mean one wanted to found a second Fatherland, in the contested lands of Palestine. No, this was precisely what it meant to him to be Italian. Italy was the Fatherland for which so many of the purest heroes of Jewish blood had died.

Later, Livia always used to berate her dead and absent father. Why hadn't he understood? Why hadn't they all left sooner? And Haffner would always reply that it was difficult to leave. Who knew when the right time was to flee? It was so difficult, abandoning the things you loved. It was difficult enough, said Haffner, abandoning the things you hated.

Haffner Delinquent

1

In his bedroom, finally, Haffner drifted into what he hoped would be the greatest of all restorative sleeps.

For a moment this was true. Then he was transformed into a baby Haffner, playing with the other children while in the next room sat Frau Tummel, taking tea, with all the other adults. Although, when he considered this, some minutes later, when Haffner had been woken up, it struck him as unusual: for Frau Tummel was nearly thirty years his junior. So what was his unconscious doing?

But really, Haffner wasn't often worried by his unconscious: nightly, his dreams were delinquent, involving all life forms, all birds of prey. He had grown used to ignoring the signs. He no more wanted Frau Tummel to mother him than he wanted Zinka to be his daughter.

Enough of the family! Let the eternal couples unite!

But Haffner was only thinking this because, as he was playing on the floor of his imaginary playpen, there came a knock at the door: this knock was then repeated. And when Haffner finally dragged his body – with patches of sweat on his back, scored creases on his cheek – to the door, he found the real Frau Tummel, who wished so urgently to speak with him.

So many things had been running through her head, said Frau Tummel. So many sad thoughts. Haffner murmured: as he had always murmured when confronted by the sadness of women. To see him there, talking with that woman: to see him with that girl. She knew that she was imagining things. And Haffner assured her that yes, absolutely: she was imagining things. What relationship could Haffner have to a girl so young? It was ridiculous.

—Yes, agreed Frau Tummel: ridiculous.

This disturbed Haffner's vanity.

Perhaps she understood, said Frau Tummel. It was as if Haffner would not trust himself, she said. What was wrong, she said, with the passion? Why always run away from it?

There was nothing, thought Haffner, that he could say to this. It seemed so obviously true, in the abstract. As a statement it had its accuracy. But not to his friendship with Frau Tummel. Only to his friendship with Zinka.

And he stood there, rummaging through his brain, like a man searching in his pockets, in his bag, for the ticket which might finally allow him entrance to the airplane which will take him away from all this misery, but finding nothing: just three coins, a key, an obediently switched-off cell phone – none of which, when proffered in a gesture of goodwill, convince the air hostess that he possesses the authority to board the plane and leave.

In this pause, Frau Tummel lit a cigarette: she only managed to light half its tip. She inhaled deeply, until the whole circumference fiercely glowed.

She appeared to change the subject. What a wonderful grandson Benjamin must be, she said: what a solace – as she busied herself with tidying Haffner's bedroom, opening the curtains, neatly folding his tracksuit jacket: its arms pinned behind itself – a straitjacket.

Perhaps, thought Haffner, he was not so wrong to dream of Frau Tummel as his mother. She represented all the domestic he had ever known, a sinful heaven of supervision. And Haffner liked to feel that he was supervised. It was how he had lived in the family home – where at Pesach the cockney maid fell into the dining room, closely followed by the cook, who had been listening in amazed curiosity at the door: a door which had been flung open by Papa in hopeful if theatrical expectation of Elijah.

But surely, thought Haffner, he wasn't here, in exile, banished, to find a second version of a mother. It couldn't be that. Haffner was here to find a house, not a family: not a mother or a wife.

Yet Haffner was still so easily won over by those who tried to care for him. Those who sacrificed themselves for Haffner! Like Barbra, the delight of his New York years, who used to keep a selection of his clothes freshly ironed in her wardrobe. The secret of a marriage? Haffner once argued with Morton. He wanted to know the secret of a marriage? You had to find someone who agreed to be the slave. Somebody had to give up. That was the only solution. Two people in love with their pride, then everything was over. Maybe not immediately, but in the end. The only successful marriages involved someone giving up on their life.

He did not tell Morton who, in the marriage of Livia and Haffner, was the masochist, and who was not.

But it wasn't just marriage. It seemed, thought Haffner, to be the secret of everything. At a certain point, you just gave up on the infantile wish to be an emperor. You stopped complaining that people were changing their clothes beside your marble statue, or carrying a coin stamped with your counterfeit face into a bathroom, or a brothel. Those were the crazy edicts of Augustus. And Haffner, now, was beyond them.

3

Frau Tummel stubbed her cigarette, half smoked, into Haffner's ceramic ashtray, engraved with a view of a mountain whose name Haffner did not know. Then, slowly, Frau Tummel began to undress.

—We don't want to talk, after all, she said.

What was the point in all these arguments? They loved each other; that was all that mattered. Her husband, he was talking to her all day. His health, it was so up and down. He planned walks in the mountains which he would never take. And to think that she was contemplating leaving him! So much strain she was under! But what could she do?

She wanted the sex. And this might have suited Haffner, but the sex was wasted on him, because she wanted to make the sex love. It wasn't that he couldn't have the two together at any point, but with Frau Tummel it was impossible. He didn't love her. The dramatics bored him. With Frau Tummel, he just wanted the purity of pure dirt. The kind of dirt Frau Tummel could have been into as well, with her lavish breasts, the tired lilt of her belly, if only she had been less in love.

She reclined: as normal, her bra still on.

—There might be no more beauty, said Frau Tummel, observing herself, but there can be a little grace.

And although this forgivable vanity touched Haffner with a remote tenderness, he still felt nothing. Yes, at this point, Haffner suddenly discovered that not only did he not love her, but he didn't even want her. It struck him as strange.

Would he put her on her stomach? Frau Tummel asked him.

He wished he could; he wished that he wanted to do this for Frau Tummel; but he could not see his way to it. Kneeling on the bed, he toyed with her bra. She looked up at him, breathing heavily.

Then there was a knock at the door.

Saved! thought Haffner. Saved!

He dreamed of the receptionist, of Viko, of the waiter in the dining room: joyfully, he considered how it could only be someone who was here to help him, to release him from this agony of politesse and sadness.

No voice came. Haffner asked who it was. Still no one replied. Frau Tummel looked at him: startled

—My husband! she exclaimed, in a whisper.

To his surprise, Haffner discovered that he was enjoying himself. The male competition of it appealed to him. Anything, so long as Frau Tummel was returned to her own life: a life which had no place for Raphael Haffner.

Did she think so? he whispered back to her. She was sure. Who else could it be? It could be anyone, he argued. Absolutely anyone from the hotel. Or even Benjamin, he argued. Whispering, she shouted at him that this was no time for argument. It was obvious who it was. They needed a plan.

Haffner had no plan. Haffner had no plan.

They looked around the room: at the desk, the window, the elegant armchair, the veranda and its view, the door to the bathroom.

Five seconds later, Haffner confdently opened the door, to discover Zinka: in her sunglasses – twin beige lenses, flat against the hollowed angles of her cheeks.

4

Haffner could understand the icons of the Orthodox Church, with their mournful expressions: the deep sadness of distance inscribed in their high cheekbones, almond eyes, the nose which Haffner always found alluring: dense with bone, its line an asymmetrical quiver.

Perhaps it was true that he had momentarily abandoned the quest for Zinka in his quest for the villa. He would admit so much. But that was no argument against the sincerity of his desire. The true desire, as Haffner was discovering – as Haffner had so often discovered – was returning. Just as it had returned when he first met Barbra, in his office on a twilit morning in November in Manhattan: a story which Haffner cherished. Just as it had recovered when he had met a woman called Olga, in an executive box at the World Series, who said she was with the Dow Jones, and who so wanted to write about his career, who would appreciate just a few moments with him in private: a story which Haffner, when questioned by his colleagues, had always denied.

Zinka stood there in front of him. She had just come because she had a message from Niko. That he would meet Haffner in the car park: after dinner. It was OK with Haffner? He understood? It was OK, said Haffner.

—So OK, she said.

Haffner did not shut the door. She noticed this. She did not move.

She observed that they seemed to get along. And Haffner agreed. So she had nothing to do now, she said: she was just here to tell him the message.

Haffner thanked her. He told her to thank Niko.

—Maybe, said Zinka, I can come in?

Panicking, considering Frau Tummel in the bathroom, a recording booth, Haffner asked her if she wanted to get a coffee. It seemed the better option: to lock Frau Tummel in, rather than let her hear who was now replacing her – in Haffner's room, in Haffner's desire. But Zinka said that no, why did they need to go anywhere else? He wasn't sure, said Haffner, if he had the facilities for making coffee.

—But whatever, said Zinka, elongating past him. And Haffner paused, anguished by indecision.

But, too late, Zinka had walked towards the window, where her silhouette asked him if she might change into her yoga things in Haffner's room. There was no way, thought Haffner, in which he could answer this with anything approaching the correct decorum. So Haffner only nodded. And as, delirious, he nodded, Haffner considered Frau Tummel, in the bathroom. Transfixed in the fluorescent light. He considered this in a different delirium to the delirium with which he looked at Zinka: a delirium of pensive concern.

Somehow, he considered, without him meaning it to happen, his actions became cruel in their effects.

And Haffner was not cruel. The emperors, of course, were not like him. The great dictators enjoyed their torture: but it was never Haffner's way – to throw a party for a father, to make his son's execution go that much more sociably.

Haffner looked at the wood of the bathroom door. It was probably just a veneer, thought Haffner: not a solid oak, or trusty beech. Harshly, he judged its inadequate soundproofing. He cursed this country. He cursed the former Communist empire for its inadequate provision of workmanship. Then he cursed the nascent capitalist transition.

On the other hand, if Frau Tummel could hear everything, thought Haffner, could hear that Zinka's was not the voice of her husband, then why had she not come out? This seemed reasonable.

Oh Haffner! He hadn't considered the depth of Frau Tummel's pride. Nor the intricacy of her sadness.

5

Zinka lay there, in no apparent rush to dress herself in the tracksuit and vest which formed her sportswear. She lay against the bolster, in a T-shirt, and socks, and panties. She took an apple from the bowl of fruit placed with professional love beside his bed each morning, bit a slim curve out of it, then put it back, on the table. It wobbled; then came to rest. She looked at Haffner.

She hooked a finger under the gusset of her panties. They looked at each other. Then Zinka withdrew her finger, let her gusset move back into place.

In Haffner's memory, this happened with an infinite languor. This was only, perhaps, because the speed of Haffner's thought was now subject to a steep acceleration.

She must like him, thought Haffner. In some way, she must like him. Haffner, after all, did not believe in the maliciousness of reality. This talent allowed him to discover so much solace where other people only saw benightedness, the end of civilisation.

Zinka asked him if he wanted to watch her touch herself.

No, thought Haffner, trying to reason, considering Frau Tummel, considering Benjamin, considering the villa which had led him into this ever more miniature trap: no, if against his better judgement the world was turning itself into a succession of traps, then what did Haffner care? The obvious reasons were there: the many ways in which Zinka might be thinking of repayment. Or she might be acting for reasons which would always remain inscrutable to Haffner. The reasons were beyond him.

And this, I think, was where the story of the villa began to truly become the story of Haffner's finale: at this point, he began to enter a world where all the usual values seemed reversed: a small gymnasium of moral backflips, with the joyful ideas walking on their hands.

He couldn't remember if any woman had ever asked him this at any other point in his history. It startled him with its poise. Usually, the women seemed to expect Haffner to do the action: Haffner was the highest executive, the producer there to give permission to the director in his folding and eponymous chair, with all the lights off and the crew observing him, expectantly, surrounded by vacant lots where the streetlights flickered in their high anxiety. He looked at

Zinka. Frau Tummel, sweating, weeping, did not occur to him, not any more. What he wanted, more than anything else, was to see Zinka touch herself.

Again, Haffner nodded.

Then Zinka flipped over on to her stomach. This was not the position which Haffner had expected: his improvised imagination had been more orthodox, more pornographic. But at this point he was not burdened with the responsibilities of the critic.

Then, he realised, there was a small problem involved in Haffner's own position.

Haffner considered sitting down. He worried this might seem too formal. It might seem rehearsed. So he stood: in the appearance of the casual. As if it were nothing more than an ordinary conversation, this exchange between a hotel guest and his spa assistant.

Standing by his desk, at the foot of the bed, Haffner could see her moving her fingers, the red fingertips emerging where she lay.

And that, Haffner suddenly realised, was it. There was nothing more to see. This moved him. It was, he thought, more intimate like this. He would see nothing, not even her face. Everything was in the noises, the small moans and inhalations, the slow exhalations. Her face was squashed against the pillow. The intimacy was musical. Entranced, Haffner stared.

She rested a cheek on the bedraggled sheet, to look back at him. Her cheek was red, as if she were blushing.

Outside, unknown to Haffner, the sun maintained its fixed decline.

6

Distractedly, Haffner saw once more the *Lives of the Caesars*, there on his bedside table. Even if this was not quite despotic, it was the closest he had really come, thought Haffner, to feeling imperial. This was Dacia, and Dalmatia. He could understand the euphoria.

No wonder they set about erecting columns, thought Haffner: the camels and the trumpets. No wonder they wanted to parade their spoils, in triumph – the chariots drawn by panthers on their padded paws. No arch, no column, was grand enough to commemorate the few grand moments of desire in a life, the even fewer moments of possession.

Yes, there had been twelve Caesars: and now here was the thirteenth – Haffner Augustus: whose image, if there were any justice in this world, should be carved on a marble tomb, its panels chased with Haffner in profile, leading his jungly train – the leopards, the chubby satyrs – to some screwed-up festival of Bacchus.

7

The lamps, in their shades, observed Haffner, delinquent.

And Haffner forgot himself. All the characters of his recent history – Frau Tummel, Niko, Benjamin – dissolved like the swoon of a television's closedown. There was only Haffner, in his second-best tracksuit: and this figure in front of him, a resting contortionist.

For Haffner was beginning to understand.

That people tended to make other people up, that friendships tended to be formed between two imaginary people: Haffner knew this. What struck him as more poignant and more touching in the friendship of Zinka and Haffner was that it was so much less imaginary than he might ever have predicted. In ways which rather tended to be beyond him, Haffner seemed to offer her some kind of playfulness. And this version of Haffner, he thought, was the truest, the most profound.

When Esther was very young, she used to play with Haffner and their schnauzer. Livia would be in the kitchen, or the garden. In this way, the three of them formed a diminishing series: for Esther would only play so long as Haffner was there, a minor role. Just as

Haffner was only happy when he knew that Livia was there, somewhere close, if out of sight. With Haffner in attendance, occasionally called on to settle some argument, or adjudicate some game, Esther played with her seven imaginary friends, while pensively chewing on the blonde curling tips of her hair.

Haffner wondered whether this resemblance perturbed him – between his daughter playing and a girl on his bed. He concluded that it did not. At that moment, he realised, he would accept whatever conditions were imposed, whatever distortions might be demanded. He would do anything: just so long as he could be there, in the sunlit room, with Zinka.

He was interrupted momentarily from this glow of happiness by Zinka reaching a conclusion which Haffner only wished might be a little softer, a little less of a crescendo. And then there was a pause in which the world, sadly, began to right itself. Finally, Zinka sighed, began to move, and then turned round and sat there, on the bed, looking at him, a leg tucked under her waist: a seductive yogi.

She should probably go, said Zinka: Haffner agreed that yes, she probably should. So, then, she said. And he sat down, by the desk, marvelling – a vague state which meant that her dressing and smiling at Haffner, then leaving the room, then the door shutting with its slow delayed click all seemed to happen in a miracle of speed, without Haffner noticing.

She was the only woman he had ever met – apart from Livia, apart from Livia – marked by such self-possession.

But Haffner had no time to consider the line of his life: its line of beauty. Out of the bathroom, in an adagio of sadness, emerged the judgement of Haffner.

Haffner Guilty

1

As in the horror films of Haffner's silent youth, the door to the bathroom swung open, and no one emerged. There was silence: except, thought Haffner, for the liquid, aquatic soundtrack of the bathroom. Then Haffner understood that he was listening to the profound whisper of Frau Tummel's exhalations, the soughing of her inhalations. She had been standing there, staring into the mirror, her profile against the door. For a perturbed exalted moment, Haffner wondered if what he could hear was maybe the after-effect of a simultaneous Tummelian orgasm: still transcendent, cascading.

It was not.

Frau Tummel emerged from her oubliette. She made hungrily for her handbag and discovered her package of cigarettes. She lit one, then relaxed into the usual minimalist rhythm, standing at the window, grinning against the light. To the mountains, the unending sky, she said that she had never been so much made mock of. She was a wife, she was a mother. Everything she had, she had offered to Haffner. And this was how he treated her. He had let her say so many things. He had told her so many untruths.

He was like a boy, she said. This monster of immaturity! Even an adolescent would be more careful with love.

—But, argued Haffner, standing uneasily in the middle of the room.

At this point in his intricate reasoning, Frau Tummel interrupted.

She could not understand it. Was he rational? When he had done what he had just done? This man who had just locked her in a bathroom, while he entertained a woman in a way which she, Frau Tummel, could not explain. No, she could not understand it. A man who was dressed, as ever, in a variant on the shell suit.

Haffner only wanted to say, he began again. Again, he was forced to pause.

And although I am Haffner's historian, I can observe Frau Tummel too. He only wanted to mock her, she thought. He must have staged the whole thing. She was feeling so suddenly desolate. Now, she had no one. It was clear enough, she thought, that Haffner would never want her in the way that she wanted him to want her; and yet she did not want her husband, not quite, in the way that she wanted to want him either – a man who was so delicate, so unlike the ideal of Frau Tummel's youth.

Why, she said, must there be so much vulgarity with Haffner? Why this obscenity? Her voice accelerated into the upper registers. What beauty was there in his behaviour? Why the dirt, Raphael? Why this dirt?

And Haffner, still in the cloud of happiness produced by Zinka – illuminated, looking down on the pitiful world of humans – did not know what to say.

But of course, continued Frau Tummel, let everything descend to his level. Because he didn't understand the higher emotions. Haffner tried to remonstrate with her. When, said Haffner, had he ever? Whereas for her, continued Frau Tummel, fool that she was, it was a fantasy: of course, it was just a romance. If that was how he wanted to describe something eternal, something real.

—You! said Frau Tummel. In your tracksuit.

This point seemed incontrovertible.

—You want, she said, to be with this girl? This teenager? It disgusts me.

Once, this accusation would have seemed just to Haffner, perhaps: but not now. Up here, in the mountains, he had discovered a delighted sense of flippancy: yes, up here, he really could dispense with thinking in terms of the up or the down. As if the healthy were really ill. Or the old were really young.

So what could he say to soothe her? She wanted love to be a refuge: the desert island. But Haffner never thought that anywhere was safe; nowhere was truly deserted. Not even a marriage. It was, he thought, impossible to desert into another country, across the border, in the blue dawn.

It wasn't Haffner's fault, after all, if the moments of love and the moments of sex so rarely coincided.

—So, said Frau Tummel. So.

Haffner wondered what that meant. He wondered if he could ask.

It was always the same, said Frau Tummel. Men would always say they were in love, when all they wanted was the body of a woman; whereas for a woman, said Frau Tummel, it was absolutely opposite. He came from an outside place. But what could this man in front of her know about a true woman?

—But I never said I loved you, said Haffner.

And then he immediately regretted this moment of pointless truth. Suddenly, Frau Tummel stalled in the headlong pursuit of her anger. But then, perhaps this was what she had expected all along: this brutal Haffner.

It didn't mean, however, that Frau Tummel was not in love. It only confirmed her in her feelings all the more. The suffering was no contradiction. It couldn't be love, thought Frau Tummel, without the suffering. It came upon you, unbidden.

She waited for Haffner to say something kind, to tell her that of course he loved her. But Haffner simply stood there, deserted by his politesse: maimed by sincerity.

He refused to agree, said Haffner, with her theory. No, love was not a compulsion. The suffering was not necessary. It was just imagination, he told her. Everyone, said Haffner, chooses if they want to fall in love.

And as he said it, he wasn't sure if it was true. It didn't seem true of his love for Zinka. It had never been true of his love for Livia.

Let me be my own author! This was Haffner's cry. He wanted to be the one who invented his own stories as he went along. Except he hadn't then; and he couldn't now.

3

No, there was nothing masculine about Haffner's desire for Zinka: it did not obey the usual categories of Haffner: pursuit, and then seduction. Instead, it represented a happy passivity, content with whatever it might get.

Perhaps Zinka understood this. She wanted a man who was beyond the normal aggression. She wanted, really, an escape from the men. Whereas Frau Tummel – who craved the masculine – did not.

If Haffner were only allowed to exist in one sentence, it would be this: he was a desire that had outlived its usefulness.

And maybe this was the universal law of the empires: the law of decadence. That was the secret history of history. The very quality that led to an empire was the reason why that very empire would no longer be able to sustain itself. No contemporary, in the words of the great historian, could discover in the public felicity the latent causes of decay and corruption. He was talking about the Roman empire. But he could have been talking about Haffner. The long peace, and the uniform government of the Romans, introduced a slow and secret poison into the vitals of the empire. And so the minds of men were gradually reduced to the same level; everyone sunk into the languid indifference of private life.

Not survival of the fittest, then, but the deeper truth: survival of the weakest. Haffner had been so intent on the pursuit of women. He had always been kind to his desires. And now this very taste for possession had led to his transformation into the greatest of fantasists – the most elegant and whimsical of imaginative artists. Because the desire was still there, but Haffner was no longer in control of where he might act these desires out.

And this reminds me of one story from a more decadent empire than our own.

The emperor Elagabalus was emperor when the empire was disintegrating. As if that wasn't obvious. His reputation as a voluptuary was awesome. It might be possible, recorded Elagabalus's historian, that his vices and follies had been exaggerated; had been adorned in the imagination of his narrators. But even if one only believed those excesses which were performed in public, and attested to by many witnesses, they would still surpass the records of human infamy. Of these excesses, the one which I most admire is the way in which Elagabalus – the instigator of a coup – loved to dress up in women's clothes. He preferred the distaff to the sceptre, and distributed the honours of the empire among his male lovers, including one man who was invested with the authority of the emperor – or, as Elagabalus insisted on being known, the empress's husband.

Laughable, maybe – but man! What possessions one could enter into, when dispossessed to this extent!

4

Perhaps, said Frau Tummel, he simply lacked soul.

This was more than Haffner had expected. Perhaps, she continued, the spirit was beyond him. She was sure that he didn't even know how to cross himself. No, said Haffner, he didn't. This, said a demonstrative Frau Tummel, is how you do it.

Was it only Haffner, he wondered, who was constantly available for education?

Like this? he wondered. No, that was wrong, she said. The forehead first? queried Haffner. The forehead was not important, said Frau Tummel. The forehead was nothing. Why was he worrying about the forehead?

Then there was another knock at the door.

—Don't answer it! cried Frau Tummel.

—Why not? said Haffner, flinging open the door, to reveal a boy bearing a tray.

It was reception, he said. They were sending Haffner complimentary refreshment.

—Why? said Haffner.

—A gift, said the boy.

—From whom? said Haffner.

—I don't know, said the boy.

And he placed on the table an inaccurate planetarium: a galaxy of white chocolates, with seven half-moons of cinnamon biscuits.

Frau Tummel looked at Haffner.

—You mock me, she said.

And, for a moment, he wanted to enfold her in his arms and tell her no, he did not mock her at all.

He was truly a monster, she told him. What right did he think he had?

He could admit, as she said this, that there were ways of finding Haffner guilty. Therefore, maybe it was right that, more and more, his life resembled some bizarre form of punishment, some gonzo idea of karma. But Haffner wasn't one to be abused by ideas of sin. The devil, like all the other gods, was one invention among many, in Haffner's improvised theology: the gods were just decoration; scribbled marginalia. The gods were doodling. He preferred to form the categories himself. If Haffner were pressed, he preferred the more charming and likeable others: the demigods. The infinite fairies: the 33,000 gods of the pagan religions. These were the gods he might have called on when he felt that he was sinning. But the prospect was unlikely, He doubted that, if the gods existed, their concern would be the soul of Raphael Haffner.

—I said I loved you, said Frau Tummel.

She said it, he thought, as if she were in shock.

—It'll be OK, said Haffner. He knew this was not adequate. But there was nothing, he felt, he could say.

Naturally, said Frau Tummel, she would have to consider whether to report the girl. It was only right. This seemed unnecessary, said Haffner. No, said Frau Tummel. It was only right. She had to consider what was right. Would there be anything he could do, said Haffner, to persuade her otherwise? Frau Tummel looked at him. She told him that no, there was not.

And she turned and left, theatrically slamming the door. Or, theatrically trying to slam the door: but the door, on its stiff spring-delay, braked, and softly, slowing, slowly, softly closed itself, in silence.

But what else had she expected? He was a monster, absolutely. A chimera, a griffin: a rabid centaur. Nor was this the first appearance of Haffner's multiple personality, his capacity for metamorphosis.

5

The night when Haffner proposed to Livia – just before Haffner was due to ship out – he had gone with some friends to the French Pub in Soho. And at that time he did not realise that the man behind the bar, with the Gallic twin-twirled moustache, was Victor Berlemont, the father of Gaston – Gaston, who after his retirement from the French Pub would play golf with Haffner twenty years later, in the other bohemia of Hendon. A man who understood the problematic species of herbs. With a Pernod in his hand – the first

time Haffner had ever drunk this strange and continental liquor –
he had talked to a girl about the higher things. Many times, Haffner
had considered the uneasy fluctuations of one's sense of beauty. In
wartime, he discovered, one could find beautiful most women you
met. Because you needed beauty, for the desire to feel rational.
Whereas the desire you felt in a war wasn't rational, and there was
no beauty. She didn't believe, the girl in the French Pub had told
him, that adultery was wrong. It was, let us say, a short story: to
the side of the novel. He did not quite understand the analogy; he
knew, however, what she meant. But that girl and her analogies
dissolved into memory – the steep amphitheatre of Haffner's
memory which he looked down on from the great height of his
longevity, perched on his seat in the gods, looking down at the rabid
lions, the dying Christians.

Haffner had left, and gone to meet Livia at the statue of Eros.

It was always like that, he thought. He wanted to be bohemian,
and the bohemian eluded him. He had kissed the girl in the French
Pub, and then left, before anything else might happen.

He took Livia for a meal on Shaftesbury Avenue. Then they had
gone to some film: of which Haffner only remembered that a man
spent a lot of time driving. This was, Haffner remembered, the main
reason, it seemed, there had been for making a film: the mania for
cars. It was so cool to drive that all any one in Britain wanted to
see, all any one in Los Angeles wanted to film, was a man getting
in and out of a car. And also, remembered Haffner, smoking a pipe.
In and out of a car while smoking a pipe. That was cinema.
Afterwards, they were in a taxi round the back of Leicester Square.
They were taking Livia home. And did Livia know, asked Haffner,
how dangerous it would be for him over there, soon, at the front?
Livia made Haffner aware that she did. But perhaps, he continued
– wishing he could not remember how the girl in the French Pub
had kissed him, the thick dry texture of her lipstick, with its waxy
faded rose perfume, like the greasepaint of his recent brief theatrical

career, which she then reapplied, open-mouthed, after they had kissed, while Haffner watched the taut ellipse of her mouth – Livia did not quite appreciate the magnitude of the danger. The danger Haffner would be in, over there, at the front.

Haffner touched her on the cheek. He was twenty-two. She was twenty. It was very possible, he said, that he would never see her again. He might never come home. So would she, he said – looking down, bashful – consent to make him happy? It would mean so much to him, he said, to know that someone cared. Livia looked at him: and, as she used to tell Benjamin, and everyone else, for ever after, she did not know what else she could do. It seemed rude to say no. So she said yes and – feeling very fast – cuddled him up, and kissed him.

As Haffner silently and helplessly compared her nervous, gentle, motionless kiss to the inspired kiss of a girl four hours earlier, whose name he would never know.

Haffner Jewish

1

Because Haffner was now in a state of introspection; because his attempt to find Zinka, to warn her about the rages of Frau Tummel, had stalled when, as he leaned casually against the counter at reception, a man sporting a slicked quiff, with a paper rose in his lapel, smiled blankly at him and assured him that Zinka had left the hotel that day; because in any case Frau Tummel was unlikely to draw the hotel's attention to her surveillance of Haffner's bedroom: because of all these reasons, Haffner went walking again. His intention was to sit and reflect on the villa. He was due to meet Niko that evening, in their clandestine arrangement. Before that, he was eating supper with Benjamin. So Haffner now had two intentions. He wanted to sit and reflect, and check that his quest for the villa was being as slickly maintained as possible. And to do this, he intended to find a coffee: the blackest, most acrid, most Mediterranean coffee.

From this search, however, Haffner was sidetracked.

He didn't always know why he did things. He didn't know why, now, he had wandered into a church: first blinded by the darkness, then gradually seeing the light. A shrine on his left was an exhibition of car crash photos: for those who had survived miraculous suffering. A shrine on his right was an exhibition of baby photos, toddlers, foetal scans. The shrine of the miracle births. Haffner sat in a pew, his back straight, his knees aching, and looked up at the crucified God. He looked back down. A woman in a headscarf was shepherding seven bags of shopping. She bent low to worship her Lord.

Just as Livia had bent her head, when she crouched there, on all fours, waiting for the entrance of Haffner. Because she liked to see it, she said. She liked to watch him moving, between her legs.

Haffner looked up. He looked back down. The only prayers he knew were Jewish prayers, and so he tried to say them.

The Jews were, in the end, his people. If Haffner had a people.

Perhaps, then, this was not the digression it appeared to Haffner. Perhaps this was just another way for Haffner to consider his commitment to Livia's inheritance.

—Shema, Israel, he said, the Lord our God.

And then he could not remember anything else. Because the way up is the way down and the way left is the way right. He was in a church, and he was Jewishly praying. Did this matter? Was this the sort of action which damned a soul for all eternity? Haffner had no idea.

2

When Livia had died, Benjamin had taken Haffner aside. As if Benjamin were the grandfather. Perhaps, thought Benjamin, Haffner might find solace if he went to shul?

—Shul? said Haffner.

—Shul, said Benjamin.

—Since when, said Haffner, did you give up on the English language?

Haffner disliked the modern trend for Yiddish. It wasn't some recovered purity of the blood that Haffner cared about: instead

Haffner preferred the distinctions of the English language, learned in the difference between a parvenu and an arriviste, a cad and a bounder.

On the other hand, the linguistics did not exhaust his irritation at Benjamin's suggestion.

Haffner rarely went to synagogue.

—You want to leave the synagogue? the Reverend Levine had said to him. Be my guest. I don't mind which synagogue you don't go to.

And Haffner had riposted with his own.

—Come on, said Haffner, winningly. What is the definition of a British Jew?

—Tell me, Raphael, said the Reverend Levine.

—A person, said Haffner, who instead of no longer going to church, no longer goes to synagogue.

Once, he had felt more allegiance to his religion. At school, he hadn't eaten the bacon, just the eggs; and when there was an exchange, and some German boys came over, he didn't want to speak to them: he had resented them being there. Yet he also went to chapel once a day, and twice on Sundays. He could have, naturally, been excused, but he still went.

—The thing about you, Benji had said to him, during one of their political discussions, is that you're so English. You're lukewarm.

—You're English too, said Haffner. Don't you be forgetting you're English.

—I'm not, said Benji. Well, I'm not English like you're English.

Just as in New York, when Morton persisted in his absolute belief that race was where it was at. That history was where it was at. That no one could be sincere if they tried to deny the world-importance of politics.

In this way, Haffner floated above the Atlantic Ocean, neither European nor American.

During the war, he had disturbed his Jewish friends – particularly Silberman, that comical Jewish soldier – with his unabashed hatred of the Stern Gang: the Zionist Jewish terrorists. With disdain, Haffner quoted from their newspaper, *The Front*, where the crazies argued, crazily, in Haffner's considered opinion, that neither Jewish morality nor Jewish tradition could negate the use of terror as a means of battle.

Haffner didn't care about birth or name or nation. He was not a stickler for such things. He was amused when Hersch Lauterpacht – Goldfaden's new friend – told him, many years after it happened, over dinner, that his nomination to the International Court of Justice had initially been blocked by the Attorney General, on the grounds that a British representative should both be and be seen to be thoroughly British, whereas Lauterpacht could not help the fact that he did not qualify in this way either by birth, by name or by education. Yes, how they had laughed, at Simpson's on the Strand, in 1980. How he had chuckled at this idea that they should in any way be seen as European.

My hero of assimilation! My hero of lightness!

Or so Haffner would have liked his story to be written. But it was not entirely true.

Haffner still treasured his family's stories from the shtetl. Or, more precisely, he treasured the story of their escape. How the final branch of the Haffner family tree to reach England had docked in Sunderland, in the midst of the nineteenth century, with Haffner's great-grandfather, a two-month-old baby, in a box. This was the family romance: the line of the Haffners had only survived the Lithuanian pogroms because of the silence and courage of great-grandfather Haffner, whose name was Isaac – the perfect silent baby. But, thought Haffner, where was the logic in this story? If one needed to hide the baby, surely one would have needed to hide oneself as well? And the chances of a baby remaining silent during a customs investigation, tight in a box, seemed highly unlikely.

So in what way would this ruse dupe an anti-Semite, in Prussia, with his sideburns and the plume of his helmet, the beige snuff stains on the crook of his thumb? But there it was: this story, invented or not, was the beginning of the Haffners' career in polite society. This silent infant generated the family law firm – which Haffner had refused – the house in north London, the servants, the cricket matches, the endless lawn-tennis lessons.

And his mother, his minuscule mother, who fasted every Yom Kippur: who stood on the steps of their synagogue in St John's Wood, asking Raphael to hold her, because she was dizzy.

Haffner thought that with these memories he was avoiding the pressing issue of the villa, the pressing issue of the women who had so invaded his stay here in the mountains. But there was passion in Haffner's indecision. He wanted to be a *flâneur*: he wanted to pretend that he had no engagements, no responsibilities. This ideal Haffner would idle through his memories – flick through them as through the pages of an outdated women's magazine, in the dentist's waiting room, while sitting beside an abandoned playpen made of multicoloured plastic. But this Haffner did not exist. No, the real Haffner was, as always, in the middle of things.

Here, in this church, Haffner tried to disappear from view. As he always tried to do. And he could not.

He was an aristocrat. Could no one understand this? Bourgeois, true, but an aristocrat! He had class. Even as they tried to force him into the Jewish working classes: the ordinary ranks of the Jews. The dispossessed; the heartbroken. No, Haffner had nothing to do with the Yiddish in London. *Koyfts a heft!* they used to cry, in the streets where Haffner was trying to find a cup of tea, after his cricket coaching in the East End. His cousins had set up the first ever mixed Jewish and Christian social club for boys in the East End locale of Bethnal Green, a club whose cricket team Haffner had coached to victory that same summer, the year before he went away to fight in the British army. Buy a pamphlet! they cried, crowding round

Haffner, with their Yiddish literary magazines, their Zionist *cris de coeur*.

Buy, thought Haffner, a fucking pamphlet yourself.

It had seemed so funny then. It seemed less funny now.

3

The aristocracy of Haffner was not a metaphor. A cousin on his mother's side was a viscount.

Yes, Haffner had history.

As a young man, Haffner's viscount had been moved by the plight of the underdog, the abandoned masses in their ghettos. He would go with his father – a liberal politician, a man of principle – to the dilapidated areas out to the east of London, where the less fortunate Jewish people lived, with their impoverished tailoring, cabinet-making, matchbox-making, fur-pulling. Then they would go to the park, to take a stroll, or a ride. The disparity between these two experiences moved the young politician: he wanted to do good. He was so moved that the syntax in his diary became impassioned, inverted. *What are they, dull, short-visioned, who see not the ground shaking beneath their very feet* – wrote the young liberal – *and angry voices, quiet, marvellously refraining yet, that are soon to rise, in ever-swelling clamour?* Later on, when he retired from public life, Haffner's viscount devoted his time to the writing of philosophy. He was, he said, a meliorist. He believed that, with only a small adjustment in our thinking, we would see that this world could indeed become the best of all possible worlds.

Whenever the business of imagining this thing called history came up in Haffner's life – on rare occasions, perhaps when rereading Churchill, or arguing with his grandson, or listening to the stories of Livia's family – he imagined history as a straight line. The line of gravity. The all-encompassing horizontal – its horizon – to which all bodies descended.

It was Haffner's viscount who had argued for the Jewish right of return to Palestine: the Arabs could not forbid the Jews to come back, he had argued, since the Jews were a people whose connection with the country long antedated their own – and especially as it had resulted in events of spiritual and cultural value to mankind in striking contrast with the barren record of the last thousand years. There could be no question, he had told the Prime Minister, Lloyd George, that the best thing for the land would be for it to be reclaimed by the Jews.

He was not dogmatic, however. The rights of the immigrants did not cancel out the rights of the natives: no, the arrival of the Jews must never be marked by hardship, expropriation, injustice of any kind for the people now in the land, whose forebears had tilled the soil and dwelled in the towns for a thousand years.

The viscount possessed the optimism of the romantic.

As the first ever High Commissioner of Palestine, the viscount had sent rare stamps to his philatelic king, painted with Churchill (whose paintings, he noted, were avowedly crude, but nonetheless effective, especially in colouring) and played tennis with Lord Balfour himself. Whose idea – along with that genius Weizmann – the whole country had been in the first place. And it was the viscount who was one half of the most famous anecdote about this country which they still called Palestine. When his predecessor, Chief Administrator Bols, was about to leave office, wrote the viscount, he asked the incoming commissioner to sign a receipt. The viscount asked for what. For Palestine, said Bols. But, replied the viscount, he couldn't do that. He couldn't mean it seriously. Certainly he did, said Major Bols. He had it typed out here. And he produced a slip of paper – *Received from Major-General Sir Louis J. Bols, KCB: one Palestine, complete* – with the date and a space for the viscount's signature. The viscount still demurred, but Bols insisted, so he signed; adding, however, the initials which used often to appear on commercial documents – E & OE, meaning Errors and Omissions Excepted. And Bols had this piece of paper framed, he was so pleased with it.

And when the viscount finally left the country, to further pursue his career back in Britain, he took with him a vision. In his memoir of his time in Palestine, he recorded the wide roads, bordered by little white single-storeyed houses, well spaced out, with creepers over their porches; around them, little gardens of flowers and patches of vegetables, with fields of waving corn and young plantations of trees beyond; groups of men and women in working-clothes, smiling girls and beautiful, healthy, white-dressed children; overhead, the cloudless blue sky. That, he said, was the vision with which he had left.

It wasn't Haffner's vision. Haffner thought it was schmaltz.

But it was with pride that, towards the end of 1942, he had learned in the newspapers of the viscount's speech in the Lords, on the reading of the declaration against German extermination of the Jews. This was not an occasion on which they were expressing sorrow and sympathy to sufferers from some terrible catastrophe due unavoidably to flood or earthquake, or some other convulsion of nature, the viscount had said. These dreadful events were an outcome of quite deliberate, planned, conscious cruelty on the part of human beings. Hear hear, the Lords had murmured. And Haffner with them, in Egypt. Absolutely.

Authority like this was what Haffner was destined for, thought Haffner. It was his inheritance: the natural deference shown to the political classes, the happy comforts of the *Finanzbourgeoisie*. A class to which he naturally belonged, thought happy Haffner, confirmed in this belief by the speech in the newspaper just as much as he was by his first ever deal – at Anzio, when he persuaded some desperate American, a friend of Morton, just for a cheap bottle of whisky, to part with his regulation, all-terrain, multi-gear jeep.

4

The viscount, however, had still been moved by the ghettos. Whereas Haffner felt more distance from the Jewish underclass. The stories from the ghettos distressed him but they were not his. Partly, this was from a sense that as a cossetted Londoner he could hardly adopt the tragedies of people he never knew. A position which seems calmly moral, precisely modest, to me. But there was also a more complicated distance. The person Haffner knew best, whose stories were ghetto stories, was Goldfaden. With Livia, thought Haffner jealously, Goldfaden possessed a tragic European past. So this meant, I think, that Haffner sometimes exaggerated his haughtiness in regard to history. For Haffner was not without his own sense of racial possessiveness. In Haffner's opinion, there was no reason for the working classes, for the Blacks and the Chinese, to avail themselves of this word *ghetto*. It was a Jewish possession. No one else had suffered like the Jews had suffered. No one else had been persecuted with such universal thoroughness.

In Venice, on holiday with Esther and her family, in the early 1980s, Haffner and Livia wandered away from San Marco: they ended up in what had been, Livia informed him, reading from a guide-book, the original ghetto (—From the sixteenth century! she exclaimed). In the bleak hot sunlight, no one was moving. On the seventh floor of a tenement building, some washing was strung on runners. A wireless was talking to itself.

In this ghetto, Haffner and Livia discussed their recurrent story of the Ghetto: the story of Goldfaden's uncle, Eli, who was now a cameraman in LA.

Eli had not been on the family holiday in London with the Goldfadens. So he was left behind in Warsaw. Before the war, he had been a member of the Bund, the General Jewish Labour Union. He believed in a strange combination of the Yiddish language and culture, and secular Jewish nationalism. Like Livia's father, and Haffner, he was not a Zionist. Unlike them, he expressed this Yiddishly, through his devotion to *doyigkeyt*, to hereness. His family lived on Sienna Street, near the Jewish quarter. And Eli, Goldfaden used to tell Livia, as they reminisced about

Europe – while Haffner glanced at the diary pieces about his financial rivals in the evening papers – Eli was so earnest in his devotion to learning that he even read the novels which were serialised in the newspapers. A man should be prepared, thought Eli. Nothing was alien to him.

In Warsaw, before the revolt in the Ghetto, and before the uprising in the city, but when everything still was bleak, Eli had been told to go with his parents to the main square. This seemed reasonable. Or, at least, not unreasonable. In the square, they were told to walk in single file to the train station, where a train was waiting at each platform. They had asked the rabbi if this seemed advisable. The rabbi, after long deliberation, thought that the best thing to do was obey those in power. Could they really wish them harm? And this, said Goldfaden, was where his cousin became heroic. He came to a decision. No one had ever heard again from those who had got on the trains to the east. Eli knew this. Therefore, concluded Eli, he would run. So what if he were shot in the back, his kidneys torn inside him? He would prefer to stage his own death, rather than sleepwalk into it. And so he ran, and managed to hide out in the rubble of a destroyed apartment block.

Here, in the ghetto in Venice, just before Haffner had retired, Livia had praised Eli once more. But Haffner, this time, had paused. Then he had asked her: what about the others? She had asked him what he meant. They paused and looked at a dark canal. What about the others, the ones the man had left behind? said Haffner. What about his parents? And Livia had replied that they all died. Naturally, they had died. The moral value of Eli's act seemed to Haffner to be complicated by this. He had chosen to abandon his friends. And maybe this was fine, maybe this was unremarkable, but Haffner thought that, at the very least, it was a complication.

She should have known, said Livia, that Haffner would be difficult.

Yes, said Haffner, Haffner would be difficult. Why shouldn't he be difficult?

And perhaps Haffner was right, even if he was only accidentally right, by transforming Eli's story into a story of Haffner: a compromise.

Haffner saw in this anecdote the grand bravery of refusing to act in the way you were supposed to act. In Haffner's rewrite, Eli's escape from the Ghetto was also a desertion.

5

According to Livia, the story of Eli was not a story of a desertion, because a desertion was morally bad. An escape, however, was morally good. But I am not so sure that the two can be so easily divided. People call a flight an escape, only after having been forced to give up the idea that it is moral to remain in a bad situation. So often, people think that if one person is suffering, then everyone else should suffer too. In these cases, if someone takes flight, then their escape is just a desertion.

Yes, the whole vocabulary of flight is puritanical. So every act of desertion is also an act of hedonism.

And maybe the deep reason for this is that no one likes a deserter, an escapee, because it proves the fact that there is always a choice. So often, it is easier to believe that life is a trap. The trap is the image of life's seriousness.

Haffner, however, my hero, did not believe that life was serious. He didn't believe that one must necessarily be faithful to the ordinary, inevitable tragedy of a life. If one could be faithless to anything, Haffner always hoped, surely it would be to one's own past?

But, however much I admire the hope, I am not so sure that this kind of infidelity is possible. And there, in the church, nor was Haffner. Because the story of Eli now made Haffner remember another story which he preferred to keep to himself: how under the patronage of the Reverend Levine, the appointed guardian of Jewish refugees from Germany, a girl stayed in the Haffners' house, in 1938. He didn't remember very much about her: he couldn't remember her name. He knew very little, but he believed that she took her own life. Not when she was staying with them, but eventually.

She must have been about twenty. He didn't remember even trying to talk to her. She must have been with them a very short time, thought Haffner. She was extremely unhappy. Perhaps they couldn't cope with her. Yes, in his mind, he heard that she had taken her own life. But his mind was a bit hazy. He hadn't got involved – but he knew that there was somebody there, upstairs, in the spare room. She was always asleep. He had no idea how it had been organised.

This was what it was to be Jewish in Britain. The East was always making its demands on you: the grief of its history entered your life and so it became your own. You were always being forced back: beyond the pale.

He couldn't remember that girl's name.

He was not sinful: he refused all ideas of sin. But if Haffner had ever sinned, thought Haffner, then this forgetting was it.

6

In the dark church Haffner called on God: —You are the Lord my God, Haffner exclaimed, in silence, in the darkness of this church, and I am a clod of dirt and a worm; dust of the ground and a vessel of shame.

But Haffner didn't need his God for such lavish repentance. The women were enough.

Haffner had used the infidelities within his marriage as the Orthodox used the eruv. They were exercises in invention; the riches of self-blame. His interior life was festooned with sagging squares of string, marking out the permitted areas within the forbidden world. He believed in marriage like the Orthodox believed in God. It was a territory for permitting the unpermitted.

And for testing the soul of Haffner.

Livia had been expert at the put-down. She was, in Haffner's language, a strong woman. This trait had endeared her to him. At the official dinners, the unofficial suppers, Haffner bore with pleased and happy grace her talent to resist Haffner's charm, believing that this public scepticism served to illustrate his moral grandeur, his lack of vanity. It was not an unusual moment in his life when, on the night of the dinner for the City Branch of the Institute of Bankers in 1982, he came into her dressing room while she was in her underwear – blue lace, white frills – and with a crooked finger, its nail tipped with a varnish whose colour Haffner would never be able to name, she pointed out to him the direction of the door. And in his socks he turned around and left.

Retrospectively, however, this moment had acquired a unique weight. For that, thought Haffner, was when he understood that his marriage had in fact been governed by forces which he did not understand or control. That night, after Haffner's speech, after the speeches reciprocating Haffner's speech, as they were driving home in Haffner's Saab – with Livia driving, because Haffner was utterly drunk – Haffner quizzed her on the significance of why he had found her sitting outside the venue, the Butchers' Hall; why he had found her sitting there with Goldfaden, sharing a cigarette while the meat-market traffic began revving and chirring around them and the rinsing smell of meat gusted and retreated: yes, why had he found them there, sitting peaceably, with Goldfaden cupping her hand as he lit her cigarette? And at the time Haffner had not so much minded about the fact that he had never seen her smoking; nor that it was a habit she excoriated in Haffner: he minded about the casual way in which Goldfaden touched her hand.

Calmly, without malice, Livia had simply told Haffner that it was not as if he could really lecture her. It was not as if he could condemn what she had done, and would continue to do.

Drunk, silenced, Haffner considered this. And what he wanted to say was that the two were incomparable: because when it came to women, Haffner had only ever got whoever came along. They loved him, true – but Haffner never really loved them back. He just amazed them with the strength of his devotion: a devotion which was indistinguishable from the fear that they would leave him. Even if no one did leave Haffner. Whereas Livia had something else. Livia, it seemed, had love.

—Do you love him? asked Haffner.

And Livia, braking gently at the traffic light by the Hampstead pond, said that yes of course: naturally, she said – and she touched Haffner, gently, on the cheek. So Haffner asked her what they were going to do about it now, to which Livia simply replied that she saw no reason to do anything.

Livia didn't believe in an escape.

She parked the car in the drive, went into the house, and Haffner sat there: listening to the rose bushes' gentle crackle in the wind. Just as now, years later, Haffner sat in a church and surveyed the wondrous mistakes of his life: his infidelity to his wife, his infidelity to his race. Or, to put it another way, his infidelity to the women he had slept with – to Barbra, to Pilar and Joan and Laure and all the other names he now could not remember – his infidelity to his nation.

All the nebulous fairies of his history and his politics, dissolving, now, on a midsummer night, in the middle of nowhere.

He was such a klutz, thought Haffner. Then he translated himself out of Goldfaden's language. He was a fool.

It was fitting, really, that one of Goldfaden's favourite party tricks was his riff on the word *dope*. As Goldfaden would explain to you, it was the trickiest word in the language: on the American side, it came from the Dutch for sauce, so meaning any kind of goo, lubric-ant, liquid, liquor, and hence any kind of narcotic, drug, medicine, adulterating agent, and hence, through the racetracks, and their need to know the inside dope, all esoteric lore, all arcana. And there it met, at its apex, the British derivation, from dupe, meaning the gull, the fool, the absolutely-in-the-dark: and where else were we, Goldfaden would conclude, if not always in the dark, drugged by lack of knowledge, unaware of the systems which eluded us and which invaded us at every moment? This word *dope* was the real thing which bound the British and Americans together: this was the real Atlantic Ocean.

But at this point, with this word *dope*, Haffner had gone as far as he could in the business of self-discussion. Because everything was obvious to him now. Everything had always been to do with Livia. And Haffner had never noticed.

It was so evident, so infinite in its evidence, that Haffner had never known.

7

Haffner stood up: he turned to go – making for the Chinese restaurant where he was meant to eat with Benjamin. In front of the church, where the baroque facade hid the brick barn of a nave, a line of floats was parked, each decorated with a *tableau vivant*. All the actors in these *tableaux* were children. Surrounding them, the adults of the town were taking photographs. Saint Peter was scratching the side of his nose with a translucent wafer, while another boy in white shirt and black trousers kneeled before him, on a plush velvet cusion, with his eyes escaping through the trickle of his fingers.

No, thought Haffner, observing the children. Some things were irreversible. The entropy of Haffner! Not everything could be recuperated. Like Haffner's gilded youth. For how can a man be young, when he is old? He knew enough of the Bible to know that this was difficult.

As Morton would have said, do the math.

Only on the last day in Cairo, in 1946, did Haffner write to Livia as his wife. Throughout their engagement and the early years of their marriage, throughout the war, he had referred to her as his darling girl, his sweetheart. Only now, in the last letter he would write to her from the war, when he was coming home, did Haffner address her as his very darling wife.

—I only pray that you will find me a better man than when I left you and that I will fulfil all your dreams, he wrote. I believe that we can do tremendous things together and that with our lives, with our happiness, we can make others happy. And that is what I think life is for, the real purpose behind it all. So Haffner wrote to Livia, the night before he sailed back to England, in 1946.

—Bless you, my beloved girl, wrote Raphael Haffner, keep you safe always.

PART FOUR

Haffner Gastronomic

1

The meals of Haffner and Benjamin were epic. In this gargantuan size, they expressed their love. They went to Bodean's on Poland Street and sucked at the burned ends and ribs of cows – which jutted out forlornly, and unevenly, like organ pipes. They were experts in the cuts of steak: both convinced that the aged hanger steaks of New York were the greatest of them all. Then there were the deep-fried marvels of Japan: the chicken katsu, endowed with its cloudy pot of barbecue sauce. Candy undid them: not the ordinary treats, but the strange, gourmet sugar of internationally local cuisines: nougat, glacé cherries, marzipan fruits, baklava. They invented festivals of junk food: on one famous occasion, they had walked down Oxford Street, eating at every branch of American burger chain they could find. But there was more. This more was the Chinese food.

There was nothing, said Benjamin, more Jewish than this – Haffner's passion for Chinese food. Nothing more emphasised, said Benjamin, his genetic roots to the scattered race.

Haffner looked at him, amazed: his own grandson, with the same weird theory of Chinese food as Goldfaden. Or perhaps he was misremembering. This was, after all, possible.

Underneath a red paper lantern, Benjamin's cheeks were carmine – incandescent. On his face shone a glaze of sweat, echoing the lacquer on the slices of pork belly which lay, unguent, on their bed of shredded iceberg lettuce set before Haffner.

—You ordered the crispy beef, said Benji.

—Yes, I ordered the beef, said Haffner. Of course I ordered the beef. Wait a minute.

Benjamin swivelled round. Or, he swivelled as much as his bulk would allow: an imperfect barn owl.

He saw no one who could help him. He turned back to Haffner.

They continued to argue over whether Haffner should keep his appointment with Niko. Haffner thought it was obvious; Benjamin thought it was less obvious. But he couldn't see, said Haffner, what he had to lose. Could Benjamin explain this to him? He wasn't so proud that he would refuse someone else's help.

It was the principle, said Benjamin. He didn't know these people. How could he trust them?

What kind of principle was that? replied Haffner. It was fear, that was all. And they were hardly, said Haffner, going to rob him – and he exhibited his Nike T-shirt; his flared turquoise tracksuit trouser.

Benji swivelled round once more: he still saw no one who could help him.

Sighing, he turned back, and introduced a new topic of conversation.

What, he wanted to know, did Haffner know about hip hop?

—Hip hop? queried Haffner.

—Hip hop, confirmed Benjamin. But not the West Coast hip hop, nor the East Coast hip hop. Instead, his new thing was South Coast: the hip hop of urban and immigrant France.

In this way, Benji combined a former craze, his craze for hip hop, with his new – and, he believed, ultimate – craze for love. In Tel Aviv, he had been introduced by the girl who had deflowered him to the classics of French hip hop: the angry *banlieusards* in the angry *banlieue*.

This was, after all, why he had come to the spa town. Benjamin was in love. He was in love, and was here to receive advice from Haffner.

So he talked about hip hop. To Benji, this seemed logical.

As he ate, Benjamin described the curious fact that his two favourite songs, at this moment, were both about terror: the French hip-hop song called 'Darkness', and the French hip-hop song called 'Mourir 1000 Fois', with its dark first line: in which the rapper told his terrified audience about his fears of death, in which the chorus simply stated that existence was punishment. They entranced Benji with their myth of the grand: the imagination of disaster. This was why he so loved the rappers from Marseilles: a city he had never been to; a city which, if he were honest, scared him with its reputation for the brutal.

Everything in Benjamin's life now seemed so fraught with significance. As if, thought Benji, he could destroy his whole life with one wrong decision.

He hazarded this to Haffner. Haffner thought it was unlikely that a life could be destroyed. It would take more than one wrong decision for that. Then he reached for the giant bottle of beer in front of him, and poured an accidentally overfoaming glass.

The restaurant advertised itself as Chinese. In its provenance, the food perhaps tended more towards the Vietnamese than the Chinese. There were moments when it was nothing but Thai. But no one here was concerned with the detail of origins: not the sullen Slavic waiters, the absent owners. Haffner, however, didn't care. So long as the effect was Oriental, then Haffner was happy. It possessed an aquarium in which melancholic fish hid themselves beneath mossy banks, munching sand. It seemed Oriental enough for Haffner.

In this setting, Haffner sat and listened to his grandson: his anxious grandson. He was, thought Haffner, the kind of kid who was so vulnerable to women that he'd probably get aroused just by the naked mannequins in shop windows, their robotic defenceless arms. Their invisible nipples and missing pubic hair, like some statue of Venus found beneath the tarmac of a Roman street.

But I think that Haffner could have gone further than this. There was so much to worry about, when considering the character of Benji.

2

Benji was the solitary only child. At fourteen he threw up in a girl's toilet after an evening of drinking whisky and was pleased at the suavity of his aim until he found out the next day that they had found sick everywhere. He used to listen to Liverpool matches on his clock radio in the dark under his Tottenham Hotspur duvet, for he was fickle. The first girl he kissed frightened him. Aged nine, he used to rehearse cricket strokes with a cricket stump and a practice golf ball in his bedroom, while listening to the classic ballad 'Take My Breath Away' on repeat. Like Haffner, the songs were always his downfall. He listened to 'Bridge Over Troubled Water' when Esmond drove him to the cricket matches.

Nothing in Benjamin's early youth had poise, or cool. Instead of cool, the miniature Benjamin hoarded Haffner's anecdotes. The stories of Haffner formed Benji's inheritance.

He treasured a portable Joe Davis snooker table – made on the Gray's Inn Road, in London, and guaranteed to add a touch of fun to family occasions – which he had found in Haffner's loft. One ball, the pink, was still in the centre right pocket, slung in the netting. It nestled there, solidly. Benjamin studied the faint lines printed on the baize. There were shiny trails of turquoise chalk. There was a line horizontally printed across the table, a little below the top. From this, a semicircle arched and settled. It reminded Benjamin of a soccer pitch. It was like a magnified penalty area. But this was not why Benji loved it. Its instructions, glued to the wooden underframe, were signed, in facsimile, by the great Joe Davis himself. From then on, in bed, with his clock radio beside him, its incensed digital digits flipping luminously and silently, Benjamin would read about Thurston's Billiards Hall in Leicester Square. Because he was romanced. For Haffner was Joe Davis's banker, in the 1950s. One day Joe Davis was in South Africa, at a hotel. He was resting. He was having some time off snooker. But then some guy challenged Joe Davis to a game. This man didn't know Joe Davis was Joe Davis. He thought he was just an ordinary person. It was, Haffner would remind his grandson, before the days of television. Joe Davis tried to refuse. He didn't want to play snooker, on his holiday. But the man was insistent. So Joe Davis played snooker. Naturally, he played with exquisite grace. And his challenger was amazed.

—What are you: Joe Davis or something? he said.

And Joe Davis paused.

—No, he said, but I know the man who sleeps with his missus.

Yes, Benji loved his grandfather: his grand grandfather. He was a romantic. And the romance was all inherited from Haffner.

So Benjamin found himself here: in a Chinese restaurant on the outskirts of a spa town, in the centre of Europe. And because he was here, he could ask Haffner anything.

—Is it true, said Benji, that you once gave away the Mercedes to someone else?

—No, said Haffner. No, it isn't.

—OK, said Benjamin.

He returned to the more familiar ground.

—This food is good, said Benji: piercing the inflated curve of a chicken dumpling with a chopstick. I mean it's exquisite.

Haffner queried this; the food, he thought, verged on the inedible:

like every cuisine in this town. But for a moment Haffner loved him – his progeny with the marvellous appetite.

3

The problem was, Benji told Haffner, how did he know that this wasn't a craze? Because he was prone to crazes, he knew this. It was just that this didn't feel like a craze. It felt true. What else did he feel but love, thought Benji, when looking at the curve of his girl's breasts, matched yearningly by the imitative curve of his penis in his briefs? But, continued Benjamin, even if it was true, how important was this, in the end? It was only desire. It wasn't everything. So maybe he should return to his summer school, and forget all about her.

Haffner raised an eyebrow.

And he considered how, in the more ordered nineteenth century, the ordinary family judgement was the father on the son. This was how Haffner's life had begun – with Solomon Haffner in judgement. Now that the twentieth century was ending, however, it turned out that there could be something different: the judgement of the grandfather on the grandson. But instead of judging him for his lack of restraint, it was the lack of chutzpah which Haffner found wanting in his descendant. He would have to educate him into courage.

—Let me tell you my story about Palestine, said Haffner.

—No, I know this story, said Benji.

—I haven't started, said Haffner.

—Your Jewish story? said Benjamin.

—I will tell you again, said Haffner.

Having missed the major battle of the war in North Africa, then served in the liberation of Italy, Haffner had been posted to Palestine. He was twenty-four at the time, he reminded Benji. He was – how old was Benjamin? He was about the same age as Benji was now. In fact, Jerusalem was the setting for his twenty-fourth birthday, on which day he announced he was going to drink twenty-four pink gins. And he did.

His battalion was ordered to keep the peace between the Arabs and the Jews: or, more precisely, between the Arabs and the crazy Russian Zionist Jews.

His people! As if those crazies were his people! What did Haffner have to do with the Orthodox, the serious – complete with dyed sidelocks and dyed caftans, the fringes of their prayer shawls ragged around their waists? In Palestine, Haffner had learned one of his very first truths. To be bohemian you had to be an absolute insider. It was the recent immigrants, the suddenly displaced, who most believed in nations and in boundaries. The ones who believed in a people at all.

Benjamin threw a wasabi pea up into the air and, to his profound satisfaction, caught it in the maw of his mouth.

Haffner ignored him.

It turned out, however, that in the eyes of the British war cabinet the crazies were Haffner's people. All members of the Jewish faith, commissioned or uncommisioned, were to leave the battalion in Palestine and travel to Cairo in the next forty-eight hours. This was the order. And yes, Haffner would concede, if discussing the matter with a benign historian, at that time the Jewish underground was conducting tactics not dissimilar to those of the IRA – but the order utterly devastated him. He had been with his battalion for nearly five years and fought through the Battle of Anzio, the only battle – he would remind this now less benign historian – in the World War which, like the Great War, had been fought in the trenches, and here he was to be kicked out because of his faith. He wouldn't stand for it. His faith, not his race. This was the important distinction. Even if Haffner still had a faith at all, which was doubtful.

Haffner was the senior Jewish member of the battalion, so he called all ranks together: about thirty of them. All felt as Haffner did, with one exception. Whose name now eluded him. Haffner went to see the CO, who took him that evening to see the divisional commander in his HQ at Mount Carmel overlooking Haifa. He was a Canadian, who afterwards became Vice Chief of the Imperial General Staff.

At this point in the story, Haffner would put on an accent which he assumed was Canadian (it was not).

—Well, Haffner, I'm a Canadian, and if I were asked to fire on my boys in Montreal, I'd refuse.

—But, Haffner replied, in his own voice, I do not regard the Jews here as my boys. I'm an Englishman and my faith is Jewish.

Benji continued to scan the empty restaurant for a waiter to bring the beef: crispy, shredded. Or the approximation to crispy shredded beef which Benjamin had hoped to see in the fried ripped beef offered to him by the menu's translation: in haphazard italics, and assorted brackets.

—It's a good story, said Benjamin.

—The divisional commander, said Haffner.

—You should do the clubs, said Benji, grinning. I'm amazed you haven't.

The divisional commander, said Haffner, gave him permission to go and see the C.-in-C., Middle East Forces, in Cairo. So Haffner went with his driver, Private Holmes. They travelled 600 miles in twenty-four hours. Across the only little metal road in the desert to Cairo. Put up in a hotel to wait the pleasure. Etc. His driver had sunstroke and went into hospital. But the C.-in-C. had been sent to deal with the Communist threat in Greece. So Haffner was seen by his deputy, who sympathised, but there was nothing he could do. It was a cabinet decision.

A cabinet decision, emphasised Haffner. This was in about November 1945. In June, the war in Europe had come to an end. It was now three years since he had last seen his wife, just after their wedding. For the early married life of Haffner and Livia was an absence: a hiatus. And here he was being questioned about his Jewish loyalty: his Eastern heritage.

—No really, like Lenny Bruce, said Benjamin.

Haffner's East!

Looking back on Haffner, he was so clear to himself – it was like he was made of the most transparent glass. He had always wanted to mean something: to reach the grandeur of the world-historical. Like all the characters in the grand novels: the American novels which Esther used to give as Christmas presents to Haffner, to further his education. But the problem wasn't Haffner, he was discovering: the problem was the world-historical. Not even the world-historical was world-historical. The instances of everything, Haffner thought, had turned out to be so much smaller than one expected. The magnificence was so much more minute than one expected.

He had gone to school with the man who later married the Prime Minister. He remembered her, from the days watching her son play cricket. Once, in the 1970s, before she became the party leader, he danced with her at a dinner at the Criterion. She was really very brilliant.

Haffner emptied his glass of its pale beer. He felt a little blurred, a little faded – a faded Haffner which dissolved even further as the tape in the restaurant came round to one of his favourite songs, in one of his favourite incarnations.

—You know this song? cried Haffner.

—No, said Benjamin.

—Then listen! said Haffner.

4

And Haffner floated away: forwards, into the past.

For when they began the beguine – according to Cole Porter, as sung by Ella Fitzgerald, as listened to by Haffner as he tried to educate his grandson – the sound of that beguine brought back the sound of music so tender; it brought back the night of tropical splendour; it brought back a memory evergreen. And then Ella's voice went higher. She was with him once more under the stars, and down by the shore an orchestra was playing, and even the palms seemed to be swaying when they began the beguine.

He had heard this song with Livia, sung by Ella, in Ronnie Scott's on Frith Street: and the shadow of the double bass's scroll on the white backing screen was a seahorse behind the Lady. She was in a gold lamé dress.

But you couldn't go back. This was the meaning of the song. But precisely because one couldn't go back, thought Haffner, was why one wanted to go back. Precisely because one had lost everything.

Yes, weakened, exhausted, melancholy, Haffner was beginning to revise his ideas of sin. It was so hard, he was finding, not to regret certain aspects of one's life, now that one considered one's life carefully.

And so the reason why Haffner so loved this song now, here in a Chinese and Slavic restaurant, was that it allowed you the romance of resurrection, of recuperation. It allowed you the dream.

For, against all expectation, the rhythm moved into a different beat; so that, as Ella's voice rose, she changed her rhythm against the beat – as she begged them not to begin the beguine; as she begged the orchestra to let the love which was once a fire remain an ember. And then again, in a contradiction which Haffner had always cherished (—Listen to this! he cried to Benji! Listen to this!), Ella with as much sad abandon contradicted herself, with the same push against the beat, the same refusal to give in to the obvious rhythm: that yes, let them begin the beguine, make them play till the stars that were there before return above them, till whoever it was who she loved might whisper to her once more, darling, that he loved her – and the song softened. And they would suddenly know, as she quietened down, what heaven they were in – she quietened to a becalmed softness – when they began the beguine.

5

—Yeah, it's cool, said Benjamin.

Haffner didn't know what to say. He was lost, in contemplation of his past.

Finally, Haffner spoke.

—You finished? he asked Benjamin. You full?

—I don't finish when I feel full, said Benjamin proudly. What kind of person finishes when they're full? Me, I finish when I hate myself. That's the treasured moment.

And as Benjamin said this, more dishes arrived: chicken in a black bean sauce; chicken with lemon. Then finally another porcelain plate, chased with fake Chinese scenes: on which cubes of beef were shivering. Then two more decanters of beer.

In a reverent silence, Benji's mind considered Haffner's ideas of loyalty. Oh Benji wanted so much to lose his loyalty! He wanted so much to leave his religion behind. He imagined himself in the backstreets of Paris, the docks of Marseilles, and it entranced him. But he found this subject difficult. The guilt distressed him. So, in defence against himself, Benji tried to talk himself out of his new temptations.

—I don't get this, said Benji.

—You don't get what? asked Haffner.

—I don't see why it's more cosmopolitan to be anti-Zionist, said Benji. It just means you feel more nationalist about Britain.

—Don't be clever, said Haffner.

Gluttonous, still perplexed by Haffner's ideas of loyalty, Benji continued to reach for the black bean chicken with his chopsticks: trembling in the air, like dowsers. Haffner continued too. On one thing were Haffner and Benjamin agreed: the absolute superiority of MSG – that glorious chemical. They adored its sweet and savoury slather – and there it was, unctuous, before them.

Through the prism of his newly sexual nature, Benjamin considered the problem of fidelity. Perhaps, he thought, there was something in what Haffner said. Maybe it was true that it was better to refuse one's own nation. And I think that I should repeat that Benji had inherited from Haffner the love of romance. So he liked the grander, political structure which Haffner's theory offered him when he considered his current predicament, more than the crudely sexual structure in which it was housed at the moment. It was nothing to do with the girl! Nothing to do with the smell of her, which Benji had caressed with his nostrils all the next day, and night, refusing to wash. Nothing to do with the wet warmth of her mouth on his penis. All of Benji's urges, he thought, were simply desires to be free. They were all about his new refusal to be faithful to irrelevant ideals.

It did seem possible.

—So then, said Haffner. Time to go.

—You can't, said Benjamin.

—I am, said Haffner. I'm meeting this man, and I'm meeting him now.

Had Benjamin, wondered Haffner, any better ideas? No, thought Benjamin. He didn't. He only knew that he had barely begun the conversation he wanted to have. He had barely begun at all.

If he wanted, said Haffner, if he was really worried, then Benjamin could call him. Haffner promised to keep his phone on. And then Haffner, replete with a final spring roll, having laid down his chopsticks on their concertina of wrapper, and given Benjamin a selection of banknotes to pay for the meal – a meal in which

Benjamin settled to the last dishes, as if to the last supper – ventured back out into the fading day.

And as he walked, he hummed. In the tropical night, the beguine washed over him.

Raphael Haffner was drunk.

Haffner Drunk

1

In the driveway of the hotel, Niko was in his car – now wearing a pair of outlandish tinted glasses – waiting for Haffner.

The sky was fading, elaborating its golden cloths. And all its other traditional effects.

—Yes we have it, he said. I have found your man.

Haffner peered into the car. There was a plastic bag full of Coke cans in the footwell behind the driver's seat. A packet of cigarettes was protruding from the open glove compartment. The radio, to Haffner's antiquarian delight, was only a radio – without even the empty slit for a cassette.

Niko's jacket had the word *death* stitched gothically at the back of its collar. He took it off, and threw it on to the back seat – so revealing a T-shirt which said *Godless Motherfucker*.

This was the company Haffner now kept. He decided that he rather liked it.

—You saw my girl, yes? said Niko chirpily, bending to slurp at the keyhole of a newly opened can of Coke.

—Yes, said Haffner, deciding that it would be best if he stopped the sentence there.

—Uhhuh, uhhuh, said Niko.

To this, Haffner maintained his politic silence.

—You like potato chips? said Niko: trying to begin a conversation as they drove off.

Niko, the athlete, was always snacking. He offered Haffner an angled tube.

—No, said Haffner: feeling drunk, and sick.

Their destination was a billiards and pool hall – on the opposite edge of the town to Benjamin's utopian Chinese restaurant, in an industrial complex – on the second floor of what appeared to have been intended as an office block. On the ground floor were a hairdresser supply shop – whose windows were hung with posters displaying the moustaches and side-partings of another era – and a shop selling carpet to the outfitters of mid-range business premises. Each window of the billiards hall was blacked out.

Their contact was already there. To Haffner's disturbed surprise, he discovered that he recognised this contact.

—I'm sorry, he said to Niko. I don't think I got his name.

—Viko, said Niko, pointing to his misprinted double.

—Ah yes, of course, said Haffner.

And Haffner gazed over at his masseur.

Haffner wondered if this would be awkward. All that was needed, he concluded, if the man could indeed do what he said he could do, was a brisk, businesslike demeanour.

He looked around: at the wall lamps, visored by green eyeshades; at a bar of chocolate on a table, its foil wrapper partially unwrapped, exposing its ridged segments – like a terrapin, or grenade.

He had hoped for something more; he had hoped for a man in a suit, with a briefcase and moustache. He had certainly hoped for a stranger. A powerful, authoritative stranger. If Haffner had ever had to imagine how this kind of business might be done, difficult as it may have been, he would have been able to be precise about the clothes. It most certainly would not have featured this man's obvious pleasure in contemporary sportswear.

As if, conceded Haffner, Haffner could talk: this man without a wardrobe.

2

Viko was a drifter; a man of travels. His career had taken him along the fabled European coasts: from Juan-les-Pins to San Remo, from Dubrovnik to Biarritz. His trade was that of the hotelier. Wherever he went, he found work in the spas of luxury retreats, the reception desks of grand hotels. In this trade, he had grown sleek. He had also become expert in the wiles of the world. Not for Viko, the moral life. He preferred corruption, blackmail: the free flow of information.

He kept himself to himself, this was how Viko put it. It was not quite how his colleagues put it. They knew him as rather more sinister: a fixer; a man who was protected, and who could, in his turn, offer protection to others. His ethics were those of the favour. He dispensed largesse. In return, he received the loyalty of chambermaids, office assistants, waiters, car-wash attendants. Often no one knew where Viko was: his movements were uncertain. His apartment was always blandly comfortable: on the walls, posters of Renaissance gods, and cubist still lives.

Yes, out of his uniform – out of the shorts and cotton sports shirt, the tennis shoes – Viko was transformed. No longer the man who pampered the pampered rich. Now, he was in power.

Viko walked up to Haffner and Niko, nodded, then walked past them to the bar. But the barman was not there. He was taking the garbage out. Viko waited. He turned from the bar and reapproached them.

—How are you, my friend? said Viko to Niko. You are like Elton John, no?

Viko was wearing a T-shirt which did not conceal the fact that his forearms and upper arms were plaited with muscle, like cholla bread. He put imaginary binoculars to his face. He grinned, behind his binoculars, scanning the limited horizon.

—In those glasses.

Niko smiled. He looked at Haffner. Haffner smiled at Viko, nervously.

The label of Viko's shirt, which lolled over the collar, was still pierced by its plastic hammerhead tag.

The billiards and pool hall in which they found themselves was reminiscent of an idealised gentlemen's club, from the nineteenth-century colonies. It was a vision of the past, where the players – dressed in waistcoats and bow ties – were meant to tend, like waiters, to the table. Portraits of forgotten stars, like imaginary aristocrats, were hung beneath lamps which bequeathed luminous rectangles to the aristocrats' foreheads, as if they were sweating. Each photograph was scribbled with an illegible imitation of a signature: as if the sign for a signature was its very illegibility.

Niko said that he would just go into the bathroom. Viko said he would be with them in one minute. First he had this little matter – they understood? He gestured over to a table, where an argument was taking place. They understood. So Viko wandered back over to the tables and took up his position, a little way off, on a bar stool; while Haffner waited on a banquette for Niko to return.

Haffner listened to the argument: like every argument, its intonations were universal.

He did not know the precise details: he did not know that a man was telling his teenage son that he was not showing any respect to Viko.

—When you were my age, he said. When you. When I was.

There was a pause.

—You're me, right, said the man.

On his bar stool, Viko lit a cigarette: aloof from the argument, in his ivory tower.

He was forty-two, said the anonymous father, and he had never said fuck in front of his mother. Never. Look, he loved him more than his bird loved him. He respected him. And he didn't need to go round saying things which weren't respectful. If he didn't show any respect.

—Him, if he wants to, said the man, pointing at Viko, he can have anyone killed.

And how was Haffner also to know, as he listened to this incomprehensible argument, that Niko was, at that moment, bending as if in solicitude over the tank of a toilet, inhaling a gram of cocaine which he had first neatly heaped in a thin straggling line? It wasn't Haffner's normal world. As he looked around, sipping the first of the vodkas which the barman brought him, he was simply trying to understand why there seemed to be such a lack of urgency; such a lack of businesslike flair. He wanted to be done with this. The urgent need to do what he had to do and secure this villa for Livia still possessed him, even in his drunken state. He wanted to be true to a domestic idyll. He wanted to be successful and in bed. But Haffner, in his finale, was fated so rarely to be in bed when he wanted, with whom he wanted.

He felt for the phone, bulging in his tracksuit top.

Niko propped himself on the patch of yellow foam under the ripped velour of the banquette, on which Haffner's hand had been resting.

—You want to play? said Niko. You like billiards? Why not? If we played a little game, for a bet?

—Really? said Haffner.

—Why not? said Niko. Why not?

Haffner was drunk. And he was good at billiards. After all, he had been Joe Davis's banker. Haffner, as the legend had often said, was a natural.

3

Along the walls of the billiards and snooker hall, a range of cues was propped – like an armoury. Haffner prised one out from its tight little omega, and rolled it on the empty and unlit surface of a dark unoccupied table. It drifted in an unprofessional curve. Haffner prised out another. The black butt of this cue was slightly sticky. He rolled this one also – noting its warp, its bias and slide.

He walked back to his table; asked if Niko wanted to break. Niko rested his cue, upright, against the table.

—You break, he said.

Haffner settled over the table, fervently. He jabbed the white, but somehow swerved his arm so the tip of the cue slid and tapped the white on top, then bounced beside it on the thin green baize.

—That's not a good shot no, said Niko.

—No, said Haffner.

—Listen, said Niko. You must keep your arm straight – no, yes, out, yes, better. Now try.

—But it's your turn, said Haffner.

—No no, said Niko. You go, you go.

Haffner recovered his form with an in-off red. He played gracefully, impressively. He relaxed into his talent. Intently – doing this for Livia, thinking of Livia, the tenderness he felt for the rashes she had been prone to, her skin weeping like honeycomb – he did not look at Niko during a series of fourteen in-offs. And then he missed.

—Come into my office, said Viko: he was standing beside their table, his arms wide, smiling.

Neatly, he sat down on a bench.

—So sorry, said Viko, nodding over in apology to the now becalmed and darkened table. A drink? he added.

A deal among men: this, at least, was a world which Haffner could understand. On his bench, as in the most masculine of steak houses, Haffner leaned forward, in the way that he had always done: the clasp of his palms dropped against his lap.

A genie, Niko returned with three bottles of beer – the flare of his nostrils, inside, was a glowing coral. He picked up his cue, scratched the turquoise block of chalk, with its shallow indentation, across its tip. He puffed the puff of chalk away. Then settled to his work.

And Viko outlined the situation. Haffner wanted the villa. The Committee was proving difficult. Haffner was interested in speeding the process up. This, so far, was what Viko understood. Haffner praised his grasp of the situation. And Viko, continued Viko: he was known as a man of honour. He liked to help his friends. And Haffner was a friend?

Haffner was a friend.

He thought he was, said Viko. So. Viko had done his research; he had asked various questions: he had made Haffner's situation known.

This was very kind, said Haffner.

4

Niko had been playing a monotonous series of in-off reds. He lifted his head from the table. What, he asked, did Haffner want the upper limit to be? Haffner wondered if 100 would be appropriate. Niko played another long in-off red.

And Viko therefore thought that, with the document he was now offering to Haffner, Haffner would find it ever so much easier to bring the matter to a close. He unfolded a square of paper from his pocket, and laid it in front of Haffner. Haffner tried to read it. As he expected, it was not in a language he knew.

This was what? he queried. It was the necessary authentication from the authorities, said Viko. It was the proof that the family of his wife were the rightful owners of the property.

—The deeds? asked Haffner.

—Not quite, said Viko. But this was all he needed.

Haffner had never imagined the world of corruption to work with such elegance, such dispatch. If only he had understood this sooner, in his career, he thought. He might have saved himself so many hours of work.

From the bar, they could hear a miniature ice-hockey match, on a miniature television, being brought to its conclusion. Niko paused: he strained to watch.

—You prefer which games? asked Niko, still straining.

—The game of cricket, said Haffner.

—Yes, the English game, said Niko, relaxing back into the real world.

From his cueing position, Niko wondered if Haffner could explain the game of cricket. Haffner thought this was unlikely. But it was true: he liked the higher games. The higher English games. Like cricket, and croquet. The games with intricate rulebooks.

—Or soccer, of course, said Haffner, in an effort to lower himself to the universal level, looking at his incomprehensible document with lavish pride.

—This is my game, said Niko. The penalties! This I love. The lottery. The goalkeeper's fear.

But no, Haffner said, putting his folded document down beside his beer, careful to avoid the ornamental water features on the scratched and sticky shelf. Not at all. The goalkeeper was never afraid of the penalty, said Haffner. The goalkeeper was in love with the penalty.

—You kill me, said Niko.

Hear him out, said Haffner. Hear a man out. What the goalkeeper didn't want was the difficult cross, the perfectly weighted through-ball. These were the tests of skill and psychology: the undramatic moments.

—Possible, said Niko. Possible.

The real dilemma for the goalkeeper, continued Haffner, was whether or not to leave his area. That was the moral crux of goalkeeping – to know when to curb one's courage. But the penalty was pure theatre. The goalkeeper, finished Haffner, in a penalty, could never be defeated.

—Interesting, said Niko, still watching the television. You like Barthez?

—Barthez? said Haffner. A showman. Just a showman. Never rated him. Now Banks, however, now there was a goalkeeper.

—Who? said Viko, bored.

5

With Niko's next shot, the red ball quivered against the angled upper jaw of a centre pocket, and settled there, unpotted. The white dribbled towards it and, miraculously, stopped – on the lower jaw of the same centre pocket.

—It's amazing what can happen, said Niko, meditatively, on this twelve by six foot table. Then he smiled at Haffner, as if for appreciation.

There only remained, therefore, said Haffner, with decorum – trying to return the matter to his hoped-for conclusion – the matter of: and then he broke off, as he had always broken off before, when negotiating with clients. He understood?

Viko understood: he had consulted with Niko, he said. They were friends. Haffner nodded. They wanted to do this as friends. Haffner nodded again. They would therefore only charge him for the merest expenses. With a small extra compensation. For a third time Haffner solemnly nodded his assent, with gravitas. With gravitas, Viko named his price.

In this way these deals were done.

Haffner, in conclusion, nodded his agreement. In response, Viko stood to offer Haffner the manly theatrics of a less reserved hug.

Haffner looked at his phone, and considered calling Benji – to boast of his success.

—You want another drink? said Niko. Sure you do!

He decided that Benji could wait.

—So, said Niko.

They walked back to the bar, and sat down on the ripped banquette. There was also, he added, the question of his money too. Haffner looked at him, sad that matters should have turned so predictably filmic: with all the usual minor sins. He thought that had been taken care of, mentioned Haffner.

—For the bet? said Niko.

Had that been a real bet? asked Haffner. He had no idea that Niko had been serious.

Niko looked at the old man in front of him, and placed a paternal hand on Haffner's boyish shoulder. Could Niko talk about Haffner? Would he permit this? Haffner said he could. Sometimes, Niko worried, Haffner didn't seem to take things seriously which he should have taken seriously. Like, he pointed out, how Haffner had behaved in the club the night before. Whereas Niko, now Niko took things seriously. But then, Niko had been in a war. In fact, Niko had fought in two wars. Against the Muslims. And let him maybe tell this story. Once, Niko was on the border, in the mountains. They were laying an ambush. It was very cold in the mountains. And Niko's friend, he had been to America. In America, he had bought a special suit, with wiring inside. It was like an electric blanket? But there was no internal power supply to this suit. There was no battery. So they were at the front, in the mountains. And his friend did not bring so many of his clothes. Instead, he brought his suit, and also a car battery. So. They got to their position. He put his suit on, and then he wired it up to the battery.

—And what happened? asked Haffner.

He fell asleep, said Niko. It was freezing, all the enemy was there, close to them, and he fell asleep. He was snoring. And this, said Niko, was Haffner. The man asleep.

—I fought in two wars, said Niko. And I fired shots in anger, I can tell you.

6

In the difficult silence which followed Niko's portrait of Haffner, Viko proposed that they should go somewhere else to celebrate.

241

There was a place near here, agreed Niko: with such girls! Then he paused. He began to smile. In his lightness of spirit, Haffner said he would also, of course, pay for the drinks. First, however, Haffner downed a final vodka. He placed the glass back on the brittle bar towel. Then he drank another final vodka. His heart accelerated. And Haffner, searching for coins in his wallet, which emerged, scissored between two figures, leaned into the sense of flight – as into the exhilaration of a speeding curve.

He knew what Niko meant. The problem had always been to distinguish whether one was wasting one's life or truly living it. This was the conundrum inherited from Solomon, his father. But the anguish of Haffner's life had therefore been in identifying which was which: the two so often hid within each other.

Libertine man! This was all Haffner had ever wanted to be. Yet now, he was beginning to think, it had always been a mirage. Although it might have looked like waste – his life in the quiet suburbs – although it had so often seemed a waste to Haffner, in fact that life was everything. Renouncing a woman, after all, can be a form of heroism; this is famous. And winning her may be a form of discipline.

The war was everywhere.

And Haffner, thought Haffner, had finally proved equal to this war – as he contemplated his finale up here in the mountains, with Zinka in the foreground, Frau Tummel in the background, and Benjamin a shadow in the distance. This piece of paper in his pocket, thought Haffner, constituted an undeniable achievement. So Haffner rejected Niko's accusation. Haffner was exultant!

In recovering Livia's villa, Haffner saw his reconciliation.

A chorus of trumpeting putti, Viko and Niko and Haffner raised their ultimate vodkas, downed the glasses on the wet surface of the bar counter, then on they went, happy, to the next whisky bar.

Haffner had always liked the imaginary travel books: the voyages to the centre of the earth, the voyages under the sea. There were the Sciapods, one-footed, but whose one tremendous foot served as a sunshade in the desert; or the Cynocephali, with the heads of dogs and a language which resembled barking. His favourite, given to him by Livia as a Christmas present, was an illustrated edition of the adventures of Cyrano de Bergerac – the comical man with the grandiose nose, who imagined a trip to the moon. But all these mythical journeys could only lead their heroes home. And Haffner was moved to realise that this was also true of him – even now, when Livia was dead. The marriage was endless.

—It kind of baffles me, sometimes, how you sleep at night, Pfeffer once said, as they sat in the Overseas Bankers' Club in Lothbury: amazed how Haffner could lie beside the wronged form of Livia.

Haffner dropped a chunk of sugar into his coffee, observing the brief spawn of bubbles on the black surface.

With Pfeffer, the family man, when trying to defend his sexual record, Haffner had then developed a theory of the wife and the mistress. Really, said Haffner, people didn't understand: the wife was safe. The really vulnerable were the other women. Pfeffer queried this. Haffner was always good, he observed, at misplacing his tenderness. His sense of what was important and what was not had never been a thing of moral beauty.

Haffner's argument had never convinced Haffner, let alone Pfeffer. Now, however, Haffner was beginning to wonder if he had been right all along. He couldn't remember the other women. They meant nothing to him. It was sad to admit this, but it was true. Whatever Barbra was doing now, Haffner didn't care. Whereas Livia was different. Livia was everything.

And me, I might add something else.

It is still the same Promised Land, it is still the same story, whether we talk of Moses and his Promised Land, or Odysseus and his Ithaca; or Haffner and this villa in the centre of Europe. And in a version of the story of Odysseus, which I once read, when Odysseus finally arrived safely home in Ithaca, he found himself utterly disappointed. And yet, wrote the author, whose name I have forgotten, what did he want of Ithaca? What else did it really offer him, if not precisely that journey home?

Just as Haffner stepped out into the midsummer night – the longest night of the year, the longest night of Haffner's life – but did not see before him the deserted nocturnal retail village, but instead entered the noblest park, and stood there observing a spreading oak tree, under which a long-lost version of Haffner sat with his beloved wife. Around them, deer munched. They were in Gloucestershire, or Warwickshire: ensconced in England. A fox was a red blur in the dark of a blackberry bush. And this lost but momentarily recovered Haffner lay watching the yellow-green where the sun lit the leaves; the black-green where it didn't.

Haffner Defeated

1

The club which Haffner was speeding towards in Niko's car was located down a side street, pretending to be a milk bar. So went its name. It opened on to the street via a metal door. When this door was opened, the clubber walked down some steps to a checkpoint where a girl waited behind a table, branding you with an ink stamp, before letting you turn left, down a further flight of stairs, further underground, into the club itself.

In the first room, there was the bar, and a selection of chairs. In the second, there was a room where two girls were DJing. On the wall was projected a selection of childhood images: though from whose childhood, no one knew. In the final room, the kids were dancing; when the DJs finished, a live set began. Tonight, it was an electro band from Hungary who were pretending they were from New York: singing their lyrics in a filmic version of American. They screamed at their appreciative crowd, drinking vodka and Coke from plastic cups; drinking beer from bottles; drinking shots of absinthe from a cache of plastic espresso cups stolen from a hospital canteen.

Into this underground came Haffner: the back of his hand – freckled, brown-spotted – now stamped with an extra red stain, so prompting Haffner to the thought of all the major crimes he could have committed, but had not. Yes, Haffner descended into the night, as he contrived to answer his phone, into which he shouted to Benji that yes everything had gone smoothly, that yes it was very loud, he was in a club, called Milk Bar, or maybe it was a milk bar, he had no idea: and then he lost reception; and the collar on his shirt seeped with sweat, and his lungs filled with the smoke of 250 cigarettes, lit from each other by the manic youth of Europe.

It was *inferno*. But to Haffner, triumphantly still reminding himself that Livia's villa was soon to be his, it seemed a blessed *paradiso*.

2

Inside, alone for a moment in the middle room, Haffner looked around. Behind Haffner, a boy was cycling along a mountain path. His path wobbled with the trembling grip of the super-8 camera which was working so hard to preserve his balance for eternity. A girl who was more real, in sunglasses and a bracelet made of pink plastic paperclips, was watching this film, intently, while shifting her feet to the beat from the DJs behind her. The boy continued pedalling, now observed by an ecstatic parent in mint-green sunglasses, encouraged by the severed hand of the camera operator.

Was this what the kids were up to? wondered Haffner. Their mania for nostalgia took them this far? This farrago of the senti-mental. The kids observing the kids. Whereas all Haffner had wanted, as a boy, was the adult. He had wanted to wear a tie, to wear a suit. The two girls DJing were drinking from the same pink straw in the same glass of Coke. Although Haffner rightly doubted if it contained only Coke.

In this setting, his tracksuit, he thought, was more appropriate than he had imagined. Around him there seemed to be no dress code, no fashion which Haffner could recognise. The laws were gone.

So much posturing at the infantile! But now that he was old, Haffner rather applauded this resistance to the adult: the spirit of the flippant. The bare midriffs; the obvious bra straps; the visible panties. Everything in fluorescent colours. He warmed to this; as he warmed to everything which seemed unimpressed with the adult world. The nostalgia, perhaps not. But the infantile, this the older, less mature Haffner could admire.

Viko was offering to buy Haffner a drink. Haffner looked round. He suddenly realised that Niko was gone. With a depressed shrug, Haffner assented. He watched Viko lean against the bar, a man at ease. And Haffner tried to understand what was meant to happen next. He had hoped to avoid this, the time alone with his masseur. Their business relationship had been maintained with surprising ease, thought Haffner. This still did not resolve the question of where they stood more privately: what conclusion had been drawn after Haffner's curtailed massage. The problem was how seriously Viko thought that Haffner had taken it. Preferably, their relationship would have ended in the fog of its ambiguity – stranded, on a mountain top, with the night coming on, and only the cowbells for company.

Viko returned with the drinks. They chinked glasses, plasticly. Then Viko moved closer to him.

Viko, of course, didn't want Haffner. He only thought that Haffner wanted him. If there were more ways to make money from Haffner, then Viko was happy to explore those ways. He was a man of mode. The older men went for the younger men: this was the story of Viko's life. They offered you money to let them touch you; or watch you. So went the ways of the Riviera.

Haffner placed a palm on Viko's chest, girlishly: in a cute gesture of rebuff. Viko looked at it. He removed Haffner's palm, and held it tight.

He was drunk, Haffner. He was gone. He was there, at the crest of his ascent – in the glory of his absolute inspiration: just before it transformed itself, as if nothing had happened, into the absolute descent.

3

The descent of the grandfather, however, was being deftly matched by the ascent of the grandson. Even if, at the moment, this ballet was suffering from problems with timing. Oblivious to his future ascent, Benjamin was depressed. He was standing at a corner of the bar: trying to lean forward enough so that the deep folds of his T-shirt could hang down in a perpendicular line. For Benji's body in these clubs became a pastoral: the hillocks of his breasts, the trilling streamlets of sweat which ran between them.

This was not the kind of club in which Benjamin had ever felt happy. His grandfather's phone call, however, had disturbed him. So here he was, in his excited fear, and he felt alarmed. Packed as the club was with assured and sexual girls, it presented multiple temptations to Benji's soul. The temptation of lust, naturally, but also the darker temptations: of self-pity, and self-disgust.

His reaction to this state, before his Orthodox training, used to be a prolonged session at the bar, followed by a session of manic dancing. And it was to this practice, haunted by his recent erotic memories, worried for the safety of his grandfather, that Benjamin, against his moral code, returned.

His yarmulke was now stuffed, shyly, in the pocket of his jeans.

How many of his beliefs, considered Benji sadly, were really just romances? It seemed so very likely that his moral code was a romance too. It was all too possible. Benji wanted to be there in the Jewish East End: with Fatty the Yid, the fixer, handing out betting slips in Bethnal Green. Could he have told you why? Wasn't it obvious? These people had cool. On one street there would be Jewish Friendly

Societies, for Benjamin's relatives, newly emerged from Lithuania; and a house which concealed a miniature synagogue, whose ceiling would be azure with gold stars, and below which, on the walls, would be engraved in gilt the names of its benefactors – the Rothschilds, the Goldsmids, the Mocattas, the Montagues. Had Benjamin not been born too late, what a member he would have made of the Bilu Group, of Hovevei Zion! A group which he had once admired for the sarcastic praise they had bestowed on their nation for having woken from the false dream of Assimilation. *Now, thank God, thou art awakened from thy slothful slumber. The pogroms have awakened thee from thy slothful slumber.* No, thought Benjamin, this was the melancholy truth. In his identification with the marginalised, the bereft, he had been wowed by the romance of belonging to an elite. Because the persecuted could be an elite, of this he had no doubt.

Inside him lay Benjamin's grand emotions: envy, anxiety, self-hatred, self-contradiction. There they were, in their plush velvet case – snug, like a cherished heirloom; a polished silver piccolo.

They seemed unnecessary now.

Beside him, sitting on the plastic pod of a stool, a girl began to talk to him. She didn't want to talk to him about the state of his soul, nor the state of world politics: the endless problems of minority peoples. She only wanted to ask him what his plans were that evening, what his girlfriend's name was. Benji sadly admitted that he had none: no plans, no girlfriend. She offered him a cigarette. Her name was Anastasia, she said. And when somehow Benjamin inveigled into the conversation a mention of his Jewish origins, she looked at him. There was a pause. This was it, he thought: the moment when everything became obvious.

—Uhhuh, she said. So anyway.

He looked at Anastasia. She was the tallest girl he had ever met; and although he could not help remembering the distracting features of the girl to whom he had lost his virginity, he also could not help feeling that in Anastasia he had discovered something so much more refined. She was wearing a black shift dress, black tights: and red high heels. Her hair was cut in some sort of slick bob. There was a plastic butterfly visible on her left, diminutive breast.

—You are American? asked Anastasia.

—British, said Benjamin.

—Is better, said Anastasia.

And at that moment, as she shifted her weight, so accidentally placing her thigh in warm proximity to Benjamin's podgy hand, Benjamin finally noticed Haffner, talking to a man. He stalled in a trance of indecision. And although this was why he was here – to protect his wayward grandfather – Benjamin did nothing. He did not excuse himself and go to offer Haffner his protection. He simply looked into Anastasia's eyes, smiled, lit a cigarette which she had offered him, and desperately, feeling sick, hoping that he would not regret this, tried to take up smoking.

4

The smoke here was mythical. It was its own clouding exaggeration – not just in the usual secret places: one's nostrils, the creases of clothes. Here, it hurt the cornea, the tonsils, the ganglia of one's lungs.

Politely, Haffner wondered if Viko could perhaps put out his cigarette. It was terribly hurting his eyes. In fact, he said, he really did feel very tired. He really thought that he might sadly have to excuse himself and end his evening here.

But Viko, by now, was dictatorial in his drunkenness: a Tamerlane. Barbaric, he looked at his cigarette, and looked at Haffner, vanquished. He could not believe it, he said. It was a cigarette. And now this man in front of him wanted it to be put out. For why? It wasn't, he pointed out, as if he was the only person smoking.

And he gave out a staccato mirthless laugh – a studio audience of one.

Uneasily, Haffner looked around, into the crowd: the extraordinary overspill of beauty in this basement amazed him with its grace. It contrasted with Haffner. It contrasted less with Viko. He looked back at him.

Viko continued to stare – the cigarette hanging limply from his lower lip.

There was nothing else for it, thought Haffner. Any conversation which might restore some poise, some grace, seemed impossible to him now. And he had done what he needed to do. So he was leaving, said Haffner. He was very grateful, but now he really must go.

And Haffner turned – to discover Niko, bearing Zinka as a trophy. Gently, with distracted distance, she bestowed her smile on Viko, and then Haffner. And Haffner stood there, confident that if Zinka stayed here for ever, then so would he. With a gesture of European politesse, Haffner kissed the raised paw of Zinka's hand. He stood there, happily smiling.

And suddenly, Viko understood.

Viko believed in desire being rewarded. He believed in the myth of the kept man. No shame attached to money. The sudden way in which Haffner had left the massage table, having solicited Viko's attention, had not been forgotten. It irked him. Especially because he had heard the rumours of Haffner's friendship with Zinka. Why should Viko be spurned? It was the more galling for being the more unjust. This, after all, was the man whose property claims would be made easier by Viko: from Haffner, Viko had expected money in instalments, he had expected cash.

In this sad way, Viko talked to himself. His monologue took place before an unseeing audience of Zinka and Haffner.

Haffner was telling Zinka the story of his nightlife: how he had known the former Prime Minister of his country, and in a bar in

London he had danced with her and talked of world finance. And although the details of this conversation were inaudible to Viko, his rage was inventive enough to inflame itself just with its visionary gifts: observing Haffner's charmingly enfeebled touch on her arm, Zinka's dimpling smile.

It was incredible, said Viko. No one heard him. He said it again. It was utterly incredible. And he began to shout, in the language which Haffner did not understand. Spurned, Viko listed the million vices of Haffner. Ignoring Zinka's calming protestations, her anxious glances, Niko's confused scowl, he listed Haffner's lechery, his financial manoeuvres, his cowardice.

Haffner mildy asked what was happening. He seemed upset, observed Haffner. Zinka silenced him with an irritated flourish of her arm.

—You, said Viko, anxious to explain, jabbing at Haffner and Zinka and Niko in confused identification. You fuck her. His girl.

Haffner, full of justified smugness, tried to explain that this was not true, not at all. He really had to say that this was quite ridiculous. Viko refused his explanations. Everyone knew, he said. So Niko might as well know too. He glared at Zinka. Zinka lit a cigarette, and exhaled a plume of smoke in Viko's face, like the most classical of zephyrs.

The character of Niko was often inscrutable: so said his teachers, his mother; so said Zinka, the girl who tried to love him. It was difficult to predict. This difficulty was made more difficult by the various heaps of cocaine which Niko had inhaled that evening, the various drinks he had imbibed.

At first, he seemed only amused. He didn't care if Haffner had been trying to get more of his Zinka. Who wouldn't? said loyal Niko.

No, said Viko, doggedly, he didn't seem to understand.

While Haffner, as he listened to what he understood to be another attack on the soul of Haffner, realised that his feelings were oddly divided. It was true that he didn't want any violence; he didn't want a display of machismo. But on the other hand, he would have preferred Niko to be more worried, more ill at ease. At least violence would have demonstrated some form of sexual contest. Whereas Niko did not seem aware of any sexual contest.

So Haffner's pride debated with itself.

5

And, in this way, the ballet of Haffner and Benjamin began to find its synchronisation. For Benjamin was also considering the nature of his sexual pride. But not, however, with sadness. In the bathroom of this club – located in what seemed to be a makeshift plastic tunnel attached to the basement, reached through an emergency door – Benjamin was delirious with success.

—When you say obscenities in another language, it's only ever funny, said Benji. You can't do it. I mean, how do you say fuck me in your language?

She told him. He tried to repeat it. She started to giggle.

—You see? said Benji. I mean, say fuck me, in English.

—Fuck me, said Anastasia.

There was a pause.

—Oh no, said Benji, softly. Well maybe no. Maybe we could continue like that.

With no shiver of distaste, her hands were stroking the softness of his breasts; they were clasping the rings of fat which circled Benji, like a planet, and still she kissed him with abandon.

—Was that a practice sentence, or a real sentence? said Benjamin.

—Maybe both, said Anastasia.

And after they had kissed, Benji smiled at her.

—I haven't seen you smile that smile tonight. It is good, she said.

—I have a greater variety than that, said Benji, winningly.

Oh Benjamin's allegiances were all awry: they were jostled, irretrievably. He thought of the girl in Tel Aviv. Perhaps, he thought, he was not in love. Perhaps she was just a beginning. He didn't want to be what others made of him. Surely that was cool. No longer did he want to be defined by his loyalty: not to a race, and not even to his family. He wanted, thought Benjamin, to be himself.

—I want you so much, said Benjamin.

A sentence said with such ardent and charming sincerity, so in excess of Benji's pudgy demeanour, that Anastasia, helplessly, began to adoringly laugh.

6

It wasn't that Anastasia was cruel. She had simply become, by accident, the audience to an ordinary kind of comedy.

Himself! Benji wanted to be himself. So he exaggerated. And this is not so unusual. Maybe this is all the self is, really: whatever is most fervently displayed. It isn't difficult, to find this kind of story. It was, for instance, a theme in Benji's family itself.

In 1940, Cesare was interviewed by the British police – trying to ascertain his loyalty to Mussolini. In his defence, Cesare had not only proved to them in minute detail how he was a Marxist, a member of the Mazzini Garibaldi club; he had not only quoted to them the words of Garibaldi himself, imploring his acolytes to have faith in the immortal cause of liberty and humanity, because the history of the Italian working classes was a history of virtue and national glory – no, this was not enough for Cesare. To clinch his point he had stood on a chair and sung the Internationale, improvising an English translation. After the third verse, with three still to come, the British police allowed that perhaps they had been wrong in their suspicions concerning Cesare.

And when Cesare recounted this story, which was often, Haffner would riposte with the story of Bleichröder, Bismarck's Jewish banker, a hero of finance. An allegory for Haffner. For Bleichröder never managed to become Prussian, rather than Jewish. He tried, but he failed. He went for walks, Haffner would begin. And then Livia and Cesare would continue – in a ritual which they did not know was a ritual, since no one ever remembered that the precise same conversation happened at regular intervals which were not regular enough to prevent this amnesic repetition. So Cesare would tell his story of Cesare. Haffner would begin the riposte of Bleichröder. And Livia would finish, reminding Cesare, in case he didn't remember, how Bleichröder kept himself apart from the Jewish people, even in his weekend walks. On the promenades along the Siegesallee he walked on the western side: eschewing the east, with its Jewish crowds. And when asked why he walked on the other side, according to the police, added Haffner – yes yes, Livia would say, she knew this line: when asked why, Bleichröder answered that the eastern side smelled too much of garlic.

Benjamin, as he kissed Anastasia, and felt for her slim breasts, in the furore of his passion, was forming the final panel in this luminous family triptych. If his God could see him, he did not care. The neon light in this plastic cubicle did not disturb him, nor the seven empty beer bottles lined up, as if posed for some pop-art portrait, on a ledge. And Benji revelled in the sensation that in kissing Anastasia, on this night which he understood marked no high point in Benji's romantic life, no moment of deep conversion, still mindful of the girl whom he felt in love with, in Tel Aviv, he had made it impossible to return to the ways he used to think. In kissing Anastasia he had crossed over – through the looking glass, out the back of the wardrobe.

7

Haffner, however, found nothing new in this world. As Viko had elaborated the lays of Haffner, Zinka had led him out of the club.

At the door, a group of girls were waiting for a taxi. He turned to Zinka, anxious to enquire quite if he really needed to leave.

No, there was nothing new for Haffner. He knew this place. It was suburbia. Like everywhere Haffner lived. The clapboard pavilion on an artificial lake, with a landscaped golf course arranged around it; the hotel with souvenirs kept in a glass cabinet in the foyer; homes which once belonged to writers now preserved as monuments, complete with shops which sold tea towels on which were stitched, in italics, quotes from these great writers; or which were instead knocked down and replaced by an apartment block which bore the great hero's name; or restaurants which advertised a return to the ethos of the nineteenth century, or advertised the cuisine of Italy, or China, even though they were staffed by white and disillusioned teenagers: all this was suburbia. And so was this youthful display he could now see outside the club, where girls in thin dresses gathered together to whisper and giggle while sporadic boys lit avoidant cigarettes, affecting to ignore them.

And so was the manifest violence.

In the dark street Haffner stopped with Zinka, anxious to prove that he was scared of nothing, a speech which he had barely begun when Niko emerged from the crowded steps and stood there, in the doorway.

Even at this point, Haffner refused to believe in violence: he refused to believe it was possible – for Haffner was surely invulnerable. He still refused to believe that his story could really be serious. So Haffner was surprised when Niko moved to where he stood with Zinka and then pushed him, in a way which Niko imagined was only gentle, a tender threat: an amused gesture of gentle reproach. It was all the violence Niko would ever offer this aged man. But, unprepared, an unbalanced Haffner swayed backwards and then, in his effort to overcompensate, swayed forwards.

And Haffner fell.

He lay there on the street, but still refused to be downcast, beneath the chemical sky, its wash of cloud – like the most perfunctory of watercolours in the window of a fine-arts dealer behind the British Museum, on a Sunday in November, when everything is closed. No, opined Haffner, bleeding, wasn't it Cole Porter who used to say that, as he lay beneath the horse which was crushing his legs to a pulp, he worked on the lyrics of 'At Long Last Love'? Surely Haffner too could discover a *sprezzatura*?

Above him, like warring and disporting gods, Zinka and Niko were shouting. He was impossible, she said. What, she asked him, was he thinking – to attack an old and defenceless man? While Niko was shouting back, arguing with the facts as he now saw them, that he had never meant to hurt him, of course he had never meant to hurt him. And, then again, who was she to put the blame on Niko? Perhaps she should hear what Viko had to say about this man now lying there beside them. But Viko, suddenly, had disappeared.

And Haffner remembered with a sensual pang how he had once woken on Viko's massage table, surrounded by the scents of candles, the cries of whales, the tenderness of towels, in what now seemed to be a forever lost vision of safety.

8

Defeated, bloodied, Haffner stumbled his way back inside, to find the bathroom. Against the basin, a girl was being roughly kissed, on her breast a man's splayed hand, a starfish: a hand which she was lightly coaxing away.

Into a stall stumbled Haffner.

Adjacent to Haffner, unknown, in another cubicle, Benjamin was gasping with abandon, as he touched the girl between the legs, his hand a little trapped by the elastic of her underwear. He was in a modern heaven. Through the bathroom's thin walls he could hear the music, throbbing. The DJs had been replaced by the Hungarian band, featuring a girl who sang her American English songs in the highest voice Benji had ever heard: as if the world were house music.

While Haffner, oblivious, the end of all the modern, observed his ancient face, illuminated by one fluorescent tube. Behind him was a bucket with an indefinable mop drenched inside it. He should have known, he thought: this was how things tended to end up – with Haffner as a clown. He dabbled with the taps: they relinquished little water.

He had always wanted to be a libertine, but now he was something else. Just Haffner Silenus – a sidekick, so prone to fall over, so vulnerable to capture, so easy to wound: the same Haffner as he had become when Livia announced, two years before she died, that she was leaving him.

—Now? he said.

It didn't seem worth the effort. But yes, she said: she was finished. She was leaving him to live with Goldfaden. It was long enough after his wife's death. It was what they had always wanted to do.

And Haffner had looked at her amazed. He couldn't understand it. It was always Haffner who was the one to leave. No one else. But there she was, announcing that she would be going to live with Goldfaden. And although Haffner pleaded on behalf of his love for her, his family, Livia was unmoved. It was what she wanted, she said. And just as now Haffner stared into a mirror, hyperbolically lit, so Haffner had gone into the downstairs bathroom – the toilet with its pink fringed bib at its base, a china cow-creamer whose back overflowed with pot-pourri – and stared at the clown before him. There he tried to be precise about what he was feeling; he tried to be composed. But he was only possessed by a gigantic feeling that he missed Livia, that he had perhaps been missing her for many years: and Haffner wanted her back. He wanted to recover things.

So he emerged, from the bathroom, ready to plead and beg – but found that Livia had gone.

Whereas this time he emerged, with wild wet hair, and discovered that, as in the puzzles of his youth – *Spot the difference, dear reader! Can you see it, kids?* – the picture had been doctored. Where Livia had been absent, there now stood Zinka, her arms folded, leaning against the bathroom's plastic walls. She unwrapped a wafer of chewing gum, and offered it to Haffner: its dusty granular surface.

She was taking him home, she said. She would spend tonight with him.

It seemed true, thought Haffner. She did not seem to be one of Haffner's visions. In the words of the very old song, the dream was real.

9

And yet, the dream life of Haffner was troubled.

It did seem all too possible that the brief moment of his triumph in relation to the villa was now over. The ordinary rules would soon reassert themselves. He doubted if the deal with Niko and Viko was still on. This seemed even less likely if he chose to allow Zinka to spend the night with him. Presumably, he could return to Viko and Niko and offer them the agreed sum. Presumably, he could try. But their goodwill might well be lacking.

Was Haffner to blame for this sudden fiasco? It seemed possible to plead that he was not – not responsible, in the end, for Niko's rages, for Viko's pride. He consulted the shade of Livia: would she really have wanted him to play the coquette with another man, simply to ensure her inheritance?

He could imagine the shade of Livia smiling.

Then Haffner was interrupted in this vision by a strong sense of nausea. A shiver took possession of his body, then relinquished it.

Yes, this, thought Haffner, was his return to the everyday. All his ingenuity had failed him. The Committee would have to be wooed all over again. So Haffner only felt a tired disappointment.

And yet, he thought, in compensation he seemed to have Zinka, in this party dress, beside him. But Haffner realised that even his joy in her was tempered. On arrival at this club he had felt so confident, so victorious. If he had been told he would leave with Zinka, it would have only made him a happy Haffner. Yet now here he was, still burdened with the problem of the villa, walking slowly through the dark streets of a spa town so marked with Livia's memory. And whether Zinka was a digression or in fact some covert route to Livia, Haffner did not know.

He still felt confident of his innocence. He had tried to remain faithful to Livia, and he would continue to try. But he was a connoisseur of Haffner's ability to be defeated. That Haffner had done his best, he was coming to realise, sadly, didn't mean he wasn't still guilty.

In this unaccustomed melancholy, Haffner followed after Zinka: his halting walk now embellished by the iambic rhythm of a limp.

But I am not so sure that Haffner should have felt so divided. Perhaps there is no such thing as a digression.

Zinka, it's true, was thinking in the same way as Haffner. She thought that it was an unusual event in Haffner's life – this dejected progress through the empty streets. She was moved by Haffner's comical plight. And it moved her more because she assumed that this comedy was all her fault. There was no way this man could have previously suffered the indignity from which he was suffering now. She didn't realise that in this story, as in all of Haffner's stories, there were certain patterns, certain repeats. She didn't know that farce was Haffner's constant mode.

This form was not new in the life of Raphael Haffner. Free from his ordinary customs, let loose in the wild East, Haffner was just allowed to become even more Haffnerian than ever – his own exaggeration.

So that every zenith was also a nadir, as usual, and all victory consisted of beatings. And, as usual, while illuminated with desire for Zinka, Haffner didn't know that a bruise was beginning to develop around his eye and on his cheek, like a Riviera sunset, the backdrop to a promenade bordered with palm trees, illuminating the night in green explosions, accompanied by the muzak of the rhyming cicadas.

Haffner Translated

1

So, said Zinka, as they entered Haffner's bedroom. Here they were.

It seemed undeniable. Here they were, at Haffner's finale. But Haffner was worried that his body was going to prove unequal to this finale. He was quite sure that he was getting ill. True, he was drunk. It could be just the drink. But Haffner knew about his body: its breakdowns and malfunctions. And this feeling was unusual: the dizzy sweating ague of it. He felt for his palms. They were sweating. He brushed the hair which still remained to him down with the Brylcreem of his sweating hand. As if to simultaneously produce a suavely dry palm and a suavely plumed forelock.

He offered Zinka a smile.

Tonight, Zinka explained to him, there was only one rule. Haffner asked what it was. The rule, said Zinka, was that everything came from her. Everything was her decision.

She liked Haffner, this was true, and she felt for his bruised pathos. But this did not mean that this was going to be Haffner's evening.

And Haffner said yes, absolutely.

He had never been one for the fantasies of permission: the allowed and the disallowed. But if rules were going to be a condition of this night with Zinka, then he didn't care. He revelled in them. He would content himself with the little which he was offered. Whatever the modern age would give him. At no point could Haffner touch himself, said Zinka; at no point could he touch her without permission. If at any time he broke these rules, the night was over.

Let Haffner submit! Let Haffner be debased!

All his life, the erotic for Haffner had been a matter of apertures: all the exits and entrances. And now he discovered that the apertures were something, but the rest was something else. There was so much else to play with.

Zinka pushed him gently to the bed, where he slumped down: his head raised, expectantly, like a yawning sea lion.

—You will do what I tell you, said Zinka. Yes?

—Yes, said Haffner, meekly.

Zinka stood between his legs, bent her head, and told him to open his mouth – which Haffner obediently did – then she let her spit dribble out: a thread slowly fastening with its own weight, then falling, gathered in by harmless Haffner.

2

Zinka went into the bathroom, crowded with the male accoutrements of Haffner, bought from a chemist in the town – a shaving brush, the tube of shaving cream, doubly creased in a sine curve which a parsimonious History had borrowed from the smudged blackboards of Haffner's prep school. With the door still open, she crouched on the toilet. She beckoned to Haffner. From below her crotch came the whispering sound of her pissing.

She told Haffner to come closer. He tried to sit down, like the men in Oriental street scenes exhibited at the Academy: a neat bobbing squat. It hurt too much. Instead, he therefore watched her on his hands and knees. Crawling, Haffner approached her closely. He could see her stream – braided, splurging.

—You like this? Zinka asked him.

—I do, yes, said Haffner.

As if there was nothing of the bodily about her, no smell emerged from Zinka. And Haffner, as he waited there, on all fours, only felt an overwhelming happiness. He was in the paradise of women; an island of intimacy, like Gulliver among the giants – whose travels Haffner had read when he was ever so young, so much younger than he would ever be again, in a miniature, octavo, red-leather edition. The eighteenth-century disgust remained with him now. It was there in his stomach, in his nervous system. But also the erotics. Gulliver astride a giant nurse's nipple! Even now, he felt himself rise up in applause. The rough pitted areolae which little Gulliver observed; by which Gulliver was entranced and perturbed. And when Gulliver – or did he? was this just a mistake of Haffner's imagination? – went on to describe the gaping maw of her crotch, Haffner, the delinquent eight-year-old, was not stricken by disgust at the human animal. Instead, he was overtaken by an acrid pleasure. The minuscule Haffner longed for this closeness to the women: the fur and softness. What was small was large, and what was large was small. The world was just a trick of perspective. It all depended, he supposed, on how good you were at magnifying, or diminishing.

Zinka came to an end. From his canine position, Haffner looked up at her, expectantly.

—Now you wipe, said Zinka.

Haffner tended to Zinka. He unrolled a small section of paper, then folded it into the most luxurious, downiest towel. He wanted to do the job with elegance: no one could ever accuse Haffner of not being a good sport.

—No. First with your mouth, she said. Your tongue.

It was for only a brief moment that Haffner paused in a qualm of indecision, before he bent his neck, uncomfortably, deliriously, and licked at Zinka's ferrous crotch. To his surprised disappointment, only a trace of her pale urine was detectable to Haffner's tongue: a sweetly sour herbaceous perfume.

—Now OK you stop, said Zinka.

Then he pushed the paper against her labia. He refolded. Pushed it again, a little harder. He dropped the paper between her legs, into the toilet bowl.

—So, said Zinka. We go through.

And Haffner followed her to the raised stage of his bed, where – earnest, dedicated – Zinka squatted over Haffner's face.

Zinka was hairless between the legs. Where the hair should have been, there was a brief tattoo: a mermaid easing herself against an invisible wave: sinuous, like Venus rising from her shell – a vision in dark green. And Haffner inhaled her.

Canine, Bacchic, Haffner thrived on the lower thrills: the women with their marine and sour aroma, the rotting rich smell of powdered roe, the ammonia rinds of cheeses. The spread of molecules in the still air was one of Haffner's most intense delights. They wafted and they drifted and they delighted him. He was undisgustable.

—You must not move, said Zinka. You move, I punish you.

Haffner wondered if this was serious. No one had ever said this to him before. Haffner had to admit that although he believed that Zinka possessed a charm he had never known in any other woman, it was true that he hardly knew her. He adored her, but she was unknown. He adored her because she was unknown. Unknown, and also young.

—Is this serious? asked Haffner, gaily.

In answer, Zinka pinched the twin wings of his nose together – their burst red cartilage poignant through the skin, like the surface of a butter bean – then pushed herself down on to his mouth. She was everywhere inside Haffner. His eyes goggled back at her, as she looked down, between her breasts.

—We do this how I like, no? said Zinka.

Haffner nodded. And she relaxed her grip on Haffner, flooding him with her delicate smell, a refined sweating bouquet.

Maybe it was better like this, thought Haffner. He began to accustom himself to the absolute relinquishment of choice. Who

265

needed to see Haffner holding in his stomach? Or his almost hollow shins – a veteran Roman legionary, the skin rubbed to a sheen? In this relinquishment, Haffner found his revolution.

3

His life had been shadowed by the counter-culture, the underground – and however much he disapproved of their childish politics, he admired the chutzpah of the protestors and the fighters, the uprisers and the deserters. Once, in New York, Haffner had helped a kid into the foyer of Chase Manhattan to extricate himself from the riot police, with their bright Lego helmets. Most orderly in his life, most savage in his imaginings, Haffner read with indulgence about the European anarchists, with their colourful cryptic names: the Black Bloc, the Tute Bianche. The Yippies in particular had gladdened Haffner's heart – especially the day they strode into the New York Stock Exchange, quietened the black security men into meek submission with raucous accusations of anti-Semitism, then stood in the public gallery and rained down dollar bills on the dealers in their braces, their visors, their pinstriped bespoke suits. He felt less attached to the Parisian revolutionaries, whom Haffner had watched on the BBC – the students in the lofts of the Ecole des Beaux Arts, attaching posters to washing lines with clothes pegs, so they could dry in time to be glued all over the city: the garish fonts and pointing hands – *Hypocrite reader! My double! My brother!* – proclaiming their escape from all the bourgeois normality, their new creation of an idyllic island, a utopia.

And now Haffner was stranded on this island, in this utopia.

Zinka, without explaining to Haffner, skipped off him and ordered him to undress. And this, thought Haffner happily, might be the moment, the reward for all his courage. In his exuberance he undressed, ignoring his habitual neatness, letting the bunched pair of his socks roll anywhere, his shirt remain in its pool on the floor.

He didn't care what form his utopia might take. Any revolution would do. If he had to be, Haffner would be the Saint-Just of the hypermarket, Guevara of the guava. And if in fact his utopia were here, in a hotel bedroom in a spa town, then Haffner would not resist. No, thought Haffner, if this was it, then he would take his place.

Leaning over the side of the bed, Zinka picked up the tracksuit trousers, and sloppily drew them up, like a snake charmer, along with the pool of his T-shirt. The trousers served to tie up one of Haffner's hands behind him, to the bedhead; the T-shirt served for his other. And Haffner was tied to the bed.

4

Stoical in his pursuit of pleasure, the true classical epicure, it wasn't the first time Haffner had been involved in the bedbound business of knots. It had been a habit of Barbra, his American secretary, to need to be tied to the bed, before being smacked with a book, struck with a cane, spanked until her buttocks turned a chaste and virginal pink. She liked to lose control, in the most controlled way possible. In her apartment in Chelsea, Haffner employed his ingenuity – even, in a moment of inspiration, lassoing a rope that had been stashed in a canvas bag left behind by her hearty and mountaineering brother over an exposed joist, so that Barbra could be tied there, standing naked, her arms above her head, her breasts raised with the tension – breasts which Haffner struck lightly but woundingly with the edge of his belt. When her breasts were raised like this you could see the mole which was usually a deft stowaway underneath the left. No, Haffner never minded these contrivances: but they were not for him. Not even medicinally. In the Russian Bath House in New York, he never understood why Morton so enjoyed being whipped with switches, beaten with birch rods.

Here in Central Europe, however, the position was reversed. Haffner was the one who was tied. Lightly, it was true: with garish sportswear. But his power had still gone.

Haffner had abdicated.

Slowly, Zinka lowered her mouth to Haffner's chest. With her teeth she tugged at a nipple – its blunt miniature nub. To Haffner, this action still felt within the limits of the normal, or the possible. It hadn't yet gone beyond the border of the pleasurable. Then she continued to bite. And Haffner began to revise his definitions of pleasure. He wondered how far he could take this before she might draw blood. Nevertheless, he thought, nevertheless. His body took over – with its strange routes to enjoyment. Zinka began to bite the other nipple. As she did so, she dragged the sharp nails of her fingers over Haffner's delicate skin. Wildly, he felt his penis stir. She held his penis, tightly, painfully. It tried to stir some more.

Then Zinka began her game of teasing.

Stupendous, haughty, grand, the diminutive form of Zinka began its travails down the length of Haffner's body. She struck him; she bit him. Soon, he knew, his old body would become a palette of bruises – the yellows and browns of a landscape from the nineteenth-century French countryside, with cows, and sheep, and a misshapen cypress. She told him to close his eyes. He could feel her hover over him – her warmth and smell. With a calm hand, she rubbed her wetness on his eyelids, on his nose: a pensive Impressionist. And then she moved further down until she reached his penis, where she waited.

Oh Haffner was adrift! He was in a new ecstasy, confused beyond the obviousness of pain and pleasure. He began to whimper. As he made a sound, she hurt him. So that then Haffner lay still, silent, blinded: in the absolute perfection of his denuded state.

And this was it, he thought. It was the final liberation.

He had found a strange detachment – like the Zen-like kids in the sixties, on Wall Street, who used to tell him the world wasn't the way everyone said it was. Everything was perspective. The real object of the game, they told him, wasn't money: it was the playing of the game itself.

If Haffner had been a mystic, he could have found in this some kind of god. But Haffner was not given to the mystical. He preferred the reckless sensual. It seemed more rational.

5

In a fleeting, floating way, this reminded him.

Long ago, when Haffner was fitter and more beautiful, he had been having lunch with Livia, in Mayfair's Mirabelle. For reasons which were already obscure to them, they were arguing about the merits of the 1968 revolutions: the revolution in Prague, the riots in Paris, the protests in London, then the sit-ins in New York, which Haffner rather saw as pitiful imitations of the European originals.

But it wasn't just the Americans whom Haffner doubted. Even the Europeans, Haffner argued, couldn't be taken seriously. The kids with their posters! They were yearning for violence. And they hadn't seen what violence was. They couldn't understand it.

But Haffner had? asked Livia. Haffner had. Of course he had. She knew he had. And these kids wouldn't have been able to contemplate it. What about the one up the tree, the poet? Who on being asked to come down by a policeman replied that he wouldn't, and, on being asked by the policeman why, answered by saying that he would not come down because if he came down then the policeman would beat him. A pacifist revolutionary! But then: he was a poet. A master of theatricals. Like his friend, the theatre critic: who left the protests because his Berlutis were scuffed. No, Haffner, she had to concede, knew about violence. And so he was best placed to ask the following question. (At this point Livia, distractedly busying herself with the tea, scalded herself on the stainless-steel teapot, where a teabag was in agony.) The following question. Could she honestly say that any of these students, these playwrights, these children, were motivated by anything except a desire to be seen in the newspapers? Could she? He didn't think she could. However much they might dress it up as something else, however much they might turn it into street theatre, or whatever, it was still the same old story: the ancient desire for glamour, for someone to notice you.

Livia asked when he would ever stop being flippant. At what point would he learn to take things seriously? Haffner considered his petits fours; the black water which was offering itself as coffee. He was, he assured her, taking it seriously.

She could put it this way, said Livia, spooning the teabag on to a saucer, bleeding its brown ichor on to the china. Haffner looked at her, and realised, with a small shock, that her hair was now white. So, said Livia, Haffner saw everything as selfishness. This was nothing new. A gangster, he thought that everyone else had the ethics of the gangster too: she knew this. But what revolution would survive the accusation? What moment of human history? Everyone only cared about themselves. This was obvious! Less obvious was how much, said Livia, anyone should really care. So everyone – Robespierre, Brutus, Lenin, Mussolini – these were all men who wanted to be noticed. But maybe, said Livia, this wasn't the truth of Brutus. And Haffner had to concede – for he was a lover of the classics – that Livia wasn't absolutely wrong. He was always on Caesar's side, true. But even a Caesar was impeachable.

The revolutions happened – nourished by a healthy sense of melodrama. Who was Haffner to judge the revolutionaries? asked Livia. Who was Haffner to judge the people who didn't care about all the irrelevant emotions – the self-consciousness, the self-pity: the people who didn't care what others thought of them?

So long ago, Livia had said this to Haffner. Now, when she was dead, it occurred to him that perhaps he finally agreed. If she was right, then Haffner was finally behaving like a true revolutionary. Like the revolutionaries, he was untroubled by the usual emotions: the self-pity, the embarrassment. Here, in the East, in the remnants of Kakania, he no longer cared about social niceties. So a girl was treating him with absolute hauteur, and he was loving it? What did Haffner care? He was his only audience.

Solitary, realised Haffner, he was shameless.

6

Haffner's room still preserved the forms of the 1920s. As well as its view of the mountains, its Zarathustrian height, the room was also equipped with armchairs, an escritoire, and a marble fire surround, on which were two silver candlesticks, containing the unlit slim obelisks of two cream candles.

Haffner opened his eyes to see Zinka pluck a candle from its niche. This baffled him. Then she told him, lying there on his back, to raise his knees to his chest, so exposing himself to whatever Zinka might want to do to him.

It was a fantasy she had always had: to use a man as a woman.

Once, Zinka was talking to her friend, about love and its ramifications. Zinka's friend had explained how her husband's favourite thing was that she should perch there, behind him, and use a dildo on him, with its pink latex bobbles. Slavenka was happy to do this. She was a dutiful wife. But when Zinka asked her if she enjoyed it, if she found it sexy – because she thought it must be sexy, she envied Slavenka her exotic and fulfilling sex life – Slavenka sighed.

—Oh no, she said. It's so boring. I keep forgetting I'm doing it. It's like doing the ironing.

It wasn't how Zinka felt. The idea of it excited her. All her life, she had felt so managed, so in thrall. The idea of being the manager herself seemed so dense with possibility.

In an amazed trance of obedience, Haffner held his knees up. It felt so insubstantial, thought Haffner, that he could not rule out the possibility that this was all a dream. He rather hoped it might be. And as he raised his knees, Zinka noticed the creases which emerged on his stomach – as on a sofa, a clubman's Chesterfield. These

271

creases, for Zinka, were tender with vulnerability. And this was what she wanted. To make the men unusual. To make them unprotected.

The unsure length of Haffner's penis was now being mimicked and outdone by the candle – slick with hand cream she had found in her handbag – grasped in Zinka's hand, like a light sabre.

There was no way, thought Haffner, that he could allow this indignity. But then again: why shouldn't he? It was his liberation. In it, he was prepared to entertain ideas for which he felt no natural wish to be an entertainer. It was not as if he hadn't done this to women himself. So why was it that he would blithely do to a woman – sure of their mutual pleasure, concerned to move with a more exaggerated tenderness – something he would not want a woman to do to him?

He had been content to let matters take their course when Zinka had entered his room that afternoon. In this way, Haffner meditated. Then, he had been moved by her pensive creativity. So why should he stop now?

The problems of philosophy were not, however, Haffner's primary concern. She let the thin candle, deftly coated in her hand cream, slip and settle slightly inside him. She watched him watch her. He could not see the oddity of it; he could not see this act's improbability – as it distended him, and enlarged him, beneath his tight testicles, as it made him wriggle and his stomach break out in sweat.

Then Zinka's other slippery hand became intricate around his penis, just as he had watched it elaborate itself on Niko's penis, two days ago: when his life, reflected Haffner, seemed so much simpler.

As she rested his rough, unpedicured feet on her soft shoulders, he felt moved to hazard the existence of a soul. Nothing else rendered his feelings explicable. And Haffner – Haffner cried out in his denuded, opened closeness to Zinka. They looked into each other's eyes and saw each other: illuminated.

Haffner's paradise! His translation to the supine, the passively cherubic!

She had begun by causing him pain. Now, gradually, she was gently moving the candle, back and forth, as she moved the skin on his penis, up and down, up and down, in front of her. She looked into his eyes and he looked back at her – comical, romantic. She didn't speak to him. Simply, they continued to look at each other, intently, while Zinka continued to make her motions inside Haffner. There was a blemish in one of her pupils.

And Haffner ascended.

With a burgeoning slow realisation, a shy astonishment, he could feel the slow progress of a climax he had not quite ever believed would be possible. Like the faintest music from a radio, playing in some car which pauses, behind an apartment block, as you lean out the window and enjoy a pensive cigarette, watching the unknown city below you, and then, when you think that no, you will never quite be able to make out the tune, that it will remain forever just beyond you, the car turns a corner and with it you recognise with an unexpected glow of recollection the full volume of some hit made famous by the genius Django Reinhardt in the music halls of New York.

In this way, Haffner finally jolted his hips, and cried out.

Zinka scooped up Haffner's tepid liquid into an enticing paw. Then she told Haffner to open his mouth. Haffner opened. Then she tapped a fingertip on his tongue: a nymph tapping an aged demigod – asleep and drunk – with a finger stained with mulberry juice, to wake him and make him sing.

Haffner paused. Then Haffner swallowed.

And Zinka smiled at him. Plucking a tissue from beside the bed, she wiped the trickling semen from his belly – then flushed the heavy tissue discreetly away.

7

When Frau Tummel had left Haffner that afternoon, he had tried to argue that he was a libertine. Because he only cared about pleasure, he told her. This was why it would never work between them. And, furious, she had looked at him: her nostrils angrily flared.

—No, she said. No: you are too frightened.

The chutzpah of it had enraged him: because Haffner knew that it was true. For if Haffner were ever a libertine, it was never absolutely. He wasn't an absolute immoralist. He lacked the ruthlessness, the total selfishness.

But now, as he rested from Zinka's labours, he wanted to say that no, Frau Tummel was wrong. In some ways – the rhetorical ways – he wished that Frau Tummel could see him now. (He wished that Livia could see him now.) He wasn't too scared. He just hadn't wanted Frau Tummel enough. He just hadn't ever understood the ludicrous crazytalk of true desire.

Because, yes: desire is the ultimate in the improvised. This is the normal theory of desire. It was Zinka's – who was just about to explain to Haffner that now everything was over. But I am not so sure.

The difficult task is to improvise the seventeenth time. Or even, say, the second. It might have seemed so incandescent, one's impromptu smearing of chocolate mousse on the palpitating body of a woman – there where her flesh is most exposed. But if the next time one again moves doggedly to the refrigerator, then the prone and lovely woman will experience in her soul a tiny qualm.

The true libertines are the geniuses at repetition. Not the artists of the one-off, the improvised. Everyone can improvise. The true talent is in the persistence.

8

He woke up, to discover Zinka leaving.

He had drifted into what seemed like the deepest night of sleep, but which was in fact only a small moment; he had hardly closed his eyes. He looked down: his shrunken penis was sticky as an orchid bud.

—I have to go, she said.

—You could stay here with me, he said. Why not?

—I can't stay here, she said. I have to go home.

—But you can't let him make you, said Haffner.

—No one's making me, said Zinka.

Haffner looked woebegone. He felt worse than woebegone: he felt as if everything was over. Yet for a brief moment he had felt so utterly reborn. But then, who was Haffner kidding? How could a man be born, when he was old? What schlub was ever allowed the victory of a second chance?

—I mean, she said. Look at you. Look at me.

It was just a moment, she said. It wasn't love.

But, thought Haffner, he loved her. This seemed plausible. The speed of it was nothing for Haffner. It simply overwhelmed him with the evidence.

He knew, however, that he had thought that he had never thought like this before on previous occasions. The repetition, he had to admit, tended to produce a comical effect. So what was true? The feeling of uniqueness, or the feeling of a repeat?

And me, I do not know. Two answers seem possible, and only one can be true. Maybe Haffner was right to feel that he was always stuck in a repeat. He had always thought, every time he fell in love, that it had no precedent in the past. Just as a perplexed critic looks at a barbaric work of art, which seems to come from nowhere. And this was precisely why he repeated himself. He recognised nothing, because he forgot so much. And since he forgot so much, he always repeated himself. He always believed he was in love, when it was perhaps just another brief moment of desire. On the other hand, maybe the opposite was also possible. Every time he said he was in love, it was true. Every woman Haffner had loved had been unique. But he forgot so much, so lavishly. And the more he forgot, the more he tended to see each story as the same. Whereas, perhaps, no story was the same.

It is all a problem of perspective.

But whatever. Haffner, in however baffling a mess he found himself, was sure of this: the desire was nothing to do with Haffner. It wasn't a whim; it wasn't capricious. How could it be capricious if it was a compulsion? So maybe nothing was an imbroglio of one's own making. Maybe nothing was Haffner's fault. A new goddess appeared – that was all. And he surrendered.

9

Abandoned, Haffner began to argue with Zinka about the faithlessness of woman. He was aware that this was the opposite of what he had argued, a few hours earlier, to Frau Tummel: when he complained about the faithfulness of women. He was aware that he was beginning to resemble a character in the farces he had watched with Livia, in the 1960s, on Shaftesbury Avenue, the era when Haffner could still happily go to the theatre without being disappointed in the quality. But then, maybe this was fine. What else was farce but the way of understanding how quick one's ideas were, how soon their showers passed?

After all: this was why he liked Zinka. It was why he had loved Livia: he was always in search of the one who would leave him.

It had always been Haffner who was the one to leave. No one else. First Livia had destroyed this illusion of Haffner. But he had been able still to preserve one place of hope: that in the one-night stands, the brief affairs, it was always Haffner who left, cold-hearted. Now even this was not true. Now that it was happening to him he was enraged by the injustice of it. Could a person simply choose whether or not they would have sex with someone else? Surely, if you had done it once, you had an obligation to continue for ever?

Although, as Zinka tenderly kissed him on the forehead, and left his room – not looking back at Haffner, naked on the bed – he could not conceal from himself the thought that this new incarnation did possess a certain logic. Maybe, thought Haffner, in a haze of contradiction, it was possible to love someone without wanting them: not to be tired with the need for possession. It didn't seem so unlikely. To want to inhabit the mind and body of someone else. For desire may involve possession. But also it might mean the opposite desire: to be possessed.

In his bedroom, Haffner was translated.

There was no reason, therefore, to be angry at Zinka. There was no reason to be proud. So what if she had left him? She entranced him precisely because she had never belonged to him at all.

Just as no one, thought Haffner, would belong to him again.

Or to put it in a way more familiar to Haffner, in the words of a great comedian . . . One day, this comedian, tired but happy, was walking down some street in Manhattan with his producer. The day's filming had gone well. Now they were off to some diner for a much needed salt beef sandwich, a much needed latke. Or whatever. As they sauntered down the street, two nuns, in wimples and solid shoes, walked towards them. And, solicitously, the great comedian took them aside, and very gently reminded them that he did apologise but they were in the wrong place. They had made a mistake. They weren't in this sketch.

In exactly the same way, what Haffner needed was the voice of a comedian, gently reminding him that now, regretfully, in the matter of Haffner, life was through.

Haffner, my hero, had outlived himself.

PART FIVE

Haffner Harmonic

1

The next morning – as the sun rose over the conifers, gilding the distant snows – Haffner woke up, raised his aching face and saw his battered suitcase: wrapped in creased and blotched cellophane, swaddled in blue adhesive tape, slashed by a diagonal tear which, according to the man who had delivered it – reception told him – could not be explained, and for which the airline admitted no responsibility.

In another era, perhaps Haffner would have instituted various legal battles. He would have written to the chairman and demanded compensation: donations to his designated charities. But not now. Haffner was no longer so proud of his property. He only felt a warm relief, as he abandoned his golfing trousers and tracksuits, and replaced the image in the mirror with a more familiar Haffner, in his brown tweed suit, his checked twill shirt, a muted tie: the handkerchief which Cesare had bought him in the Milan arcades stuffed with elegant negligence in his pocket.

Then he put on his glasses, and was fearful at his suddenly precise reflection. A livid stain was spreading across one cheek. A gummed splinter gelled in the tear duct of his right eye.

The reflection, however, perturbed him less than the pain within. His body seemed exhausted: he was shivering, worried Haffner, and his pulse was erratic. He felt for his clammy forehead: it seemed hot.

His first step, thought Haffner, in the life of this renovated, broken-down version of Haffner, should be breakfast. Then he should find Benjamin, and admit that perhaps Benji had been right all along. Though would he still believe that for a brief hour Haffner had been successful? Perhaps not, thought Haffner: perhaps not.

The dining room, by now, at this late stage of the morning, was empty. Haffner moved slowly along its buffet: with its sacks of grains and cereals, the contraption – which resembled no toaster Haffner had seen – for toasting bread, from which each slice emerged with its black insignia: a franking machine. All of these Haffner ignored. He took a croissant from some imitation of the rustic *panier*, and poured himself a coffee from the dregs of three silver Thermoses.

Haffner felt sick.

With flakes of croissant caught in the fibres of his tie, Haffner wandered out into the hotel's lounge: where the windows looked on to the mountains: their blues and greens and mauves. The absolute blue of the sky. It suddenly made sense to bespectacled Haffner now: this perfect view. He made for the bookshelves, but Haffner, whose flesh was sad, had read all the books he could. Humming to himself, he moved on to the miniature but eclectic collection of CDs – on a shelf, beside a book of mountain views, and a guidebook to the mountain walks, in French, from four years ago. And *Anne of Green Gables* in Spanish, and Volumes I and II of the *History of Nottingham* from the 1930s – but not the crowning Volume III.

Without expecting much, Haffner ejected someone else's CD featuring the classics of reggae from the 1970s, slid his own random choice into the waiting machine, and pressed play.

And Haffner discovered that he was in the orchestra stalls at the opera house.

2

As he gazed in the darkness, while fairies disported themselves on stage, Haffner was distracted by the surprise which had persisted, throughout the ballet's first half, at the smallness of Pfeffer's shilling tip to the cloakroom attendant in Rules, where they had eaten their theatre supper. In Haffner's opinion, no largesse was too much for the everyday retainers. So Pfeffer baffled him. But then Pfeffer often baffled him. Beside him, in the darkness, Pfeffer was holding opera glasses to his eyebrows like some marine instrument. They seemed to be directed at the mechanics of the flies.

Their respective wives were watching the ballet intently.

Haffner tried to settle into his velvet chair. He had accepted patiently this proposed outing, to celebrate Livia's birthday, to the Royal Ballet. It hadn't fit Haffner's idea of entertainment. But when he saw Bottom shrugging away his sorrow with a neat bend of his legs, Haffner began to enjoy himself. These people had humour, after all. While Livia watched beside him, on edge, transported – plucking at the plush velvet with her fingernails.

This theme recurred in Haffner's life. Twenty years later, in the living room of his daughter's house, he heard Benjamin trying to sight-read the same melodies: the cover of the score was worn like blotting paper. And in Benji's clumsy chords, Haffner rediscovered the sad emotion he had felt for the actor playing Bottom – the pirouettes, the tender holds! – in his massive ass's head. The sadness seemed to make sense to him now.

For what else was it as you lumbered across a room, towards the body of a woman, the prong of your penis straining to beat you in the race to touch her? It was farcical, always.

In the lounge of the hotel there was a curved bar made of vertical strips of pine, a collection of sofas, a box of board games. Into one sofa sank Haffner, as he played to himself, in the morning, the nocturne from Mendelssohn's ballet.

The horns, softly, their own echo, lay on the bed of the violins.

And as they did so, Haffner made a loop, descending from the childhood of Benji, back through Livia's birthday, to where this theme had first emerged. It was Haffner's theme tune. His first ever delicate kiss had occurred to this accompaniment, the music played with the film he had watched at the Ionic Picture Theatre, after which Hazel had allowed him to kiss her cheek.

In the window, outside, on the hotel veranda, he could see a woman emptying her rucksack – polyester in primary colours – of its crumbs, its lost cellophane wrappers from drinks straws, its crumpled tickets, its creased promotional leaflets to the most inauthentic restaurants.

Haffner contemplated the peaceful scene. There was no one in the lounge. Only Haffner. Everyone else was out walking, or swimming, or lying beside the pools. Or being cured of whatever they wanted to be cured of. But Haffner, instead, was lost in his persistent sense of floating, unattached.

Yes, checked Haffner, as if feeling in a pocket for his passport, the feeling was still there. Haffner was free.

3

As the soft nocturne continued, Haffner mooched among the CDs. He rejected showtunes from the movies; he rejected a selection of fados from the backstreets of Lisbon. And then, to his excitement, he found the Cole Porter songbook, as sung by Ella Fitzgerald.

If Haffner had an ideal musical form, it was the wordless harmonies of Duke Ellington's scat. But if there had to be words, then he wanted them to be Cole Porter's, with Ella's accent. She sang the songs so precisely, so simply. She confessed to her audience, as she had confessed to Haffner, that time in Ronnie Scott's, that ev'ry time they said goodbye, she died a little. And now, as he read the liner notes, he noticed the weird old-fashioned elision. Ev'ry! He'd only noticed the poetic quality of Cole Porter's title now, after – what was it? Sixty years? He rather liked it.

He was in the mood for preserving outmoded things.

—Benjamin! said Haffner, delighted.

Benjamin paused, and pointed a finger at his cheek, like a tearful harlequin.

—You've got a huge bruise on your cheek, said Benji.

Haffner asked him if he knew this one. Benjamin repeated his sentence; Haffner repeated his. Benjamin replied that no, not really. It was kind of not what he listened to, really. Then he should listen, said Haffner, raising a hand. As for the bruise – as for the bruise: the bruise was nothing, said Haffner.

Together they listened to Ella Fitzgerald explain to her silent audience how every time they said goodbye, she wondered why the gods above her thought so little of her that they allowed her lover to go. And then, once more, the strings came in, a trampoline for her voice.

—I'm not sure I like it, said Benji.

—How can you not like it, said Haffner, when it's true?

He had always loved this song for the frankness of its melancholy: its admission of being defeated by love. Perhaps this was the real America of Haffner – not so much the happy improvisation, as the stoic openness about pain. The acceptance of vulnerability was what moved Haffner now. He loved the Ella of this song, just as he had been charmed by his meetings with the innovative businessmen in the early seventies: the gunslingers, the white sharks. Sometimes, he had dealings with James Ling: the man who regarded the portfolio as a work of art, providing an escape from real life, and all its attendant risks. With his theory that one could diminish the risk of disaster by betting on everything. Patiently, over the years, Haffner had listened to their jargon – derivatives, risk arbitrage, hedge funds – all of them trying to pretend that these new ideas could diminish risk. And Haffner had listened to them, unconvinced – amazed by their ability to invent the idea of the rational bubble. So frank an oxymoron! So fragile a hope!

But Benjamin, this morning, was euphoric with optimism.

—Have you fixed things? Because I think I'm going to go back, said Benjamin.

—To bed? queried Haffner.

—Home, said Benjamin.

—To that summer school? said Haffner, looking down the song titles.

Benjamin said nothing.

—But this one, said Haffner to himself, is the real marvel.

—No, said Benjamin. I'm going back to her.

At this point, Haffner noticed something.

—You're in the same clothes as last night, said Haffner. You brought nothing else?

—I'm in the same clothes, said Benjamin. And then he grinned. To which Haffner offered a happily sceptical eyebrow.

—When did you arrive? said Haffner. Yesterday? I've hardly seen you.

Haffner had converted him. The legend of Haffner had now created the legend of Benji. For this would always be Benji's great story: the story of how he abandoned the practice of his religion, having slept with two girls in one week: in Tel Aviv, and then an Alpine spa town. Even if Haffner, in the mountains, had a finale all of his own. His story was all about the dismantling of his legend: the sudden zest for abandonment.

And, sultry in the mountainous morning, Ella began again to sing Cole Porter's classic: 'Begin the Beguine'.

—You're going to leave your school? asked Haffner.

—But have you fixed things? said Benji. I won't go if you still need me.

And Haffner considered this.

—No, he said.

—You haven't fixed things? said Benji.

—I don't need you, said Haffner.

—But no, began Benji.

—You ever heard of Artie Shaw? said Haffner, holding up the liner notes. Eight wives. Now let me tell you something, old boy.

But before he could continue Benjamin's education in the art of jazz, before he could continue to praise Benji for his liberation, before he could go on to explain that in fact uxorious panache wasn't what had made Artie Shaw remarkable – that in fact Artie Shaw's talent was his extension of the clarinet's upper range – there was an interruption.

4

Frau Tummel, clasping Herr Tummel's hand – like exhausted Olympic victors – appeared at the door of the hotel lounge. Like the overcrowded lounge at the end of a Parisian farce, an English murder mystery. Behind the Tummels, there was a man who was wearing his name pinned to his chest.

—He is here, announced Frau Tummel.

—Who? said Haffner.

—You, said Herr Tummel and Frau Tummel, in concert.

He had at least, thought Haffner, brought them back together. If this was the only good he had accomplished in this spa town, it wasn't nothing. Surely someone should acknowledge that?

The man with his name on his chest was the manager of the hotel. It was a pleasure to meet him, said Haffner, welcoming him with a handshake. This handshake was declined with a gentle cough, a gentle incline of the head.

Benjamin busied himself with the neat arrangement of a pile of magazines, dating from two years ago, concerning the niceties of couture.

Then the manager began his speech. He regretted to say it, he said, and he was sure that everything could be explained – just as, he added with what he imagined must seem an engaging twinkle, a teacher had once told him that everything, yes, must have an explanation, a rational explanation. So: he regretted the situation, but there it was.

Haffner watched him, silently.

Benjamin, in an attempt at disappearance, debated within himself the eternal oppositions: between the one-piece and the bikini; the bronzing or the elegance; the virgin or the whore.

So. There had been accusations. There had been comments raised to him of a personal nature, concerning Mr Haffner.

Haffner began to read the songbook's liner notes, with scholarly exactitude.

Yes, continued the manager, these allegations involved Haffner and a member of staff.

Haffner discovered with surprised satisfaction that the record – Haffner's vocabulary was not always modern – not only included Ella's renditions of Cole Porter, but also included a selection of live recordings: so that here, even here, in the least smoky and least cool environs of a spa town high in the backward Alps, Haffner could listen to Ella's improvisation of 'Mack the Knife' – an improvisation she delivered at the jazz festival in Juan-Les-Pins on the French Riviera with Duke Ellington in 1966. Which Haffner himself had annoyingly missed. An improvisation, he then found out, which was in fact a staged version, since it went back to 1960 in Berlin, where Ella had first improvised these new lines to a song she couldn't remember.

Of course this could all be settled amicably, said the manager. He just needed to be aware of the facts. The facts as they had been made known to him by this lady here beside him. But he was sure that, perhaps, there had been a mistake.

—Present the evidence, said Haffner, simply.

Then he selected a new track, and pressed play. Because now he was truly bohemian: which is to say, he was bored.

Frau Tummel looked away, distressed.

—I'm sorry? said the manager.

He would of course have to determine the full facts, said the manager, raising his voice over the beginning big band. But naturally if this were true, he was afraid that naturally the young lady in question would have to be let go by the hotel.

—The evidence! shouted Haffner.

Furious, he turned away to the window, with his arms folded, and considered how he was going to save Zinka. It seemed unlikely. But Haffner wanted to try. For even if the world were a trap for Haffner, he saw no reason why it should be a trap for anyone else. Other people, he thought, could be done with being caught up in the farce of Haffner.

5

In other words, he no longer wanted to be Mack the Knife. It had always seemed to Haffner to be universal: this song which had begun in London, been rewritten in Berlin, then transatlantically re-rewritten by Louis Armstrong, Bobby Darin, and finally Ella and Duke. This universal ballad used to seem a statement of the universal facts as Haffner knew them.

But now, Haffner was less sure.

For Macheath was the perfect criminal. With Mack the Knife, anything was possible: on the Thames, a body was found; or there you were, in Soho, and a woman was discovered, raped;

or in the City of London, on a Sunday morning, there on the sidewalk was a body oozing life, and someone was sneaking round the corner.

This was how the song had gone, in Europe. Mack was the emperor of crime: the rewrite of a man like Tiberius, who made his guests drink lavish vats of wine, then tied a cord around their penises, so that their bladders burst. That was the usual story of how humans liked to be animals. But now that Ella sang it, something new occurred. Suddenly, realised Ella, the chorus had disappeared: and so that great singer, with her own bravado, had made up her own words.

Just like 'Begin the Beguine', the song had a way of extending itself. It went the distance. It possessed a final flourish of pure happiness.

For oh Bobby Darin, and Louis Armstrong, they made a record, ooh what a record, of this song, she sang. And now Ella, Ella and her fella, they were making a wreck, a wreck, such a wreck of the same old song. Oh yes yes yes yes they'd sung it, yes yes yes yes they'd swung it, they had swung Mack, they'd swung old Mack in town – for those people there, there, at the jazz festival, they were gonna sing, they were gonna swing, they were gonna add one more chorus.

And the Duke took over, with his big band.

Haffner, at the window, hummed along. And Benjamin, amazed at his grandfather's odd insouciance, amazed that one more time his grandfather was being accused of monstrous fidelity to pursuing love, went out on to the veranda. The prickly hair between Anastasia's legs returned to him, in the memory of his lips, his soft thick hands. It made him happy. While the manager, having been engaged in theatrical conversation, at this point left the hotel lounge with a final severe glance at Haffner: sweeping away in a flounce of Tummels.

It must, thought Haffner, have been Frau Tummel's doing: this catastrophe. And he could see why: always, the wives wanted to reassert their dignity: the sanctity of their marriage. Betraying Zinka was simply Frau Tummel's way of doing this. He couldn't blame her. What else was Haffner doing himself – if not trying to reassert the sanctity of his marriage?

No, Haffner wasn't hurt by Frau Tummel's malice: the melodrama of everyone's feelings. He was really done with all the theatre now. Because this was the point when Ella's scat began: the scat she had learned from Duke – the scat which Haffner admired. Twice she used it to push once more through, into a new repeat of the chorus. And then once more. And then finally again she sang: could they go with one, just one, one more? And oh they had swung it, yes they had swung it, they had swung old Mack, they'd swung old Mack for you. And once again they'd like to know, to let them know they were through.

And as the applause died down a voice said: You're the Lady – a voice which may well have come from the audience but which Haffner had always imagined, for Haffner liked his heroes to be friends, to be the voice of the admiring Duke himself.

6

Frau Tummel returned in the doorway. She called his name.

But Haffner was done with the romance of others. From the window, he walked across the room. As Frau Tummel motioned to speak, he held out a silencing palm. Instead, Haffner returned to the masterpieces of classical music.

Randomly, he chose a melody from the era of grand opera.

Oh but everyone knows the famous music where the music soars above the circumstances: like the beautiful aria sung by an unfaithful woman who is in love, without knowing it, with an unfaithful man. Or the song which is sung for a girl who is about to die beside her lover, immured in a tomb – music which somehow, as the master said, manages to leave behind the true circumstances of the singing, that two people were being buried alive; they would die together or (what was even worse) one after the other they would die from asphyxiation or hunger. Then the horrendous process of disintegration would set in until only two skeletons would remain, two inanimate objects quite un-affected by the presence or absence of the other. And yet, while all this was true, they continued to sing the most ethereal of melodies.

This is one version of music. It was the version which Frau Tummel believed in. Just as she believed in the eternal power of the feelings. But, for Haffner, music offered no lofty and irrefutable soothing enhancement to life's unadorned and crude ugliness. He did not believe in music's triumphant power of transfiguration.

He stood and stared at Frau Tummel, who stared sadly back.

In this final meeting of Haffner and Frau Tummel, a gorgeous melody enveloped them. Unknown to both of them, a woman sang about her sad realisation, that the sincerity of passion is no argument against the corresponding truth of its comic portability. When a new god arrives – sang this woman, in a desert – we surrender.

Everyone moves from God to God.

But then, Haffner already knew this. He could have comforted Frau Tummel without the music. Think about it! Haffner could have said – if he had wanted to care for Frau Tummel in her romantic distress, sad at Haffner's betrayal, the speed of his feel-ings. Their liaison may have been brief, but it was still longer than many other more celebrated love stories. And the tempo of a love story's demise was no argument against it being a love story. The plot of *A Midsummer Night's Dream* takes just one night. In that night, so many couples swap over. The plot of *Romeo and Juliet* takes less than a week. Three days and three nights were all that was needed for a fairy tale. While the story of Frau Tummel and Haffner had lasted more than a week. Their love, in relative terms, was endless.

And I think that it is possible to add one further comforting thought for Frau Tummel. There is a link, perhaps, between the transience of passion and the irony of the love songs. In the same way that a passion is always so much more fleeting than it believes itself to be, so a passion is always bestowed on an inappropriate object. But just because a passion might be bestowed on an inadequate object doesn't mean that the passion isn't real.

Everyone was on their desert island, waiting to be rescued by another god. It was true of Frau Tummel; it had been true of Haffner too.

Haffner auf Naxos!

Was Haffner laughable? Perhaps. But no more laughable than anyone else in love. To go for a young woman at seventy-eight was simply to add to the comedy of passion the comedy of the object.

7

The manager reappeared, with Viko.

—Yes, said Viko, looking bored.

That was the same man. Absolutely, improvised Viko. He had seen him kiss her too. Well then, said the manager. There seemed nothing more to say. He was sorry, but the matter seemed unambiguous.

Haffner had thought that a spa town would be a paradise of liberation. In his imagination, it was a bohemian idyll. And maybe it had been like this, for him, in some secret way. But the overt facts were disappointing. The morality of this place was so depressingly limited: a bourgeois, communist morality – unoriginal even in its rules.

Haffner looked down, at his suit, at his shoes; at the tie which had been unaccountably crumpled by some customs official in Boston or Tehran. It seemed an adequate outfit for his own banishment.

There would be no need to let the girl go, he said. Instead, he would leave himself. He trusted that this would end the matter. The girl had done nothing wrong. He was sorry if he had behaved in an unbecoming manner.

This was really not what he had in mind, said the manager.

But no, Haffner halted him. It was the only just solution. He was sorry for the inconvenience.

And in the halo of his grandeur, Haffner nodded goodbye to Frau Tummel, to Viko, to the manager of his hotel, and strode out on to the veranda – where Benjamin was standing, looking out at the sky and its clouds, considering the phenomenon of Haffner.

—I am leaving in protest, said Haffner. This is a scandal. I will find another hotel.

—It's always like this, said Benjamin. It's kind of amazing. Everywhere you go, there's a crisis.

Haffner tried to protest. Once again, he had been the victim of an extraordinary set of circumstances. Benjamin said he had no idea.

Haffner changed the subject.

—So you're leaving as well, said Haffner.

—I'm really not sure now, said Benji.

—Come now, said Haffner.

—But Mama, said Benji.

—We will manage her, said Haffner.

And Benji, newly criminal, smiled.

—But you're sure you can handle this business? said Benji.

—It's paperwork, said Haffner.

He put his hand on Benji's shoulder, in his manly gesture of camaraderie.

—I always stick up for you, said Benjamin, looking out at the sun and the sky. Always.

And he broke off. He tried again.

—Even when she left, said Benjamin, – I still defended you.

And Haffner contemplated, for a moment, in an access of irritability at this kid's sincere demonstration of love, telling Benjamin the truth. For a moment, he imagined the conversation where he revealed, here, to Benjamin, and so to his family as well, the story of Livia with Goldfaden. How Livia had left Haffner not because she was enraged by Haffner's minor infidelities, not because of his refusal to take the art of ballet nor the religions of his forefathers seriously, but because she had been in love with another man. And then Haffner could have continued, and explained that the reason why Livia then lived for two years, the last two years of her life, on her own, in her flat in Golders Green, was not because she had so taken against the selfishness of Haffner that she had finally decided to abandon him, as her family believed, but because Goldfaden, when confronted by Livia's proposal that they could finally live together, now that his wife was gone, had gently but irreparably told her that this was a very bad idea. He was quite happy as he was. He couldn't understand what had come over her. There was no need for such theatrics, he had said.

This was why she had left, and not come back. She would not admit that she had been humiliated.

But Haffner would never tell Benji this. He would never tell anyone. No one would ever know about her defeat. He loved Livia with all the passion he was capable of; with an overwhelming care for her secrecy.

And maybe, I now think, as I watch Haffner stand there, that is how to truly be a libertine: to accept the libertinism of others.

For a final time, Haffner looked at the hotel's private landscape, the giant mountains, the infinite sky; then he patted Benji's shoulder again.

—You're a pal, he said.

And Haffner left the hotel.

Haffner Fugitive

1

Haffner stepped out into the midsummer afternoon, carrying his suitcase. It still trailed rags of cellophane.

The question was, thought Haffner, what he was to do next. Some form of shelter seemed imperative.

Wearily, Haffner made the long walk across the park, into the town, in search of a new hotel. The square was empty. The square was metaphysical. It was a Platonic form of sun. He passed a sports shop with a crate of plastic balls outside, printed with pictures of more leathery, more professional balls; he passed a patisserie with trays of greaseproof paper in the window. On a café terrace, a woman was pushing a folding chair flat with a pensive knee. On and on went Haffner, homeless in the heat. He was ancient. Everywhere was ancient: the imprinted gas vents were fossils in the pavements.

He couldn't stay just anywhere. He had his standards, his distastes. One hotel Haffner rejected because of the canaries kept behind the counter; another he rejected because of its incorporation of a nightclub.

So Haffner continued to walk, past the former medical institute, past the baths for men and the baths for women, and then, ahead of him, was the Metropole Cinema: its sign in handwritten squiggles of pink neon.

In general, if Haffner were forced to discuss the matter, he felt disappointed by the film industry. He did not feel the pictures had, as a rule, distinguished themselves. First the films were American. And these, Haffner had admired. Once, he had been Jayne Mansfield's banker: and she was a very handsome woman. Then there was a fashion for the French, which – as Haffner would inform the dinner party, the work colleague – left him cold. He never understood them: with their inexplicable cuts, their disdain for plot. Then Italian, then Japanese. Now they were God knows what. They were Mexican. But whatever their provenance, it really didn't matter, because one thing was sure: the new cinemas, with their speaker systems, were too loud for Haffner.

But Haffner, today, was tired. He wanted succour. At this point, Haffner would take anything.

He looked at the posters in front of the cinema. He recognised nothing; or no one. The language – as always, written in the language which for ease of reference Haffner was calling Bohemian – escaped him. The faces were foreign too. But Haffner didn't really want the film. He wanted the cinema instead: the rich festooned interior, the air conditioning and the darkness and the popcorn. He wanted peace.

So Haffner made his tentative way in.

In the foyer, a depressed salesgirl stood behind a stall which offered multicoloured packets of multicoloured chocolate. This combination tempted him. He bought two bars of chocolate. Then he approached the cloakroom. He lifted up his destroyed suitcase. The girl behind the counter looked at him.

—Is possible? asked Haffner, in his best imitation of foreign English.

She continued to look at him. Then she tore off a perforated ticket, and pushed it flat on the counter towards Haffner, letting it come to rest beside her magazine, which boasted of its proximity to the lives of the stars. Haffner heaved his suitcase up on to the counter, where a protruding plastic wheel caught the pages of her magazine, a circumstance which for a moment Haffner did not notice. As he pushed the suitcase across, he heard, to his alarm, a tearing sound, identical to the sound of glossy paper ripped.

She put the suitcase in a corner.

And Haffner turned round, to discover his interpreter from the Town Hall: Isabella.

—Is you, she said, pleased with this chance meeting.

—Is me, said Haffner.

—So how are things? she asked him. All good?

—Kind of, said Haffner.

—You will be glad to go home, stated Isabella.

Haffner considered this. He said nothing.

Isabella asked him where he was from, in Britain, and Haffner replied that he was from London. Isabella, she told him, had been to London herself. It was many years ago. She stayed at a hotel near Westminster. She told him its name.

—I don't know it, said Haffner.

He knew it? asked Isabella.

He felt for his forehead. Now he was sweating profusely. He wasn't well: he wasn't himself.

—I don't know it, said Haffner.

And Isabella paused, lost in memories of bygone times.

Sweating, craving rest, Haffner excused himself, turned round, and – refusing the usher – entered the auditorium.

2

He realised that the reason for the usher's reluctance to let Haffner in – bearing though he did bars of chocolate and tickets, all the normal signifiers of an ordinary spectator – was that the film had started almost twenty minutes earlier. And perhaps, thought Haffner, if he had arrived at the beginning, then maybe he could have followed the plot. Now, it seemed unlikely.

Ahead of him, gigantic, loomed the dead.

He didn't really know, poor Haffner, why he was there. But then, the question of what he was doing anywhere had been posed so deeply to Haffner in the last few days that now he was tired of it. Happy, he settled into his bewilderment.

The film, it turned out, was in French, with subtitles; but Haffner no more understood the subtitles than he understood French.

One thing, at least, was clear. It was a war story. At first, he thought it took place in his war. Gradually he realised that it was taking place in his father's war: the Great War. Often wrongly called a World War. Whereas it was to be distinguished from Haffner's War, which was a truly World War. Though Haffner was increasingly unsure of both the greatness and the world.

Bereft of language, Haffner watched the slapstick. It seemed a reliable guide. Like so many war stories, this film was about escape. Happily, he watched as the prisoners propped a chair against the door, hooked a blanket over the blank window, prised up a floorboard. The alarm system was a tin can pierced by a string.

These escapes repeated themselves.

While, in the occasional background of an occasional shot, Haffner recognised what was left of his youth: sunlight, a horse passing by – its hooves and white ankles – watched by a slumped bored sentry.

How important could a man's life get? wondered Haffner. At what point would it ever become symbolic, or cosmic? Haffner was beginning to get a pretty shrewd idea. He was beginning to understand the abysmal length of the odds.

On the screen, the boredom continued. The prisoners tried to amuse themselves with amateur theatricals. They dressed up as girls, in stockings and heels. And Haffner with approving assent noted the silence, the deep hollowed silence as the prettiest kid emerged on stage in his chemise and stockings and hairband. The parody of the wife you hadn't seen for the last three years. The parody which broke the obvious rule: you couldn't think about sex, not in a war. But you only thought about sex. The last thing you needed was the reminder. And then a singing comedian came up on stage, who could neither sing nor make his audience laugh: a vampire, backlit, in white tie and tails.

And this was Haffner's past. He knew it intimately. The boredom was Haffner's domain – an infinite suspension. One had always lived, during the war, under the illusion that everything would be over very soon. Whereas now Haffner wondered whether both victory and defeat were forever deferred. Although Haffner could not have said why – because one was endlessly defeated, or simply because the war was never over.

In the life of Raphael Haffner, maybe a truth became obvious: the great illusion – the true schmaltz – was always the illusion of victory.

3

Above him glowed the tired and blissful face of a French actor, licking his way along the rim of a cigarette paper: a harmonica. And although Haffner was almost happy here, in this cinema, after the initial coolness, the initial comfort of the velvet and the chocolate, he was still finding it difficult to focus.

He looked at the audience instead. It was sparse. The usual collection of misfits, the bedraggled loners: the geeks, the academics.

Then Haffner noticed a tall lean angular neck, with a crest of hair, and seemed to recognise it. Was that Pawel? He couldn't tell. Pawel from the Committee waiting room: Haffner's exposed twin.

Haffner tried to get his attention – coughing, leaning forward – but Pawel simply sat there, entranced in the picture. And then, in Haffner's bored scan of the audience, his heart jolted.

Was that Zinka sitting a few rows ahead of him, diagonally across? He could not be sure. But before he could try to look closer, there sat down, late, a woman whose face was darkly hidden from Haffner, but whose scent clouded towards him: the delicious mixture of perfume and sweat. He had a thing for the imperfectly adorned, did Haffner. For the sorrow and the pity. But not now. Now he only wanted her to move.

He was going mad, he knew this. As if suddenly, in this back-street backwater cinema, everyone he knew would have gathered, for Haffner's finale.

Concentrate! Concentrate!

And Haffner settled back into his seat, begrudging the cheapness of the velveteen, the dead springs inside.

He was oddly adrift from everything he knew. Haffner, now, had no one. Not even the troubles of his heart. No, not even the women troubled Haffner's thoughts.

On their holidays, Livia always had her little ritual. Happy at their escape, she used to ask him how far they were from the West End – the bright theatres – snug in her couchette above him, as they sped through the mountains of Italy to Venice, or Lake Como. Their daughter, with her husband and their son, was in the adjacent compartment. And the rain fell, wriggling in jerky zigzags down the pane. Against the wall was pinned a bulging net for Haffner's book and glasses. Yes, thought Haffner. She was always intent on putting distance between them and the rest of their known world. So how far was he now from London? He tried to imagine the distances. And in this way, making this calculation, in the full emergence from his chrysalis, Haffner fell asleep.

But maybe, to understand the full happiness of Haffner, I should contrast it with another metamorphosis: For Benjamin had undergone his own metamorphosis, his conversion to a world of pleasure. But this conversion had not led to a happiness impervious to fear.

In his room, the twin buds of his earphones in his ear, he was once more listening to his favourite hip-hop song of the moment, called 'Darkness'. And as he listened, he brooded, darkly.

The song called 'Darkness' was by Saïan Supa Crew, rappers from Marseilles. It opened with a sample from the most romantic song: 'Anyone Who Had a Heart' – with an abrupt drum roll and first faint orchestrated crackle, like the oldest radio in the world. And then, almost simultaneously, began the wistful violins. But the words – oh the words – Benji could not understand them. The rap, apart from one moment which he was sure mentioned the metro, eluded him. All he could recite, without understanding, was the chorus.

Ho, c'est le darkness, recited Benji, grandly: adieu à l'allégresse, c'est le darkness, c'est Loch Ness, c'est le madness, la lumière se baisse.

The first time he heard the song was in Tel Aviv, in the apartment of the girl whom he once hoped would become his girlfriend. Or, more precisely, whom he once hoped would let him see her naked. He wasn't ambitious. She shrugged a nonchalant record from its sleeve and made it frantic. On the cover was a black-and-white photo of a cream block of flats in the most modern version of Paris, with a patchy sky and burnt-out cars.

Since then, he had listened to this song called 'Darkness' over and over. And he still did not know precisely what it meant. But to him it was so beautiful – with its plush American romantic violins, crackling with nostalgia, and sarcastic clever French rhymes (rhymes whose meaning he did not understand). It seemed so poignant with poise, so world-weary with sadness.

Luxuriously, therefore, romantic, Benji contemplated his fears.

It wasn't the first time. Three years earlier, Benji had been stricken by a vision of his death, in some club in an industrial part of north-west London: for the first time in his life he had not only taken a tab of LSD but had added, recklessly, a pill as well. So Benji could soon be found sitting on his own, carefully near the accident and emergency room, feeling sick, and terrified, as hippies with matted dreadlocks bent forward to leeringly if kindly ask about his health. He had decided that he would not go into the emergency room until it was absolutely necessary. He was mortified by appearances. This tendency to be mortified was adding to his panic, since all too easily he could imagine the headlines in the newspapers the next morning: the school photo, the tearful parents, the charity estab-lished in his memory. It would have to be him, the amateur who died after taking a pointless and accidental overdose: the bourgeois boy adrift in the world of cool.

The great screw-up: this was Benji's constant anxiety. He always went in fear of doing or saying the minute thing which would place everything in the greatest danger.

Really, thought Benji, there was no need to understand the words of this, his favourite song. He knew what it was about. True, the moments of incomprehension were everywhere. He was not convinced, for instance, that in the chorus of one of their songs, a hip group of French hip-hoppers, whether from the graffiti'd *banlieue* of Paris or the graffiti'd suburbs of Marseilles, could really be saying c'est Loch Ness. Maybe Loch Ness, with its monstrous Scottish depths, connoted darkness to a group of French hip-hoppers, but this seemed hopeful and unconvincing. This seemed his provincial, unlikely mishearing. But then, what did this mistake really matter?

He knew what this song was about. The song was about the fear.

The voices were all he needed, because the voices were grave, and delicate: they were, for him, the meaning. The meaning of this song was in the collage of serious, careful voices, trying to resist the melancholy romantic violins.

Because they couldn't. No one could resist the romance, he thought: as he contemplated the screwed-up mess which was the life of Benjamin.

5

When Haffner woke up in his uncomfortable velvet seat, he discovered the black-and-white outlines of a new prison for the characters on the silver screen: a grander, more feudal kind of prison. It was some kind of schloss – with pines and stones, and Gothically written signs warning against escape. The scene took place by night. And this time a man with a French accent and a man with a German accent were talking to each other in English: a fact which led Haffner to wonder if he was still dreaming.

—Have you really gone insane? said the man speaking with a German accent.

—I am perfectly sane, said the man speaking with a French accent.

He really couldn't be sure, thought Haffner, at what point any of this had been a dream. From the moment he met Zinka until now. From the moment he met Livia until now. With depressed accuracy, however, he felt compelled to admit that no moment of his life could really be excused or explained by a theory of unreality.

The German and the Frenchman continued their elegant debate in English.

—It's damn nice of you, Raffenstein, but it's impossible, said the Frenchman.

And with that, he began to climb, while the Germans trained a searchlight on him, like a music hall artiste: the famous actor in his follow spot. As, presumed Haffner, he was. In another version of the world entirely. And when Haffner then saw the man halt, arch his back, and stumble; when he saw the Frenchman on his deathbed, tended to by the German who had shot him, he wished he could believe it. He wished he could be moved. But partly there was the problem that he could hardly be moved by a film he had barely seen, and barely understood; and also there was a deeper reason.

Haffner didn't care about nobility. He didn't care about the soul. Just the beauty of escape.

All of Haffner's dreams of escape were suddenly incandescent. He sat there. And when the house lights came up – revealing to Haffner's placid eye the empty drinks cartons, packets of sweets, the crisp cellophane from cigarettes – and the credits rolled, he sat there while the small audience filed out, checking the footwells for coats, for wallets, for all the human belongings. The man he thought was Pawel was just conceivably Pawel: he could not be sure.

The girl he thought was Zinka turned out to be a teenage boy.

6

And Haffner, left behind in the cinema, considered how, on the one hand, there was the myth of the escape. Everyone understood the need for this myth. But maybe the need was explained by another wish: the safety of a refuge.

He had always assumed that he would go back home, to London, when the paperwork on the villa was completed. It wasn't as if he was here as an exile. But then, anything could become an exile, if it became impossible to go back.

And Haffner considered this spa town.

In Haffner's mind, his vision of Livia's villa was now merging with his vision of the cottage in the film, a cottage where the Frenchman had conducted some form of love affair with a lonely woman on her farm. The husband, presumed Haffner, must have been away, at the war. This cottage represented some kind of idyll. And now Haffner was wondering if he was beginning to understand the need for this cottage, he understood the need for a refuge. It was the deeper meaning of every escape. Just as he now understood how deeply he missed the girl who had stayed with them, in 1939: the girl whom none of them could understand, who took her own life. She was looking for a refuge, and she had not found it. And just as how – if one discovered the most minute version of Haffner, the slimmest, most concentrated fraction of Haffner – in some way, he thought, he understood what their marriage had represented to Livia. It might have seemed inconceivable to the outside observer, but to her it was a place of safety. For she knew he would never leave her. Haffner mimed the act of leaving, but he never would.

He had always believed that there would always be another girl; just as he had always believed that he would always have another city. However much he might have made mistakes, however unsure he may have been that he had made the right decision, he could always start over again. But now, he thought, he didn't.

And me, I might put it more sadly. I might use the words of the poet – the poet of a disappeared empire – who once said that in the way a man destroys his life here, in this little corner, so he has destroyed it everywhere else. But Haffner's pessimism was more euphoric. The problem had always been in finding the right elopee. But surely the elopee was obvious. It was always only Livia. If he added up his women, he decided, he had only ever had two: Livia, and then everyone else. Yes, thought Haffner. He had always seen everything in terms of repetition. And now it turned out that there was such a thing as a singularity. And love proved it.

The *trompe l'oeil* of the ending! The false bottom of the ending!

Could he manage one more? wondered Haffner. He thought he could. Let him swing it one last time.

His century was over, and all Haffner wanted to take from it was the memory of Livia. He only wanted, now, to assert his constant fidelity.

Why did he need to go back, when the paperwork was completed? Why couldn't he, thought Haffner, live there in the villa – surrounded by the history of Livia? And in the excitement of his decision, Haffner wanted to see the villa, now – the villa which he had not thought he ever wanted to visit. He wanted to pay homage to Cesare's famous ceiling – executed in the dining room when he was sixteen, when he still believed in his destiny as a great European painter. Homeless, he wanted to observe what would be Haffner's final home.

7

Haffner marched out into the foyer. The window to the cloakroom was shut. At the ticket booth, he pointed to the cloakroom. The woman in the ticket booth shrugged, helplessly. Haffner mimed, like a monkey, the heaviness of twin suitcases, invisibly weighing down his arms.

—No no, said the girl.

—No? said Haffner.

The girl said a word which Haffner did not understand. She turned to the calendar behind her on the wall, one half of which was a series of mountain views, underwritten by romantic poetry; the other half of which was a grid with numbers. She pointed to one square, containing one number.

And finally Haffner understood that he would only be able to recapture his belongings the next day.

With a renewed sense of triumph, therefore – since what more could he now lose? – the untold story of Haffner reached its conclusion. He would go to look at the villa, unencumbered by his possessions. And eventually he would live up here, in this spa, in this place of his escape: in the solitude of their infinite marriage: its absolute irrelevant immortal secrets.

For this, thought Haffner, was the true version of Haffner – a husband.

In a bar out on North Beach once, in San Francisco, he had talked to the barman about DiMaggio. DiMaggio, said the guy behind the bar, had been a regular. And the barman confided in him that when Joe was dying, he used to say that it was no sadness to him. At least, he said, it would maybe give him another chance with Marilyn.

It had shocked Haffner then. Now, however, it seemed bleakly accurate. It seemed adequate to the facts.

Always, he had wanted out, thought Haffner. And now he didn't.

Haffner Mortal

1

As the twilight began, the subtlest twilight, Haffner walked up the long road towards the villa. He tended to his memories of Livia. It was his triumph, his procession through the city's streets: with his conquered slaves before him – and his personal freedman behind him, whispering that Haffner was mortal.

And that slave, for now, is me.

Yes, the conjuring with tenses was now all over. For Haffner had indeed caught a cold two mornings ago, when he swam in the lake with Frau Tummel: finally, the symptoms were for real. And in two weeks' time this cold would develop into a virulent form of pneumonia, which would be imperfectly treated, here, in the Alps, by a junior doctor whose concentration was distracted by his concern to keep calling his girlfriend and assure her that he loved her, stricken as he was by his lone moment of infidelity, an impulsive regretted kiss at a soirée after a conference; so that by the time Haffner was flown home to London – successful, true, in his legal pursuit of the villa – he would have already suffered a stroke. And in that weakened, muted state, began the long dying of Haffner.

It wasn't the defeat he had intended, or predicted: like everyone's defeat. It was just the one that Haffner got.

But at this moment, Haffner was still happy in the bliss of his escape. Up the hill he walked, out of the town, into the depleted suburbs: his natural habitat.

On reaching the drive which led to the house, however, he was struck by a problem. What Haffner had not considered, in his moment of emotion, was the legal problem. He did not own this property, obviously. He knew this. The company who used it as a holiday home still owned it. It now struck him that he had no idea how he might explain why it was that he was here: a bedraggled ancient madman with a bruise above his eye and around his cheek.

For a moment, his bravado disappeared. A homesickness overtook him. In Benjamin's bedroom, which had already not existed for years, he began to describe to Benjamin, in his bunk bed, how easy it was for Santa Claus to fly: he was buoyant, said Haffner. He simply floated.

In this cloud, Haffner stopped at the gate of the house. Perhaps, thought Haffner, no one was there. It could be standing empty.

Haffner paused.

He was here, thought Haffner, so he would brave it. And Haffner walked across the grass, and opened a door.

2

Haffner found himself in the kitchen: bare, lined with white tiles. A spiral iron staircase seemed to lead to all the other floors. Haffner stood at the base of the stairs, listening. He could hear nothing. So Haffner ascended and found himself in a corridor – covered in grey wallpaper, with brown stains, like stock market graphs, rising from the skirting – which led to the roofed veranda. Haffner knew about this veranda. On this veranda, Livia's father used to sit, watching each Alpine sunset. It used to have wooden floors, with zigzagging parquet. Now, the floor was lino; and the view had been glassed in.

It seemed to be a dining room: two Formica tables were lined up against each other. On one of them, there was a plate with a slick of butter flattened on its rim.

Haffner stood there. He looked down. Just like Uncle Eli, who – so Goldfaden told him – at one point in his late escape from Warsaw reached a wall: and there below him was a courting couple. They were sitting on a bench. A plane tree was growing in its wire netting beside them. The man was begging his girl to come inside with him, up to his apartment. It was just up there, he said. Her mother would never know. The girl was not so sure. And Eli had perched there, looking down on them, begging this girl silently to ignore her moral scruples, to go into the room. This resistance fighter, said Goldfaden, his slight jowls shaking with laughter – imploring her to give up her resistance!

Even now, Haffner found this amusing.

From the veranda, another door led into an empty room, containing just a photo of the President, and a plastic sign advertising the various ice creams to be found in a miniature freezer, there in the corner, humming to itself. So Haffner did not know that this, in fact, was the room which had once contained the grand brick fireplace beloved by Livia's mother, which had now been blocked up and plastered over. Nor did he know that Cesare's treasured ceiling, on which he had depicted *The Dream of Europa*, being squabbled over by two women who represented two continents, had been boarded over by another dropped ceiling, twenty years ago.

Everything was missing.

Upstairs, the bedrooms were filled with bunk beds; and more grey wallpaper. The bathroom which had been Livia's mother's personal project, obsessed as she was by all the conveniences of modern hygiene, with bidet, toilet, mirrors, handshower – all the delightful gadgets – had been replaced by a stone floor and three doleful showerheads, hanging their heads from the ceiling.

And when Haffner ascended, finally, into what had been the eaves, where Cesare kept his painting things and Livia kept her costumes from all the plays she had ever been in, there were now four small mansard rooms. Above each door there was a sign demanding that no one should smoke.

Haffner pushed one door open. Again, there was a bunk bed. A bra was resting on a chair. He turned to go, and as he turned he saw the notice which was on the back of every door, extending a most cordial welcome to this vacation home. Haffner was wished a wonderful stay. To guarantee order in the home, however, he was asked to observe some simple house rules. Sadly, Haffner read the times for meals, and the pickup of picnic lunches; the time for the afternoon rest period. During this time, Haffner was asked to refrain from playing the radio: instead, he should walk quietly on the stairs, and close doors quietly. In the immediate vicinity of the house, children were also required to play quietly. Lying on the beds in day clothes was not permitted. Requests and complaints should be addressed to the house manager.

All the ornament, all the marginalia and doodling were gone.

Unlike Solomon Haffner, his son believed in inheritance. The European museums always left Haffner sad. He saw no reason why a home should be given to the state. If Haffner had his way, if Haffner were a president, or a mayor, he would restore these ancestral homes to their rightful families. The pleasure of the chateau tour always eluded him. He could not help thinking of the dispossessed. This sensation returned to him now.

Yes, Haffner wished that he could bring everything back. He wished everything could be revised. In this, Haffner's last judgement, everything he had once consumed would be made whole again: the cigarettes would ravel themselves back into neat cylinders, the wines would loop back into their bottles; all the newspapers he had ever thrown away, all the detritus, would be restored in Haffner's sight. And finally the women. Everyone would be returned to him – resurrected: all the people he had loved. Because the problem with Haffner, really, was that he loved too many people. Thought Haffner.

He tugged at a venetian blind's toggle. It snapped up, like an aperture.

And Haffner, ignoring the landscape, remembered how, ten years earlier, when Morton was dying, he had gone to see him in Brooklyn. And because he couldn't think of anything which seemed in any way adequate to the monstrous fact of Morton's death, he tried, as he had so often tried to explain to Morton, the nature of a draw in cricket. It wasn't the simple matter of the scores being level. As always, this was where the foreigner became confused. But this time Haffner didn't bother with the detail. He didn't try to explain the technicalities: he just tried to explain its beauty. What it meant, he said, was that in cricket you could never be sure of victory or defeat: you could snatch defeat from the jaws of victory and victory from the jaws of defeat. And this was wonderful. It meant, Haffner tried to explain, that there was no reason for the strong to win.

Morton's contribution to this had been to tell him a story.

Was it like this? said Morton.

Man, said Morton, Haffner didn't know what the British had missed, sitting outside Rome, waiting on the Americans. When they had gone into Rome, said Morton, it was crazy. And Morton then told him a secret. So there Morton was, in Rome, in bed with two girls. One of them was his girlfriend, the other one was not. They were simply trying to sleep. Because everything was a mess. He had no idea why they'd ended up in the same bed. And in the middle of the night, he turned to the girl who was not his girlfriend. For she undid him. She was so beautiful. And they kissed. He shivered with the memory of it. They kissed and kissed. He put his hand down her skirt. He felt her, there where her legs became so intricate with flesh. The soft cleft with the strong bone above it. And this was the great moment of his life, said Morton. Beyond anything he had ever felt with his adored wife. It was the moment of absolute excitement.

—And? said Haffner.

—And nothing, Morton said. Nothing happened. My girl woke up. So we both pretended to be asleep.

3

No doubt about it: Morton understood.

In the end, you had to get over the victories and the defeats.

—You know, said the celebrated movie star Hugh 'Tam' Williams, on the way to Aldershot in 1939 for their training, you're going to make it. You've got it in you. You have star quality. I can tell these things.

And Haffner had never forgotten this. Slick compliment it may have been, to pass the time in some station café more pleasantly, but Haffner believed he meant it.

He didn't need his wallet and its mute photograph album now. Haffner was quite happily his own mausoleum. The pictures came back to him so easily.

What had been Haffner's victories? The Athletics Cup in 1934. The Divisional Cricket Championship in Jerusalem in 1946. The presidency of the City branch of the Institute of Bankers in 1982.

But the real victory, thought Haffner, was elsewhere. It could take place anywhere: not just in the eternal cities, with the Colosseum for backdrop, or disporting in the Roman swimming pool, watched over by a Fascist eagle. And Haffner, remembering that night, when Rome was liberated, then thought of another swimming pool – in LA, where Goldfaden's Uncle Eli lived. He was having some kind of pool party. And Eli had begun to reminisce about the Ghetto in Warsaw. Of course, said Eli, after the third year people started reminiscing. It wasn't like this in the beginning, they used to say: then things were so much better.

With a bottle of beer in their hands, tipped with a crescent of lime, Haffner had guffawed.

In this humour, in this privacy, Haffner reckoned the true triumph might be found.

And then Cesare – who had wandered over, dressed neatly in his European and academic suit, refusing all West Coast dress codes – entered the conversation and reminded Haffner and Eli of a resistance fighter's great interview, twenty-five years after it was over, when he pointed out that the history of the Warsaw revolt wasn't going to be one for the military historians. The outcome had never been in doubt. It wasn't notable for its strategy. But if there was a school to study the human spirit, then it should be a major subject. The importance was the force shown by the Jewish kids, after years of degradation, to rise up against their destroyers: and choose their own death. Was there, asked this hero, a standard which could measure that?

This man here, said Cesare, pointing at Haffner, he didn't want to be Jewish. He would never acknowledge, said Cesare, how much the Jews were hated. How much strength they had to be capable of. And Haffner, only wanting to locate Livia and go with her to the edge of the garden, to look out over the city, disagreed. It was true that he loved the image of the Jews as musclemen, the men of steel. But really what he admired was something else entirely. It wasn't Jewish – the revolt. This was Haffner's theory. It was a triumph of something much more universal.

Such confusion! said Cesare. But it was only to be expected. This was the constant problem. You try to assimilate, and in fact you just lose everything: you lose your family, but you also can't make friends. You can neither go forwards nor backwards. Wasn't this right, Raphael?

Oh he had loved Cesare so much, thought Haffner. Cesare had courage. But even Cesare was not as courageous, thought Haffner, as he should have been. The deepest courage belonged to those who chose to withdraw. To be doubly rejected, encircled by rejections – by the Jews and the non-Jews – allowed you an absolute freedom.

Haffner didn't care if he was a contradiction, an impossible hybrid. After all, he liked the hybrids. The greatest piece of music in the world was Mozart's Clarinet Concerto, as improvised by the great Benny Goodman. Haffner went for such impossible beings: the sphinxes, the centaurs.

And maybe, I think, Haffner was right – as he stands there at the window of a dismal bedroom, which had once belonged to Livia. His century had been a century of metamorphoses. And at its centre was his greatest invention of all: the strange winged beast of Haffner's marriage.

4

In the darkening sky, the reticulate constellations were nets, hauling in Haffner.

He had left Frau Tummel behind. Zinka, it is true, troubled Haffner's thoughts: but gently, tenderly. She still eluded him. He could only think of her obscured: taking off her T-shirt, an arm making shadows of her face.

So, for one last time, I want to go in search of Zinka.

She was in her apartment, in front of her television: in the living room decorated with prints of haystacks, a cathedral facade disintegrating in the twilight. She sat there until the light went, then went to sleep. And then that night, as usual, Niko came home, and made for Zinka's bed, where Zinka was doing her best to form the letter S. Her bed was in fact a sofa. It disguised itself as a bed in the darkness of the night. Its covering was ribbed polyester, dyed grey. Niko tried to follow the breathing which made her chest ascend and descend, cleanly silhouetted in a sheet. He tried to synchronise his breathing to hers. In the same way, in the dark mornings, before school, when he was eight, and it was snowing, he had crept into bed beside his mother, and tried to match his breathing to hers. Someone once had told him that men's respiration was quicker than women's, which was why women lived longer. So he tried to calm his breathing down.

Very slowly, Niko then began to move.

He felt his usual combination of the erotic and the uncomfortably sad. As he laboured inside Zinka – as she lay on her stomach, her legs cramped in angles which he could not alter, which would not let him extend himself in the way which Niko might have liked – he tried to tell himself that although it was not the life of desire he had imagined, perhaps it was enough. Perhaps Niko was happy.

But he could not.

No, long after he had finished with Zinka, who was pretending to pretend to be asleep, Niko lay awake, watching the shapes of the books melt and blur against the wall, in the dark, in dawn's twilight – yes, long after his bleated, blurted defeat as he reared over her, stabbed in the back by his soft orgasm. While Zinka lay there, imagining all the other lives she could be living.

And then they fell asleep.

5

Haffner walked downstairs, and went on to the villa's enclosed veranda. He looked out into the landscape: where the colours were. Yes, there they were: pure, like the colours Haffner had seen in the museum in New York – more neatly arranged there, true, more vibrant, but with the same lightness, the same absence of any human mistake. They obeyed their own mute logic.

Haffner was horticultural. He knew about the breeds of roses: how they formed an ideal order, invisible to the human brain. His life had often led him to gardens. Like the gardens of Ninfa, near

Rome. Or Haffner's own rose garden, where Solomon had taught him the two possibilities for a life: to live it, or to waste it. As if the choice were Haffner's.

The forest was a smudge of greens and blacks: a giant discarded palette. Through the trees, the sun was a precise gold disc pressed on to the horizon.

It was an industrial pastoral, with the sounds of the sibilant freeways in the distance: the twentieth century's automobiles and dryads, its fauns and chemical plants. He tried to hear the tune which had been playing at his first ever dance with Livia in Southwark. Naturally, he could not. He was not romantic enough for that. There was now just the sound of the wind in the trees, and the sound somewhere of the cattle bells – those bells, thought Haffner, which must so irritate the proud cow, reminded with every move of their ownership by others. Or maybe, thought Haffner, it was no more irritating to them than the weather. Maybe the bell was part of the bovine condition.

But before he could continue his meditation on the limits of a cow's perception, he was distracted by a bumble bee, hovering against the glass. And then another. And Haffner, in his exasperation and fever, began to wave the bees away: so that from a distance, from the position of the imaginary spectator, all that could be seen was Haffner, standing at the window, beating time to the grandest and most transparent orchestra.

6

And maybe, as he stands there, I should balance Haffner's faults and virtues. Perhaps this is the point to decide whether Haffner was a hero or a monster. But even if I could truly describe him now, as he looks out of the window, in his wife's villa, would that portrait equally apply to the soldier in Palestine, the husband in New York, the romantic in London?

He always saw himself in poses. And this series of receding Haffners could continue diminishing, into infinitely vanishing fractions.

I wanted to preserve the real Haffner. I wanted to resurrect him. The Haffner I actually knew was a man of reticent privacy. I only had the stories to work with. I only had my inventions. But whether they were true or not, Haffner was inescapable, in all the stories he gave rise to . . .

And this was, perhaps, how history worked.

As an admirer of the classics, Haffner wanted to understand what caused the great empires' decline. I was more modern. I wanted to know how the emperors had turned into legends. But maybe both these questions possessed the same solution. The law of unintended consequence – the law which governs every empire's decline – was so definitive that every emperor became a legend: enveloped by their own defeat. No historian, after all, could ever know all the causes. So they had to write a legend. A legend is just a story which is missing most of its causes; a legend is just a feat of retrospective editing.

The more I knew of Haffner, the more real he became: this was true. And, simultaneously, Haffner disappeared.

7

Haffner walked away, down the steep road back into town, towards the spa, to find a hotel. In the same way as that classical king who, as the poet says, when deserted by the Macedonians did not behave like a king. Instead he threw away his golden robes, borrowed someone's everyday outfit, then left – like an actor who, once the play is over, changes back into his clothes and wanders away.

As he walked, he remembered Livia's funeral: how from the window he had seen the undertakers waiting outside, like paparazzi, for the body; and the organist, playing the funeral march as everyone shuffled away, finished with a comic trill, a final flourish, when he thought that everyone had gone – a squiggle of pure flippancy. Just as Haffner would have told her, afterwards, in the refuge of their bedroom, if it hadn't been Livia who had died.

Think about it, thought Haffner.

Exiled on St Helena, Napoleon continued to be chic. He cared about his waistcoats, the gold stitching of his shoes. Yes, it was unbelievable, but it was true. All the victors were masters of retreat. They cultivated retreat. Even Tiberius, the ruler of the world – a god with his giant pied-à-terre in Rome – preferred the quiet island of Capri.

But me, I might put it like this: there you are, dear reader, at the pool party, by the sea, in the sunlight, with the pine forest sighing behind you, and the blue sea sighing in front of you, ceaselessly bringing you tribute, while in the distance the dolphins show off the sheen of their backs; and then, from somewhere invisible, out of your field of vision, you hear a deep splash, a forsaken cry, and when you turn to look – there it is, the surface, settling in circular ripples, which enlarge, and then enlarge some more: until they enlarge into nothing.

Postscript

This book contains quotations, some of them slightly adapted, from works by W.H. Auden, Saul Bellow, Bertolt Brecht, Mel Brooks, Constantine Cavafy, Blaise Cendrars, George Eliot, Ella Fitzgerald, F. Scott Fitzgerald, Gustave Flaubert, Edward Gibbon, Alfred Goldman, Robert Graves, Alfred Hitchcock, Courtney Hodell, Hugo von Hofmannsthal, Christophe Honoré, Horace, Bohumil Hrabal, Peter Stephan Junk, Franz Kafka, Velimir Khlebnikov, Ladislav Klíma, Stéphane Mallarmé, Thomas Mann, Groucho Marx, Thomas Middleton, Vladimir Nabokov, Marcel Ophuls, Georges Perec, Petronius, Alfred Polgar, Alexander Pope, Cole Porter, Alexander Pushkin, François Rabelais, Saïan Supa Crew, Viscount Samuel, William Shakespeare, Tupac Shakur, Stendhal, Laurence Sterne, Alexander Stille, Suetonius, Tacitus, Junichiro Tanizaki, Leo Tolstoy, Paul Valéry and Virgil.